Books by Edgar Hilsenrath

NIGHT
THE NAZI AND THE BARBER

The Nazi
and
The Barber

EDGAR HILSENRATH

The Nazi
and
The Barber

TRANSLATED BY ANDREW WHITE

1971

DOUBLEDAY & COMPANY, INC., GARDEN CITY, NEW YORK

In memory of my father

I would like to acknowledge the help of the following people, who offered me a combination of encouragement, advice, and friendship, without which the writing of this novel would have been more arduous and perhaps, even, impossible: Maximillian Becker, Lawrence Freundlich, Gisela Meyer, Elisabeth Bachtler, Eveline Neumann, and Marion Gid.

E.H.

𝕭𝔬𝔬𝔨 𝔒𝔫𝔢

I

I am Max Schulz, illegitimate though purely Aryan son of Minna Schulz . . . who at the time of my birth was a maid in the house of the Jewish fur dealer Abramowitz. There can be no doubt of my pure Aryan origin, since the family tree of my mother, Minna Schulz, while it does not go back to the Battle of Teutoburger Forest, nevertheless has roots which reach back to Frederick the Great. Who my father was I cannot tell you with any certainty, but he must definitely have been one of five men: the butcher, Hubert Nagler; the locksmith, Franz Heinrich Wieland; the builder's mate, Hans Huber; the coachman, Wilhelm Hopfenstange; or the butler, Adolf Hennemann.

I have had the family trees of my five fathers carefully looked into and I can assure you, the Aryan origin of all five can be certified beyond doubt. So far as the butler

Adolf Hennemann is concerned, well, in his case, I can say proudly that one of his forefathers bore the nickname "Hagen the Keybearer," a cornet of the valiant Knight Siegismund von der Weide, who bestowed upon him a certain key as a sign of his great trust. I refer to the key of the chastity belt worn by his spouse . . . a guilded chastity belt renowned at the court of the Mighty Monarch, which later made history.

Itzig Finkelstein lived in the house next door. He was exactly my age or . . . to be more precise . . . and if I may be allowed to express myself in this way: Itzig Finkelstein first saw the light of the world exactly two minutes and twenty-two seconds after the midwife Greta, nicknamed Fatty Greta, liberated me from the dark womb of my mother with a hearty tug . . . that is to say, if life can be called a liberation, which—after all—is fairly questionable.

Two days after Itzig Finkelstein came upon this world, the following announcement was featured in the *Jewish Spectator* in our town . . . Wieshalle in Silesia:

I, Chaim Finkelstein, barber, proprietor of the renowned gentleman's hairdressing salon "Man of the World," corner of Goethe and Schillerstrasse, Wieshalle, Director of the Jewish Bowling Club, Acting Secretary-General of the "Jewish Community," member of the German Association for the Prevention of Cruelty to Animals, member of the Club for the Furtherment of Interest in Plants, member of the League "Love Thy Neighbor," member of the Wieshalle Guild of Barbers, author of the booklet *Haircuts Tailored to the Head* . . . have the honor to announce the birth of my son and heir *Itzig Finkelstein*.

The very next day a second announcement appeared in the *Jewish Spectator* with the following text:

We, the Jewish Community of Wieshalle, have pleasure in congratulating Herr Chaim Finkelstein, barber, proprietor of the renowned gentleman's hairdressing salon "Man of the World," corner of Goethe and Schillerstrasse, Director of the Jewish Bowling Club, Acting Secretary-General of the "Jewish Community," member of the German Association for the Prevention of Cruelty to Animals, member of the Club for the Furtherment of Interest in Plants, member of the League "Love Thy Neighbor," member of the Wieshalle Guild of Barbers, author of the booklet *Haircuts Tailored to the Head*, upon the birth of his son and heir Itzig Finkelstein.

Can you imagine what Hilda—scraggy Hilda, maid at the Finkelsteins—said to Frau Finkelstein when the announcement of the birth of little Itzig appeared in the *Jewish Spectator*?

"Frau Finkelstein," she said, "that's something I don't understand! Herr Finkelstein is in other ways no show-off. But this announcement of little Itzig's birth . . . it's a little too much!"

Scraggy Hilda: over six feet of scraggy body, face as thin as a bird, hair as black as pitch.

Sarah Finkelstein: petite and rotund, pince-nez gripping her nose, her hair plaited round her head, already graying—even though she was not in the least old. Yet she seemed filmed over with the dust of age, of another era, like the venerable family pictures in Finkelstein's old-fashioned living room.

Chaim Finkelstein: still shorter than his wife, but not chubby. A tiny, thin dwarf of a man . . . his left shoulder sagging as though two thousand years of exile and two thousand years of suffering were hanging from this single shoulder. From the left shoulder, the shoulder nearest to the heart.

Chaim Finkelstein's nose is difficult to describe. I would say . . . always dripping a little . . . and always a little inflamed by a chronic cold. But not bent. His nose was neither long nor hooked. It was normal. To all intents and purposes normal. And he didn't have flat feet either.

Hair? You want to know if he had any hair? Chaim Finkelstein the barber? Oh no, he didn't have any hair. At least not on his head. But he didn't need it. Because Chaim Finkelstein, that tiny little manikin, had expressive eyes. And whoever looked into those eyes could not possibly be offended by the bald pate. Nor by the inflamed nose that was always dripping just a little bit, or even by his undersized body. His eyes were large, and clear and kind and wise. Eyes that shone with the poetry of the Bible and with compassion for his fellow men.

That was Chaim Finkelstein, the Jewish barber from Wieshalle.

On the 23rd May, 1907, at Finkelstein's house, an event of enormous importance took place: the circumcision of Itzig Finkelstein.

I assume that you are well aware of what circumcision is and that you, if you are a Jew, have not only from time to time contemplated your own mangled member, sizing it up as it were, but that you have also occasionally cogitated upon the symbolic cause of the missing foreskin. Am I not right?

Circumcision is a symbol of the bond between the Lord and the people of Israel and as such it is also given the name *Brith Mila*. A conscientious reader of encyclopedias, I have been able to ascertain that the circumcision of Jewish little boys is supposed to represent a kind of symbolic castration, a metaphor, intended to symbolize the following: the

[12]

Ennoblement of Man, the taming of his bestial instincts and passions, a symbolic act, which I, speaking as a mass-murderer, cannot praise highly enough.

On the occasion of Itzig Finkelstein's circumcision, a festive mood reigned in Finkelstein's home. The gentleman's hairdressing salon "Man of the World" was closed. Finkelstein's maid, scraggy Hilda, asked my mother to help out a little since she had much too much to do, and my mother, who was all for cooperation between neighbors, went across to the Finkelstein's and helped scraggy Hilda in the kitchen. There they baked honey cake and apple strudel, flat cakes with sweet raisins and almonds and all sorts of other tasty morsels. The hosts were not skimpy with the hard drinks, and my mother and scraggy Hilda, who had nothing at all against good liquor, drank to the health and wealth of the Jews and the health and wealth of Itzig Finkelstein.

It's true that my mother drank to the health and wealth of the Jews in the kitchen with scraggy Hilda, and to the health and wealth of Itzig Finkelstein, because she liked good liquor and because she was having fun, but she didn't have the slightest idea why it was that there were so many visitors streaming into the house and what sort of strange festival it was that was being celebrated at the Finkelsteins, and when she finally made inquiries of scraggy Hilda, Hilda laughed and then said:

"What's all the fuss about? Little Itzig is eight days old today. And so he's having his willy cut off. That's always what happens with Jews. Always on the eighth day after birth."

"But that's horrible," said my mother. "The poor little kid will never be able to have a proper piss again—and later won't be able to fuck."

"Oh it's not so horrible," said scraggy Hilda. "His dick will grow again."

[13]

And then scraggy Hilda explained to my mother what happened at the ceremony,

"Now just listen, Minna," said scraggy Hilda, "this is what happens: there's a fellow called the 'mohel.' He has a long knife with two sharp edges. He cuts the little Jewish boy's willy off then mumbles a few magic words and then the cock he's cut off starts to grow back again . . . till it's neither too long nor too short . . . and is exactly the right length . . . but on the other hand especially thick and strong. That's why Jews are blessed with so many children."

"Well that's fantastic," said my mother. "I've never heard anything like that before."

"It's all done as a sign of the bond between the people of Israel and the Lord," said scraggy Hilda. "At any rate that's what the barber Chaim Finkelstein said not so long ago and the rabbi who was in our house just recently said something similar. He even spoke about a certain prophet—the fellow is called Jeremiah—who is supposed to have said to the Jews: 'Circumsize yourselves to the Lord and take away the foreskins of your heart.'"

"Just the foreskins?" asked my mother.

"Yes, the foreskins," said scraggy Hilda.

"Then all they should only cut off from little Itzig is his foreskin," said my mother, "and not the whole thing. It's the same with the heart."

"Oh well," said scraggy Hilda, "that's right of course . . . but you see a dick is no heart . . . it grows again . . . as I explained to you." Scraggy Hilda laughed wickedly.

My mother shook her head and said: "That's fantastic. I wouldn't have thought it possible."

"How old is your little Max?" asked scraggy Hilda.

"Eight days," said my mother. "Exactly the same age as

little Itzig, or, to be more precise: two minutes and twenty-two seconds older."

"Then in your place I would have his willy cut off too. You see, Minna, it'll grow back again, just as it does with the Jews, neither too long nor too short, exactly the right length, but especially thick and strong."

This is probably the place where you will ask yourself how it is that I know all this so exactly, but with the best will in the world I can't tell you.

The circumcision of Itzig Finkelstein completed, my mother ran excitedly home, alerted my five fathers, dragged me out of my cot, and placed me on the kitchen table, with the intention of separating me from my member, of slicing it off so to speak. The Abramowitz family was not at home . . . and I, a poor, helpless, defenseless little worm, was completely at the mercy of them all. Do you suppose I somehow sensed what was in the air? At any rate I screamed as if the devil had got me and neither my mother nor my five fathers could quiet me. The locksmith held my arms, the builder's mate my legs, my mother stuck the pacifier in my mouth, the butler and the coachman stood around shamefacedly, while the butcher grinned and brandished a long knife.

"Don't cut it off," my mother suddenly said, "it was just a joke."

"No joke," said the butcher. "This is something that's done in bitter earnest."

"Perhaps it won't grow again," said my mother. "After all he's not a Jew. And besides, the mohel is not there to mumble his magic words."

"Oh, to hell with the mohel and his magic words," said the butcher.

[15]

"Don't do it," said my mother. "Or else we'll all wind up in jail."

The butcher was just about to put the blade to my member, when something strange happened: I, Max Schulz, eight days old, suddenly spat out the pacifier, leaped at the butcher's throat with a yell, took a powerful bite, even though I still had no teeth, let myself drop to the ground, crawled like the wind to the window, pulled myself up on the window sill, and saw, for the first time in my life . . . the street . . . a street, a completely ordinary street, with a pavement and gutter and flagstones. . . . I saw brick houses, with sloping, colored roofs, and carriages, and a swirl of two- and four-legged creatures. Gazing up to heaven, I saw ash-gray and black clouds—with spots and splashes—and dark birds circling. But I saw no little angels. Oh no, no little angels. Below us on the street the people were beginning to form a crowd. Somebody shouted: "What the devil is going on up there?" And my mother, who in the meanwhile had stepped over to the window, took me into her arms, and shouted back, "What's supposed to be going on?"

You're probably thinking I'm pulling your leg? Or perhaps that's not what you think, maybe you're just saying to yourself: Max Schulz has a screw loose! He's got a mania that somebody wanted to kill him . . . because he was a bastard . . . and all done under the disguise of a circumcision, executed, as is the custom among Jews, on the eighth day after birth. What is Max Schulz up to? What's he trying to say to me? Who is he trying to blame? His mother? The Jews? Or God? And all that stuff and nonsense about the baby acting in self-defense, scuttling off, climbing up on the window sill . . . it's all nonsense! There's no such thing as that! A nightmare! And nothing more! But I just want to tell you my story, the story of my life in systematic sequence. Is that how I should express myself? However, I am not telling you everything, only the most important things, or those that I, Itzig Finkelstein, at the time still Max Schulz, consider to be the most important.

My five fathers visited my mother every evening. They stood in line in front of her door. Usually the strongest one, the butcher, was the first to go to her, then the locksmith, then the builder's mate, then the coachman, finally the butler. Yes, the butler was always the last, because he was the weakest, a delicate little man with a castrato voice, who was left with no alternative but to stir his cock around in the semen of my other four fathers.

These goings-on did not exactly please the Jewish fur dealer Abramowitz, which I, Itzig Finkelstein, at that time still Max Schulz, can well understand. Not that the fur dealer Abramowitz had anything against me or against the fact of my existence; that is to say: so long as he was convinced that I was the son of his coachman, Wilhelm Hopfenstange or his butler, Adolf Hennemann, since both of those gentlemen belonged as it were to the family. . . . the real trouble came when the fur dealer became suspicious. One day he said to my mother,

"Now just listen here, Minna. It can't go on like this any longer. I thought it was just my coachman and butler. But five men in line, that's too much. After all, this is supposed to be a decent house."

"Good things come in threes," said my mother.

"But not fives," said the fur dealer. "Certainly not fives. This is a decent house, and I have to give you notice."

II

One rainy July day—I was just seven weeks old—my poor mother packed her suitcases, took me on her arm, and left the house. My five fathers helped her to move of course. My mother's luggage consisted of three trunks, a rucksack, a grocery bag, and an umbrella. The butcher carried the heaviest trunk, a yellow box made of wood with an iron lock and bolt, the locksmith carried the brown leather suitcase, the builder's mate carried the blue canvas suitcase, the coachman the rucksack, while the weakling butler just took the umbrella and the grocery bag, a bright green shopping bag filled with groceries and a few other utensils such as garters, hair curlers, ribbons, and so on.

You've got to keep in mind that my mother was a pretty big hunk of woman. She looked like a wandering beer barrel, jacked up on stilts which just managed to bear up her gigantic body with dignity. I should not forget to mention her luxurious blond hair, and her steely blue eyes, or her turned-up little nose, which was as gay as her double chin on which she had a bright brown wart. Her lips were sensuous, her teeth strong and white. They never failed to send the butcher into ecstasies, and he was always saying to my mother,

"You know, Minna, when I see your teeth I get scared you're going to bite off my cock." Whereupon my mother used to say,

"Oh come on, Hubert, that could only happen to the butler Adolf Hennemann, because his piece is so flabby. I'm not going to break my teeth on a steel prick. Or do you think that's just what I want to do?"

"No, Minna," said the butcher. "But teeth are no joke."

When we left the house I was sleeping peacefully in my mother's arms. I awoke when we passed Finkelstein's hairdressing salon; then I began to yell. Right away Chaim Finkelstein rushed out of the salon, even though he was just lathering a client's face. Scraggy Hilda opened the window on the second floor, saw what was happening, and rushed down into the street. Kissing and hugging was all in vain. Finally my mother said,

"I don't know what's up with the boy, Herr Finkelstein. Your barbershop has put some spell on him."

"What's this 'shop' business?" said Chaim Finkelstein. "I don't have a 'shop,' I've got a 'salon.'"

"Well then the salon's put a spell on him," said my mother. "Or else he wouldn't cry so much."

"Oh come on, Minna," said the butcher, "don't gab so much with the Jew . . . and besides this wooden box is too heavy."

"Yes, we should keep going," said the butler, and my other four fathers agreed with him.

We didn't know where we should go. Chaim Finkelstein's hairdressing salon was situated, as I mentioned already, at the corner of Goethe and Schillerstrasse. The butcher was adamant about staying on Goethestrasse, I suppose because of "The Erl-King Pub"; although I am not sure he knew Goethe's poem. Perhaps the butcher had heard something about the mad ride through the forest at night or something about the father and the son or about a temperamental horse and perhaps the madness of Goethe's poem had made an impression upon him. However the butler favored "The Bell," and in his case I have no doubts, for every evening he would recite from Schiller's great poem as he rang for supper. And as for him, he absolutely wanted us to stay on Schillerstrasse. My other three fathers couldn't have cared less. The locksmith thought that the locks in Goethestrasse were no better than those on Schillerstrasse. The builder's mate nodded his head and said,

"Yes, the houses in Schillerstrasse have just as many bugs as those in Goethestrasse."

And Wilhelm Hopfenstange, the coachman, observed that

[19]

the flagstones on both streets were just as bumpy and full of broken glass and other garbage. Eventually my mother made the ultimate decision. She said: "Let's cross the street first!"

Do you know the German town of Wieshalle? The streets are crooked and narrow, so narrow that from the opposite side of the street you cannot only see everything but also hear everything going on in front of the hairdressing salon "Man of the World."

There Anton Slavitzki was standing . . . Anton Slavitzki, the child rapist . . . standing there grinning and looking over at our group. By trade Anton Slavitzki was a barber, just like Chaim Finkelstein, only not so good. His barbershop—not a gentleman's hairdressing salon, he was not so classy—was directly opposite the hairdressing salon "Man of the World," and built in such a way that both barbers—Finkelstein and Slavitzki—could gape at each other through their respective windows—and that they often did: Finkelstein smiling and condescending—Slavitzki spiteful and envious.

Slavitzki? He was a long thin fellow, with bushy eyebrows, baggy, slightly squinting eyes, oily hair, bony nose, and a cock so long that according to rumors in the town it hung down way beyond his knees, and which people said was the reason why Slavitzki always had it fastened to his thigh with a rubber band.

We crossed the street. As we walked by Slavitzki's barbershop—my five fathers groaning under the weight of the luggage, my mother, looking like a two-ton beer barrel wavering upon two thin stilts, was holding me on her arm. I was no longer yelling, and was about to go to sleep. As we were walking past Slavitzki so innocently, the child rapist took a sudden step forward and pinched my mother in her fat behind. My mother, outraged, stopped.

She said, "What's the big idea, Slavitzki! I'm a decent woman!"

Slavitzki began to stammer. Yes, that was what happened. He stammered—some sort of stupid excuse—and my mother was so pleased she said,

"Well, well it doesn't matter, my behind has done for many a man before now. What is it you like about me anyway?"

And Slavitzki said: "Your behind."

My mother said: "So."

And Slavitzki said: "My good lady. If ever you want to have a fashionable hair-do, I'll do it for you for nothing, even though I'm not really a woman's hairdresser."

And my mother said: "You'll give me the latest hair-do?"

"The latest hair-do," said Slavitzki.

"I'm going to take you up on that," said my mother. "When do you want to do it? And I mean: for free."

"If you like I'll do it right away," said Slavitzki.

"Fine," said my mother. "If we put it off, we'll forget it. So let's do it now."

My mother disappeared with me into Slavitzki's barbershop. My five fathers waited patiently in front of the door but when two hours had gone by the butcher said to my other fathers, "Minna's not coming out. No wonder. He has the longest poker in Goethestrasse."

And the butler said: "You can include Schillerstrasse in that too."

And the locksmith said: "The longest and strongest, that's well known. He's a master fucker."

And the builder's mate said: "Yes, that's right. But he's a Pole after all. That makes him suspicious."

And the coachman Wilhelm Hopfenstange nodded his head and said: "And besides that he's a widower. That's still more suspicious."

[21]

My five fathers consulted among themselves for a while. Then they unloaded my mother's luggage in front of the doors to Slavitzki's barbershop, crossed themselves and made off.

"Shabby." I can find no other word to describe the barbershop owned by Anton Slavitzki. Dull mirrors, scratched barber chairs with burst seats, with the stuffing squeezing out, a single washbasin that was yellow and sloppy, cracked walls, damaged floors, bad lighting, everything mean and mousy, dusty, neglected. A curtain at one end of the room hid a kitchenette, right by the emergency exit leading out into the back courtyard, where there was a water closet. The barber Chaim Finkelstein and his best customer, the fur dealer Abramowitz, had a pet name for Slavitzki's clientele, namely the "rag and bone rabble."

Slavitzki's belongings were stuffed away into three chests of drawers arranged in a row by the emergency exit. Slavitzki claimed that he once had his own apartment but that was a long time ago. Now the barbershop was his home.

"Why should a widower need an apartment," said Slavitzki to my mother. "At nights I just set up the folding bed and take it down again when day comes. That's my way."

"I can understand that," said my mother, "but if you want me and Max to stay here with you, all that will have to change. Because we need an apartment."

"Very well then," said Slavitzki. "We'll have to see. All in good time."

Can you imagine a lonely widower's folding bed being changed into a double bed in which not only the lean widower but also a fat woman, weighing over two tons, despite the fact that her legs were thin, were supposed to sleep together, that is to say: can you imagine two persons of completely different bodily dimensions sleeping in such a bed?

The very first night Slavitzki was immediately at my mother. But my mother was having the curse and fended him off with her thin legs and fat hands.

"That would not be proper," said my poor mother. "I've got 'the curse.' It wouldn't be proper."

But Slavitzki would not listen. He kept up his tries. I guess he unfastened the rubber band the people used to talk about and stood there before the marriage bed, naked, showing off his stiffened masterpiece, making my poor mother's head spin, nagged at her, crept back at her under the bed sheet, whined and pleaded, tried to convince her, finally began to swear, then to shout. That's the way it must have been.

My mother remained firm. God be my witness, so it was. What is not proper is not proper. A person must have principles.

As soon as Slavitzki realized he had lost, his rage knew no bounds. He leaped out of the marriage bed like a wild man, naked, his sword erect, foaming at the mouth, beads of sweat across his forehead, his hair sticking to his skin . . . and stilled his rage and his itch on me.

Can you imagine the extent of such a crime? I, Max Schulz, just seven weeks old, future mass-murderer, at the time, however, innocent, lay like an angel in my new cradle, the washbasin, the same washbasin into which Slavitzki habitually peed, but which was now dry because my mother had wiped it off. There I lay wrapped in warm diapers, covered up and tucked in, sleeping peacefully, dreaming of my friends the angels. Dreaming and smiling I was suddenly wrenched from my sleep, and thrown into the air . . . wanted to shout to the angels perhaps, but couldn't shout, my eyes flew open in horror, out of sheer terror I wet my diapers, nearly choked on a bad swallow, threw up my mother's milk on to Slavitzki's hand, stretched out my tiny hands and legs to defend my innocence, saw Slavitzki's mighty instrument without knowing what it was, began mumbling prayers even though I had not yet learned to pray, wanted to die, longed to be back into the dark but secure womb of my mother . . . then all of a sudden landed on my stomach on top of the barber's chair, the one in front of the washbasin.

There was my mother standing next to the folding bed: two tons of heavy, shaking, female flesh, freezing, her night-gown in disarray, her breasts hanging down . . . standing there on her thin, long, hairless, female stork legs, not trembling, just cold and freezing, standing there and gaping, gaping sleepily with a glassy look, saw Slavitzki, saw the barber's chair, saw my Aryan, snow-white, innocent, velvety skin. She licked her lips, testing her teeth, wanted to bite, but thought otherwise, groped for a cigarette, finally found one behind her right ear. Not the left one, mind you, the right, stuck it in her mouth between her large white teeth, then found a match, not behind the right ear but behind the left one, raised her thin leg, her left one, scratched the match across the sole of her slipper, saw the flame, lit her cigarette and gazed shamefacedly upon the mammoth tower of the barber Slavitzki.

I, Max Schulz, future mass-murderer, at the time, however, innocent, let out a scream which would strike to any marrow, arched my back, clawed at the stuffing bursting out of the barber's chair, strained my little head into the air, felt the blood rushing to my brain, made wet again, began to tremble, heard the angels singing, heard their hallelujahs, saw hovering angels with harps and the pipes of Pan, saw tiny feet climbing the musical spheres, saw all kinds of keys, musical keys and other kinds, saw too the great iron keys of my predecessor "Hagen the Keybearer," heard him gnashing and grinding his teeth, saw the gilded chastity belt of his lady, saw her nakedness, heard giggling and whispering, saw sins scaling the passages, saw the sink of corruption, saw neither angels nor harps nor pipes of Pan, heard our Lord God laughing, wanted to pray and could no longer. . . .

I know what you're saying, "Max Schulz is going off his rocker! A nightmare! Nothing but a nightmare!"

But why do you insist on that? Is it not true that God invented innocence in order to have it trampled in the mud . . . here on earth? And is it not true that the weak and defenseless are always trodden upon by the strong, clubbed to the ground, raped, despised, buggered? And at times in certain periods simply done away with? Is that not so? And if it is so . . . why is it that you maintain that Max Schulz is going off his rocker?

III

There is not much I can tell you about my early childhood. So let me skip it and just mention that big war.

Can you remember it? They called it World War I. As for me, I remember it well, since I was seven already, a big boy who knew quite a lot that many grown-ups don't know, had frog eyes of indefinite color, which saw a great many things, even things they ought not to have seen.

We had moved into a basement apartment below Slavitzki's barbershop, a place full of rats. From there—the perspective of a basement window—the war seemed quite droll. Day after day long convoys rumbled by. Marching music crashed through my room. From my basement window I could see the underbellies of heavy artillery, and of men and animals, too. I became a devotee of horses' hooves, and was overjoyed when they clip-clopped by above my window. The spectacle of soldiers' legs tramping in unison thrilled me, indeed I had had no idea that there were so many legs in the whole world. What I especially liked was the goose-stepping boots of the officers.

[25]

Shining black, they crunched their way across the streets, careless of broken glass, gaily scornful of the hard plaster of the streets; toes curved into the air, the officers' boots flashed at me and filled me with secret wishes.

My stepfather, Slavitzki, went away for a while, leaving behind him only a large notice on the door of the barbershop: "Closed!"

During his absence the traffic to and from our basement apartment took on a merry pace. My mother was seldom without visitors, soldiers on holiday I suppose, nice boys, who brought me licorice and rock candy.

At the beginning they came singly, but eventually they came in teams. My job was to keep watch—in front of the blue bedroom door—and to give out little papers with numbers on them to the people standing in line—and I used to show the soldiers into "the waiting room"—the name we now gave to our living room. I gave them all sorts of information and told the new boys who had not seen my mother before that her legs were long and thin like those of a stork, but to make up for that she had a fat ass, weighed two tons, had a friendly nature and even an understanding of children's games. I told them that she could even bark like Satan the dog next door, that she could creep on all fours and chase around in a circle.

Does it interest you to hear what went on during the First World War along Goethe and Schillerstrasse? Do you want me to tell you how we played at war, Goethestrasse children against Schillerstrasse children? Or shall I tell you about the new gramophone in my poor mother's bedroom, with a huge horn that looked like a monstrous trumpet and which made such a din that the rats in my traps became quite wild? But that doesn't interest you, I guess.

One day my stepfather came back from the war—even though the war was not at an end at that time—took down

[26]

the notice from the door of the shop, put up a new one with the words: "Barbershop Open Again!"—threw the visitors out of my mother's bedroom, even threw out those in "the waiting room," now called the living room again, smashed the gramophone, called my poor mother a whore, cursed from morning till night, beat her up, drank himself silly—and then, the old life began again, continued as it was before, before Slavitzki went to the war.

The Jewish community of Wieshalle numbered ninety-nine souls. When you think that the Wieshalle we lived in was a city of 33,099 inhabitants, then you'll have to admit there were not really many Jews. But since most of the Jews lived in Goethestrasse and Schillerstrasse, it came about that my stepfather was able to get into the habit of saying: "Minna, this damned city is completely Jew-ridden."

Perhaps you will permit me to describe to you now the following conversation that took place one day at lunch between my mother Minna Schulz, who because of Slavitzki's perversions was standing up because she couldn't sit down, and my stepfather who was sitting down at his usual seat in a bad temper, a bit drunk already, even though it was early in the day, dressed in a dyed T-shirt and underpants from which protruded his flabby member.

"If this sort of thing goes on, Minna," said Slavitzki, "then we might as well pack our bags. The city's nothing but Jews now. And where do you think the Jews have their haircuts? At Chaim Finkelstein's. Because he's a Jew too. It's clear enough."

My poor mother shook her head. "That's not right, Anton!" she said. "That's just not right. The super told me there were ninety-nine Jews, that's all. That's what he told me. Ninety of them live around here. Fifty-three in Goethestrasse and

[27]

thirty-seven in Schillerstrasse. That may seem like a lot. But it's not too many. Just start adding up: How many houses are there in Goethestrasse and how many in Schillerstrasse? And how many apartments? I'm telling you, Anton! In this district there are more Christians than Jews. So what do you think of that? And where do the Christians have their hair cut? At Chaim Finkelstein's!"

"He must have put a spell on them," said Slavitzki, "otherwise they wouldn't be going to him all the time! They'd be coming to me!"

My poor mother shook her fat head again. "I don't think so, Anton. Because otherwise Hans Baumeister, the cobbler next door, who's a Catholic, wouldn't do such great business—in spite of the fact that there are Jewish competitors right across from him. The customers in Goethestrasse and Schillerstrasse don't let themselves get spellbound by Jews. It's just that they expect to get some sort of decent service for their good money."

"And what's that supposed to mean?" Slavitzki asked with a glare.

"That's supposed to mean," said my mother slowly, "that Chaim Finkelstein is doing better business then you because he's a better barber! And he doesn't pee into the washbasin either! And when he's cut a head of hair it doesn't look as though someone has been holding a basin over his head!"

As a boy I did the strangest somersaults. I was also able to do cartwheels, to pull off all sorts of double-jointed tricks, stand on my hands, do splits, suck my big toe, pull faces, howl with laughter without reason, stammer, throw stones at little girls, kick little boys smaller than me in the behind, break windows, climb on roofs, and pee on the street from roof tops, and so forth.

[28]

One day Slavitzki said to my mother: "I think this boy has a screw loose."

My mother said: "You know, Anton. The first time did it."

"What do you mean?" said my stepfather.

"Your cock was quite simply too big," said my mother, "and too long. It banged right up against his brain box, batted his belfry good and proper. And the result: a good hole in the head! Bats in the belfry!"

My stepfather was not pleased when he saw me playing with Itzig Finkelstein, son of the barber Chaim Finkelstein, his competitor. But I liked playing with Itzig. I showed Itzig how to set up rat traps, how to push long, sharp sticks into the backsides of drugged rats, explained to him that worms, even without their heads, still keep moving, which I interpreted to mean that the worm and its kind don't want to give up their worm-like existence and in the end survive the hand that cuts them up.

I showed Itzig Finkelstein how to play marbles, showed him that it was not the color that made the difference but the size of the marble, even though I, for instance, preferred blue marbles to green ones and the shiny ones to those that did not shine. I explained to him that the hole in the earth in which we were trying to shoot the marbles always had to be bigger than the marbles themselves—because otherwise they would stick and not go any further—and anything that sticks and still wants to go further has to have a will of its own, but marbles have no will of their own; they do not push themselves further, they do not move on through the earth on their own initiative, they have to receive a small nudge from a human finger, and that's against the rules. I showed him also the flagstones in Goethestrasse and Schillerstrasse, because although he knew them he did not know them as well as I did, and I showed him how to count the flagstones and which ones were suitable for playing hopscotch and which were not.

The saying goes that one hand washes the other. My friend Itzig Finkelstein showed that he was grateful. Since we went to the same school and were even in the same class and sat on the same bench, Itzig was happy to have me copy from him, and he helped me with my homework, did arithmetic with me, explained to me why after a period it's necessary to begin with a capital letter: because a period is not a comma, but a period, and a period marks the end. And whoever wants to begin again after an end is well advised to begin big, because who wants to begin small?

My friend Itzig Finkelstein's parents were from Pohodna, a small Jewish city in Galicia, from where one day they emigrated to Germany . . . because as the barber Chaim Finkelstein explained to me,

"The Jews in Pohodna were dying of hunger, but Germany was an advanced country, a country where the dignity of man was respected, where even a Jew could earn his daily bread and look to the future calmly and with confidence."

At the house of the Finkelstein family, Yiddish was the language, since that was the mother tongue of the barber Chaim Finkelstein and his wife Sarah Finkelstein. Yiddish is a kind of Middle High German, a language which has more affinity with the German character than our own High German, which is basically only, as the barber Chaim Finkelstein said to me once "a butchered, distorted, affected Yiddish."

You want to know whether all the Jews in Wieshalle spoke Yiddish among themselves? Is that what you would like to know? No, they did not. Just a few families, so-called new settlers. The others spoke German even at home. Because most of the Jews in Wieshalle were German Jews, who had settled there a long time ago and had been living for many generations in our beautiful fatherland.

I, Max Schulz, illegitimate though pure Aryan, son of Minna Schulz, learned Yiddish at the Finkelstein's, and with the help of my friend Itzig was able to become familiar with the Hebrew alphabet, accompanied my friend every Saturday to the small synagogue in Schillerstrasse, said my prayers with him, because it was fun, sat quietly in the synagogue next to the Finkelsteins, stood up when the congregation stood up, joined in their singing, let my body sway to the rhythm of the prayer, and whispered fervently: "*Shema Yisrael Adonai Elohenu, Adonai Echath:* Hear oh Israel: the Lord our God, the Lord is One!"

Often we spoke of Jerusalem, Itzig and I. One day I said to my friend,

"Do you know . . . when we are grown up . . . then one day we'll take a trip across there. We'll take a look at it together."

The boys who played in the street around our neighborhood had formed two soccer teams: one Gentile and one Jewish. It was taken for granted that I, as the best friend of Itzig Finkelstein, should play for the Jewish team. All the goals were shot by one of us two, usually taking turns. Itzig did his shooting with the right foot, I with my left foot. We both became famous and were often booed, as is often the case when one is famous. But we didn't give two shits and said to ourselves, "They're just jealous"—and stuck to each other like tar and feathers.

My friend Itzig was blond and blue-eyed, had a straight nose and finely shaped lips and teeth. I, on the other hand, Max Schulz, illegitimate though pure Aryan son of Minna Schulz, had black hair, frog eyes, a hooked nose, bulbous lips, and bad teeth. The fact that we were often confused you will, I hope, be able to understand. The boys in the other team all called me Itzig, said I had somehow put a spell on the ball, asked me whether my father, Chaim Finkelstein, also peed in the washbasin like the stepfather of my friend Max Schulz, if he too whipped his wife on the backside, and if not why not? If I had told my stepfather all that he'd have said, "Well, what did I tell you. Don't play with Itzig. He has put a spell on you. It's obvious. How come he has your blond hair? And you his black hair? And your straight nose? And you his crooked nose? To say nothing of the eyes, lips, and teeth."

But I of course did not tell that to my stepfather, but only to the barber Chaim Finkelstein.

"Don't give it another thought," said Chaim Finkelstein. "There are no Jews who look like you. But that's something they don't know. Just understand it. They're prejudiced. And it so happens you have that certain look."

Itzig Finkelstein knew of course that my stepfather was in the habit of raping me now and again, but he did not know that my stepfather was also in the habit of beating me. One day I showed him the thick red stripes on my behind.

"How did he do that?" my friend Itzig Finkelstein asked me.

"With a rod," I said, "with a black rod. We have a yellow one, but that one is only for my mother. After the whippings there's a place that hurts, or sometimes several places, for a few hours. It's not so bad. No, that's not what's bad. What's bad is when he whips my mother. Every time he whips my mother, my own behind begins to give me pain! And how!"

"That I don't understand," said Itzig Finkelstein.

"Me neither," I said.

[32]

There was much I could understand, and much I could not understand. My dreams for instance: often I dreamed of a long knife. I used it to cut off Slavitzki's member: which I then stuck on myself because it was longer than mine, and then ran around in the children's room with the long hunk of cock, doing somersaults, cartwheels, doing splits, headstands, running into the living room then into the bedroom, looking at the memberless Slavitzki lying in bed next to my mother, watching his envious look, watching the way he crept away from me, made room for me, saw how my mother looked up with joy, stroked me, stroked my member—the long one—with her fat fingers, then I would wake up.

I also dreamed of the yellow rod, and of the black rod, saw both of them in my hand. Slavitzki I couldn't see in my dream, but I heard him shout things—quite plainly—heard his voice, knew who the blows were meant for, could only hear. I could not see him, but I could hear the squashy sound of rod against flesh. And I knew.

IV

When Itzig Finkelstein was ten and made the move, as was customary in those days for the rich and the clever, from primary school to high school, I decided to do the same.

"And what's a boy with a hole in his head going to do at the high school?" asked my mother. "I think you'd better stay at the primary school."

"Not a chance," I said.

"Why?" asked my mother. "Why?"

"Why not?" I said.

"You're talking like a Jew," said my mother. "Your answers are all screwy."

"Itzig is going to the high school," I said, "so I'm going too."

[33]

"So that you can copy from him again, eh?"

"Yes," I said. "We'll have to sit on the same bench. That's important."

"I won't hear of it," said my mother.

"Do you want me to tell Slavitzki that the super comes to you? Every second afternoon?"

"So you want to blackmail me?"

"The super," I said. "Or am I not right?"

I don't know whether that's something you could call blackmail or not. At any rate, I got what I wanted. I went to the high school.

My mother—and I—let Slavitzki continue to believe that I was still going to the primary school. We knew how envious he could get. In the end, however, he learned the truth, and called me with a sneer: a fine gentleman . . . high school pupil . . . a student . . . a would-be professor—and beat me every day because I had "bees in my bonnet." But I did not let myself be distracted.

My poor mother paid the school fees from the money the super gave her; books and exercise books, pens, erasers, and all that sort of stuff I bought myself, because I began earning money when I was ten, helping cripples and blind people across the road, putting to sleep the child of the Catholic cobbler Hans Baumeister or cleaning out his workshop with a long straw broom, and doing the same for the Jewish cobbler Fritz Weber—about whom my stepfather Slavitzki used to say, "That's a Jew who's pinched a German name"—doing errands for housewives, and making myself generally useful, getting tips, sweets, sticks of licorice.

The years at the high school gave me, Max Schulz, son of a whore, stepson of a child rapist, rat-torturer with a hole

[34]

in his head . . . quite a new stamp. I began to develop, became an educated young gentleman who knew Latin and Greek and even algebra, a young man knowledgeable about many things, especially about history and mythology. Yes, especially about history and mythology, even though sometimes I mixed up the two, somehow got the two mixed up with each other in my mind.

It's true that I was not the best student, but under the direction and stimulus of Itzig Finkelstein who sat next to me on the school bench, I was able to suck all kinds of things worth knowing into my bastard brain. You know, even scraggy Hilda began to have a certain respect for me and used to say now and then, "Max Schulz might be a little idiot, but he's still a young gentleman who's had an education!"

Itzig Finkelstein used his leisure time to read good books, including the works of great poets and thinkers who were not on the school curriculum—and since I, Max Schulz, imitated everything that Itzig Finkelstein did, naturally I too read the same books, and became even cleverer—almost as clever as Itzig Finkelstein.

When he was sixteen years old Itzig Finkelstein founded a poetry club. Can you imagine that? Itzig Finkelstein, the son of barber Chaim Finkelstein—a poet? But it really was so. Really and truly so. Naturally I joined in the endeavor, not wanting to leave my friend in the lurch, began to write poems myself, and discovered I had a poetic strain in my blood.

Itzig Finkelstein's poems were perfect in form where mine were formless; his were harmonious, mine dissonant; his well reasoned, mine completely irrational; his were real and normal, mine absurd and perverse. We both became famous at the high school, were gazed at, stared at, envied, hated, often had to put up with beatings—it was just as it had been in former times at the soccer games—but, we kept on writing our poems without allowing ourselves to be distracted!

As the year 1923 crept to its end—a year in which we had inflation, a tedious year, a year that crept along, even though it was in a hurry to see the new calendar—my friend Itzig Finkelstein said to me: "Right! Now it's enough. Now we have had an education. We are both great poets, each of us in his own way. Now I'm going to have my father teach me his trade."

I asked: "What about me?"

"You too," said Itzig Finkelstein.

"And what about all the studying we've done?"

"Oh, to hell with that!" said Itzig Finkelstein. "In Germany everything's being ruined by inflation. Everything's shot anyway. The best thing to do is learn a trade. You can always make a living if you have a trade."

"What does your father say to that plan?"

"We both share the same opinion."

I said: "Actually, you're right. We wouldn't have made it anyway. The university's the next step—we'd have had to go through all that—and all that goes with it—then years and years after that—and then—there's no money in poetry."

"None at all," said Itzig Finkelstein.

"And then there's the inflation," I said. "Nothing makes sense anymore. You're right. A trade's the thing. That's something you can fall back on."

Itzig Finkelstein nodded, and we understood each other perfectly. He put his hand on my shoulder and said: "Now listen, Max. The day will come when I'll be taking over the shop. And I'm going to make you my partner."

"Good," I said. "But why do you say, 'shop'? Aren't you

[36]

talking about the gentlemen's hairdressing salon 'Man of the World'?"

"That's the one I mean," said Itzig Finkelstein.

I said: "The 'Man of the World' is a gold mine."

"That's right," said Itzig Finkelstein. "It's a gold mine."

V

Slavitzki was of course furious to learn that I was going to be an apprentice with his competitor, but my mother said:

"The boy has to learn something properly. And the 'Man of the World' is a real hairdressing salon!"

In this respect my mother was completely on my side, and deflected Slavitzki's attacks of rage, backed me up, covered me so to speak! Yes, I, Max Schulz, entered the service of Chaim Finkelstein as an apprentice.

Itzig and I were already a little too old to be apprentices, indeed, we were almost seventeen—and we found ourselves the butts of all sorts of joking, teasing, kicks in the ass, laughter—but none of it disturbed us very much. The others were just jealous of our education—envious because we knew Latin and algebra and a lot of other things too, and had read good books, could write poetry and so on. The regular hair-cutters jibed us with nicknames like "Professor Itzig! Professor Max!" But as I say, nothing disturbed us. We knew what we were after!

As for me, the profession of barbering had always interested me. After all, is there anything more noble than the human cranium? And is it not pleasurable to shape something noble, to form it, to make it beautiful . . . just because at the same time, when doing this and other similar kinds of work one has the feeling that it would be just as great a pleasure to smash that noble creation to bits? At every moment the temptation

[37]

is so near. At one's fingertips. The hands itch—it's so very peculiar, you know. That's a head! Completely at the mercy of your own hands!

Was I ambitious to learn? Is that what you would like to know? Yes, I was. I wanted to become a good barber. Because barbering is no ordinary trade. But above all, I wanted to do better than Slavitzki, in order to be able to say to him one day: "I, Max Schulz, the bastard, am a better barber than you!" The booklet *Haircuts Tailored to the Head* became my bible and its author Chaim Finkelstein became my great model, my teacher.

Chaim Finkelstein explained to me that a man has a hundred thousand and two hairs on his cranium. While there are certain craniums, according to Chaim Finkelstein, which have more, that applies only in cases of extremely silky hair, because it is thin and has to provide a cover. Therefore it grows luxuriously. On the other hand, the number of hairs on a head which has short, curly hair, that is to say thick, strong hair, is mostly smaller, all of which is a special arrangement organized by our dear God, who knows how to distribute everything equitably when He wants to.

"What if He does not want to?" I asked.

"Well, in that case it's different," said Chaim Finkelstein. "Everything is in His hands. He is the one who breathes life in and snuffs it out again. He is a 'Great Concealer' but also a 'Great Revealer.'"

"Is that the reason why some people have bald heads?"

"That's the reason," said Chaim Finkelstein.

It was Chaim Finkelstein who taught me how to do a short back and side cut without making it look as though a bowl had been placed upon it. It was he who taught me to distinguish among hair lotions, shaving lotions, face lotions; he who taught me that creams used during the day should be without

[38]

fat, that creams for the night should have a great deal of fat; he who taught me that a mustache should be trimmed with a special type of mustache scissors; he who taught me how to go about a razor cut in the right way, using a special blade when the hair is dry, but just a plain razor when the hair is damp.

Chaim Finkelstein explained to me how a gentleman should be shaved: first come the hot compresses—dip a face cloth into hot water, wring it out, then put the middle of the cloth under the client's cheek (it being of no import whether the chin is single or double), slowly roll up the cloth so that mouth and nose stay free.

"The customer should after all be able to breathe at our shop, and not have to smother!" said Chaim Finkelstein.

The technique of lathering is important. A good lather is half the shave. You can shave with or against the grain. Or both at the same time. If you nip the client and he bleeds, don't use alum stone but alum water, because that's more hygienic. It goes without saying that when the shave is finished the face should be washed thoroughly and then—and that is very important—the skin should be carefully massaged with a lotion containing alcohol, preferably eau de cologne.

Chaim Finkelstein emphasized to me that a good barber never forgets to sharpen his blade. He explained to me that there are three kinds of razorstrops, the most handy one called "Adam" with a handle at one end and a ring at the other.

Have you ever tried to sharpen a razor blade? Do you know what a footrest is, and a headrest? Do you know that a good barber puts paper over the collar of his customer, but that only a strip, roughly one and a quarter of an inch wide, should be folded over the top of the collar, that is to say the strip which disappears between neck and collar, being stuffed into that space as it were?

[39]

If I were to tell about everything I learned while in Chaim Finkelstein's tutelage, I would go forever.

Do you know what a handbag mirror looks like? . . . I mean one that belongs to a lady who is no lady? I'm talking about the handbag mirror my mother owned . . . the one in her large, cheap handbag . . . kept there between the powder compact, nail varnish, lipstick, hairpins, handkerchief, sewing things, and all sorts of other knickknacks all squashed together . . . a small mirror, stained and sticky with lipstick and nail varnish . . . a little chipped, just a little too much . . . laddered with cracks.

One day I borrowed it and held it up in front of my face . . . and saw what I saw! Between the many cracks in the glass of the mirror a multiplicity of faces: the face of a barber . . . the face of an educated gentleman . . . the face of an idiot . . . the face of a poet . . . the face of a pervert . . . the face of a normal man . . . the face of an Aryan . . . the face of a Jew . . . the face of a soccer player . . . and other faces too—especially when my frog eyes began to drip tears from the constant staring . . . and then between the glass cracks swirling across the broken handbag mirror I saw . . . a whole host of other faces . . . faces out of a far-off future which I did not yet know . . . broken hosts. Rows and rows of faces . . . and one especially . . . quite a specific one . . . one that moved, tried to dance away . . . dance out of the rows, the rows of faces . . . as though it did not belong . . . that one . . . that one: that one was the face of a murderer . . . but it was a strange murderer's face, because it seemed to bear at one and the same time the traits of all mortals upon earth created according to His Image . . . but I could not say with complete certainty, even though it was quite a specific face that I saw, because everything was blurred . . . because my eyes were dripping with tears . . . those damned frog

[40]

eyes . . . because I did not know whether I could place my trust in the handbag mirror that belonged to my mother, who after all was a whore.

Standing in front of my mother's handbag mirror I asked myself: Who are you actually? Asked, just as my mother had asked . . . wanted to choose one . . . one of the faces . . . but could not because the faces did not want me . . . they did not want to have anything to do with me; they just gazed at me furiously, strangely distorted, because I was grimacing and sticking out my tongue.

VI

Not much happened during the next years. So I will skip over this period. The only thing worth mentioning would be the fact that I became a good barber, passed all my examinations, remained living at Slavitzki's house with my mother, but worked in the gentleman's hairdressing salon, "Man of the World," which, by the way, had been expanded from five chairs and two barbers to ten chairs and eight barbers.

In the early thirties my stepfather began to grow noticeably older, and to put on fat. The hair around his temples grayed, and so he dyed it and combed his thinning hair onto his forehead in order to look impish, shouted louder than ever, drank more liquor than ever, and began to grow a mustache.

My mother had changed too, become fatter, had no neck anymore, could hardly move, had lost the desire to play "doggy," couldn't even bark anymore. And her legs had become still more skinny.

At our place in the cellar, Adolf Hitler was often the subject of discussion, and Slavitzki perked up considerably every time my mother said,

"Do you know Anton: Ever since you started to grow a

[41]

mustache and comb your hair onto your forehead you've begun to look a bit like the Führer."

And Slavitzki said: "Yes, indeed, Minna. Hans Baumeister, the cobbler, said the same."

Slavitzki, who otherwise was not a great reader of newspapers, had been buying regularly since 1930 the tabloids of the rising new Nazi party, *Stürmer* and *Völkischer Beobachter*. He spat whenever he came across the word Jew and enjoyed especially the juicy national socialistic slogans, which he had the cobbler Hans Baumeister explain to him, and which he then in turn explained to my mother, who after that began to underline them with nail polish, mostly red or rose-colored, clip them out, and stick them onto the long wall in the barbershop. Above the washbasin into which Slavitzki was in the habit of peeing were stuck quotations like: Blood and Soil . . . International Jewish Conspiracy . . . Shameful Peace Treaty of Versailles . . . Disgrace of the First World War . . . Down with Loan Sharks . . . and so on.

In other things, Slavitzki and my mother were never of the same opinion, but in everything that concerned Herr Hitler —as Slavitzki called him—they always agreed.

"He will be the savior of us all," said my mother. "He will revenge us upon the strangers who have soiled our hearth, he will annul the shameful Peace Treaty of Versailles. He will clean up the business of war reparations and help unmarried mothers of Aryan descent to get back their honor."

And Slavitzki said: "Yes, Minna. He'll do that, all right. You can bet your life on it. And he'll get those Jews out of Schiller and Goethestrasse also. And that includes the barber Chaim Finkelstein."

"Do you know, Anton," said my mother, "every day you look just a little bit more like the Führer—with your hair across your forehead and your mustache. He had a long wagger too, just like you, although he didn't keep it down with a rubber band; but his shrunk because he's a vegetarian."

"Yes," said Slavitzki, "that's right."

"It's just your name we'll have to do something about," said my mother. "You'll have to change it."

"It's not the name that matters," said Slavitzki, "but blood and breeding. I'm no damned Pole after all."

"What are you then?" asked my mother.

"A genuine German and a pure Aryan," said Slavitzki. "My forefathers were immigrant Germans. That's why I have a Polish-sounding name."

"So—I didn't know that," said my mother. "Why didn't you tell me?"

"Because I'm no boaster," said Slavitzki.

"But can you prove it—that bit about your forefathers?" asked my mother. "Do you have a family tree?"

"No I can't," said Slavitzki. "But I'm willing to swear an oath. And when a true German swears an oath, that's a real oath."

"Yes," said my mother. "That's right."

Slavitzki had bought a secondhand radio and both of them— my mother and Slavitzki—sat before the set evening after evening, talking about politics, and working out in their heads when Herr Hitler would most likely come to power. They talked about German honor, blood and soil, a nation without living space, about our basement apartment and Chaim Finkel-stein's apartment, about the dignity of the German barber . . . even one with a name that by chance sounded Polish . . . they talked about the dignity of the Aryan mother with or without a wedding ring—for what's a ring after all? said Slavitzki—"I shit on rings; because a ring is made of gold: and who is it that's so fond of gold? International Jewry!"

My mother, who weighed *three* tons in those days, made a

girlish face, nodded her head, began to darn socks, though sometimes she interrupted this job in order to continue knitting a woolen jacket for Slavitzki. She smiled at Slavitzki, who was drinking his liquor, played around a bit with his long flabby member, stole a furtive look at the yellow rod—although not at the black one, because, in the meantime, I had come of age.

VII

Did I tell you that I was a member of the Wieshalle Association for the Prevention of Cruelty to Animals? Well, during the spring of 1932, a few of the most influential members of our organization joined the Nazi movement. Soon the slogan was flying around: Adolf Hitler loves little animals! There was a huge selection of such slogans in our clubroom: The Führer Loves Animals! Or, Adolf Hitler Loves Animals and Animals Love Him! Others: Animals Can Feel whether They Are Loved! Vote for the Animal-Lover Adolf Hitler!

One day excitement in our city rose to fever pitch. The news got around that the Führer was coming to Wieshalle to give a speech on the Mount of Olives.

Do you know the Mount of Olives? It's called that because every year the firm, Meyer's Vegetable Oils, organizes an archery contest there, a sophisticated publicity stunt for its famous product, Meyer's Olive Oil.

When the great day dawned, our city began to look like Mecca and like a town under siege. I had never in my life seen so many policemen. The people were mumbling: Look out, as soon as he comes, the Communists will be after him. Others were saying: They won't dare try anything.

The streets were swarming with people wearing swastikas. They were swinging their arms gaily, while those who were not wearing one kept their arms still and quiet, did not swing them, and looked like they wanted to tuck in their arm as a dog or a poodle tucks in its tail when water is thrown on it.

Farmers and others from the neighborhood all streamed into town—going into the local inns for a drink, flirting with housemaids and children's nurses, who were all out on the street, reveling in the sweet sense of anticipation and the warm May sunshine—before it was time to go to the Mount of Olives.

On that epoch-making day I worked in the gentleman's hairdressing salon "Man of the World" only during the morning. At twelve o'clock I took leave of Chaim and Itzig Finkelstein, saying that I had to have the day or rather the afternoon free because I wanted to see "Him."

"To see whom?" asked Chaim Finkelstein with a cough. "The son of Providence—risen from the dead?"

"Stop that coughing," I said to Chaim Finkelstein, "that coughing will be the death of you!"

I hurried home, changed into my best suit—for I had no uniform—I was not even a member of the party—put a swastika on my arm, threw down some lunch, and said with a jeer to Slavitzki . . . he should put one on too, but not with a rubber band, and not with safety pins or drawing pins, but sewn on! Slavitzki said I was getting fresher every day, told me he had not thrown away the black rod yet, and assured me that he would put one on—and a real one too—for after all, he was a German—and a real one too! That's what Slavitzki said.

At two o'clock—or to be more precise, at five minutes before two—all three of us left the basement apartment, very happy that the sun was shining, believing that Herr Hitler had arranged personally for the good weather—for that was well within his power—or so Slavitzki said—and all three of us were

[45]

wearing swastikas, yes, my mother, too. Mother's swastika was the most ostentatious, and looked as though at any moment it would burst from the fat of her upper arm.

The whole town seemed to be out on a pilgrimage to the Mount of Olives—and everybody from the neighborhood seemed to be there too. You really should have seen Weishalle on that afternoon. I especially liked the windows decorated with flowers. You could see all the colors you could think of there. The Jews in Schillerstrasse and Goethestrasse had put wreaths in their windows, as had the pacifists, the Communists were using hate blossoms, the supporters of weaker parties and those who had no party affiliation were sporting colorless flowers which drooped silently and wearily, while the others seemed to be shouting and yelling in desperation. But the flowers of the Nazis were cheering in jubilation; they were carefully chosen and arranged and made use exclusively of the colors of joy.

I lost Slavitzki and my mother in the crowd, then tried to find my Association for the Prevention of Cruelty to Animals but could not; however I did find, or run into by chance, my former German teacher Siegfried von Salzstange, who had since become headmaster at the school, which news was gladdening and I congratulated him, shook his former teacher's hand, now the hand of a headmaster, pushed myself to the front in his company—as far as the holy of holies. Siegfried von Salzstange knew just how to get through a crowd, showed me his technique, showed me how to use elbows to push intelligently, whenever that was necessary, though sometimes it was not. Finally we were successful in finding a good place to stand not too far from the altar. When I took a look back I got a shock, because behind us were millions of people.

"And I thought—that only people from Wieshalle and the

[46]

neighborhood were going to be here," I said to Siegfried von Salzstange. "But there are more here than that. Many more! I can see millions!"

"Almost all Germany is gathered here," said Herr von Salzstange.

"What do you mean: almost all Germany?"

"I mean the discontented," said Siegfried von Salzstange. "Germany's discontented, all of them, are massed in this place today!"

"The Communists?" I asked.

My former German teacher shook his head. "The others," he said, "the other discontented. Because there are a whole lot of other kinds of discontentment which communism cannot cure."

Herr von Salzstange gave a weak grin—then said: "Or at least not so thoroughly."

"Who can, then?" I asked.

"Adolf Hitler," said Siegfried von Salzstange. "He is the Great Healer."

My former German teacher picked his nose for a while in a ruminative fashion. Then he said: "All those are gathered here today who ever had a knock on the head—whether from God or from man."

"So," I said. "So that's it?"

"Yes that's it," said Siegfried von Salzstange. "Here you have a conglomeration of shattered lives, including asthmatics and professional ass-lickers, people who couldn't get anywhere in life, either because they couldn't catch their breath and had never learned to creep properly or because the asses they licked were never satisfied."

My German teacher grinned for a while in a forlorn sort of way. "And naturally others too," he said, looking at me solemnly. "As I said before I am talking about those who at

[47]

sometime or other have had a knock on the head—whether from God or from man: people with bald heads for instance, they too are here today—just take a look around you—people who are too thin and people who are too fat, people with legs that are too short and people with legs that are too long, people who are too old and people who are too young, perverts who can't find a partner and impotent men, people with a lust to strangle who have not been allowed to strangle before, being told they were allowed only to stroke; men who wear glasses have come too and women who wear glasses, because 'He' said: 'Suffer the little children to come unto me.' But 'little children' —here that means the frustrated—yes, there's the crux of it," said Herr von Salzstange. "Above all—those who would very much like to do something and can't."

"And why are you here, Herr von Salzstange," I asked. "There's nothing wrong with you, is there?"

"I'm here because of the pepper," said Siegfried von Salzstange.

"Pepper?" I asked.

"My wife puts some into my coffee every morning," said Siegfried von Salzstange poutingly.

"Why does she do that?"

"I don't know," said Siegfried von Salzstange.

"And is there nothing you can do about it?"

"Nothing at all," said Siegfried von Salzstange sadly. "There's nothing at all I can do. I snore at night by way of revenge, but it doesn't do any good."

"That's bad," I said. "And I always thought that anyone with such a good job as you could afford to have a smile on his face all the time!"

Herr von Salzstange gave a wry grin, stuck his cigarette in his mouth shamefacedly, blinked in an absent-minded manner, crushed his cigarette between his headmaster fingers, then

[48]

suddenly spat it out again as though he did not dare smoke on the Mount of Olives.

I really would very much have liked to have asked him: and why, Herr von Salzstange, did the others not come to the Mount of Olives to hear the Sermon on the Mount . . . tell me, Herr von Salzstange, how about the others . . . the hangers-on, I mean. . . . I think you know what I mean . . . the big and the small and the very small . . . the whole bang-shoot of different interest groups, as the word is, I believe, if I'm not mistaken, dear Herr von Salzstange, from within and without our beautiful German town of Wieshalle . . . of course I'm referring to those who wanted to get on the bandwagon with our Führer . . . they're always there at other times when he's giving a sermon . . . and none of them has any frustrating impediment . . . and those who have are here . . . and those who haven't are not . . . and do you think they can afford that . . . I mean not to be here with those who have an impediment . . . or perhaps they're car drivers . . . and can't come today because they'd have to come on foot . . . and that's somehow beneath the dignity of a car driver . . . because it's the Mount of Olives after all . . . and the sermon is the Sermon on the Mount . . . and why is it that car drivers can't go on a pilgrimage without their cars . . . is it because they all have flat feet . . . but I have flat feet too! And have you a headache too, Herr von Salzstange? Do you think it's from the sun? It's damned hot. And I really shouldn't be standing here . . . because of my head and the hole I have in it. . . .

But at that point I got separated from him in the melee and when I had found my way back to Herr von Salzstange he made a sign to me to keep quiet. I don't know how many millions of cripples there were gathered together that day on the Mount of Olives, but I thought to myself: if the Lord our

[49]

God looks down from above and sees it, it really must look like an anthill. Because the mountain seemed to be in constant motion. But we were not ants, were we? And it was not our wish to carry the mountain away? Or is that what we wanted? Were we not after all standing on the slope of the Mount of Olives? Did we not, in truth, bear the Mount of Olives on our shoulders? Or did other shoulders perhaps bear the Mount of Olives, which in turn bore us?—The mountain seemed to be shaking, waving in the wind, beneath a shining blue May sky and a happy sun; sometimes it seemed to stretch itself and then contract, began to tremble as the Führer arrived, cocked its ears like a beast, wanting to rear and shy, but unable to, noticed that it was being carried, and became calm—quite suddenly calm.

And do you like birds? Do you feel yourself sometimes tempted to observe the flight of birds? Especially birds that sing? Do you know what it looks like to see a bird plummet down from sky to earth? Or many birds, a whole swarm? Does it make you feel glad to hear birds singing? Especially in May?—and do you know what it feels like when the voices of the birds are stilled suddenly and unexpectedly?

When the Führer stepped up to the altar, the entire crowd drew in its breath . . . and yet we all had to continue breathing, because otherwise we would all have suffocated.

But we closed our mouths and continued to breathe through the nose only. I had a huge shock when I laid eyes on the Führer for the first time because I thought it was Slavitzki; then I said to myself: no, that can't be Slavitzki, because Slavitzki eats meat and has a long cock, but this fellow has a tiny cock and is a vegetarian. And Slavitzki has the eyes of a drinker and a lifeless expression in them, but this fellow has the eyes of a prophet. I caught sight of one last squadron of birds, zoomed in from nowhere, suddenly there, settled by the Führer on both sides of him, looking like birds of death, making no sound, not singing, sitting still and silent on the oak of the altar and the cloth of the flag, forming strange configurations: one, then nine, then three—then three again—1933—the formations stuck in my mind: what could be their meaning? I nudged Siegfried von Salzstange and whispered the question to him "What could it mean?" Even though I was not supposed even to whisper—"It means that in 1933 He will come to power," Siegfried von Salzstange whispered back. "That is after all as clear as the Rhine."

"How do you know whether or not the Rhine is clear?" I asked.

"Anyway, keep your mouth shut now," said Siegfried von Salzstange. "Can't you see that He is raising His eyes to heaven? He wants to implore the help of heaven. And in a moment everything will begin."

"What will begin?" I asked.

"The speech, you idiot!" said Siegfried von Salzstange.

First Adolf Hitler spoke about the origins of the movement, described the march to the Feldherrnhalle—reminded us of the blood of fallen comrades, of the dead who were not dead because they lived on in us, explained to us why it was necessary to build cannons, that He would build some—very special ones—because that was an oath He had sworn to His father, the Lord of Providence, and he made clear to us that ordinary cannons shoot cannonballs, but that his would belch forth also butter and black bread and Harz cheese and hot dogs with sauerkraut. Hitler explained to us that brown shirts were better than others, tight trousers better than loose-fitting ones, explained to us that puttees looked ridiculous because shins are best sheathed away in the shafts of boots, like everything

[51]

else below the knee, which is to say of low position, and not above the knee, which is to say of lofty position. He spoke about the Versailles Peace Treaty, pledging its annulment, and explained to us that a zero was a circle with a hole in its middle, a real hole, because there was no such thing as half a hole: "A hole is a hole!"

Hitler spoke of misers and bloodsuckers, of soiling and tearing to shreds, explained to us that honor is hereditary just as is courage and loyalty, spoke about the conspiracy of world Jewry that was holding German honor, German courage, and German loyalty in its net, to prevent its developing and its flowering.

I hardly listened, because I knew it all already, had heard it all so often over the radio and read it in the newspapers. I just looked at the vultures, looked at the altar of oak draped with flags, compared the hair on His forehead with Slavitzki's, compared His mustache and Slavitzki's. It was only when the Führer began to speak about history, and began to go back in time until finally he was speaking about Jerusalem, that I became attentive again and clicked my heels, began to breathe through the nose, and stop comparing mustaches and locks of hair, began to forget the vultures on the altar of oak draped with flags, and to look only into His eyes.

The Führer had opened the Bible. First of all, he leafed through the Old Testament, then through the New Testament, pushed the lock of hair on his forehead out of his eyes, wrinkled his forehead and said finally, "St. Luke twenty-three, verses twenty-seven to twenty-nine."

Then He began to read in a hoarse voice: "'And there followed him a great company of people, and of women, which also bewailed and lamented him. But Jesus turning to them said, Daughters of Jerusalem, weep not for me, but weep

[52]

for yourselves and for your children. For, behold, the days are coming in which they shall say, Blessed *are* the barren, and the wombs that never bare, and the paps which never gave suck!'"

The Führer banged the Bible shut, folded his hands, raised his prophetic eyes toward the heavens, and said: "Verily, verily I say unto you: the Lord has condemned them, and the curse has been enchained. But I have come to unchain it."

And the Führer said:

"Blessed are the strong for they shall inherit the earth.

"Blessed is the fist because it will strike a hole in the circle, and make it a real hole and not half a hole. Because there are no half holes!

"Blessed are those who are thick of blood, because they will be lord of all beneath the sun. For when blood loses its virtue to water, it evaporates. And what has ceased to exist can exist no more. And what then with the Lord and Master?"

And the Führer said: "You heard what was said to the men of old: thou shalt not kill; and whosoever shall kill shall be in danger of the judgment. But I say unto you: whosoever shall kill the enemy of our nation shall make my name holy. And whosoever shall make my name holy shall share in my holiness."

And the Führer said:

"You heard what is ordained in the Old Testament, an eye for an eye and a tooth for a tooth. But I say unto you: is that not the justice of publicans? What is an eye and what is a tooth? Take one eye—does not another eye remain? Take one tooth—do not thirty-one teeth remain? Verily there is no real revenge there. Therefore I say unto you: two eyes for one eye. And thirty-two teeth for one tooth. Blind your foes and make them toothless for all eternity. . . . For the blind man can see no more. And the toothless man can bite no more. If you will be Lord, then strike with strength. And if you will inherit the earth that I wish to give you, do as I command. Amen."

And the Führer said:

"Cursed be the rod in the hand of the false master. But when the rod changes its master and the new master is the true master, let it then be sacred."

And the Führer said:

"Blessed be the rod in the hand of the true master. For behold, it is not the rod that makes the hand holy but the hand which makes the rod holy. Verily I say unto you: in the hand of the true master the rod becomes a sword, and the hand that holds it may rule in all eternity. Amen."

As the Führer spoke the final words, the heavens became outraged, for His words were mighty. Thunder and lightning began. Clouds massed over the Mount of Olives and circled above the altar. But the rain was afraid and the clouds made themselves scarce again. The crowd stood still as death.

During the latter part of the speech I felt a powerful itching. My backside, I thought. Why is it itching like that? Then the itch became stronger and stronger, burning painfully. I saw the yellow and the black rod, saw Slavitzki's cock hanging down from the black and the yellow rod, becoming a part of it, grinning jeeringly, an omen of my impotence. Without pause the words of the Führer hammered in my brain. "Cursed be the rod in the hands of the false master. But when the rod changes its master . . ." I began to grow dizzy. Felt a lump in my throat. Choking me. And I wanted to spit it out. . . . "Blessed be the rod in the hands of the true master. For behold . . ."

And I said to myself: Yes, but why? Enough! And I said to myself: Max Schulz, never again will you hold out your backside. It's high time that you held the rod in your own hand. The yellow one as well as the black one.

[54]

Next to me stood Siegfried von Salzstange. Looking in front of him, stupidly, fixedly.

"Germany's discontented, all of them, are massed in this place today."

Isn't that what he said a while ago?

"All those are gathered here today who ever had a knock on the head—whether from God or from man."

I would very much like to have asked my former German teacher whether everyone here, everyone standing here and looking straight into the mouth of the Führer or into his eyes knew a false master—one with a rod—but I didn't dare because Siegfried von Salzstange was looking ahead of him so strangely and so fixedly. Perhaps there are different kinds of rods for the others, I thought, it doesn't absolutely have to be yellow ones or black ones. Perhaps it can be green ones or blue ones, red ones or violet-colored ones?

It is certain that there were other kinds of rods, many kinds of rods, probably in all kinds of possible colors. And as I was thinking along those lines, the thick lump in my throat began to choke me again and I absolutely had to spit it out. And suddenly I saw millions of rods hissing over the Mount of Olives and the manifold colors were mirrored above us, now no longer blue but an ocean of colors. No wonder the Führer had driven away the rain!

Standing to my right was an old woman—an old woman with a gray face, a face in which the God of love had dug ditches and furrows mercilessly as though it were not a face created in His image. The old woman was moving her lips as though in prayer. I understood only one of the whispered sentences: "Heaven and earth shall pass away but my words shall not pass away."

When the old woman began to pray the others began to pray too. Gradually the mass of bodies began to move. And then

. . . yes, that's how it must have been. Quite suddenly! Suddenly came the first scream. Then we all began to scream. The right hand. Without warning it flew upward. Everybody's. As though on its own. We were screaming like lunatics. Screaming: Amen, amen, amen! One man excited the next. We screamed. We went into frenzies. We wept. He was our savior. Then someone in the crowd sobbed: "My Führer, I want you to give me a rod too." And another cried: "Me, too, and I want to have faith in you!" Soon there was a chorus of voices on every side. To our left people were screaming: "Behold the blood on our backside!" And to our right people were screaming: "Let us be true masters—we wish to have faith in you!"

Do you know how to spit out a lump in the throat? And do you know what it looks like when millions of men spit out the lumps in their throats and watch them glide through the air?

Naturally you will want to know whether I took the rod away from Slavitzki—I mean later—at the right moment? Or both rods, and whether I put him over my knee as he had done to me? And whether I raped him as he had raped me?

No. I left him the rods, because they were old and worn. Like Slavitzki was. And after all, had not Slavitzki too known a false master—sometime in his life? Perhaps he still knew one and couldn't get rid of him? Think about it for a moment.

After all, who is Slavitzki. And anyway was there really only one Slavitzki in my life? Were there not perhaps many Slavitzkis? And was not the dear Lord also a Slavitzki? One with a rod? And apart from His rod, the rod of the invisible Slavitzki and the yellow and the black rods of the earthly Slavitzki--were there not also other rods in my life? Perhaps

[56]

no principal rods, but certainly some subsidiary rods? Not lilac and red or green and blue, because those were the rods of the others, and they were first-priority rods, were they not? Right now I am talking only about all the colorless subsidiary rods, the rods of my five fathers, which projected me, Max Schulz, a nothing who didn't even exist, with one single jerk of a rod into this life. And just think of the colorless subsidiary rods my soccer opponents had, or my teachers, who tortured me, or my school friends, who made fun of me, and of whom I have so far, not told you a word—for after all I cannot tell everything—and I really don't want to put your patience to the test. And as far as the yellow and the black rods are concerned, was it then really only Slavitzki who swung those rods? Did not rather my mother help him do it? And did she not also give a little help to my five fathers with their subsidiary rods? At what point does the dance begin? And when does it end? Now where is God's place in all this round? Is He part of the dance? Or is He above it? Who is it I should really hit with a rod?

No, I let Slavitzki keep his rod. I got new rods for myself, better rods . . . better than the old ones even when the old ones were new. And I picked rods that were neither yellow nor black, but colors of my own choosing. And I wanted to find more than one victim. Because what is a single victim? I wanted a victim for every wound, a victim for every jeering grin, and didn't care two hoots whether God or the world had been the one to hurt me.

Today I can understand why the lumps in our throats which we spat out that day glided aloft through the air until they hit innocent bystanders—because we had not taken aim. We had merely spat them out.

But at the time I did not understand.

VIII

On the day following the Sermon on the Mount I joined the party of the Son of Providence—became, as it were, a member. My mother too. Slavitzki also, who was not a Pole but a German. Slavitzki and I also registered in the fighting battalions of the storm troopers but decided to wait before buying the prescribed boots and uniforms until the Führer actually came to power—because to acquire boots and uniforms required a wad of money—and a wad of money is a wad of money—and a man can never tell—it's better to be sure.

When the great day came and Hitler mounted us, swung himself as it were into the saddle and shouted "giddyup" in our ears, Slavitzki and I galloped to the nearest shop, bought two smart uniforms and two pairs of bright, shiny boots, snapped on the storm trooper's belt, drank ourselves silly, staggered through the streets, running everywhere across groups of uniformed men in the process of beating up enemies of the people, decided to lend a hand, joined in the beating, sweated, burped, laughed, masturbated, farted . . . it was great fun. Take it from me. Later, Slavitzki got a bag for groceries and we staggered noisily in the direction of home, but instead of going right away to the basement apartment, we first of all staggered down Goethestrasse and through Schillerstrasse, smashing Finkelstein's windows on the way . . . apartment and business windows, then staggered into the gentleman's hairdressing salon, "Man of the World," smeared swastikas all over the expensive mirrors, and little pig's tails too, stuffed everything we could into our grocery bag: face lotion, shaving soap, expensive creams, soap, brushes too, the latest models in shaving sets, scissors, combs, brushes, kicked Chaim Finkelstein in the ass and Itzig Finkelstein too, and shouted: "Jewish

Pig!" Shouted: "Itzig!" Slavitzki yelled: "My son gives notice effective today! Heil Hitler! You've put a spell on him! He looks like an Itzig! Yes, goddamnit! . . . like Itzig Finkelstein!"

When we got home in our boots and our uniforms—our so elegant uniforms—my mother raised her eyebrows in amazement, shook her fat behind, giggled, showed off her skinny legs, became quite excited, then said to Slavitzki: "Now, Anton, now you look like a man."

And Slavitzki said: "We went shopping. We didn't forget you. Here is an assortment of creams. There's one for your behind too."

And my mother said: "Oh come on, Anton!"

And Slavitzki said: "Oh come on, Minna!"

"What about the rats?" I asked.

"Let the rats be," said Slavitzki. "The Führer didn't say anything about rats."

"But he did say something about the Jews," I said. And I clicked my heels and said: "The Lord has condemned them. And the curse has been enchained. But I have come to unchain it."

"That's not what the Führer said at all," said Slavitzki. "You're batty."

"And I told him he shouldn't stand in the sun without something on his head," said my mother.

"Besides, I don't understand that," said Slavitzki. "Do you understand that, Minna?"

"Me neither," said my mother. "That's too highfalutin for me."

"He wants to get rid of all Jews," I said.

"Well," said Slavitzki, "have you something against that maybe?"

"All I was thinking about was the rats," I said, "the rats in our basement apartment. When there are no more Jews in

Goethestrasse and Schillerstrasse—won't that mean there are enough free apartments to go round?"

"Yes, for God's sake!" said Slavitzki.

And my mother said: "Jesus, Mary, and Joseph!"

"Well, then we'll move into Finkelstein's apartment," I said, "and then we're rid of the rats."

"Yes, for God's sake!" said Slavitzki.

"Jesus, Mary, and Joseph," said my mother.

"True, I have begun to get used to the rats," I said, "have always enjoyed playing with them. But that has to stop sometime."

"Obviously," said Slavitzki.

"There are rats with two legs too," said my mother.

"Right," said Slavitzki.

IX

Do you know how it is when two brothers are fighting for power? You don't know? I'm not sure about it myself either, because I, at that time still Max Schulz, am an only son of my mother, the whore Minna Schulz. I have no brother.

What happened in our party was something like a fight between brothers: between those who wore brown uniforms and those who wore black ones . . . they fought each other for power . . . the brown SA and the black SS.

Slavitzki's uniform and mine . . . were brown, or, to be more precise, shiny brown—one day my mother said to us: "Like watered-down cocoa. I liked them at first, but I don't like them anymore."

My stepfather Slavitzki said: "So what?"

"Anything that looks like cocoa is going to get licked," said my mother. "Just you watch out! It's going to be the black uniforms that take the biscuit!"

[60]

Naturally my mother was right. After the Röhm Putsch in 1934 and the assassination of the great brown general, the farsighted members took off their brown uniforms and replaced them with black ones. Only the shortsighted ones among us didn't do that—but that's because they were shortsighted. I was convinced my mother was right and Germany's future could not in any event be brown, and would be black. And so I too chose black. A few weeks after the liquidation of the great brown bear, I, Itzig Finkelstein, at that time still Max Schulz, decided to have myself transferred to the SS. I also gave up my membership in the Association for the Prevention of Cruelty to Animals. I, Itzig Finkelstein, at that time still Max Schulz, had made my choice.

My former German teacher Siegfried von Salzstange said to me once: "Max Schulz. Everybody who can fart can get into the brown SA. But not into the SS!"

Because the SS, that was the union of the "Black Puritans," the elite of the new Germany. For mice like Max Schulz, who did not look like supermen, but like inferior mortals . . . yes, that's what they looked like, really, no joking . . . who looked as though they would not be able to understand the ethics of genocide . . . never understand it . . . for them admission to the SS was anything but easy.

What did I say? Not easy? That's right. That's what I said. However, I have to add here that good connections often play a decisive role in life. Did I have connections? Do you want to know? Of course I had connections. My former German teacher had been in the SS for some time. And he had something to say there. Because Siegfried von Salzstange was blood cousin of the SS General Helmut von Schaumbeck, a man who had one of the top jobs in Berlin.

Siegfried von Salzstange took me under his wing—and he

was not the only one—because two former comrades of mine from the Association for the Prevention of Cruelty to Animals were on the racial commission of the black corps in Wieshalle.

Like all new SS candidates, I too, Itzig Finkelstein, at that time still Max Schulz, had to go through the mill of racial and background investigation by the black corps. That was painful and time-consuming. But I made it. My blood had not lost its virtue to water and my face was simply bewitched.

Slavitzki! Of course he wanted to join the SS too. Just because he wanted to show off wearing the elegant black uniform and the cap with the skull-and-crossbones.

But who was there to stand up for him? The SS refused him. There was something wrong with his family tree. With that long hunk of steak of his too. It had got flabby. And stayed flabby. And a fat behind and a yellow rod couldn't change anything about this fact of life. What was flabby and what stayed flabby and showed no will had no chance of rising with us.

Nevertheless, Slavitzki and my mother were better off than ever before. My mother had put a new sign on the door of the barbershop, which read: "Aryan Business. Minna Schulz and Company—Family Tree Available."

Since the notice on the door was not enough, Slavitzki had to help a little and act as the publicity manager of the firm Minna Schulz and Company—sometimes he plunked himself down menacingly on the other side of the street . . . yes, right in front of the gentleman's hairdressing salon "Man of the World," stood there in his stained barber's apron wearing a swastika on his arm, an awesome apostle of the Third Reich, shouting in a thunderous voice at the customers who wanted to go to Chaim Finkelstein's shop: "What, you have your hair cut at a damned Jewish barber's! You want to help an enemy of the people? Are you behind our Führer Adolf Hitler, or not?"

The nervous ones fairly streamed into our shop. Those with a bit of courage stayed by Chaim Finkelstein.

As for me, Itzig Finkelstein, at that time still Max Schulz, I was doing all right. I was working for Slavitzki. Now we had a much better clientele and Slavitzki needed a good barber. He needed me. I was earning well, getting big tips, for none of our customers dared to be mean with his tips to an SS man and bearer of the black uniform. I had nothing to complain about.

X

The Jews! They had a bad time under us. We in the new Germany showed those Jews what it means when a man has blood in his veins that hasn't lost its virtue. "For when blood loses its virtue to water it cannot be restored!" We in the new Germany began to remove Jews from key positions and official offices, put them properly in their place, blackmailed them, bit by bit took away their property and eased them out of most of the professions. The Jews were thrown out of the Army, degraded publicly with the help of the press, radio, films, and other public mass media, by all means available to us at the time. Their ugly mugs began to appear on publicity columns and on the front page of the *Stürmer*. Mobs smashed in their store windows and threw stink bombs into their businesses. Jews were mugged in broad daylight and were not allowed to issue complaints. Under any sort of pretext Jews were arrested and disappeared for indefinite periods of time, sometimes forever.

[63]

Those were bad times for the Jews. Even so, that was nothing compared with the events due to come, just a prelude in fact, a prologue to the great Jewish catastrophe.

I myself was in those days just small-fry. I had made my pact with the devil, had placed my booted foot and uniformed frame on the wheel of history, but my weight was of no account. For after all what difference can small-fry make? And what is a uniform after all? And what are a pair of boots? Millions of small fish . . . sometimes in uniform, sometimes out of uniform . . . boots on and even boots off . . . all the small fish who in those days said yes and alongside me put their feet and their frame on the wheel of happiness—they were the ones who set the bandwagon rolling.

Did I kill any Jews in those days? Is that what you'd like to know? Not in those days. That came later. At that time I was just a member. Common or garden variety of the SS. I was trained. Trained for my mission.

That's the long and short of it. I was a member. And I remained a member. The SS would not let me go. They needed me just as Slavitzki had always needed me. They needed my hands. And they needed my ass too as something that could be stuck out for the blow that one day would come when the bandwagon lost its momentum, the bandwagon which we all wanted to jump on and make history.

The Jews in Germany were well aware that the rope around their necks was being drawn ever tighter. That is to say: the clever Jews knew it. Only the dumb Jews still believed in 1936 that our government could be felled from within. Many Jews emigrated or had emigrated already. Many however had not.

As far as the Jews in Wieshalle were concerned, that is to say, the Jews in Goethestrasse and Schillerstrasse—they stayed.

In other words: they did not emigrate! Were they hoping for a miracle? I don't know.

And the Finkelsteins did not emigrate either, so I must have been mistaken: Chaim and Itzig Finkelstein were stupid Jews, who did not know what was coming to them from our government. And I have to say the same of our third Finkelstein, the wife of Chaim Finkelstein and the mother of Itzig Finkelstein.

My boss, SS sergeant Franz Sauer could not in those days possibly have known that I, Max Schulz, would in the course of the next few years myself become a sergeant in the SS. . . . He treated me, Max Schulz, the small fish, with fatherly condescension.

One day the SS sergeant Franz Sauer said to me over a beer: "Max Schulz! The Jews in Wieshalle are stupid Jews. They don't seem to want to leave!"

And I said: "Yes, Sergeant."

My sergeant burped from an excess of beer, gaped at me out of his small, foxy, blue eyes, grinned, flicked off some invisible threads and dust from his uniform . . . yes, dust too . . . from his elegant black uniform, burped again, then said: "Max Schulz! Max Schulz! It won't be held against you that you worked for that damned Jew Finkelstein a few years ago. What has been has been, am I not right?"

"Right," I said. "I gave the Jew notice long ago."

Sergeant Franz Sauer nodded. "And it doesn't matter that you were a good friend of the Jew Itzig Finkelstein. What has been has been, right?"

"Right," I said.

"Your mother told me that the Jew Itzig Finkelstein wanted to make you his partner, right?"

"Right," I said. "But nothing came of it. First of all because

[65]

old man Finkelstein is still as healthy as hell and secondly because I am a member of the party."

"Right," said my sergeant. "Right."

"Right," I said, "that's how it is."

My sergeant drank his beer, pushed the cap with the skull and crossbones back on his head and smoothed down his greasy hair.

"Don't you think, Max Schulz," he then asked foxily, "that it's high time the Jews in Goethestrasse and Schillerstrasse were thrown out of their businesses—and that the businesses were, so to speak, Aryanized?"

"It's high time, Sergeant," I said.

"Those are streets named after German poets and thinkers," said Franz Sauer.

"Let's drink to that," I said.

Franz Sauer nodded. He drank his beer, ordered another and drank that too. We were silent for a while, staring at each other. Franz Sauer ordered more beer and still more beer. His thirst seemed unquenchable. Between drinks he stood up and staggered outside. When he came back he shouted at me in a drunken voice.

"And what sort of houses are they, the ones in Goethestrasse and Schillerstrasse?"

"Full of bugs," I said.

"I don't give a damn about that," Franz Sauer said, sitting down. "Bugs won't bite an Aryan ass."

"Very good, Sergeant," I said. "Bugs won't do that. And what about the Jewish apartments?"

"Let the apartments be," said Franz Sauer, just as my stepfather Slavitzki had said: let the rats be.

"We'll take care of the businesses first," said Franz Sauer.

"Yes, Sergeant," I said. "The businesses!"

"And first on the list—that Jew Finkelstein's!"

[66]

"Very well," I said.

"Are you a good barber, Max Schulz?"

"Yes, Sergeant," I said.

"And do you know what the Führer Adolf Hitler said about the Aryan barber?"

"Yes, Sergeant," I said. "The Führer said, 'An Aryan barber is not a Jewish barber!'"

"Right!" said Franz Sauer.

Franz Sauer burped, ordered more beer, burped again, let out a huge fart, scratched himself, banged the table with his fist and shouted:

"Max Schulz! I order you—to take over that damned Jew Finkelstein's barbershop!"

"That is not a barbershop," I said. "It's a gentleman's hairdressing salon! And it has a name: 'Man of the World.'"

"Then I order you," shouted Franz Sauer and banged the table again with his fist, "to take over the gentleman's hairdressing salon 'Man of the World'!"

Make a note, please: Max Schulz never took over the gentleman's hairdressing salon "Man of the World" on the corner of Goethe and Schillerstrasse! His sergeant was just drunk.

That's the truth of it. He was just drunk. There was no warrant out for the arrest of the Finkelsteins—at least not in 1936. And I couldn't do anything, even though I would have liked very much to take over the shop, that is to say the hairdressing salon. But I couldn't arrest the Finkelsteins all on my own, because I was only a small fish at that time and my sergeant was only a small fish, even if he was a little bigger than I was.

So that's about the way things were. We let the small Jewish businesses in Goethestrasse and Schillerstrasse exist for

[67]

a while longer, that is to say: let the smaller fish among the Jews swim around a bit.

Why? You want to know why? How should I know? I myself was only a little fish—perhaps because our SS General Helmut von Schaumbeck had said: "Take it slow! And keep an eye on the foreign press! It's important to choose the right moment!"—I really don't know.

Often at night I lay awake in my bed staring into the darkness in the direction of the basement windows—saw newspaper clippings, saw headlines, seemingly written in fluorescent writing across my imagination:

THE JEWISH BARBER—A NATIONAL DANGER! PUBLIC ENEMY NUMBER ONE! DOES BUSINESS ON PURPOSE CORNER OF GOETHE AND SCHILLERSTRASSE. THE CORNER! RIGHT THERE WHERE TWO GERMAN POETS JOIN HANDS! RIGHT THERE HE SQUATS DOWN BETWEEN THEM. THE JEW! ON PURPOSE! GETTING BETWEEN THEM LIKE A HYPHEN! DIVIDING THEM! SO THAT THE HANDS CANNOT JOIN! SPLITTING UP OUR CULTURE! OPPOSE THE JEWISH BARBER! GERMAN MEN AND WOMEN: IF GOETHE AND SCHILLER MEAN ANYTHING TO YOU . . . IF YOUR HANDS WANT TO JOIN . . . THEN GET RID OF THE JEWISH BARBER ON THE CORNER!

And others:

PARTY COMRADES! THE RIGHT MOMENT! IT HAS COME! ALL JEWISH BUSINESSES WITHOUT EXCEPTION MUST BE CONFISCATED! NEW ARYAN PROPRIETORS TO BE FINANCED BY THE PARTY!

During the day I frequently stood in my white barber's apron by Slavitzki's side looking across the street through the window at the competition, and found myself facing a blurred notice on which was written: New Proprietor . . . Max Schulz . . . Aryan Business . . . Family Tree Available. . . .

[68]

There is not a lot more to tell. Our superintendent died in 1937. That was a sad blow for my mother. But then a new one came—a new super.

That's the truth. Does it interest you? Or should we throw the calendar away—the 1937 calendar? And hang a new one up? The 1938 one? Why? Where? When? That doesn't matter two hoots! And why not! And anywhere at all and any time at all? On the basement window as far as I'm concerned. In the fall too! If you like! Why in the fall? Why not?

In November 1938 there was a pogrom, which we called the Night of the Broken Glass. That's when we really started hitting. But we didn't finish then.

The Jewish synagogues across the whole country were burned down. Jewish businesses were looted. Streets were covered with glass—broken glass. A lot of glass. A lot of broken glass. In Wieshalle too.

The synagogue in Schillerstrasse burned the whole night. A few of the neighboring houses caught fire. But the November wind was to blame for that. Yes. That damned wind. Finkelstein's gentleman's hairdressing salon burned down too. Yes, that's what I said. It burned down. That corner of German culture, the corner of Schiller and Goethestrasse, ceased to exist. In its place there was a huge hole. A cultural gap. Has it grown together again? The hole? I don't know because I didn't stay in Wieshalle for much longer.

But I'm taking up your time unnecessarily, right? What you want to know is when I became a mass-murderer?

And so I, Itzig Finkelstein, at that time still Max Schulz, will try to be as brief as possible. You're losing your patience—and so am I.

[69]

Well, here's what happened: I continued to work for Slavitzki. I can't say I was having a bad time . . . not bad at all. Then—then came the war, the damned war. Yes, the damned war came!

Have you ever heard of the invasion of Poland? That was just like a short promenade. There was not much on in 1939.

Did I take part in that? No. I missed it, unfortunately. The SS did put me into a crash training program for active duty out in the country somewhere, but it didn't crash fast enough . . . because when I got to my unit in Poland . . . that was during the winter, 1939 . . . a Polish winter . . . and that means a damned cold winter . . . yes . . . well, by then the war in Poland was over.

So what did I do . . . in Poland . . . in the winter? Is that what you want to know? Well, I got bored. There was nothing doing! At least not where we were. We had to keep watch over just a few villages . . . and a few cemeteries . . . and a bit of forest . . . and a country road . . . near the Russian border or not far from it. There was nothing doing. I didn't see any partisans or resistance fighters. And the governing classes in Poland had long ago been liquidated . . . by comrades in the SS who had arrived in earlier units . . . liquidated . . . I said . . . just like other elements opposed to Germany . . . I mean right there where we were, near the Russian border or not far from it.

Out of sheer boredom we began shooting at the icicles on the trees, and now and again we did away with a few Jews because we had nothing better to do . . . did away with them . . . in the forest and then in the cemeteries . . . just to keep our hand in. I can hardly remember anymore what went on there—it was so little—where we were . . . in Poland . . . in December 1939.

Just one real thing happened. It has stuck in my mind: We marched a few Jews up to a cemetery to shoot them. But it was the wrong cemetery. There were crosses on the graves. There they were standing in front of the crosses stammering, afraid even to cry. And on one of the crosses, the smallest and simplest cross, hung Jesus Christ. And he was crying. And was saying to my lieutenant: "That was not what I meant! It's true that I cursed them! But I simply wanted to frighten them! So that they would convert!"

And Jesus wept and said no more.

And my lieutenant flew into a rage and shot a few bullets into the stomach of the wailing Christ. And Christ fell down from the cross, but was not dead.

Then my lieutenant said to me: "Max Schulz! Stop that fake saint's foul mouth. You're the best one at that!"

So that's what I did.

After I had shot Christ, we marched the Jews out of the Christian cemetery, because my lieutenant said: "Sure is sure. One can never know. A guy like that Jesus Christ is a bit of a magician. He might all of a sudden go and rise up from the dead again!"

So we marched the Jews up to their own cemetery. There were no crosses there. And we shot them. There weren't many.

It only began to get gory when the march into Russia started. Mobile Killing Unit D in the South Russia section. But that was later, in 1941.

Have you any idea how one shoots thirty thousand Jews in a forest? And do you know what that does to a non-smoker? It's there that I learned to smoke.

Can you do arithmetic in your head? Are you good at figures? If you are, then you'll know that sort of thing is not easy.

In the beginning I counted the victims; although the way

I did it was rather like the way I used to count the flagstones as a child when we were playing hopscotch—and it's easy to make a mistake in counting. Later that method didn't work. It was too laborious.

Yes, and what happened next? Well, I had a little heart attack and I found myself transferred into the hinterland. I mean to say, still further into the hinterland, because those were the days when the German Army was advancing gaily every day, and as for our section in southern Russia: that was already hinterland.

I was transferred to Poland. So there I was in Poland again. That was a country I knew. There the cemeteries had strange crosses.

Do you know the concentration camp Laubwalde? At one time the place had a Polish name. But we gave it a new name: Laubwalde. It was a wonderfully beautiful place, surrounded by woods.

There were two hundred thousand Jews in Laubwalde. We killed them all. Two hundred thousand! Even so, that was a small camp because most of the prisoners were done away with almost as soon as they'd come in. That was practical. It meant that we never had to keep guard over too many of them. As I said: it was a small camp!

Two hundred thousand. That's a number with five zeros. Do you know how to knock off a zero? Or two zeros? Or three zeros? Or four zeros? Or five zeros? Can you imagine how a man knocks off a zero? And in the end the number two also . . . even though that is no zero? Do you know how that's done?

I know, since I was one of those who were involved, even though today I can't remember what happened too exactly, and can't remember exactly how many prisoners I shot, or beat to death, or hanged. Nevertheless those days in Laubwalde

[72]

were pretty peaceful when one considers that others were at the front and had to risk their necks.

Right up to the last day of the war I served in Laubwalde— that is, right up to that memorable day when the war was for me, Max Schulz, later Itzig Finkelstein, good and properly over.

𝕭𝖔𝖔𝖐 𝕿𝖜𝖔

I

Frau Holle had two legs: one Aryan leg and one non-Aryan leg. The non-Aryan leg was made of wood, and was strapped on during the day and then, late in the evening, before she went to bed, taken off.

Frau Holle had the bad habit of reading in bed by candle-light, because there was as yet no electric light in Nietzsche-strasse. When Frau Holle was absorbed in her reading, she never thought about the wooden leg hanging from a rusty nail on the long wall of the cellar apartment . . . hanging at the foot of the bed. But sometimes, when the candlelight flickered a little, she looked up, actually without intending to, saw the wooden leg, and saw the dark shadow on the wall as well, saw the shadow move, got scared, started to jump out of the lonely bed, but then thought about it and decided instead just to pull the other leg in a little, that is to say the Aryan leg.

The shadow cast by the wooden leg was a strange shadow. Because it didn't only have a body, it also had a face. Frau Holle understood very well how it was that a shadow could move when cast by a flickering candle flame. She also understood how the shadow could jiggle about a little, even though its hoppings were sometimes strange . . . on the long wall . . . looking sometimes as though at any moment it would jump on the lonely bed, upon the lonely, scared woman herself, an Aryan woman, who during the day had two legs, and during the night only one, an Aryan leg, that would fold up out of sheer fright—but what Frau Holle did not understand and could not understand was that the shadow could also grin, and that its grin was always different.

In 1942, when the German troops reached the Volga, the shadow of the wooden leg, which after all was not Aryan . . . just as the wooden leg itself was not Aryan . . . wore a very strange grin . . . it was a desperate grin, the grin of a person who would like to cry and cannot. Then, after the fall of Stalingrad, the grin became more hopeful. And later, much later actually, when the Russians were almost on the threshold of Berlin, the shadow put on an impish grin, yes, an impish grin, just like a Russian would have or a Jew when confronting a defenseless German woman or a bunch of defenseless German women. But since the collapse of the great German Reich the shadow had been grinning with sheer pleasure and even seemed to have been laughing to itself.

At night Frau Holle was afraid. But in the early morning, when it became light and the ghost had gone, her fear disappeared and the rage she had contained within her burst out in a fury. Only then did Frau Holle dare to curse the wooden leg. And did she curse! And how she cursed!

"You filthy Ivan," Frau Holle cursed, brightening up all the time. "You filthy God-forsaken Ivan, you sex maniac, vagabond, Jewish pig, Itzig, assassin, lay-about, slant-eye, you Siberian slob!"

This morning too, Frau Holle was cursing the wooden leg, but after a while she quieted down, swallowed, spat out, rubbed her left ear, then her right ear, scratched her backside with the left hand, then the right hand, crept out of her lonely bed, took the wooden leg off its hook, strapped it on, rubbed her eyes, yawned, then got to thinking that the Aryan leg would fold up if it were not for the non-Aryan leg—simply fold.

"That's a disgrace," she thought. "Today you've slept a bit longer . . . there must be a reason. Today is the fifth of August, 1945, your birthday. Damn it, I suppose I should celebrate. But how? And with whom?"

Frau Holle began to sing a little because she was in a birthday mood. She leisurely got dressed, put on a black headscarf, even though in summer it was not really necessary. But Frau Holle said to herself: "I better put it on because my hair is so gray and filthy!" Before leaving she threw a glance into the half-broken mirror which hung on the short wall next to the old, scratched wardrobe. She felt annoyed and began to curse again.

"You look just like an old farmer's wife: one with a wooden leg. A face with wide bones, a four-square face. But where's the fat? Your face looks like a triangle under the black headscarf, and how about those big yellow teeth that stick out so much . . . they've got yellower and yellower . . . but not shorter!"

Frau Holle closed the creaking door of the basement apartment carefully. One couldn't be too careful. She wanted to go

[77]

shopping on the black market. She had had nothing in her stomach since lunch time the previous day and was beginning to feel a little sick.

"You'll just have to sell your wedding ring," she mumbled, as she dragged herself up the steps. "There's no way out of it. If Günther knew—ah well, the Russians have got him for sure—and maybe on the black market I can get a few eggs, milk, and cigarettes—oh, how I hate the damned bombed cellar steps—I'll break my neck one of these days—that's all I need, an accident now that the war's over—this bloody, wooden leg—this goddamned wooden leg."

She had just got to the top of the stairs and was about to step out of the house into the warm post-war sun in the German town of Warthenau, when she heard behind her a noise in the vestibule, heard a door creak, heard someone whistling softly, heard the door shut, and thought:

"That will be Willy Holzhammer." Then she turned and waited.

II

Willy Holzhammer's father had been killed in Russia. He had left behind him a whole pile of good clothing, which Willy's mother had sold. Even the double-breasted blue suit, which Willy had always had his eyes on. Willy had to run around now in a T-shirt, cavalry pants, a GI beret, and added to this outfit the old sandals his father had worn in 1938, because his own didn't fit him anymore.

Willy Holzhammer was sixteen, a tall boy with freckles, short-clipped red hair, a turned-up nose, small, black, beady eyes, and a big mouth which always seemed to be grinning. When Willy laughed, it was possible to see that three teeth were missing—three front teeth. He had pulled them out himself.

It was very seldom Willy Holzhammer worried about anything. The only thing that bothered him was that he had no hairs on his chest; and he didn't seem able to grow any. In order to do something for his manliness Willy had had himself tattooed—had had a naked woman with generous breasts drawn ostentatiously on his left upper arm.

Willy Holzhammer lived with his mother on the ground floor directly above Frau Holle's basement apartment. The upper stories of the house having been destroyed by bombs, the ground floor was now the top story. Willy Holzhammer's apartment had no ceiling and was only suitable for the warm seasons. Willy could take sun baths in bed or at night watch the stars. During the summer the apartment was fun. Only when it rained was it not quite so cozy. Then, Willy's mother covered the few pieces of furniture with cloth and packing paper and Willy and his mother crept away into the old tent, preserved from Willy's time in the Hitler Youth Movement, which was always kept ready in the living room.

The walls of the huge living room were solid. The floor too was not dangerous and there did not seem to be any immediate chance of its falling through. There was just a big hole in the floor near Willy's bed that really had to be walled up sometime, but Willy put off doing it because the hole in the floor was—as Willy put it—not without its advantages!

It was situated at a convenient angle above Frau Holle's lonely bed, and when Willy from time to time looked down into the basement apartment, he was able to see a few things that many a man would like to see. "It's better than the movies," Willy would say, "and after all the movies cost money, and the performances in Frau Holle's basement apartment are free."

This morning Willy Holzhammer had gotten up early. He

had been awakened shortly after six by some loud knocking at the door of his room: a stranger. A man with frog eyes. Asking for Frau Holle. Willy had said to him:

"She used to live on the fifth floor. But it was knocked out by bombs—the other stories too—you can see that, can't you! Now she lives in the cellar underneath us!" Whereupon the man made off.

After that Willy didn't go back to bed. There was no water in the house and Willy said to himself:

"Better to go and get some water now before the line gets too long."

So he left to go to the big water pump in Fleischerstrasse and brought home two bucketsful of fresh water. His mother had made him a good breakfast: sticky post-war bread, home-made marmalade, and ersatz coffee. He was not allowed to smoke in her presence—right after breakfast he had made himself scarce in order to have a quick drag in front of the door outside . . . on a Philip Morris . . . and as soon as he came out of the door, his GI beret slanted over his forehead, his hands in his pocket, whistling—he saw Frau Holle waiting in the doorway.

"Now, Willy," said Frau Holle.

"Good morning," said Willy.

"When are you going to wall up the hole in my ceiling?"

"When I have time," said Willy.

"And what about the potatoes?"

"What potatoes do you mean?"

"The ones you promised me."

"We have none right now."

"So!" said Frau Holle. She grimaced. "It's my house after all, isn't it? And if you don't mean to pay rent the least you could do is get me some potatoes!"

"And how about the rain?" said the boy. "And where's the

ceiling, the roof . . . but don't worry about it. . . . You'll get the potatoes as soon as we have some."

Frau Holle eyed the boy from head to foot. What she saw was: a GI beret, a young face covered with freckles, a dirty neck, a T-shirt, khaki pants, and sandals. She thought to herself: fifteen, maybe sixteen? Sixteen? Just the right age! Her face became smoother.

She said: "Okay. Give your mother my regards. Tell her not to forget! The potatoes I mean, and come down and see me when you have time . . . and make sure your mother doesn't notice."

The boy grinned. And said: "You're too old for me. Besides I've got a girl already—a young girl."

"What do you mean, too old?" said Frau Holle.

"Fifty-nine," said the boy.

"Forty-nine," said Frau Holle.

The boy laughed. He saw Frau Holle spit and limp off. He wanted to shout after her: "And yesterday I laid a virgin— for just one Philip Morris," but suddenly another thought crossed his mind.

"Frau Holle!" The boy ran after her and took her by the sleeve.

"Well, now what's the matter! You accused me of being fifty-nine?"

"It was just a joke," said the boy.

"That's not a joke," said Frau Holle. "It's only the Russians who go in for jokes like that."

"Yes," said the boy.

"Or the GIs," said Frau Holle. "They make jokes like that too."

"Sure," said the boy.

"Now what's wrong? What is it you want?"

"Nothing at all." He started to finger his cap. "Early this

[81]

morning . . . a man knocked at our door, asked if there was a Frau Holle living here."

"So," said Frau Holle. "And who was it?"

"He didn't give a name, but I told him you live in the basement."

"Ah, well," said Frau Holle.

"Did he knock at your door?" asked the boy.

"Maybe," said Frau Holle. "But today I slept longer than usual. Probably I didn't hear the fellow."

"He was a real strange guy," said the boy.

"Oh," said Frau Holle.

"With frog eyes."

"I don't know anybody with frog eyes," said Frau Holle.

"And a hooked nose, and bulbous lips. And bad teeth."

"I don't know anyone who looks like that," said Frau Holle.

"Looked like a Jew," said the boy.

"I don't know any Jews," said Frau Holle.

Frau Holle wanted to walk on, but the boy kept on talking: "Now's the time they're all coming back out of the concentration camps."

"You mean—the ones—who are still left?" said Frau Holle.

"Yes," said the boy. "Have you read the paper?"

"I don't read newspapers," said Frau Holle; "it's all fraud anyway."

"Six million Jews murdered," said the boy.

"It's all swindle," said Frau Holle.

III

Frau Holle limped her way across the ruins. The war had been merciless. Nietzschestrasse was still not cleared for traffic. In the middle of the road were bomb craters and between the slag and piles of rubble, corpses of vehicles and burned-out tanks, some sunk in the ground, some overturned like dead carcasses. The ruins at the edge of the broken pavement seemed to stand holding in a scream. The sun belonged to the victors, blazing into the hollow eyes of windows, spotlighting the battlefield as though God above were illuminating a snapshot, grinning at the people walking aimlessly, dressed in torn clothing, or staggering and limping, jeering at the wooden leg of Frau Holle.

Frau Holle did not bother her head about the sun. She crossed Adolf Hitler Square, fouled by the summer birds, asking herself what could his name be now? She could see no street signs, cursed the summer birds, thought of the dead Führer, swallowed her tears, thought of the wedding ring she wanted to sell, of the bread and eggs, of the milk and cigarettes. She thought too of the conversation with the boy:

"You are too old for me." And then, "Fifty-nine!" What a wretch of a boy!—and who was the man looking for? The one with frog eyes?

In Mozartstrasse she noticed groups of disinterested workers trying to clear away the rubble. As though there were still a point to clearing away the rubble, with the whole world in ruins. Mozartstrasse was not so badly destroyed as Nietzsche-strasse, and the occupation forces were able to drive their vehicles along it. And Frau Holle, who was not bothering her head about the sun at all, asked herself:

"Yes, my dear God—why did it have to be Nietzsche's street? Was he not just a music maker too?"

From time to time Frau Holle ran into American officers and soldiers chewing their gum, and others who were not chewing. Some were on foot and some in jeeps. But Frau Holle did not bother her head about them either. It was a long walk from Nietzschestrasse to the black market at the other end of Warthenau. And to limp through the bombed-out, rubble-filled streets on an empty stomach and with a wooden leg of questionable origin . . . that was no fun for a fifty-nine-year-old woman who was only forty-nine.

Frau Holle had been raped by the Russians. It had happened in Berlin during the first days of May 1945.

Fifty-nine times exactly. Frau Hole tried to hop along a little more quickly, although she knew that it was not the Russians who were in Warthenau, but the Americans. Fifty-nine times! No wonder she looked fifty-nine! And the swines had not even cared that she had a wooden leg.

At the end of May, Frau Holle had moved back here to Warthenau, where she had a house. In Nietzschestrasse, Number 59. Fifty-nine was her unlucky number. But she couldn't do anything about it. Only the officials were allowed to change numbers. And how about moving? She didn't want to. After all, it was her house. And Günther's house. And Günther was her husband. When he came back from the war he would ask people:

"I am looking for Number 59. And a woman with a wooden leg."

"Don't stay in Berlin!" That was what her husband, Günther Holle, had written from Poland—at the time when Poland was still Germany. And she had sent him the answer:

"Our house is being bombed down. The fifth floor has had it. The fourth floor too. And the third floor. And the second floor. And the first floor. Only the ground floor is still there. But that doesn't have a roof. And the cellar is still standing—yes, the cellar too. And that has a ceiling, even though there's a hole in it—a pretty big hole. But my dear Günther, are people like us expected to live in a cellar? No, of course not!

That's just not possible. I'm going to live with your parents in Berlin. The apartment in Berlin hasn't been bombed yet."

Then the Russians had come and raped her fifty-nine times. And they had not bothered about the wooden leg. And it had certainly not been easy to get out of the capital and move to Warthenau with one Aryan and one non-Aryan leg, not broken, but limping, with pains in the backside and the genitals, breasts chewed up, fingernails broken. When Günther came back from the war, then she would say to him:

"Günther! The fifth floor has had it! And the fourth floor. And the third floor. And the second floor. And the first floor. There's only the ground floor still there . . . and that doesn't have any ceiling. But the cellar, well it's a cellar after all! Well, just the house number should be changed. How about it, Günther? You're in the SS, an SS corporal. Can't you do something about it?"

The black market was in the old town, in the winding, narrow little streets behind the town hall and the Gate of Good Hope. In spite of the daily raids and the club-brandishing of the MPs in white helmets, trading remained as brisk as ever. Even though Frau Holle did not understand a great deal about black market deals, she was convinced there was nothing in the world that one could not get at the black market in Warthenau. Every time Frau Holle thought secretly to herself:

"My God—what a lot of swindling goes on here! If only the Führer knew! He'd turn in his grave!"

Frau Holle hated the black market, and not long ago she'd said to young Willy:

"Germany is one big happy hunting ground for spivs. Everywhere the black market is flourishing. You'd think that's what we've been fighting for. It's a disgrace."

And the boy said: "Yes, Frau Holle."

[85]

And she said: "The German people are going hungry. Everybody's running to the damned black market to sell the last bits of what they have. It's a disgrace."

"That's what we have to thank the Jews for," Willy said. "Not long ago I was in the country—as guest of some farmers—they had a hidden store of groceries—but they were asking the sort of prices Jews ask for."

"Yes, Willy—German farmers are a lot of old Jews."

"Yes, Frau Holle, that's right."

"Do you believe that the Führer knew that German farmers are old Jews?" Frau Holle said.

"How do I know, Frau Holle?"

When Frau Holle got to the black market she was dripping with sweat. Her right foot was hurting after the long walk, and her left stump was hurting also, her wooden leg sending jabs of pain through her whole body.

The old town had been spared from the bombs. The houses were still standing, looking as glorious as ever, still had their roots in the soil, did not seem to be angry at the heavens, appeared to be purring like cats lying in the sun, looked down drowsily and a little meditatively from the small spy-hole-like windows beneath the sloping slate roofs, upon the tiny streets behind the town hall and the Gate of Good Hope. Knots of people were moving around in the shadows of the old houses, whispering, and Frau Holle asked herself:

"Yes, my God, why is it that only the roofs can sun themselves? Why is it that the streets are in the shadow? Perhaps that has something to do with the black market? And as for all that crew around here . . . yes, my God, that's just a mob of lay-abouts afraid to look at the sun or have the light shine on them! And what am I doing here? If Günther only knew! And if the Führer only knew!"

[86]

Soon Frau Holle was sucked into the crowd, jostled from side to side, carried away. An old woman next to her whispered:

"You want a pair of stockings? Or a frying pan? Dollars changed? Do you know someone perhaps who has a gold tooth? Or who wants to take out one of his own?"

The hag had gripped her arm and Frau Holle angrily freed herself.

She thought: "Gold teeth? Do I want to tear out one of my own teeth? But I don't have any. And I'm hungry. But I do have a wedding ring. Made of gold!"

The old woman dropped out of sight. The confusion of faces around her made Frau Holle's head spin, and she felt faint from hunger in the sticky heat, from the clatter of voices around her. In the shadow of an entrance way she caught sight of a peasant woman with a gigantic straw box, and next to her a well-dressed man. The two were whispering. The farm woman pulled some bacon and bread from the basket while the man bared his lower arm and showed her a collection of watches.

"My God," thought Frau Holle, "so many watches on his forearm! Just like the goddamned Russians in Berlin!"

She wanted to stop in order to observe what went on, wanted to look at the bacon from closer up, and the bread and the watches, but was jostled on to the pavement, and from the pavement on to the road, and from the road back on to the pavement.

A crippled man in the gutter, with both his legs gone, looked enviously at her healthy single leg. Next to him stood a small girl about twelve years old, flirting with an American major. Just at that instant Frau Holle was pushed so forcefully from the rear that she stumbled and would have fallen down if the major had not caught her.

[87]

"Sorry," said the major.

Frau Holle did not know what that meant: "Sorry." It sounded like worry. She grinned at the major with a grimace. She was back on both feet again, the Aryan leg and the non-Aryan leg.

"Who is there these days who doesn't worry?" she said to the major. "Right? Better to have worries with the GIs than safety with the Russians. Because they're a bunch of sex maniacs and lay-abouts."

The major nodded, even though he didn't understand a word of German. He said something to her in his own language, and she didn't understand but nonetheless nodded because the major nodded.

The cripple in the gutter was still looking enviously at her healthy leg. Frau Holle stuck her tongue out at him. The major saw that and laughed.

"He's not allowed to talk with you," said the cripple suddenly, "because that's against the non-fraternization regulation."

"What does that mean?" asked Frau Holle.

"It means that he can't go to bed with you either," said the cripple, then gave a loud laugh and pushed himself nearer to her, showing her his black tooth stumps.

Frau Holle was just about to say: "Oh, drop dead . . . he's talking with the little girl too," but never got around to it because the crowd moved her away. The major walked next to her and so did the little girl.

"The major's long, lean and sloppy," she thought. "They're just a lot of gum chewing dummies! But he doesn't seem to have any in his mouth! Maybe he's one of the better sort? But old. Sixty, anyway? And he's got a crew cut too. A gray one. Ice-gray!"

"Do you want to buy a gold ring?" asked Frau Holle and

showed the major the marriage ring. "My husband Günther must never know. But I have to sell it."

The major laughed and said nothing, merely showed her his own wedding ring, looked for a while into the air, then suddenly began to talk like a waterfall—in his own language. Meanwhile they had gone past the town hall—actually had been shoved past it by the crowd and had now arrived at the Gate of Good Hope. Frau Holle cast her eyes around her looking for the little girl, but could not see her.

"Disappeared," she thought. "Okay. Well maybe it's just as well. Twelve is young. At that age I was still playing with dolls."

The major said something, then pointed to the black Mercedes, which was standing in the Gate of Good Hope directly under the stone arch. When they got to the car the rear door opened and Frau Holle got in, even though she had never intended to. The major got in too and sat down beside her. There was another GI at the steering wheel, younger than the major. He also had a crew cut, but had blond hair. The major spoke with the man at the steering wheel, then the driver turned round and said to her in perfect German:

"The major would like to know whether you like eating canned foods."

"Yes," she said, "I love eating them. Are you German?"

The driver laughed and said: "No. But my parents were. I am American."

"So," said Frau Holle, "and he would like to know whether I enjoy eating canned foods. Of course. I love eating them."

"The major would like to know whether he can sleep with you tonight," said the driver.

"If he likes," said Frau Holle. "What sort of canned foods are they?"

"Corned beef," said the driver.

"Actually I wanted to sell my wedding ring," said Frau Holle.

"A wedding ring should never be sold," said the driver.

"Yes, actually that's right," said Frau Holle.

"I suppose your husband is still in a prisoner-of-war camp?" asked the driver.

And Frau Holle said: "I really don't know. He was in Poland. And I have no news."

"And what did he do in Poland?" the driver wanted to know.

And Frau Holle said: "I don't know."

Frau Holle made herself comfortable, stretched out her wooden leg, pulled in the healthy leg, leaned right back into the upholstered seat, grinned at the major, and thought to herself: "There's no need for him to know that Günther is a mass-murderer. He won't understand anything like that. You could try to explain to him: they were enemies of the people and Günther was only doing his duty! It was an order from the Führer! And an order is an order! But a man like him doesn't understand that. He's just a GI."

"Listen," said the driver, in a solemn voice this time: "The major will give you three cans for the first bang, five for the second, seven for the third. And so on."

"Well, okay," said Frau Holle. "But ask the major whether he's seen my wooden leg."

"Yes, he's seen it," said the driver. "But that doesn't bother him. Just the opposite!"

"What's that supposed to mean?" asked Frau Holle.

"His wife in America has two legs," said the man at the wheel, "two real legs. But his wife can't do it properly even though she has two legs."

"So," said Frau Holle. "What sort of woman is she?"

"An American woman," said the driver. "She reads the newspaper when the major's doing it with her."

Frau Holle nodded her head. "I don't read newspapers," she said. "Anyway, they only print a pack of lies."

The driver pretended not to hear. He lit himself a cigarette, blew the smoke against the windshield, then turned back to her and said, "Now listen. The major has a complex. Do you know what a complex is?"

"No," said Frau Holle.

The driver grinned. "Well," he then said to her. "The major has been psychologically castrated by his wife in America. Now he has an inferiority complex. And he is afraid of women with two legs—two proper legs. So he wants to have one with one leg."

"Is that a complex?" asked Frau Holle.

"Yes," said the driver. "That is a complex."

At this point the major lit a cigarette too, stammered out something as though trying to excuse himself, then offered her one, saying: "A Philip Morris!"

"A Philip Morris!" said Frau Holle. "I'll take one and smoke it later. It's not good on an empty stomach." Frau Holle took the cigarette without saying thank you and put it away into her handbag. Then she bent forward and said to the man at the steering wheel: "I lost the leg in 1933 . . . on the day the Führer came to power . . . it was all gangrened the doctor said . . . and it had started to give me a lot of pain . . . yes that's the truth, cross my heart . . . and Günther said . . . it was the Jews that had put a spell on it . . . and it happened in the winter . . . on that day of all days . . . but there's nothing one can do about it . . . and that's what my Günther said."

"Well how about it?" said the driver. "Do you agree?"

"Okay," Frau Holle said.

"The more you bang the more you eat," said the driver.

"Okay then," said Frau Holle. "But he doesn't look like a man who has a lot of bangs left in him. Surely he's sixty?"

"Fifty-nine," said the driver.

IV

They drove to Mozartstrasse at the corner of Adolf Hitler Square. There the Mercedes had to stop, because the road had been bombed and was full of rubble and stones.

Frau Holle said to the driver: "It's not much further from here. We can walk the rest of the way."

Before they got out the major pulled a big grocery bag from underneath the seat and Frau Holle could see that in addition to the cans of food there was whisky. The major took her arm. They walked slowly, even though Frau Holle would rather have gone quickly, because her stomach was rumbling like a mad dog and she felt dizzy. But the major took his time.

Not only did Frau Holle double lock the door of the basement apartment from the inside but she also put down the iron bar. Then she stuffed the cracks in the door with packing paper, so that the fellow with frog eyes, just in case he stopped by again, couldn't peek into the apartment. After she had done all that, she took care to hang both the curtainless windows with sheets.

The major seemed to be in a hurry, because he had already undressed and was standing next to the kitchen table naked, his member thick and stiff as a poker, his legs hairy, his stomach slack, a bottle of whisky in his hand, watching Frau Holle as she fussed around the basement, making sure the door was really locked, testing the key and the rusty bar, the brown paper in the door cracks, and the sheets covering up the windows of the cellar.

[92]

"What's your name, baby?" the major asked.

"Okay," said Frau Holle, even though she didn't know what the major meant.

"How about this wooden leg of yours?" asked the major.

"You're probably a bit surprised that I've stuffed up the cracks in the door," said Frau Holle, "but that has nothing to do with little Willy, even though he does sometimes creep around and look through the cracks . . . he can look into my apartment anyway . . . I suppose you know already . . . up there . . . through the ceiling . . . I just thought—if the fellow with frog eyes comes back . . . he will certainly try to look through the cracks. I know what I'm doing. One can't be too careful."

Other than that Frau Holle didn't bother herself about the major. She just folded back the lonely bed covers, freshened the pillow up a little, for it was all creased.

"Some of the feathers are coming out," she thought, "and that's a good stiff cock he has, but pretty short. And with that he wants to raise the stakes. Still, the more he bangs the more I eat—and I'm very hungry—but I'll bet he'll never manage more than one—at fifty-nine—or?"

Frau Holle began to undress. She folded her dress carefully, placed it over the shaky chair next to the bed, then her underwear—piece by piece, one after the other—took off her wooden leg, hung it up—in its usual place, the place where she put it every night before she went to bed—on the slightly bent nail at the foot end of the bed of the long wall. The major was still standing by the kitchen table and drinking. Frau Holle hopped on her one leg to the other end of the bed and sat down, suddenly cold, rubbing her shoulders.

"There isn't much furniture," she said to the major. "As you see: a kitchen table, two shaky old chairs, a bed, an old wardrobe, a broken mirror, a box with a candle and a second

[93]

box—for coal—and the oven in the corner—I organized it all for myself, by the way, like everything else in here. All the furniture I once had went long ago. Oh well—I'm thin and I guess my breasts are too long, aren't they? That's what my husband Günther used to say. They hang down over my stomach! And I've gray hairs down there too. But they can be dyed. And if I get enough to eat I'll put on weight again."

Frau Holle grinned at the major who nodded as though he had understood everything she said. Then he started to slither slowly over to her, holding the whisky bottle under his naked arm. He stopped in front of the bed for a few seconds ruminating. He looked at Frau Holle, who made room for him, then he slithered away again to the foot of the bed, took a good swallow out of the half-empty bottle, then suddenly, with a quick nervous grab, unhooked the wooden leg, put it under his arm, the other arm, not the arm with the whisky bottle, came back to her and put the wooden leg next to her in the bed.

V

Yesterday had been her birthday—and she had allowed herself to sleep a bit longer. Usually summer birds woke up Frau Holle every day at the crack of dawn. It's true that the birds had made a terrible mess of Adolf Hitler Square—which was a disgrace—but in spite of that Frau Holle was grateful to the birds, because she said to herself: early to bed, early to rise, makes a man healthy, wealthy, and wise! And who would have dared to doubt it?

Today, too, a twittering of birds roused Frau Holle from a deep sleep. As was her habit, the first thing she did was curse her wooden leg, although this time it wasn't hanging on the long wall, but lying in bed between the thighs of the major, but after a while she calmed down, yawned, then pulled the leg slowly and carefully away from him.

Frau Holle strapped the leg on and hopped over to the oven. She lit it, looked to make sure there was still some water in the kettle and began to sing like the birds. Then she took some pots and pans from the carton under the bed purposely making a lot of noise in order to wake up the major. But he didn't move.

"Oh well," thought Frau Holle, "he's having a real good sleep!"

A little later she shook him, then turned him on his back. Faced with two staring blue eyes, she belched from sheer fright, and thought, "He's really dead! A heart attack!" She belched again, felt her wooden leg hurting her, and put her hand to her mouth.

Frau Holle had no idea what she should do with the dead body. Best thing, she thought, would be to lie him behind the oven. So that he would at least be out of the way.

Frau Holle got to work right away, pulled the corpse carefully out of the bed and dragged it across the bumpy floor. "No," she thought, "he's not very heavy. Americans are filled with chewing gum."

She didn't feel like breakfast and thought to call the authorities. Breakfast could come later. Then it occurred to her to telephone. Naturally. She could telephone. On Adolf Hitler Square.

Frau Holle left the basement apartment hurriedly, hopped over to Adolf Hitler Square, saw the telephone booth—which was pre-war—but still standing, then saw the notice: Out of Order!

Desperate, Frau Holle started to hop across the large square, filled with bird droppings, turned into Mozartstrasse, and asked a few people. But no one knew where there was a telephone. A man said to her:

"Wait until you see an MP."

Frau Holle said: "You mean the ones with the white helmets and the bands around their arms? But they're no better than the Russians!"

So Frau Holle limped back in the direction of Nietzsche-strasse.

"Better go home first! And think about what to do with some leisure! That's the best thing to do! And besides, I need to have breakfast. After all, a woman is only human."

When she got back home again, she found a note in her mail box.

"Am back from the war! With a message from Günther! Can't stay long! Have to leave again! How's your wooden leg? Max Schulz."

Max Schulz! The man with the frog eyes. The man with the hooked nose, bulbous lips, and bad teeth! The man who looked like a Jew but wasn't!

"Aha!" thought Frau Holle. "Now you know who that was. It's Max! Why didn't you think of him right away! Naturally! The concentration camp in Laubwalde in German-occupied Poland. Right there where Günther served. And Max Schulz! —and wasn't that 1943? Günther visited you. Brought Max Schulz with him and said: 'This is Max Schulz. He looks like a Jew but isn't one!'

"Max Schulz laughed and said: 'I'm not one!'

"And Günther said: 'Back home at last!'

"And Max Schulz said: 'Yes, Günther.'

"And Günther said: 'It's cozy where we are, Max. And we have a beautiful view from the fifth floor. Airy in the summer. Warm in the winter. And when Frau Holle shakes the feather beds out in the winter it seems to be snowing on our beautiful German town.'

"And Max Schulz laughed and said: 'At least that's different.'

"And Günther said: 'Yes, Max.'

"And Max Schulz said: 'Yes.'

"And Günther said: 'When the war is over, Max, don't forget you always have a home at Frau Holle's.'"

VI

Willy Holzhammer was repairing his old bicycle. His mother couldn't stand the noise of the hammering. And also didn't want to have the living room become a pigsty, and so Willy Holzhammer had had to bring the bicycle into the fresh air, even though the living room without a roof was really in the fresh air too if truth were known—but that was different—and so he'd taken the bicycle into the fresh air in front of the house, taken the bike apart, and put it back together again. The hand brake was in order, the headlamps and dynamo were working, the chain was freshly oiled, and the mudguard in front was firm again. Now he just had to mend the back wheel. It was lucky that he had rescued his tool box from the bombing; he even had sandpaper, rags, glue, and round and square puncture patches.

Early in the day the sky had been heavily clouded over and it had looked as though the rubble in Nietzschestrasse was going to get a free shower, but then the cloud masses had moved away and the morning sun had included the street in its rays.

Willy Holzhammer was working hard. If he managed to get the bicycle ready before noon, he intended to go to Solendorf to see his friend Rudy Schalke, whose father owned an inn. There was always something good to eat there. Willy had taken off his T-shirt, and was letting himself get a little brown, whistling, taking occasional puffs at a cigarette.

An hour before Willy had seen Frau Holle limping out of the house in a hurry—in the direction of Adolf Hitler Square. She had not greeted him. Then she had come back, looking a little distressed, had nodded to him fleetingly and disappeared in the house.

He hadn't seen her again till this instant. In her right hand she was carrying a water bucket, swinging it exuberantly, and this time she winked at him and stopped. Willy noticed that her face was strangely flushed.

"Going to the pump in Fleischerstrasse?" asked Willy.

Frau Holle nodded.

"What was going on this morning?" asked Willy.

"Nothing at all," said Frau Holle. "What do you think was going on?"

"I saw the major," said Willy. "He's a real nut."

Frau Holle was just about to say: he *was* a nut—but then it occurred to her that Willy, from his hole in the ceiling, could certainly not see as far as the oven where the corpse lay, and so she just said:

"Yes, he's a nut."

"He slept a long time this morning," said Willy.

"He drank too much," said Frau Holle.

"Has he gone already?"

"Yes, he's gone. Crept out. Probably was scared."

Willy grinned and blew some smoke into her face. He said: "It's the non-fraternization regulation!"

"Or something like that," said Frau Holle. She tugged at her dress, stared for a while at his bicycle without a word, then told him briefly that she had got a letter—from the fellow with the frog eyes—and that the fellow had wanted to bring her a greeting from Günther. Then she went off, limping, swinging her empty bucket—to the big water pump in Fleischerstrasse.

After Frau Holle had gone, the man with frog eyes suddenly appeared. Willy Holzhammer noticed him only when he was already right in front of him: suit crumpled, thin, frog eyes—an old sack on his back.

"Now," said Max Schulz. "Here I am again!"

"What sort of funny sack is that?" asked Willy Holzhammer. "You didn't have that yesterday."

"Oh, I hid it," said Max Schulz, "in the rubble."

"What have you got inside it?"

"That's none of your business," said Max Schulz.

"Old rags I suppose," grinned Willy.

"That's nothing to do with you," said Max Schulz.

Max Schulz dragged himself over to the cellar window to look whether Frau Holle was at home, but the windows were curtained up and he couldn't see anything.

"She just went to the water pump," said Willy to Max Schulz. "And the windows are curtained up still—I have no idea why!"

"Oh well," said Max Schulz, "it doesn't matter. I can wait here until she comes back."

Max Schulz sat down on the threshold, stuck his old sack between his legs, took a Camel cigarette out of his pocket, lit it. Willy put his bicycle against the house wall, shut the top of his tool box, pushed it next to the bicycle with his foot, and sat down next to Max Schulz.

"Want to swap? A Philip Morris for a Camel?"

"Okay," said Max Schulz. "Why not? It's all the same shit."

"Frau Holle told me you bring greetings from Günther. Is that right?"

Max Schulz pursed his frog eyes and laughed. "That was just a bad joke—that message about the greeting. Günther's dead."

"I don't believe that."

"He is. You can believe me. He's as dead as a stone. The partisans killed him."

"How did it happen?"

"It just happened!"

"Ah well," said Willy, "that will certainly be a shock for her, for Frau Holle. And how did it happen? What do you mean by 'it just happened'?"

"Scalped," said Max Schulz. "And disemboweled. The partisans cut his cock off in a snowed-up Polish forest."

"And it happened just like that?" said Willy.

"Yes, just like that," said Max Schulz.

Next they saw Frau Holle on the street corner, carrying the bucket in her right hand and waving with her left. Max Schulz waved too and laughed.

"Were you with the SS too?" asked Willy.

"No—I wasn't," Max Schulz lied. "I was just with the Army. During the retreat through Poland we happened on the unit to which Günther Holle was attached. Actually, his unit came upon ours. I used to know him. Just a little."

"Oh I see," said Willy Holzhammer.

"Yes, that's how it was," said Max Schulz.

VII

Max Schulz sat silently on the coal box, to the right of the oven, while Frau Holle made the bed with nervous haste, as though his presence embarrassed her. Then she limped over to the kitchen table to wipe it clean. Max Schulz had put his sack down near the door, then taken off his sweat-stained jacket and had thrown it down carelessly on top of the sack. Why had Frau Holle covered up the windows? It took a while for his eyes to get used to the gloom of the basement apartment. A big brass bed, thought Max Schulz, a bed in which an aging woman sleeps—a lonely bed—and a kitchen

table, a box with a candle to read from, two rickety chairs at
the long end of the kitchen table, two low cellar windows . . .
in one corner an old wardrobe and a half-broken wall mirror.
Only when Max Schulz turned his head a little toward the
back did he notice the naked corpse lying behind the oven.
With not even a twitch of the limbs did Max Schulz show
any sign of reaction. He just scratched himself on the backside
and thought—it doesn't itch anymore.

Max Schulz tried to make clear to Frau Holle that his story
of bringing greetings from Günther had just been a bad joke
—and that Günther was dead—yes, dead!—that is to say, dead
as a stone!—scalped and disemboweled in a Polish forest!
—no better than a stone—even though a stone couldn't be
scalped and disemboweled—but nevertheless: dead as a stone!
    At first, Frau Holle didn't seem to understand what it was
all about. And even when she did understand, she did not
immediately start yelling. First, she shot her eyes up—opened
them wide. And then she began to yell.
    Max Schulz looked at his watch. When Frau Holle began
to cry it was exactly twelve minutes and thirty-three seconds
past ten. When she at last stopped crying and the last tear
had dried away, it was exactly twelve minutes and thirty-four
seconds past twelve.
    Frau Holle lay on the bed. During the whole period Max
Schulz had been sitting waiting on the coal box, counting
the seconds and staring in the air. Now Max Schulz stood
up and slithered over to the bed, sat down next to Frau
Holle on the bed edge, sitting there grinning, stiffly—then
said suddenly:
    "So—now that's enough! Two hours and one second is
enough tears for a fellow like that—it's enough to make me
laugh!"

[101]

"Why should it make you laugh?" Frau Holle wanted to know.

"Because he was ten years younger than you," said Max Schulz. "And because he had someone else. And she was twenty years younger than Günther. That's thirty years."

"What are thirty years?" asked Frau Holle.

"The difference between you and the other girl," said Max Schulz.

"Oh, I see," said Frau Holle.

"In any case, Günther would not have come back!"

"Oh, I see," said Frau Holle. "So it's that way."

A little later, Frau Holle said: "Do you see the hole in the ceiling right over my bed? Well, Willy sometimes looks through it at me."

"But he's standing outside in front of the house door," said Max Schulz, "repairing his bicycle—outside."

And Frau Holle said: "Yes."

And Max Schulz said: "Now he can't look at us."

And Frau Holle said: "Yes," and giggled.

In the intervals between love-making Frau Holle told him that the corpse behind the oven was a former American major, who had managed seven orgasms at the age of fifty-nine. And who had then died of a heart attack.

"We will have to tell the authorities," said Frau Holle. "He can't stay there!"

"Oh yes he can," said Max Schulz. "And then again he can't. In any case . . . that's out of the question!"

"What's out of the question?"

"What you said . . . about the authorities."

"Why?"

"Because the authorities are after me."

[102]

"Oh I see!" said Frau Holle. "What should we do then?"

"I'll get rid of him. As soon as it's dark."

"Good idea," said Frau Holle.

"We'll just have to wrap him up in something. In a sack perhaps."

"But you've got a sack! Couldn't you empty it? What's in it? Old rags?"

"I can't empty it," said Max Schulz.

"What could you have that's so important?"

"That's none of your business," said Max Schulz.

"We'll just have to put some clothes back on the corpse," said Max Schulz. "I saw a roll of brown paper behind the oven. I'll wrap him up in that. Then when it's dark I'll carry him to Adolf Hitler Square. There are some benches there. I'll sit him upright on a bench. And tomorrow—yes, tomorrow —you'll see a notice in the paper: 'American Major Dead of Heart Attack on Park Bench—Adolf Hitler Square—Near Ruins of Führer Monument. Did Major Die of Fright? Did He See a Ghost or Not? Another Victim of National Socialism? When Will the End Be In Sight?'"

"My God," said Frau Holle. "You're really a nut! If the Führer only knew! He would turn in his grave!"

"I can't stay here for long," said Max Schulz. "I was looking for Slavitzki and my mother. But they have fled from the Russians. No one knows where they've gone to. So I came here. But I can't stay long. I have to hide. Somehow and somewhere! North America perhaps. And find another name. And a new identity."

"Günther told me everything . . . that in Laubwalde you murdered two hundred thousand Jews. That's what he said."

[103]

"He shouldn't have told you that at all. Talking about it was strictly forbidden. We all took an oath to keep quiet . . . Günther too. The rule was pummeled into us: Strictest Secrecy."

"But after all I was Günther's wife. . . ."

"Nobody was supposed to know . . . that's what we were told . . . not even wives and children. Nobody!"

"Was murdering forbidden then?"

"No," said Max Schulz. "That wasn't forbidden. Only the spreading of false rumors . . . that was forbidden!"

"But those weren't false rumors?"

"Now just you shut your trap," said Max Schulz, "they were and they weren't. I can't do anything about it."

"Oh, Günther," said Frau Holle, "he was a real man."

"Yes," said Max Schulz.

"And Günther always said: 'Max Schulz too. He's a real man.'"

"Once maybe," said Max Schulz.

"He told me everything . . . Günther did . . . about the long graves too . . . how the prisoners plopped into them one by one . . . one on top of the other . . . and Max Schulz, Günther said . . . Max Schulz usually sat on the edge of the long trench . . . rifle across his knee . . . a cold cigarette stub in his mouth . . . sticking to his lips . . . that's what Günther said . . . and grinning . . . Max Schulz I mean . . . he always grinned when he shot them."

Max Schulz nodded. He helped himself to another Camel, lit it, smoked it, stroked the stump of the aging woman, stroked the gray triangle of hair, tugged at it a bit, scratched himself, scratched his backside, thinking: "It doesn't itch anymore . . . once it did."

"We had a few different methods," said Max Schulz. "Sometimes we had the prisoners stand while we shot them . . .

[104]

stand in front of the long trench . . . in a line . . . had them look down into the long trench while we shot them from behind. Sometimes we had them look at us and we shot them from the front. Sometimes we had them jump into the trench alive and ordered them to lie down. Then we shot them from above. That was my specialty. To shoot them from above. From the edge of the trench. When one was dead we had the next one lie on top of him. One after the other."

"I killed my first Jews in a cemetery in Poland in 1939. Once we took the Jews to a Christian cemetery. There was a little Jesus on one of the crosses. Weeping. My lieutenant just couldn't stand the sight of it. And whether you believe it or not . . . he shot that Jesus down from the cross. But he just wouldn't die. So my lieutenant said to me: 'Max Schulz! Stop that fake saint's foul mouth! You're the best one at that!' And that's just what I did.

"Later we were in Russia, with Mobile Killing Unit D in the South Russia platoon. There we captured Jews like hares. We had long trenches there too. In 1942, I had a slight heart attack and was moved back to Laubwalde."

"And that's how you got to know Günther?"

"Yes, there," said Max Schulz. "But you know that already."

"Yes," said Frau Holle. "But I just wanted to hear it again."

"Is it true . . . that you were a barber once?"

"That's right."

"A real barber?"

"A real barber."

"Where was that?"

"In Wieshalle, before the war."

"So you could cut my hair for me sometime."

[105]

"Yes, I could," said Max Schulz, "but I'm no lady's hair-dresser."

"What were you then?"

"A men's barber."

"And can't one of them cut women's hair too?"

Max Schulz grinned. "Well, for women like you . . . that could be arranged."

"My hair is too long," said Frau Holle. "And wiry . . . and I'd like to dye it as well."

"I'll have to see," said Max Schulz. "I don't carry my business around with me . . . and in that big sack . . . there's something else in that . . . that has nothing to do with my trade. But let me think it over."

"I have a pair of scissors," said Frau Holle. "And a comb . . . I have one of those too. And something to dye my hair with. I've got that also."

"Okay then," said Max Schulz. "Tomorrow perhaps or the day after. Or maybe next week."

"What about today?" said Frau Holle. "Don't forget that a woman is better in bed too if she knows that she looks good."

"In Laubwalde . . . I never thought of my trade there," said Max Schulz. "But afterwards . . . when everything was over . . ."

"Yes," said Frau Holle.

"A man has to do something," said Max Schulz. "And the war is over."

"Perhaps you could go on the black market," said Frau Holle. "A lot of people are doing that today."

"I'll try it," said Max Schulz. "But that's something that you can't do forever . . . the black market . . . perhaps for a time . . . but it has to stop sometime."

[106]

"Are you going to open up a barbershop then?"

"You mean . . . 'a gentleman's hairdressing salon.'"

"Yes. A gentleman's hairdressing salon."

"You can bet on that," said Max Schulz. "A man has to do something. And the barber's trade . . . that's a decent, honest trade."

"A fine trade, I find," said Frau Holle. "It has plenty going for it . . . it's . . . what's the word I want?"

"Artistic," said Max Schulz, "a good barber is an artist. But an artist who makes a good living and one who can feed his family."

"But you don't have any family?"

"That will come," said Max Schulz.

"A fine trade," said Frau Holle.

"As for Laubwalde . . . that's in the past," said Max Schulz. "There's only one thing to do now."

"And what's that?" Frau Holle wanted to know.

"To strike roots again," said Max Schulz. "And lead a decent life again."

"Please tell me what you have in the sack!"

Max Schulz hesitated. Then he said slowly: "Gold teeth."

Frau Holle let out a startled cry, drew in her good leg, sat herself half upright, and stared at Max Schulz.

"And a few old rags," said Max Schulz, "and groceries, some supplies, and a diary and a prayer book. I've got one of those too."

"A prayer book? A diary?"

"Yes."

"And underneath?"

"Gold teeth," said Max Schulz.

"Gold teeth," Frau Holle whispered.

"Yes," said Max Schulz.

[107]

"And what do you want to do with the teeth?" asked Frau Holle.

"Begin a new life," said Max Schulz.

VIII

Shortly after three o'clock Max Schulz became aware that he was hungry. Frau Holle too felt as if there were a big hole in her stomach. Max Schulz helped her make a fire, chopped up wood, cleaned the oven, found a cardboard box in the coal scuttle, filled it with the ashes and the burned-out coals, went outside, emptied it on the rubble behind the house, stayed there for a while, had a pee, looked at the sun and where it was, calculated how long it would last before it became dark, wondered whether the corpse which he would have to carry away would not be too heavy, then thought: "You really should take a bath; you stink like a goat."

"Willy's mother has a washtub," said Frau Holle, "I could borrow it. It's just a question of water," said Frau Holle. "You'll have to get that yourself. There's a big pump in Fleischerstrasse."

Max Schulz nodded. He opened his sack carefully, took out a long piece of salami, some hard-boiled eggs, a loaf of bread, which he gave to Frau Holle, then closed the sack and said:

"With that and the tins of corned beef we'll have a real banquet. And we have some whisky too."

While Frau Holle made the meal, laid the table, and brought in the washtub, from time to time she combed herself surreptitiously, scratched her leg, or giggled to herself. Max Schulz gathered water from the large pump in Fleischerstrasse. After making several trips, he filled Frau Holle's cooking pot, heated the bath to the desired temperature, poured the water into the round tub, undressed, and climbed in.

Frau Holle rubbed his back with a good hard soap. Then Max Schulz stood up, dripping, steaming, let Frau Holle soap his stomach and legs, then said: "You can do my backside and my long snaky thing if you like."

And Frau Holle said: "That's not so long at all. It's just normal."

And then Frau Holle soaped his face, and his hair, was happy that Max Schulz was feeling good, and asked: "What about the gold teeth? Do I get something out of them?"

"You do," said Max Schulz. "But I have to sell them first; I won't leave you without money."

"And what about when you go underground," said Frau Holle. "Are you going to take me with you? I could cook for you . . . could look after you . . . and I'm not so bad in bed, am I? . . . And I'm easy to please . . . wouldn't be a burden to you . . . and if you find a younger girl . . . well, I can understand . . . and I won't say anything. . . . But I don't want to stay here all by myself . . . and you can do with me whatever you like."

"For example?" asked Max Schulz.

"You can whip me."

"And play doggy?" asked Max Schulz.

"And play doggy," said Frau Holle.

"With one leg?"

"That'll be my worry," said Frau Holle.

"You shouldn't have told Willy that I brought news about Günther. It made him ask if I was also with the SS."

"And what did you tell him?"

"That I was just with the Army. And that I met Günther by accident in the Polish forest and that I'd known him slightly from before the war."

"I didn't tell Willy anything else about you."

"Good," said Max Schulz. "And if he asks again, leave it just at that: I was just with the Army."

Afterward they both ate their food as though they were dying of hunger. They made a real banquet of it, drank whisky, gabbled on with all kinds of nonsense, but spoke about serious matters too, and especially about how to start a new life.

"And how about the six million Jews?" asked Frau Holle. "That was in the papers. Willy said so too. It's all a fake, I suppose?"

"That I really don't know," said Max Schulz.

"I bet it was two million at most," said Frau Holle.

"I can't tell," said Max Schulz.

"Or three, or four. Maybe even five. But certainly not six!"

"I don't know, I really don't," said Max Schulz.

"Do you think . . . that it possibly could have been six?"

"Perhaps," said Max Schulz. "It's possible. I didn't count them."

Max Schulz actually had eaten too quickly, and was feeling pains in his stomach. "Where is the bathroom?"

"It was bombed out," said Frau Holle. "I always go behind the house."

Max Schulz shuffled outside and when he came back he said to Frau Holle, "It's time for Max Schulz to take a nap."

"Lie down for a moment," said Frau Holle, "and I'll wash up and then go upstairs to give the tub back. Don't let anything disturb you."

"I couldn't sleep all night," said Max Schulz. "I spent the night in Mozartstrasse in the ruins and I was scared that someone would pinch the teeth."

"Yes," said Frau Holle. "Rest awhile. I'll wake you up when it's time to get rid of the corpse."

IX

Max Schluz snored like a power saw and when he woke up shuffled over to the window and pushed the curtains to one side. He could see the ruins were one big ball of fire . . . but that was just an optical illusion. Sundown.

"You know," his stepfather Slavitzki had once said to his mother, "Minna, if ever we get rich we'll move out of the cellar. A cellar, Minna, that's not right for a barber. It's okay for a damned cobbler. That sort of guy likes to look out of a cellar window, and count the shoes of people going by above. He likes looking at heels, and at soles. But that's nothing for a barber. A barber, Minna, should live above the street."

They put clothes on the corpse. Frau Holle helped him.
"Do you think Willy knows anything about the dead man?" asked Max Schulz.
"He thinks the major took off a long time ago."
"And what about the hole in the ceiling?"
"He can't see as far as the oven."
Once the major was completely dressed they leaned him up against the wall not far from the foot of the big brass bed.
"Better not to put him too near the oven," Max Schulz said, "I'm going to light the fire in a minute."
"Are you hungry again?"
"Yes," said Max Schulz.

"Do you know," said Max Schulz, once it was dark outside, "I have been thinking."
"And what have you been thinking?"

"The plan we had . . . with the corpse. Too conspicuous. Especially now in the evening."

"I suppose it would have been better to take him away in broad daylight?"

"No," said Max Schulz. "Not that either. The best time is just before daylight. When the sun is just coming up and the people are going to work. At that time a man with something on his back doesn't strike anyone as odd."

"So you'll do it early tomorrow?"

"Yes," said Max Schulz.

"So we don't need to wrap him up right now!"

"There's time for that. The wrapping paper won't run away from us."

"Good," said Frau Holle.

"But maybe if you can find some string," said Max Schulz, "and give it to me right now, so that we don't have to waste time looking for it tomorrow morning."

"Yes, I have some string," said Frau Holle. "But what do you want to tie him up for?"

"It's just in case there are strong winds," said Max Schulz. "To keep the wrapping paper from blowing away."

Max Schulz cut some wood up again, cleaned the ashes out of the oven, took the cardboard box with the ashes and the remaining coals behind the house, had a pee in the dark, aiming randomly at rubble and bits of walls, rolled his eyes upward toward the sky, looking for the Great Bear, but couldn't find it, but did find the Milky Way and wished he were a long way away.

X

"The war was over for both of us on the nineteenth of January, 1945," said Max Schulz, "over for me and for Günther too, because Günther was lying dead on a forest path covered with snow in the damned Polish forest and I was running as though Stalin in person were breathing down my neck, running anywhere into the forest. The thing I would have most liked to do would have been to sink into the ground."

Frau Holle was chewing. She had warmed up the remains of the salami and eggs, opened up another two cans of corned beef, and fried the corned beef a little too much, but that didn't seem to bother Max Schulz, because he didn't seem to notice what he was putting into his mouth. He continued staring beyond her to the window.

"The war was not really over, it was just over for me and for Günther. And for the other SS people in Laubwalde. And for the prisoners."

"Tell me about it!"

"Later," said Max Schulz. "Later I'll tell you everything."

They were both a little tipsy, had drunk a whole bottle of whisky, had drunk to the health of the major, and held hands across the kitchen table.

The major stared at them through wide-open eyes, sitting silently, propped up against the long wall at the foot of the brass bed.

"We'll have to shut his eyes," said Frau Holle. "I can't stand it."

"We never shut the eyes of the corpses," said Max Schulz, "that's something we never did. Besides, the major has been dead too long. It can't be done now."

Max Schulz got to his feet, stumbled across the room to the dead man, gazed into the corpse's staring eyes without touching him, then staggered back to the kitchen table and plunked himself down on the stool opposite Frau Holle.

"And what about the affair in the Polish forest?" asked Frau Holle.

With his head sagging heavily down on to the cushion of his arms, Max Schulz appeared to be dozing off but then rolled his frog eyes upward, looked at Frau Holle, cocked an ear for noise from the street and from the ground floor rooms above the cellar, raised his head again, put the bottle to his mouth, just wetting his lips, appeared suddenly to come back to life again, and said: "Yes . . . that's how it was. The day before. In the forest. I got a bellyache. So I said to my lieutenant, 'Lieutenant, I have to tell you, respectfully, that I cannot shoot the prisoners. Because I have a bellyache!'

"My lieutenant replied: 'Then go and have a good shit. And be quick!'

"I said: 'I did that already. No use.'

"The lieutenant said: 'What's the matter with you, Max Schulz?'

"I said: 'It's Warsaw, Warsaw's gone!'"

Max Schulz flashed Frau Holle a knowing smile and grabbed hold of the whisky bottle, but instead of drinking slapped the bottle back onto the kitchen table, felt something sticking to his bottom lip . . . cold . . . dried out . . . the last shreds of a cigarette butt. He took it, crushed it in his fingers, and licked his lips.

"Warsaw had fallen. The Russians were on the outskirts of Krakow, of Lodz, and Tilsit. They were about ten miles from the concentration camp at Laubwalde. In the camp everything was being broken up. The SS were packing their bags. There were a hundred and twelve of us. And we were all obsessed by a single thought: Out! Before the Russians got there. Out! To Germany!"

Max Schulz helped himself to a Camel, looked around for matches, Frau Holle pushed them over to him.

"Yes, that's how it was," said Max Schulz. "There were five lorries waiting for us. We had to get away. And we couldn't

[114]

take the prisoners with us. There weren't many left. And the ones who were still there were to be shot.

"We had the prisoners carry the heavy boxes to the lorries and load them up. We couldn't take too much with us: a few groceries, a bit of ammunition, a crate of jewelry, and another crate filled with gold teeth from dead prisoners, just a few leftovers that couldn't be sent back to the Reich anymore because of the short time.

"Yes, that's how it was," said Max Schulz. "And then it happened—when the last crate was being loaded on—that was the one with the gold teeth in it—we had a slight mishap—the crate fell down on the ground and broke and all the gold teeth clattered out.

"I was standing next to the lorries and taking everything in, even though I did have a stomach ache. But I kept my teeth together—my own teeth—because that's what we'd been taught to do.

"So that's how it was. The gold teeth clattered onto the ground. Another empty crate was simply not to be found. We just didn't have one. And so I ordered one of the prisoners to bring a few cardboard boxes. The gold teeth were picked up, put into a few middle-sized cardboard boxes, and loaded on to the lorry.

"Next I got the order to shoot the prisoners. As I said, there weren't too many left. I had counted them: eighty-nine. The last survivors. Eighty-nine? What does that mean! It only takes one man to do them in. But I had a stomach ache so I went to my lieutenant and told him that. But he didn't want to hear anything about it."

Max Schulz puffed out gray clouds of smoke. "Ah well," said Max Schulz, "so I just shot them with my stomach aching."

Max Schulz stared at Frau Holle. "When we broke camp," he said, speaking slowly, "it began to snow. At the time there was no wind and snowflakes fell from heaven like white bird feathers. We drove through the Polish forest in the direction of Germany. The forest looked like a German fairy-tale forest, with a calm sky, lofty trees, and snowdrops drifting down like the feathers of white birds. Just like the forest over which the Frau Holle in *Grimm's Fairy Tales* looked when she shook out her feather beds. *Grimm's Fairy Tales* . . . Itzig Finkelstein's favorite book . . . when Itzig Finkelstein was a small boy . . . and when I was a small boy . . . *Grimm's Fairy Tales* . . . he read to me frequently from it . . . he liked it so very much . . . his fairy tale book . . . a book of German fairy tales. . . .

"But then the wind started up. And the German fairy tale forest was transformed, seemed to disappear in a blizzard of snow, and became a Polish forest again—with the battlefront hard by us. Lurking just behind us in the forest. Prowling around us somewhere, lurking behind us in the forest like a goddamned salamander juggling fire, and did not lurk unseen for long, but crept up behind us, creeping along as fast as ourselves, even though we were driving and not creeping, and enveloped us in its fireworks.

"I was standing next to Günther. In the lorry. The last lorry. And beside us stood the camp commandant Hans Mueller, standing next to the boxes containing the gold teeth, guarding the gold teeth. He didn't seem to trust any of us anymore, stood there next to me and next to Günther, keeping an eye on the gold teeth.

"We were freezing. We had huddled ourselves deep into our coats. I was clinging to Günther. The lorries had low wooden sides but no roof. We were covered with snow.

"I said to Günther: 'Germany!'

[116]

"And Günther said: 'Yes. Germany!'

"The camp commandant Hans Mueller said: 'The front is getting nearer and nearer. This blizzard is a damned nuisance. If only we could get ahead a little faster. And, gentlemen, I am willing to take a bet that the guerrillas are waiting for us!'

" 'Which guerrillas?' Günther wanted to know.

" 'The partisans,' said the camp commandant Hans Mueller. 'At the other end of the forest.'

"And Günther said: 'How can you tell which end of the forest is which?'

" 'The partisans,' said the camp commandant Hans Mueller, 'they're waiting for us. Just you watch. Perhaps not at the end of the forest. Perhaps before the end.'

" 'And we're on our way back to Germany,' I said. 'Between the front and the partisans. We'll drive right through them. We'll drive right through the gap, won't we?'

" 'Of course we'll drive right through,' said the camp commandant Hans Mueller.

"I got a stomach ache again, but this time it wasn't the fall of Warsaw. This time it was the partisans. They were all around us. And I knew we were driving into a trap!

"I didn't ask for permission. I staggered to the back of the lorry, let the clapper down, pulled down my pants, and let my backside hang out into the cold air. I held tightly to the side of the lorry, keeping my head between my knees, and let a few droppings stain the snow-covered forest path.

"When the camp commandant saw me in action he grimaced, but caught the urge from me, staggered to the back of the lorry, tore his pants down much faster than I had done, squatted down next to me and said: 'That's no way for an *Übermensch* to shit!' But he groaned in pain, leaving a dark-colored trace behind us on the forest path, the path covered with snow, left his stain next to mine.

[117]

"The others, our comrades, just laughed, turned their heads toward us, stood covered with snow in the open lorry, stood there packed like sardines, stood there without cover, laughing, joking, Günther too."

"Suddenly the first lorry in the convoy stopped. Quite suddenly. The whole convoy stood still. There was something lying across the forest path. A felled tree. Then the firing started. Started suddenly too. And what a barrage of fire! Shots. The partisans. All they had were old guns. But they were good shots.

"I was squatting next to Hans Mueller, the camp commandant. And he was squatting next to me. We were not hit. But the others, who were standing up, laughing, in the open lorry, standing without cover, suddenly stopped laughing and folded up."

"You should have seen how quickly I pulled my pants up, I've never pulled my pants up so fast in all my life. The same goes for the camp commandant. He was even quicker than me. He had his pants up in a flash. And leaped to the front of the lorry right into the bloody heap of the wounded and dead. He grabbed a gun and started firing salvos one after the other into the forest.

"Naturally I did the same. Imitating him. I was a pretty good shot. And my stomach ache was gone. You should have seen that."

"What should I have seen?" asked Frau Holle.

"How we put a spell on the forest," said Max Schulz. "Because that was our last battle. When we had shot our last bullet, it became quite still. The forest was silent. And the front was silent too. And the partisans were silent also. Even the wind calmed itself, and the snow stopped falling.

[118]

"'Out! Get out!' the camp commandant Hans Mueller screamed.

"And I merely said: 'Yes, for God's sake!'

"We chucked our guns on the pile of wounded and dead. Hans Mueller grabbed one of the cardboard boxes with gold teeth, lifted it up and threw it into the bushes. Then we jumped down, ran off, and disappeared into the forest."

"But what happened to Günther? Was he dead right away?"

"That I don't know. Günther lay among the others. I didn't see him until the next day."

"Tell me how it happened. How you came to see him again."

"Yes," said Max Schulz. "Later on."

"And how about that bit about the forest? Was it really under a spell?"

Max Schulz nodded. "The forest was silent. But when we ran away the forest began to laugh."

"I think you're going weak in the head," said Frau Holle. "A forest can't laugh."

"Oh yes it can," said Max Schulz. "A forest can laugh. It came to life again. And the front began to rage again. The partisans came out of their hiding places and started shooting at us from behind. And the clouds opened up again. The winds whined through the trees, whipped fresh snow into our faces. We ran and ran with sticky underpants, ran in a manner not at all like *Übermenschen*."

"I lost sight of camp commandant Hans Mueller. How long I wandered around in the forest I don't know. A few hours maybe. Later I found a deserted bunker, climbed into it and spent the night there."

"The night?" asked Frau Holle.

"Yes, the night," said Max Schulz.

[119]

"I slept for a few hours, and while I was asleep the whole front line trundled above me, without my noticing. Then I awoke feeling scared and asked myself what was going on.

"I climbed out of the bunker. It was still pitch dark. I brushed my uniform down with my fingertips, clicked my heels, and hurled imprecations against heaven:

"I shouted: 'Let there be light!'

"I shouted: 'Let there be light!'

"I shouted: 'Let there be light!'

"But nothing happened. For years I had hurled imprecations against heaven in the early hours of the morning, and heaven had always listened, and now . . . there was no reaction. The heavens did not listen.

"I lit a match and looked at my watch. It had stopped.

"Only a little later did it begin to dawn."

"You *are* a nut," said Frau Holle. "I should have known that right off. It's impossible to tell when you're serious. And I can't be sure even now about what happened to Günther."

"Later, when it got lighter, I went back to the place where the ambush had taken place. The partisans had made off with the lorries. They had wiped us all out except for the two of us, camp commandant Hans Mueller and myself. They'd thrown the dead and wounded out of the lorries and they were all lying around in a confused mess on the forest path. Naturally the partisans had killed all the wounded. Only dead men were lying in the snow-covered path. I scratched the snow away from the faces . . . from only a few . . . from their bodies also . . . and at last from Günther . . . Günther . . . scalped and disemboweled."

"How did Günther look . . . disemboweled?" asked Frau Holle.

"Like a menstruating woman," said Max Schulz, "with a red hole between his naked legs."

"Naked?" asked Frau Holle.

"Yes," said Max Schulz. "They were all naked."

"Do you know what a Polish forest looks like in January," asked Max Schulz, "early in the morning, shortly after sunrise?"

"No," said Frau Holle.

"Well, it's just like it is in the picture in the Finkelsteins' living room . . . a winter landscape. A foreign landscape with a cold red sun, dark trees with icicles hanging down from the knotty twigs like dragon's teeth . . . hanging teeth, baring their gums at the earth, as though they wanted to gobble up the soil . . . all that and more was still covered with a white linen sheet and interlaced with strange gray wisps of mist. The only thing missing from Finkelsteins' picture was the naked corpses lying on the forest path."

"Who were the Finkelsteins?" asked Frau Holle.

"The Finkelsteins were the Finkelsteins," said Max Schulz. "Who else would they have been?"

"And so there I was, standing in the damned Polish forest, next to the dead corpses, thinking: 'Oh my God, Max, how are you going to get to Germany now?'

"At that moment, I would have liked to cry, but could think only that my tears would immediately change to ice. In Poland it's cold in January. So cold that a man's own spit freezes if he opens his mouth too far."

"So it was better to keep your trap shut," said Frau Holle.

"I had no choice.

"And so I stood on the forest path staring at the dead men,

stood there freezing, still tired from too little sleep, my teeth chattering, my stomach empty.

"The partisans had of course taken everything with them . . . including the food. I knew that without food and the right kind of shelter I could not survive. Somewhere I had to find a roof over my head, a place where there were matches, because I had used the last ones. I had to find a place where I could make a fire and where there was something to eat. And I had to get myself some civilian clothes, throw away my uniform, and try to get back to the West from behind the Russian lines . . . somehow get as far as Germany. It was imperative that no one know who I was. They wouldn't waste too much time dealing with me otherwise. Not with us. Not with the SS."

"Yes, here's what happened: before going any further I looked in the bushes for the gold teeth. They were still there. The cardboard box was covered with snow. I cleaned the snow off, heaved it onto my back, started walking along the path, then took a turn off to the right to lose myself between the high, icy trees, because that was safer. After I had gone some distance, I stopped, took the box with the gold teeth off my back and buried it in the snow. I marked the trees in the vicinity with my pocket knife in order to indicate the hiding place.

"I knew commandant Hans Mueller was wandering around the forest just as I was and was somehow happy that I had lost him. Nothing could be more certain than that Hans Mueller would go back to the place of yesterday's ambush to look for the gold teeth. I said to myself: better for you to have the teeth than him. When the right time comes you can go back and get the teeth, dig the teeth back out again—before the thaw comes . . . perhaps in a few weeks or so—and then you can march on . . . with the teeth . . . as far as Germany. And there you can sell the teeth and begin a new life."

"The forest was swarming with partisans. I was scared. And I thought about Günther. And about the red hole between his naked legs. The fear drove away the feeling of hunger. I crunched my way through the deep snow, and slowly began to get warm. After a while I heard the sound of engines and the grinding of heavy tank chains, and thought: that's a Russian tank convoy . . . and over there is a road. You'd better keep your eyes open this time! Russians don't joke around! The Russians . . . and the partisans. They don't joke. And the tank convoys, they're rolling their way right through Poland. They're rolling toward Germany.

"I made another turn before noticing that I was wandering around in a circle. I looked at the position of the sun and calculated in what direction lay the West, and began walking.

"Toward noon I saw smoke, saw a glade, crept carefully a little nearer, sniffing the air like an animal.

"First I saw only a roof . . . a sloping straw roof with a short chimney made out of dried clay. Black smoke was belching from the chimney, circling above the straw roof before getting caught in the tips of the trees near the roof, then being whipped toward heaven by gusts of wind. I let my eyes follow the trail of smoke, looked willy-nilly up to heaven and felt terrified. Because the heavens above the straw roof looked like a lake of ice. Blue ice with a yellow yolk of sun frozen into it."

"I have never seen blue ice," said Frau Holle. "Nor a sun like a yolk that was frozen into it. But go on with your story!"

"Yes, that's how it happened," said Max Schulz. "It was only when I got a little closer that I saw the rest of the hut . . . I mean the building that was under the roof. It wasn't much.

[123]

A small farmer's hut made out of pressed clay and cow and horse dung, and limed-over in white. I couldn't see any stables. Nor any barns. Just a hut. And the hut had narrow windows, frosted and draped with ice-fern."

"Ice-fern?" asked Frau Holle.

"Yes," said Max Schulz. "Ice-fern. It only blooms in winter . . . and especially on windowpanes . . . and especially on the windowpanes in Veronja's hut."

"Veronja?"

"Yes," said Max Schulz. "Veronja!"

"And what happened was: all of a sudden one of the windows was opened. I saw a face. The face of a shriveled-up old hag. An ancient face."

"How old?" asked Frau Holle.

"I don't know exactly," said Max Schulz; "but the old witch was at least twice as old as you."

"Twice forty-nine," said Frau Holle, "makes ninety-eight."

"Twice fifty-nine," said Max Schulz, "makes one hundred and eighteen."

"Yes that's how it was. It happened just like that: the window was shut again just as quickly as it had been opened. For a time there were no further movements, and I had begun to think: what rotten luck! The old woman saw my uniform. She's probably terrified!

"Then the door opened. Quite slowly. Creaking. Creaking in a quite comical way."

"Just like in the fairy tale *Hänsel and Gretel*," said Frau Holle. "I can feel the chills down my spine already."

"There were chills running up and down my spine too," said Max Schulz. "Suddenly there she was on the threshold.

An ancient old hag. A strange grin cracking her face. I had never seen a grin like that before."

"What was it like?"

"She grinned the grin of a vampire," said Max Schulz. "A female vampire. I couldn't help thinking of a giant cooking pot and seeing my backside swimming in it . . . pink and red . . . ready for the carving knife . . . saw my big frog eyes swimming around in the brew. And my eyes saw her face: the grinning face of a withered old witch . . . bending down over the cooking pot."

"I suppose you got out of there as quick as you could," said Frau Holle.

Max Schulz shook his head. "No, of course not, where did I have to go? I was hungry and cold. And there were partisans lurking in the forest. And Red Army tanks on the move to Germany not far from there. I was a member of the SS . . . and not just a member but one of those who had done the dirty work for those who had made the plans for the New Order . . . that's who I was . . . Max Schulz . . . a mass-murderer . . . a fugitive . . . but apart from that: behind enemy lines! They were all around me in the forest and in tanks on the road . . . and there were more following the tanks . . . whether with eyes or thoughts or feet . . . standing behind the tanks with fingers crossed . . . there were plenty of them, looking for me, Max Schulz, the mass-murderer, thirsting for my blood, and also, no doubt . . . at least I thought so then . . . for my cock too, to use the knife on it . . . as they had with Günther . . . and with the others lying there . . . with Günther . . . in order to do the whole job on me, even after my death.

"I looked at the old witch. And I saw Günther. Just as I had seen him the last time. And I stammered from sheer terror. And I said to myself: 'Here I stand, I can do no other!' "

"I followed the wrinkled hag into the house. I stumbled over a few words in Polish . . . the few words I had managed to learn. But the old hag just laughed and said: 'I can speak German too!'

"The hut had two rooms and a loft. The witch showed me around. First we entered the big kitchen, at once a living room and a farmer's kitchen, filled with roughly made chairs and stools, a square table, a long bench, a rusty stove, and a baker's oven with a chimney corner and bench. Beneath one of the windows was a large black box that looked like a coffin, and on the long walls hung all kinds of strange woodcuts and drapes. Between the stove and the oven was a large bundle of straw. That's where I saw the goat. A tiny goat no larger than a lamb. It was nibbling at straw, and as I walked past the stove the goat turned its head, looked at me, opened its mouth and let out a bleat.

"In the second room there was only a large wooden bed with a mattress of straw. Apart from that the hut was empty. The loft the old hag did not show to me, and I assumed it was probably used as a hayrick or lumber room.

" 'You've come from Laubwalde, haven't you?' the old hag said to me in a wheezing voice. 'From the concentration camp . . . five miles from here!'

" 'No,' I said, 'not from there—definitely not.'

" 'You're lying,' said the old woman. 'I can see that.'

"The old witch began to laugh. It sounded just like the bleating of the goat."

"Yes, that's how it happened. There was a good fire in the kitchen stove. The old witch moved a stool closer to it, invited me to sit down, then pulled off my boots, my socks too, went outside, brought back in a handful of snow, squatted down at my feet, and rubbed my naked frozen feet with the snow. Massaged them, breathed on them, then said hoarsely: 'You're frozen stiff. But not just your feet . . . everything else about you too. Now, take off your uniform, your underwear too . . . everything.'

"I did as I was bid. Soon I stood naked in front of the stove. The old hag brought in more snow, rubbed me down from head to foot, massaged me, and said: 'Outside you would have frozen to death. What kind of blood do you have? Is that the blood of an *Übermensch?* Get dressed and stay in front of the stove. I'll make you something to eat. Are you hungry? How long were you in the forest? And how long is it since you last ate?'

" 'Yesterday noon,' I said, 'twenty-four hours.'

" 'That's not so long ago,' the old witch said, 'and yet you look as though you were starving. So *Übermenschen* don't last any longer than ordinary folk.' "

"It was clear that the old witch had plans for me. But I didn't know what they were. Perhaps she was planning to slit my throat during the night? At any rate I was certain she wanted to kill me!

"The meal she had made tasted good. It was borscht with potatoes and farm bread. The old witch didn't eat much. She just watched me and seemed to be saying with her watery, tiny eyes: 'You're thin! I'll have to fatten you up a little!'

"We were on first-name terms very quickly. 'You look like a Jew,' she said, while I still had my mouth full with potatoes, bread, and borscht. 'But I know that you're not.'

" 'That's right,' I said.

" 'Tomorrow you'll have to stay here by yourself, because I'm going into the village. Have you ever seen a Polish village?'

"I said: 'Yes. Polish villages . . . I know enough about them.' "

" 'My last husband was younger than I am,' said the old witch. 'Much younger! And he had a daughter from his first marriage. She lives in the village!'

" 'And what do you want from this daughter?' I asked.

" 'Groceries,' said the witch. 'Once a week I get a few potatoes, beet roots, bread, and vodka. Enough for a week.'

" 'Is that what you live off?' I asked.

" 'Yes,' said the old witch. 'That's what I live off.'

"Then we drank vodka and became more and more friendly.

" 'You can't leave now,' the old witch said to me. 'In the winter you would never make it as far as Germany. You would freeze to death in the forest. And where do you think you would get something to eat? If you dared to put one foot into a village, they would beat you to death. Or one of the Russians would get you. Or the partisans. Or the police. It's impossible that you leave now.'

" 'So what do you suggest?' I asked.

" 'Wait until it's spring,' said the old witch. 'The groceries I get once a week from the village are enough for both of us to live on if we divide them carefully. And when spring comes round again you can get going. Before that day comes I'll sell your boots and your watch and buy groceries. We'll divide them equally. Enough for me. And enough for you too, to last until you get through to Germany.'

"We drank more vodka. In spite of all she had said and all I had drunk I remained afraid. The old witch was right. I was trapped. There was only one reasonable thing to do: to wait until spring came. The war might be over in the spring. Then

[128]

I could go. I would be happy to give her the watch and my boots. The old witch was certainly lying and just trying to lull me into a sense of security. Why should she feed me right up to springtime? A useless mouth. She was really going to slit my throat one night. And take my watch! The boots too! Or did she have something else in mind for me?"

"The whole night I lay sleepless, my eyes open, on the long bench in the kitchen, listening to the old witch's snores from the next room, and from time to time I stood up and stirred the fire in the kitchen stove. Outside the wolves howled and the wind sang in the trees. I could easily have done the old girl in, of course, but if I'd done that, who would have provided me with food till spring? I couldn't go into the village myself. I needed the old woman.

"There was the goat whose name, whose name I found out was Katjuscha. But it was thin, and tiny as a lamb. If I did away with the old witch, I thought, I could at least slaughter the goat and live off it. But for how long? A small, thin goat? No! I was dependent on the old witch. I needed her. The old witch could do what she wanted with me. If she wanted she could feed me until spring. She could hide me under the bed or somewhere else if the partisans were to come . . . or the Russians . . . she could protect me. But she could give me away too. I was completely in her hands.

"That thought stuck in my mind the whole night."

"Next morning the old witch said to me: 'You could do me in, but I wouldn't advise you to!' as though she had been reading my thoughts.

"I said: 'Do you mean because it's you who gets me food?'

"'Not only for that reason,' said the old witch, 'my stepdaughter is used to having me come to the village once a week.

[129]

If suddenly I didn't show up she would come here right away to check what's wrong with me. That could be embarrassing for you—and if you were to do my daughter in too—before she could get to the police—that wouldn't do you any good either. The village folks would notice. And they would check up.'

"I said: 'Veronja . . . how can you possibly think such thoughts? Why should I do you in? Or your stepdaughter? Or both of you? People would notice that right away! I know that!'

"'You can leave in the spring,' said the old witch, 'and until the spring you will have to do what I want!'

"'What is it you want from me?' I asked.

"'You'll soon see.'"

"While we were eating we drank a lot of vodka. The old girl still had a good stock from better days. Soon I was in a good mood, but I was still afraid, even though I didn't show it. I told her that for years I had been in the habit of shouting at the heavens, and I showed her how. 'Let there be light! Let there be light! Let there be light!'

"The old witch said: 'You're drunk.'

"And I said: 'And heaven always heard me.'

"'Now too?' asked the old witch.

"'Now too,' I said, showing off.

"'I don't believe you,' said the old witch.

"'I can prove it.'

"'Then prove it.'

"'Very well. Any time you like.'

"'Tomorrow morning at dawn,' said the old witch. 'Before daylight. I'll wake you up. And then if you like you can shout up to heaven. As much as you like. But watch out if you've been making it up!'"

[130]

"The old witch woke me up next morning before dawn. I got into my uniform and my boots. We opened one of the windows, and together stared out into the darkness. I clicked my heels and shouted:

"'Let there be light!'

"I shouted: 'Let there be light!'

"I shouted: 'Let there be light!'

"But nothing happened. Then the old witch began to laugh and groped her way over to the kitchen table to the petroleum lamp. She lit it, held it in her hand up above her toothless mouth, gave a loud belly laugh, slithered over to the large black box beneath the window, opened it, pulled out a riding whip, still laughing, a strange giggling laugh, gradually calmed herself, then said to me in a croaking voice: 'I can do with you whatever I like! I can hand you over. I can let you go hungry.'

"And I said: 'Yes, you can. But you won't!'

"'Oh yes, I might,' she said, 'and I will, if you don't do what I want you to.'

"'I will do what you want me to,' I said.

"'I never whipped a god before,' said the old witch, 'and I would very much like to whip one.'

"'A god?' I asked.

"'Someone who once was a god,' said the old witch.

"And then she raised the riding whip and croaked: 'This is it! Get your pants down! Fast!'"

"Life in Veronja's house was dull. Three times a day the same sequence: red borscht, potatoes, bread, vodka, and whippings.

"Veronja might have been as old as stone, but she had the strength of a witch. She performed her whippings with power and precision, giggling whenever I yelled. She seemed never to tire. She slithered about on her old legs faster than I could run, pursued me underneath the kitchen table, underneath the bench, under the stove . . . even under the wooden bed in the other room. I was able to take a lot, but from time to time I lost consciousness.

"After the whippings it was Veronja's habit to fill one of the washtubs with ice-cold snow water. Veronja maintained that the open wounds healed quicker this way. I was convinced that Veronja wanted to beat me to death, and refrained from doing so only to enjoy me for a longer time."

"One night Veronja woke me up. She was standing in front of my bench, dressed in a black apron, holding the petroleum lamp in her hand. Her ice-gray hair fell in a crumpled mess over her shoulders and her back. Giving me an evil grin she ordered me to follow her. We went into the next room. Veronja pushed me down onto the straw mattress then knelt beside me.

"'Now you listen, Max Schulz,' she said in her croaking voice. 'I have a serious word to speak with you. Because fucking is no joke.'

"'What is it you want, Veronja?'

"'I want to know how many orgasms you can have at one go, Max Schulz!'

"'That depends,' I said.

"'Now don't try to pull any fast ones with me,' said Veronja, bending over me menacingly. Her panting, evil breath made me feel sick.

"'More with a fat woman than with a thin woman,' I stammered. 'Probably because my mother was fat.'

"I tried to edge away from her, but could not because of the wooden bed-end. 'And, of course, it's a matter of age,

[132]

too,' I said, trying to gain time. 'The younger and fatter she is, the more I can do . . . the older and thinner she is, the less I can do. But I have my principles.'

" 'What sort of principles are those?' Veronja wanted to know.

" 'I only sleep with women under seventy-five.' "

"Veronja laughed at me. She ordered me to stay on my back, went into the kitchen, stirred the fire, brewed a strange drink out of herbs, then came back and had me drink it.

"Veronja screwed down the wick of the petroleum lamp, and put it next to the wooden bed. Then she slithered over to the window, and stood there for a while . . . in her black apron, mumbling to herself, moving her gray-haired head in rhythm to her mumbled incantation, pressing her wrinkled forehead against the cold glass of the window, peering out with her piercing eyes through the ice-fern on the glass into the winter's night, seeming to listen to the howling of the wolves, and the singing of the forest wind, then suddenly turned around to face me, slowly edged back to the bed, where I was still lying, having drunk my herb tea to the last drop, afraid, a sense of sheer disgust in my marrow. . . . There she stood, in front of the bed, staring at me—piercing eyes gazing into frog eyes—then she clambered onto the bed, squatted down next to me, and grinned.

"And then it happened. My whole body began to tremble. As soon as Veronja noticed that she tore my pants down with a single yank, threw them to the ground next to the bed, next to the dimmed lamp, gripped my thighs, pressing them down tightly onto the straw mattress, began to tremble, let a purring noise throb in her throat, licked her lips, her tongue coated, sticky spittle trickling from her mouth, mumbled something, opened her black apron, bent down closer over me, so close that her breasts . . . dried out and black with warts . . . touched my skin, stroked my knee with gnarled hands, stroked my thighs, then suddenly stretched out her fingers, fingers with long fingernails, fingernails with large white moons, and with these ancient fingers grabbed as though at random at my cock, squeezing, hanging on.

"Outside the wolves howled. And the wind sang in the trees. And the night looked into the room, its eyes dimmed.

"'That herb tea,' said Veronja, 'can wake up the dead. Including that lifeless snake between your naked legs. Yes, that's what, Max Schulz, it's waking up now, and shedding its skin. Really is shedding its skin. And growing. Like the geni captured in a bottle.'"

"I made love to Veronja the whole night. And Veronja kept giving me herb tea to drink. In between I told Veronja about my heart attack . . . in Russia . . . told her about the mass executions . . . before I got to Laubwalde . . . in Russia . . . in southern Russia . . . Mobile Killing Unit D . . . said to Veronja: 'I had a heart attack. I was not used to killing. At least not then. To shooting so many at one go . . . women and children as well . . . and those eyes . . . those eyes, Veronja . . . it was too much . . . and I thought it was just because of smoking and drinking . . . but it was because of the eyes . . . and I had a heart attack, Veronja, in southern Russia . . . and what did the company doctor say: don't exert too much! Be careful with the women! Once a week is enough! And just one bang! Understood! One times one is one!—and not two! And certainly not three! And definitely not four! And on no account five! And certainly not six! And whatever you do not seven!'

"But Veronja wanted to kill me."

[134]

"The next night I was again awakened out of a deep sleep, led into the next room, had to drink tea—the love potion . . . not the strength-giving drink—then again had to do my stuff . . . seven times.

"That was the routine for the next days and nights. During the night Veronja stoked a nuptial fire in my loins, coiled herself around me like an octopus, sucking me up, rolling about on the giant straw mattress groaning and full of desire, while during the day she played nurse, giving me tonics to drink, making sure my blood pressure was normal, taking care of me, pouring vodka for me, and fattening me up."

"During the seventh night I had the heart attack I had expected. It came shortly before daylight.

"Veronja pushed me down from her bed, dragged me into the kitchen, levered me up onto my sleep bench with the help of the sooty poker, laid me on my back, put the flickering petroleum lamp at my feet, waited until it was daylight, then extinguished the lamp, squatted down next to the bench . . . and the window . . . beneath the ice-fern . . . her face wan . . . as wan as the dawn . . . her eyes piercing . . . as piercing as swords . . . and her mouth . . . a narrow grinning slit . . . her teeth huge.

"I watched Veronja as though through a fog, lay on my back retching, my eyes wide open, thinking I was going to die, heard violins and harps, saw angels on the window sill where the ice-fern grew . . . saw the angels sitting in the cups of the flowers . . . singing and playing and waiting . . . saw Slavitzki too . . . saw myself as a baby . . . saw my backside . . . pink and red . . . saw my mother . . . heard her barking . . . noticed somehow that Veronja was slipping away . . . heard the poker among the ashes . . . knew Veronja was making a fire . . . thought of the large cooking pot . . . saw

[135]

myself cooked already . . . looked down into the thick brew
. . . saw my backside . . . not the backside of the baby . . .
saw the backside of the mass-murderer . . . saw my eyes . . .
saw millions of eyes. . . ."

"And what happened then?" asked Frau Holle. "Why did
you not die? That would surely have been better."
"I was not allowed to die," said Max Schulz. "That is the
point. Veronja did not want to kill me. I understood that as
I lay on the bench . . . when the angels appeared in the
frozen petals of the ice flowers. I was there to be tortured.
Nothing more. Veronja wanted to tell me something."

"What happened next?" asked Frau Holle.
"Slowly I began to get well," said Max Schulz. "Meantime
it was March. Or at least the end of February. Around noon
the sun was strong enough to warm. The ice-ferns were afraid
of the sun and in their fear were watering the windowpanes.
In the forest the snow was thawing, but at night froze again.
"As soon as the sun stood high in the sky, we opened the
windows. From time to time the wind blew to us the cold
thudding sound of ax blows, the shrill whine of saws, and
the cracking of felled trees. At such moments Veronja would
say: 'That's the lumberjacks. They're cutting the trees in the
forest, all the trees around the concentration camp at Laubwalde . . . everything within a radius of seven miles.'
"And I asked: 'Why are they doing that?'
"And Veronja said: 'Because of the evil spirits nesting in
the leaves of the trees.'
" 'But the trees have no leaves,' I said. 'The trees are still
bare.'
" 'They will be getting leaves again,' said Veronja. 'The trees

will be covered with foliage again soon if the lumberjacks are not quick.'

"'And where are the spirits now?' I asked.

"'Sleeping in the barks of the trees,' said Veronja. 'But they will wake up again in the spring . . . and climb onto the leaves and make their nests there.'"

"It became markedly warmer. The thaw was all around us. Snow still surrounded Veronja's hut, but it was like a cardboard covering which every day seemed to cuddle closer to the earth, seeming as it were to melt from within, as though it wanted to collapse. Here and there I could already see large puddles, above all in front of the house door and underneath the roof. Over by the grove in the woods a waterfall had formed. The trees were still bare, and here and there a remnant of snow still lined the twigs, seeming to cling desperately. Yes, indeed, the snow was desperate. But the sun . . . was laughing . . . laughing scornfully at the desperate snow. The whole forest was wet, Veronja's hut also.

"I was almost completely recovered again, and every day at noon took little walks, in my boots of course, which were firm and watertight. Veronja made sure that I did not go too far, but had nothing against my leaving the hut for short periods.

"One day I stayed away more than two hours. I wandered through the forest in the hope of finding the place where I had buried the gold teeth. My sense of direction had always been good. After I had walked around for a while I saw the trees I had marked with my pocket knife. I had buried the box with the teeth deep into the snow, but when I got to the hiding place I noticed to my horror that the box was sticking provocatively out of the melting snow.

"Unsure of what I should do, I stood there undecided, cocking my ears. The forest had a language of its own. The trees were weeping softly to themselves, shedding tears of snow . . . in drops . . . sometimes stiffening against the wind, which no longer was really strong, and neither sang nor whistled, but rustled. There was a swishing noise also in the dying snow, and I felt myself surrounded by all kinds of wild life, although I could see nothing. The earth had ended its sleep and was beginning to stretch itself. I was already able to distinguish between the different voices of birds, but one thing in particular unsettled me at that moment . . . the sound from the blows of the lumberjacks' axes. It came from not too far away!

" 'Max Schulz,' I said to myself, 'if you had a shovel, you could bury the damned teeth in the ground. But that would be stupid. Because when the trees here are felled, how will you find the place again? The best thing would be for you to take them with you now. Just take care that the old witch does not see you. You can hide the teeth behind the hut in the bushes, and then at night you can take Veronja's big shovel and slip out of the hut while Veronja is asleep . . . and bury the teeth.' "

"When I was about a hundred yards from Veronja's hut, I left the straight forest path leading to the glade so that I could get behind the hut without being spotted. I wanted to be able to hide the gold teeth in the bushes. I was certain that Veronja could not see me from the kitchen window, but I had miscalculated. Veronja had seen me. She was waiting in the bushes behind the hut and I almost stumbled right over her.

"I felt limp . . . numbed. I stood opposite her, silent, unable to say a word, the box on my back, and gaped at her.

" 'I was in the loft,' said Veronja to me, grinning, 'and saw you through the window. What's that you're carrying on your back?' Veronja asked.

"'My things,' I said. Slowly I managed to collect myself.

"'What sort of things?' Veronja asked.

"'My things,' I said. 'Every man has something that belongs to him! Isn't that true?'

"'Surely,' said Veronja, grinning.

"'I must bury the things,' I said, 'because there are documents in the box as well, and some other stuff that is no concern of the Russians.'

"Veronja nodded. She said: 'Fine! But the box is wet. If you bury it like that, everything will rot. It's best to let the box dry out by the kitchen stove. I'll give you a thick sack to wrap it up in. After that you can bury it.'

"I agreed. We went into the hut and I put the box next to the kitchen stove."

"That night I lay awake on my sleeping bench, wondering about what I should do if Veronja should get the idea next morning of opening the box. The more I thought about it, the more tired I became. And I inadvertently nodded off. During the night the goat Katjuscha nibbled at the damp box and chewed a big hole into the cardboard . . . and the gold teeth tumbled out . . . tumbled out over the floor. I didn't wake up until Veronja came into the kitchen, still sleepy. I raised my head, saw what had happened, saw Veronja, and thought: too late!"

"When Veronja saw the gold teeth strewn out all over the kitchen floor, she began to scream, rolling her old eyes like a mad woman, tearing at her hair. Then she ran to the kitchen stove, kicked Katjuscha, grabbed the ax from underneath the stove, started to scream even more loudly, ran around Katjuscha, her body bent, mouth open . . . her teeth huge . . . dripping spittle . . . her eyes flashing . . . her hair scraggly and in disarray . . . suddenly began to make small leaps . . . like a goat . . . in spite of her old legs . . . then, with one jump leaped right over the goat, ran towards my bench, and began to attack me with the ax.

"I was quicker than Veronja. I ducked away from the blow, threw Veronja to the ground, grabbed the ax, which was still sticking in the bench, pulled it out and smashed the witch's brains out with three quick blows.

"Three blows! As the saying goes, all good things come in threes. Veronja's scalp flew underneath the bench and slapped against the wall.

"A part of her head shot off in the opposite direction, coming to a halt at the door of the bedroom. But Veronja's face . . . slid across to the kitchen stove, slid between the legs of the goat Katjuscha, which sprang back horrified toward the oven door. Cold ashes showered down on Veronja's face. I fetched a coal shovel, swept the face and ashes onto it, threw it into the oven, and made a bright fire."

"Then I searched around for the remains of the dried-up old head, found them and threw them into the fire. I lifted Veronja's headless body onto my shoulder and carried it to the well behind the barn. The well was deep. I threw the headless body into it.

"'Max Schulz!' I said to myself: 'Now you'll have to skip! Spring is on the other side of the forest. But you can't wait for it. You'll have to go now! You'll have to go and meet the spring on the way.'"

"I slaughtered the goat Katjuscha, chopped it into small pieces, made a fire and cooked the remains. Then I poured gold teeth from the box into an empty sack, burned the box, stuffed the remains and parts of the goat into the sack, put them on top . . . on top of the gold teeth, packed vodka too and the remaining provisions of potatoes, bread, and beets. I took my uniform off. My boots too. In the black box beneath the kitchen window, I found, apart from the riding whip, a number of articles of clothing which had once belonged to Veronja's husband. I picked the best ones out for myself: a Sunday suit, a good pair of boots, underwear, and shirts. I changed clothes completely, put extra underwear into the sack . . . threw it over my shoulders and left the hut."

"I walked towards the spring," said Max Schulz. "The ground in the woods became drier. One day we met: the spring and I."

"Do you know what a Polish forest looks like in spring?" said Max Schulz. "In the spring the sun and earth eat up the snow. And the trees cease to weep. They yawn and shake themselves. And earth, sun, and rain drive away the funereal cover and weave a new, colorful carpet of grass and flowers and other things like them. It's beyond my head exactly . . . I mean . . . how it is done. I only know that every year spring comes to Poland . . . whether the Russians are in Poland or I am there. It will always be so . . . I suppose. Spring does not stop for the Russians. Nor for me. And when I met the spring, in those days in the Polish forest, spring grinned at me a little. In the eyes of the spring, I, Max Schulz, was nothing more than a croaking beetle, a beetle that had been shouting for a while and lost its voice.

"Yes, that's how it happened," said Max Schulz. "For weeks I walked through the Polish forest. And I walked over fields and meadows. And one morning I came to the frontier.

[141]

"And when I came to the first German village, I stopped as though rooted to the spot. The houses had been burned down. The inhabitants had fled from the Russians. I saw a sign, the arrow pointing upward . . . toward heaven. I tried to read the name of the village but it was unreadable."

XI

The candle had gone out a long time ago. It was black in the basement apartment.

Although Max Schulz had not noticed it, Frau Holle had gone to sleep on the kitchen chair. For quite a while Max Schulz had gone on talking, drinking whisky, smoking cigarettes, and staring into the darkness with drunken, glassy eyes. It was only when Frau Holle, her head resting peacefully against the arm of the chair, gave out a few loud snores, that he became aware of the real reason for her long silence.

Annoyed, Max Schulz poked Frau Holle with the empty whisky bottle, whereupon Frau Holle's eyes popped open, startled.

"What's wrong?"

"There's nothing wrong," said Max Schulz. "You slept the whole time."

"Not the whole time," said Frau Holle. "I kept on waking up."

Max Schulz got to his feet unsteadily, stumbled against the chair, staggered across to the bed, his legs shaky, groped around for the candle on the bed table, lit it, came back to the kitchen table.

"You're drunk," said Frau Holle.

"Not really drunk," said Max Schulz.

Frau Holle laughed. She poked her finger up her nose, screwed it around for a while meditatively, stroked her hair,

[142]

looked for bread crumbs on the kitchen table, rolled them into balls, flipping them away playfully with her finger, aiming at Max Schulz's hand.

"You know, Max Schulz . . . I like listening to you."

"You were asleep," said Max Schulz. "You were not listening to me at all."

"Oh yes I was," said Frau Holle. "I heard the beginning of the story. And I asked some questions. And spoke with you. And later on . . . yes, later on . . . I went to sleep . . . but I didn't really mean to. And I did keep waking up . . . but I told you that already . . . and I did listen a bit . . . I mean to the rest of your story . . . almost to the end."

"So . . ." said Max Schulz. "Oh well, why should I give a shit."

"You know, sometimes you talk just like a poet!"

"Sometimes I'm able to do that," said Max Schulz, "even if not always."

"Not at all like a barber," Frau Holle whispered. "And especially not like a mass-murderer. But just like a poet."

Next Max Schulz went on to tell her that he had avoided country roads and railroad stations. Even after the capitulation of the Great Fatherland. "Always on foot," said Max Schulz. "Even though I had flat feet like a damned Jew. And I went to Wieshalle too. And there I looked for Slavitzki. And for my mother. But they had fled from the Russians. And I went to other cities too . . . marched through them . . . as a civilian . . . but I kept my eyes open . . . was very careful . . . I had no papers after all . . . and I wanted to sell the gold teeth . . . yes, that's what I wanted. But I preferred to wait.

"Yes, that's how it was," said Max Schulz. "And then I came to Warthenau, you see, and now I'm tired. I am bloody tired."

They slept only a few hours. Frau Holle had no alarm clock. Often she woke up out of fear that she might sleep too long, looked at Max Schulz's wristwatch, peering hard at the green, luminous dial, then closed her eyes, her mind at ease, went to sleep again, but soon woke in a panic.

Shortly before daylight, she poked Max Schulz in the ribs, shook him, and said: "So! Now it's time to get rid of the corpse!"

During the night the major had fallen down and had rolled a little across the uneven cellar floor. He lay there in front of the large bed.

Max Schulz brought over the wrapping paper, rolled out a long piece, and pushed it underneath the body of the dead man. Then he wrapped him up in it. Frau Holle helped him with the string, tying bows and knots as though it were a Christmas parcel.

A little later, when Max Schulz left the cellar apartment with his package, Frau Holle opened the window in order to watch him. But she was not able to see very far.

"That's what you get," she thought, "for living underground."

It seemed to Frau Holle that the first light of dawn brought with it whisperings and murmurings throughout the ruins of the quarter. The bombed-out houses seemed to be mouthing curses, pointing heavenward with their brick-walled fingers . . . toward the bared heavens, which had betrayed them . . . winding off slowly the black bandage of night, uncovering their wounds to the new day. The open mouths of the walls formed mistrustful grins directed toward the dawn, and unseeing brick eyes gazed toward the horizon from hollow, paneless windows.

Frau Holle waited for Max Schulz in front of the door.

When she at last saw him from afar, the sun had already arisen, bathing the ruins of Nietzschestrasse with a fresh, yellow tint.

There were only a very few pedestrians to be seen on the street, all of whom looked a little tired and seemed to be walking aimlessly straight ahead. It would be a long time before the bomb craters would be removed from the roads and traffic could be brought back to normal.

Max Schulz walked at a deliberately slow pace, fearing to be conspicuous. When he reached Frau Holle he didn't say a word, merely nodded to her, winked with his frog eyes, and gave her to understand that he would rather talk to her in the cellar than in the open street. Silently they descended into the basement apartment. Only after Frau Holle had closed the door and made certain that the face of young Willy Holzhammer was not to be seen above the large hole in the ceiling did she ask him, in a whisper, "Where did you dump him?"

"Just like we said! On a bench in Adolf Hitler Square!"

"Did anyone notice?"

Max Schulz laughed softly. "I followed a troop of workers. Most of them were carrying something on their back. No one noticed me. Later . . . on Adolf Hitler Square . . . I sat down on a bench . . . with the package, of course . . . it was next to me on the bench. I just waited for the right moment . . . and when no one happened to be looking . . . I unwrapped the parcel . . . sat the major up straight . . . and cleared off."

"And the paper? And the string?"

"Threw it away later on!"

"And the major?"

"He's sitting there and can't take his eyes off the Adolf H.tler monument," said Max Schulz.

[145]

XII

Since neither of them had had much sleep during the night, they lay down after breakfast in the large brass bed, fell right off to sleep, and didn't wake until afternoon.

Max Schulz got up before Frau Holle, went behind the house to pee, came back a few minutes later, and busied himself with the sack of gold, unpacking the rest of the groceries, taking out shirts and underwear and finally also two books: one brown and one black.

Frau Holle watched him. "Have you unpacked everything?"

"Not everything," said Max Schulz. "The gold teeth are still in there."

"And what sort of books are those?"

"I found them somewhere on the way," Max Schulz said. "In an abandoned village near the frontier. The brown one was a blank diary, although, of course, I've now made some entries myself."

"And the black one?"

"That's a prayer book," said Max Schulz. "A prayer book."

"Are the groceries from Veronja's hut?"

"No they're not," said Max Schulz. "The food I took from Veronja's hut I ate long ago . . . the goat Katjuscha as well."

"And where did you get this food?"

"By a swap," said Max Schulz, "for a few gold teeth."

"Single ones?"

"Yes," said Max Schulz.

"Why don't you sell the whole bagful?"

"Because I'm biding my time before I do that. It would be too conspicuous right now. If I sell the teeth one by one, I can always say that I pulled it out of my own mouth or that they fell out."

XIII

In bed, during the night, Max Schulz said to Frau Holle: "You know . . . I read all the newspapers. Since I've been back in Germany I have been reading everything I can lay my hands on . . . even scraps of newspapers from garbage cans and out of the gutter . . . and I know that the authorities are sure I'm still alive!"

Frau Holle turned right around to him, cuddled her old head into his arms, and asked: "So they know that then, and are sure of it?"

"Yes," said Max Schulz. "And they also know that the camp commandant Hans Mueller is still alive and hiding out somewhere."

Max Schulz spat on his fingers and snuffed out the burning candle stump. "There's just one mistake we made," he said softly to Frau Holle. "When we left the camp the Red Army was just a few miles away. It's true that we knew about the danger of ambushes by partisans . . . and Hans Mueller especially was scared of that. Just to hear about the partisans made him shit in his pants. We were completely convinced, on the last day when we were packing up, that the Red Army would not overrun us and that we would get through the ring of partisans. Because we believed that we would escape and get back to Germany alongside the retreating German troops, we didn't throw away our papers. Every man had his identity card and all sorts of other stuff. And all that fell into the hands of the partisans. And it was in the papers, too.

"The partisans gave the papers of the men they had ambushed and of the comrades they had lost in the forest to the Soviet authorities. Then they sent a party into the forest and photographed the dead corpses. It's true they didn't have any private parts and a lot of them only had half their heads left, but, still the Soviet authorities and the Russians . . . they knew exactly who had fallen and who hadn't. And there's something else. We had burned the lists of the dead . . . but not the list of names of members of the SS. That was in a file in my lieutenant's lorry. That too fell into the hands of the partisans and later into the hands of the damned Russians. And now they know exactly, that I, Max Schulz, and Hans Mueller the camp commandant . . . that both of us are still at large.

"Yes, that's how it is," said Max Schulz. "And the new German authorities who are sucking up to the GIs and to the Russians . . . and to everyone else . . . they know it too. And above all, the new Polish authorities know it. They're the ones who most of all would like to get my head . . . perhaps more even than the Russians. It's the Poles who would like my head more than any others . . . yes, and Hans Mueller's head too, because of our murders on Polish soil . . . even though they shouldn't give a shit that it was Polish soil or some other soil . . . but that's life. And I can't do anything to change it.

"And do you know what?" said Max Schulz. "I have a long tongue. Sometimes it's a little coated . . . and sometimes not . . . but it's long . . . and sometimes I try to see in my mind's eye what that long tongue would look like if I were hanging from the gallows."

"Well I'll be goddamned," said Max Schulz, "but that's how it was. That's how it still is. Not any other way. And as for the dead Jews from Laubwalde, they spewed out their gold teeth so that I could have it a little easier in this life. Perhaps I'll be able to work out a deal on the black market. And perhaps not. But one day . . . yes, one day . . .

[148]

I'm going to open up for myself a new barbershop. I mean
a gentleman's hairdressing salon, a real salon, with all the
trimmings. And when I really am settled down . . . and I'm
somebody again . . . and when people are saying he's so-and-
so . . . and no vagabond . . . no lay-about . . . he's a barber
. . . and he earns his money with the sweat of his brow . . .
and he's a good barber at that . . . a real good one . . .
and a member of this and that . . . and a real good member
at that . . . yes . . . you know . . . then the sun can go up
in the morning . . . and down at night . . . I won't care one
shit . . ."

"When I was a boy I had a Jewish friend," said Max
Schulz. "His name was Itzig Finkelstein. He had blond hair
and blue eyes. And many other things that I did not have.
And I had a Jewish mentor too, called Chaim Finkelstein.
And he was a real mentor, let me tell you. You're lucky to
get his sort.

"I went to the synagogue often with the Finkelsteins. And
on the Sabbath in the evenings I ate with them. At Passover
too. And on many other Jewish holidays. I know how to
pray just like a Jew. And can do a lot of other things that
the Jews do. And do you know," said Max Schulz, "for
months I have been thinking how I can best go into hiding . . .
and the more I think about it, the oftener I say to myself:
'Max Schulz! If you are going to have a second life, you
should live as a Jew. After all . . . we lost the war. The
Jews won it.'"

"The worst thing is that I'm going to have to so some
knife work on my cock," said Max Schulz.
Frau Holle had been listening to what Max Schulz had

[149]

been saying without a word. But suddenly she gave a twitch of horror.

"What's that supposed to mean?"

"I don't have to cut everything off," said Max Schulz solemnly. "Just the skin at the front. Then, I'll be circumcised . . . just like Itzig Finkelstein."

"Where's this Itzig Finkelstein you always talk about?"

"I don't know exactly," said Max Schulz. "Itzig Finkelstein arrived in Laubwalde during the summer of 1942. When I saw him for the last time—that was in September—September 1942—on the seventh day of the month—he was already deep under the sod. But perhaps he's in heaven now? I can't say exactly."

Book Three

I
Berlin 1946

I have insomnia. And so I am reading a lot. Sometimes for half a night at a time.

I cannot make a list of all the books which I am reading. Actually I just wanted to tell you that I am also reading newspapers . . . among others the Warthenau *Advertiser*, even though this newspaper is a very boring provincial rag. I buy it only for sentimental reasons.

A short time ago I read in the Warthenau *Advertiser* the news of Frau Holle's death. I could hardly believe my own eyes. There it was in black and white: "The widow of the SS corporal and mass-murderer Günther Holle stepped on a mine while collecting old iron in the no-man's land between Moltke and Hanauerstrasse!"

A typical post-war death! Did she go hungry after I had

cleared off? I presume so. And she wanted to collect old iron? Did she want to sell the old iron?

Do you want to know what I said to myself? "Itzig Finkelstein," I said to myself, "Itzig Finkelstein, formerly Max Schulz, the German Woman is hungry! The German Woman is collecting old iron! And the German Woman is stumping around the ruins of the thousand-year-old Reich in order to collect old iron. Because the German Woman does not want to go hungry. But the German Woman did not see the no-man's land warning sign. When the hell are the GIs going to clear away the last of the mines that our boys dug into the soil . . . into German soil?"

God knows . . . I wanted to take Frau Holle with me. But then I thought about it, and I said to myself: "Max Schulz"—in those days I was still Max Schulz—"Max Schulz," I said to myself, "you can hide. But a woman with a wooden leg, she can't. At least not so easily."

After all, I know how it is, sooner or later the police would have put her under observation because she was Günther's wife! And I was Günther's friend! They have good nostrils . . . I mean those who are after me. And every track is a good one for them . . . every track that seems it might lead to me . . . even a Frau Holle.

I told Frau Holle something about Itzig Finkelstein. And I told her also that I had the intention of becoming a Jew. Just like Itzig. But I did not tell her at the time what name I intended to take.

Well, now I am Itzig Finkelstein. Of all people . . . Itzig Finkelstein! That's the truth. And I can't change it anymore. And between you and me let me tell you. . . . Itzig's doing well:

Itzig Finkelstein has struck it rich!

Itzig Finkelstein has sold the gold teeth. . . . The whole caboodle!

Itzig Finkelstein became a black marketeer and traded with everything you could think of, from black cigarettes . . . to black virgins.

Itzig Finkelstein is living like a gentleman. Yes . . . like a "Man of the World."

Itzig Finkelstein has changed. The top of his head is shaved bald. He has a pointed beard and wears spectacles. He looks like Lenin, although not quite. Because Lenin didn't have frog eyes.

Itzig Finkelstein's private member has become a shade shorter because the foreskin is now gone.

Itzig Finkelstein's private member may well be a shade shorter, but it's no shade weaker.

Itzig Finkelstein is living with a beautiful woman . . . with a countess. More about that later.

Itzig Finkelstein takes pleasure in beautiful things, good music, instructive books. And naturally the countess encourages him.

Itzig Finkelstein is living it up!

Frau Holle had been shopping on the black market. And when she returned home in the late afternoon, Max Schulz had gone. Had packed his rags into the sack with the gold teeth. And had put the sack on his back and cleared off. Just like that!

Did she cry for long?

Life is cruel, dear Frau Holle. Not even summer birds have an easy life.

And it is not easy to travel in occupied Germany, especially as a German without papers. And with wanted signs out. But you can rely on Max Schulz. He got through . . . with his sack . . . with his battle-worn face . . . and his worn clothes . . . by roundabout ways . . . inconspicuously . . . as far as Berlin.

Have you any idea how an *Übermensch* completes his invasion of the smashed-up capital of the Thousand-Year Reich? Wearing shoes full of holes! Stinking clothes! With a tired face and reddened frog eyes! And an old sack on his itching back, an old sack in which the teeth of dead Jews shine and grin!

Immediately after my arrival in Berlin, I buried the teeth among the ruins. In the American sector. Marked the spot. Then looked for somewhere to live. It was not easy in Berlin. I found a room in the basement of a bombed-out house. There I could snore away beneath the street. I was used to that.

I had many comrades. And one of them was called Horst Kumpel. He was an SS man, an idealist, a fanatic.

Horst Kumpel did not have a proper profession. For a while he had been a sailor, later a waiter in the "Three Moors"; when the fair came around each year he made a business out of tattooing in Wieshalle . . . rented himself a corner in a shooting booth.

Horst Kumpel was once a tall man, but Horst Kumpel had bad luck. An accident. On a motorcycle. And in the year 1936 he lost both his legs.

In Berlin I said to myself: "Max Schulz! Horst Kumpel didn't have to go through the war. He has no record. And he doesn't have to hide. And his parents used to live in Berlin. They're certain to know where he is. And you can find him. And he was a good guy. A fellow who could even tattoo. And he surely can still do it. And there's something else he can do: he can keep his trap shut!"

The house where Horst Kumpel's parents had lived had been bombed, just like all the other houses in the Tulbeck-strasse. But the basement! It still existed!

I found Horst Kumpel's parents. The two of them were cringing down in the cellar like two old rats. Didn't know me. Had never seen me before. Looked at me suspiciously. Naturally I didn't tell them who I really was. I told them that I was a friend of Horst's, and that like him had no record, and said that I owed Horst some money and would like to speak to him.

Horst was living in a basement, too. Not far from Tulbeck-strasse.

Horst Kumpel: an SS man. Without record. Without legs. Wept when he saw me. Slithering around on the ground. Gesticulating with his arms.

"For heaven's sake, Max. I read your name in the paper. Kept my fingers crossed for you. Said to myself: 'They won't get him!'"

"Yes, Horst, I knew it . . . that you would be keeping your fingers crossed for me."

"That was quite some job you pulled . . . in Laubwalde. Two hundred thousand. It was in the papers."

"Jews, Horst! They were just Jews. Enemies of the people. Inferior people."

"You did 'em in good and proper, Max."

"Tell me, Horst, where is your wife? I don't want her to see me."

"Don't be scared, Max. She's gone to the country. To get

food. Things to eat are scarce in Berlin. But in the country . . ."

"Good, Horst! I can't stay long. But one night . . ."

A room in the basement . . . a narrow bed for Horst and his wife. Right away I thought to myself: he's no bigger than a four-year-old. He doesn't need much room. A table and two chairs of raw wood. A stove. A coal shovel. A washbasin, splintered. A window . . . and a slice of drab autumn sky.

Horst Kumpel slid busily hither and thither, lit a fire in the stove, cooked soup for both of us, and conjured up a bottle of liquor.

"Now listen, Horst, can you still do tattoos?"

"Of course, Max."

"Do you still have your tools and everything?"

"Yes I do, Max."

"Can you tattoo me, Horst?"

Horst grinned. "What do you want: a woman with large breasts? Strawberries for tits? Or cherries? Or toads? . . . A cunt or two? Or a rose?"

I said, "A concentration-camp number, Horst. What I want is a concentration-camp number."

For a while we cracked jokes. Then Horst said: "My God, Max, it seems to me that you're a damned Jew after all. And they just forgot to give you a number."

I grinned and said nothing.

"How could that happen, Max, with a mug like yours!"

I said: "Number one-two-three-one-four! And in front of the number, a letter. The letter A!"

"Why an A? Why not an L? You were in Laubwalde, weren't you?"

"In Laubwalde there were no survivors, Horst. That was just a small camp."

"What do you mean it was a small camp? You did two hundred thousand of them in, after all."

"That was a small camp, Horst. Most Jews were killed right away. Immediately after being delivered there. You understand? That way we never had many to watch over and keep."

"Oh I see, Max."

"Yes, Horst. That was a small camp. With just a few prisoners. And not one of them got away. We were well organized."

"That seems very true, Max."

"The letter A, Horst."

"Very well then, Max. An A, then."

"Auschwitz, Horst! That has a better effect! It's better known!"

I got my concentration-camp number. And Horst Kumpel also gave me the address of a doctor . . . one who could keep his mouth shut.

Dr. Hugo Weber was eighty-four years old. A man who had gone into retirement in 1930. Too old to have been around during the war. Therefore without a record. But a Nazi. A theoretician. An anti-Semite. Sentimental. An idealist.

I told him frankly who I was: "Max Schulz. A small fish." This man would not betray me.

The first thing Dr. Hugo Weber did was remove my SS tattoo from below my left arm—a pretty unsightly tattoo, a small letter denoting my blood type—then, his withered hands trembling, lined up my penis, trying to hold it steady, and sliced off the foreskin, performing a last service of love for Führer and Fatherland.

All he said was: "Max Schulz! That mangled cock . . . goes well with your ugly face."

I would have liked to have replied: "My dear Doctor: such prejudices are anti-Semitic, my face is not Jewish." But I preferred to remain silent.

During those first weeks in Berlin I changed my quarters frequently, sleeping in different cellars or remains of cellars, sometimes in the open air, somewhere among the rubble, once even in a ruined church. Tramped around. Among the ruins. Thinking up plans. Ruminating. Inventing lists of Jewish names, but finally clinging to one . . . to the name Itzig Finkelstein.

Max Schulz, the mass-murderer, illegitimate though pure Aryan son of Minna Schulz, was born on the same day as the Jew Itzig Finkelstein. He knew his past. And he had the same profession.

II

My story is simple: I am Itzig Finkelstein, a Jewish barber from Wieshalle. Not many Jews lived in our town. It was a small community. The Nazis had warned us. But we did not believe them. We believed that the whole nonsense would pass. We believed in a better Germany. And we waited. We did not emigrate.

And then the war came. And we waited for a miracle. And the miracle did not come. One day we did want to leave. But it was too late then.

Then one day . . . they came to fetch us. In the gray of the morning. All the Jews from Wieshalle. Not one was forgotten. We had to climb into lorries. In the gray of the morning.

We were brought to Dachhausen, a concentration camp in Silesia. There a few of us were executed. But not all.

In June 1942 Dachhausen was evacuated. We were brought to Laubwalde, a death camp in Poland. No one ever returned from there.

But I, Itzig Finkelstein, never arrived in Laubwalde. The transport train carrying us went through Poland. For days on end. We got hardly anything to eat and water was scarce. In my car there were a few dead. At a small station in Poland the doors were opened and the corpses were carried out. I took this opportunity and jumped out of the train.

Where did I flee to? Where can a Jew in Poland flee to? Into the forest, of course. I did not trust the Poles, because they were worse anti-Semites than the German Nazis. I stayed in the forest. Gradually I set my sights in the direction of southern Russia, the Ukraine. And there I joined the partisans. Fought for a while incognito. Wanted to revenge my parents. But then—shortly after the fall of Stalingrad—I was captured. My unit had walked into a trap. Once again I succeeded in escaping. For a while I was alone. Wandering around the area. Again I was captured. I worked as a grave-digger for a German unit. Was sentenced to be shot. But I managed to get away again. This time I fled back to Poland. There I was captured once more . . . and deported to Auschwitz.

Auschwitz! Yes . . . there the prisoners were put into the gas chamber. But not all of them. I was assigned to a work unit. I, Itzig Finkelstein.

And the front got nearer. Nearer and nearer. Then one day Auschwitz was liberated by the Russians.

And was I liberated by the Russians? No, gentlemen. A part of this monstrous transit station for millions was evacuated shortly before. And sent where? Toward Germany! Do you know what a death march is? I cannot describe it. But I was on one. En route I managed to escape.

I fled back to Poland. Into the forest, naturally. What other place was there to go? And one day . . . yes . . . one day the forest was taken by the Russians. I, Itzig Finkelstein, was free. The Russians freed me.

But I did not trust the Russians. And I did not want to stay with the Russians.

No, gentlemen. I, Itzig Finkelstein, was not so stupid as to want to stay with the Russians! I, Itzig Finkelstein, am going to Berlin! And where in Berlin? The American sector, of course!

In Wieshalle we were a small, isolated community. My Jewish friends and acquaintances were dead. My parents also were dead. There is no one left whom I know. I had relatives in Poland, or to be more precise in Galicia. But I have never known them. Where are they? I have no idea. Shot, probably. Or their brains beaten out. Or gassed. I really have no idea. What am I doing in Berlin? In the American sector? Gentlemen! What a question! How should I know? I was crucified and have bats in my belfry! And I didn't want to stay with the Russians.

Berlin is swarming with refugees. And I am one, too. We refugees are like frightened ants. We scurry about among the rubble of the city. All possible kinds of ants. German ants . . . displaced persons from the occupied Eastern territories . . . former forced laborers from Poland, Italy, Greece, people from all sorts of countries. But I, Itzig Finkelstein, am a quite special ant. A Jewish ant. I can scurry about the city today without fear. Because I was a victim of the toppled regime. And of all the victims I was the most cruelly treated. And for that reason all doors are open to me today. The conquerors do not love

[160]

me. For no one loves me. But they feel compassion toward me. And doors are open. For how long still? That I don't know. But as long as they are open I can slip through.

I cleaned my glasses every day . . . for the sake of keeping the view clear . . . and I kept my frog eyes open . . . I watched how organizations for the aid of surviving Nazi victims sprouted up from the earth like mushrooms. I think they embodied the conscience of the victors. These aid organizations overwhelmed the victims of the toppled regime with their retarded love and welfare. Naturally. A little late. Because millions of us were dead. But better too late than not at all.

I, Itzig Finkelstein, put myself in contact with the American-Jewish aid associations for surviving Jews of the Nazi regime. They had money. You can believe that. Because the American Jews . . . had not been crucified. But I, Itzig Finkelstein, their blood cousin, had been crucified. And my cousins had sympathy with me . . . a sympathy that was bigger and stronger than the sympathy of all the other conquerors, above all, of all the official ones. But sympathy is a form of suffering. And suffering is a cross. And everyone wants to rid himself of his cross. And so there was available to me, Itzig Finkelstein, tear-stained dollars, to enable me, Itzig Finkelstein, to get back on my feet, to heal my bleeding limbs, to help me to forget my cross. And to help them forget theirs.

And so . . . hear me out.

Along with many others, I, Itzig Finkelstein, was sent to the displaced persons camp at Lichtenberg near Berlin. No one puts questions to a Jew: like, were you with the German Army? Were you a member of the party? Or were you a member of the SS? A Jew is clean. He doesn't even have to prove that he was the victim of the toppled regime. Because

"Jew" is synonymous with victim of the toppled regime. Of course we had to prove that we were indeed Jews. Most of us had no witnesses because the witnesses were dead. And most had no papers. Of course all of us who had hung from the cross had been born somewhere and sometime. But what way was there of documenting it? Our world had gone up in flames, and who was there who knew us still?

We came before an examining commission. A pure formality. A doctor examined us men to see whether we were circumcised. We were given a prayer book to check whether we could read Hebrew. We were asked to name the Jewish holidays. Everyone had to tell his story.

You can probably well imagine that many of us who did not look like Jews were hauled over the coals more closely than others. I had an especially easy time. When my turn came around and I stammered out my name, a gentleman on the examining committee laughed. One of them, who had a bald head, said: "Herr Finkelstein. We know you are Jewish."

I showed them my Auschwitz number. And the men just nodded. I opened my fly and showed them what was there. The men laughed. The one with the bald head said: "Herr Finkelstein. We don't need a demonstration."

I do believe that those men thought I was batty. I was given neither a prayer book nor asked to name the Jewish holidays. I also was not obliged to undergo a medical examination. My identity as a Jew had been established to them without question. In spite of that I did not allow myself to be fended off so cheaply. Because I did not want to be given preference: why should I be tested less than the other Jews? And so I gave a recitation of the Jewish holidays even though I had not been asked to do so, intoned prayers that I had once learned from Itzig Finkelstein, by heart. But the men waved me away. They laughed. The one with the bald head even allowed himself a little joke. He asked, "Herr Finkelstein. How many gods do we have?"

I said: "One."

The one with the bald head asked: "And are you sure?"

And I said: "Quite sure. Only one. No son of God, and no Holy Virgin. And our God is no magic fucker who gets innocent virgins pregnant without deflowering them. He doesn't go in for such jokes."

When they heard that, the men stopped laughing. I read their thoughts. "He's mad!"

All those gentlemen just kept their eyes glued on my Auschwitz number because I had buttoned up my fly again. I could read their thoughts. I read them silently to myself with my lips tightly closed: He was in Auschwitz! He's mad! No wonder!

For a few weeks I stayed in the Jewish Rehabilitation Camp at Lichtenberg near Berlin. There I was able to eat well. The administration of the Jewish camp did nothing short of force their goodwill upon me. I received an entirely new outfit of clothes. I was given injections of vitamins. I got papers again, or, to be more precise, a provisional displaced person's identity card. I now had no need anymore to hide myself, because my displaced person's identity card proved in black and white, that I, Itzig Finkelstein, its owner, was the crucified Itzig Finkelstein, barber by profession, born on the fifteenth of May, 1907, in the formerly German and now Polish city of Wieshalle.

How long is such a provisional displaced person's identity card valid? I do not know exactly. In any case: until order is restored here in Germany . . . until the ruins disappear . . . and the displaced person's camps . . . until the day when the

[163]

whole place is functioning again . . . until the occupation ceases . . . until the day when we are able to drag the cart out of the mud. And it is certain that will take some time yet.

After I had rested myself thoroughly, I returned to Berlin in order to sell my gold teeth. I found a place to sleep . . . in a cellar of course . . . a cellar room with its own entrance . . . dug up the gold teeth . . . and took them home.

I, Itzig Finkelstein, no longer needed to sell the gold teeth singly and to tell people: "I broke this tooth off myself"— now I could sell them by the dozen because I, Itzig Finkelstein, was beyond all suspicion.

Naturally it was not my intention to sell the whole caboodle of gold teeth all at once because, after all, that would have been too conspicuous. Don't you agree? But by the dozen? Why not!

Do you know the black market in Berlin? Let me tell you; you missed something! In that place the heart of every black marketeer leaps for joy. Especially to be recommended is the area around the Reichstag building. It was just the right thing for me, the small-time Jewish black marketeer Itzig Finkelstein.

I made contacts: dentists, goldsmiths, middlemen, smaller and middle-sized fences (the big-time boys I avoided). Gold was scarce in the autumn of 1945. I sold my teeth by the dozen. I always told the same story: I am Herr Finkelstein. I buy gold teeth. I buy them up mostly from poor German women and men, who break off their gold teeth to exchange them for groceries.

It was all the same to the black marketeers. But the dentists and the goldsmiths . . . they hated me, the Jew Itzig Finkelstein, even though they said nothing. I could see the glint in their eyes, wordless showers of sparks: you shabby Jew. They should have put you in the gas chamber. What are you doing in Germany? Buying up gold, are you? From teeth of poor German women and men!

I would very much have liked to tell them: "Those are teeth of dead and murdered Jews!" But I couldn't do that. It wouldn't have been worthwhile . . . I mean . . . to discuss the matter with anti-Semites.

I sold all the gold teeth but I kept three as mementos. Wrapped them in a handkerchief. And I had a few melted down, for my own use as it were. Because my own teeth were bad, and I wanted to have them done in style.

I went to the best dentist in Berlin. And said to him: "My teeth are bad. A man shouldn't go around in the world with bad teeth. Please make me a mouth full of gold teeth. I want people to see the gold. It should glitter when I laugh."

I have a mouth full of gold teeth. And there are still three teeth wrapped up in my old handkerchief. A memento.

I had sold the remainder, and I had made a packet of money, enough to begin a small black market trade. The gentlemen's hair dressing salon had to wait. One day I again wanted to open a gentlemen's hair dressing salon of my own. Quite definitely. I wanted very much to strike roots again. Because that is what life is all about: striking roots! And leading a decent, orderly life. Perhaps start a family. Yes, why not? Why shouldn't Itzig Finkelstein start a family?

But as I said: there was time for that—1945 was the year of black marketeering.

I started with black cigarettes, then dealt in black coffee, later with all kinds of things. In time Itzig Finkelstein became notorious all over the black market in Berlin. He really had no reason to complain.

[165]

Berlin was still a heap of ruins. At night, as I lay in my bed, I could see the birds of prey above the burned-out ruins. I snuggled down under my covers. Berlin had collapsed like a pack of cards. I couldn't change it. That was no longer my concern. One day they would rebuild the city again. I could see the day coming. And the rest of Germany, too. Yes. They would rebuild everything again. All Germany. And then . . . yes . . . perhaps they will bring back the Führer from heaven.

III

Do you know Kriemhilde, Countess von Hohenhausen? Allow me to introduce the countess to you!

Now just imagine to yourself:

A black marketeer's party in a Berlin night club. In a cellar of course. The room is full of smoke. Somewhere in the room Itzig Finkelstein is sitting . . . the smallest of the big-timers. Smoking Camels . . . that's Itzig . . . and somewhere among the big-timers sits the countess . . . and she is smoking a cigar.

Dimmed lights. Candles of course. Small, fluttering, flickering, blinking flames . . . throwing shadows like the small flame of the candle in Frau Holle's cellar. They take the place of the sun, which is sleeping. And of the moon, which does not cast its gaze into the cellar. And of the electric light, which was cut off.

Perspiring, blurred faces . . . waiters in evening dress. Champagne! Flowing here from German beer barrels . . . in the background, gypsy music. Russian. Rumanian. Hungarian. Jewish, too. Sadness. Memories.

Smoke, music, champagne. And the countess.

Shall I describe the countess to you? For me she was just blond.

Perhaps tall, too. Tall and blond then. Not more. Itzig didn't see more than that. A big blond woman. A countess.

But my neighbor at the table, a pious man, a former monk, later a wandering preacher, who now dealt on the black market . . . as did believers and non-believers . . . he could see more than I could.

"Take a real good look, Herr Finkelstein," said my table companion. "What do you see?"

"A blond, tall woman," I said. "Not more."

"You don't see how perverse she is?"

"No," I said. "I don't see that."

"Everything is in those eyes," said my table companion, the monk and wandering preacher. "Negro slaves yelling their eyes out. And laughing slaves. Riding whips. Horses' hooves. Blood. White linen cloth with red dots. Colored sweat-covered cushions. A seat or behind or buttocks or bum or anus or ass . . . from the tenderest flesh and with peach skin. 'Domini craeatio magnifica!'—and there's something manly and muscular, froggy and eyeless, erectile, moaning soundlessly. Whatever is joined in this way laughs and moans and cries, sounds that only angels can hear. And don't you see, Herr Finkelstein . . . movements like spirals . . . and a damp tongue, and long female legs stamped with their ancestry, plucked smooth, as brittle as a bird's . . . and the bull neck of the man? And all that wrapped in an embrace? And the legs laughing at the tongue and almost breaking the man's neck! While tenderest flesh and peachy skin squeeze the marrow from his bones. And the bones are the last of a chain thousands of years old, with limbs damaged and spat upon! And the bed silent and patient. And the canopy of Heaven behind the window. And don't you see the rosary? And the Torah scroll? And Christ without a cross? Christ liberated? Naked? Christ, who discovered the flesh?"

I said: "Be damned and keep your trap shut! I never heard anyone talk like that!"

[167]

"Once she was very rich, farms, property in the country, a castle, too. Everything in the East. Confiscated by the Russians. Everything taken over by the state."

"Does she live from black marketeering now?"

"Indirectly," said my table companion. "She is the mistress of a black marketeer."

I said: "Oh I see . . ."

"That is to say, she was the mistress. She is not any longer, because the black marketeer died last week. From a heart attack. Because of a whole wagon of black cigarettes which fell into the hands of the military police. That's too much for a heart to bear."

I, Itzig Finkelstein, live in constant fear of a new heart attack. Nonetheless I could not resist the temptation. Everything was clear: I wanted to make the countess my mistress.

For days I wandered through the ruins of Berlin as though in a dream, and also took long walks in the suburbs . . . which were not quite so completely destroyed . . . looking here and there at villas . . . experienced the first snow fall . . . at the end of 1945 . . . began to think of the new year . . . thought of Itzig Finkelstein . . . the real one . . . the dead one . . . and of the false one . . . thought of my bent nose . . . and my circumcised member . . . thought, how is it going to turn out? I, Itzig Finkelstein, the little Jew and the beautiful blond countess . . . thought of insurrection, revolution . . . thought of horses' hooves and of the laughing and the crying Negro slaves, of horsewhipping and the white linen cloths with red dots . . . thought of tender flesh, thought of peaches, thought of her backside . . . and of my own cock that was circumcised as had been the cock of the Lord Jesus Christ.

I wrote a letter to the countess. I wrote:

[168]

Countess,

I, Itzig Finkelstein, am doing very good business on the black market, trading with black cigarettes, black coffee, black chocolate, black weapons, and many other things; sometimes, too, with black virgins, who usually have blond hair and blue eyes or possibly green or gray eyes. I am on the ladder of success. If you could find the goodness to comfort a lonely, industrious man and could see your way to sharing the fruits of honest work with me, then I, Itzig Finkelstein, would be very much obliged to you.

Respectfully yours,
Itzig Finkelstein

The answer was not long in coming. The countess wrote to me:

Dear Herr von Finkelstein,

Success ennobles you. Are you trading only with American or also Swiss chocolate, for instance: Alpine milk chocolate? It's one of my favorites. Please let me know!

Dear Herr von Finkelstein, I give you my hand for a kiss (do you know how a gentleman kisses the hand of a lady?).

Sincerely yours,
Kriemhilde,
Countess von Hohenhausen

IV

I trust there is no need to tell you that the union between the Nordic countess and me, the Jewish black marketeer, Itzig Finkelstein, came to be. The countess wanted money. And I wanted social status. We were in a position to benefit each other. We stretched out our feelers, found ourselves, and could function.

I visited the countess in her villa, a real villa, which had survived the war . . . not far from Berlin . . . in the suburb of Blankenstein . . . fruit trees, gravel paths, a well-kept wood, pine trees . . . covered with snow, of course . . . surprised by the winter . . . the winter of 1945–46 . . . a post-war winter.

The countess welcomed me, smiled like the chaste Kriemhilde surprised by Siegfried, let me kiss her hand, led me into the smoking room, offered me a cigar, pressed me into a leather armchair, sat down herself, and immediately explained to me that money offered more protection than dragon's blood, asked whether I could protect her, inquired after black cigarettes, black chocolate, black coffee, black virgins, smoked nervously, rang a small bell, ordered the butler to serve tea and bologna sandwiches, crossed her long, thoroughbred legs, showed me surreptitiously the tip of her tongue . . . blue-blooded and rosy red . . . spoke about finances, stock exchange news, music, books, then waved to me with her little finger, had me stand up and come closer, smiled, with gentle fingers opened my fly, palmed my penis, watched it grow, took a ruler, measured it for length, width, and diameter, and said: "Yes, that's normal! It will fit!" . . . then handed me a small golden key and said: "Just symbolical! Have you read Tagore? And Zweig? And Dostoyevsky? And Courths-Maler? And do you like Mozart?"

The countess had only rented the villa. It cost a fortune. Her former lover—the black marketeer Nikolaus Wanja Stubbe, the son of a white Russian and of a Berlin auto dealer . . . Nikolaus Wanja Stubbe, nicknamed: "Zarewitsch"—was one of the big-timers and for him the expense didn't make any difference. But I, Itzig Finkelstein, the Jew, was only one of the small-timers even though I was doing good business and was on the ladder of success. But anyway, it was simply more than I could afford . . . such an expensive villa which had every possible convenience I could not . . . or . . . I should not permit myself to afford.

Naturally the countess had a staff: butler, chambermaid, cook, cook's wife, gardener, personal attendant, chauffeur. In the garage was the car that had been the black marketeer's, Nikolaus Wanja Stubbe's, and now belonged to the countess; of course it was at my disposal.

After I had moved in with the countess it was soon drilled into me that big-time success has a close connection with life-style. Twice a day I was driven to the black market in a black Mercedes. This did not escape the attention of the real big-timers, who then came to me in order to do business. Regularly the countess gave parties in our villa and invited the big-timers, wrapping them around her gentle fingers, securing commissions for me, which were bigger than anything I'd ever dreamed of. And credit, too. Whereas before I had only worked on small deals and handled sums that an ordinary man can do in his head, now the figures had so many zeros that I had to buy myself an adding machine. In our circles one did not speak of single cartons of cigarettes or single cartons of chocolate or single cans of coffee, or single virgins . . . one spoke of a cart-load of coffee, a cart-load of virgins.

If you think that immediately after moving into the villa, I climbed into the countess's bed, beside my legal concubine, as it were, then you are wrong.

During the first week I was not allowed to go near her. Instead I had to share a bed with the butler . . . a solemn-faced, conscientious, dedicated man of experience, who had been especially commissioned by the countess to tutor me in the arts of love.

The butler explained to me that body and soul are one, and that while the soul in the living body cannot be dead, it may

[171]

well be slumbering, and that the slumbering soul has to be awakened just as has the slumbering soul of the violin at the touch of the virtuoso. The butler explained to me the difference between the feeling of joy and the expectation of joy and told me how the one is heightened by the other; he spoke about the theater and about the art of play, spoke about the importance of foreplay to impassion the climactic act, the throb of which continues as the play subsides to its end. The butler explained to me that man has or should have imagination, but not the beast: it has none! That the strength of love lends wing to the imagination and gives it the power to transform earthly things: until a finger is no finger, a tongue no tongue, until toes are not toes and noses not noses, until a penis is no penis and a cunt no cunt, until an ass is no longer an ass and a come no longer a come. And so on!

The butler explained to me that bees thrust their eager feelers down deep into the orifices of flowers in order to rake at their honey, that the earth is female, but rain is male just as the sun is male, that the woman receives the man and not the other way around, that mountains open themselves to the spring breeze, that the sweet birds of the air are God's creatures just as is the horse . . . and that these teeny sweet birds are not ashamed to peck at tasty grains among stinking horse muck, because corn is God's fruit and is not man better than a bird?

The butler spoke about the art of whipping, about tanned and untanned leather, about hard and soft knobs . . . with ornamentations in silver or bronze . . . about silk and velvet coverings to increase the thrill of touch. He spoke about the sting of nettles, about olive oil, foam baths, vaseline, perfume, hair curlers, nectar and champagne, spoke about smooth, round upward-curving bottle necks, about vaginas moist with champagne and nectar, about sweet cherries soft and mushy inside,

[172]

about house slippers, wagged his butler's fingers threateningly while passing on the admonition that to suck loudly was permitted only when the champagne was not tongued from the glass or directly out of the bottle, spoke about the folly of hemp and about the spirit of the vine.

My head roared from a surfeit of philosophy, and for me it came almost as an act of salvation when the butler at long last called the chambermaid into the room to convert theory into practice. Yes . . . that took up the rest of the week. I learned all manner of things; learned above all the seven most important positions, including the final one . . . the position "of pure contemplation."

Have I made you curious? Are you eager to find out how the Jewish black marketeer Itzig Finkelstein alias the former Aryan mass-murderer Max Schulz came through the first night of the great test with the beautiful, noble Frau Kriemhilde Countess von Hohenhausen?

Do you know what a failure is? Have you studied psychology? Do you know anything about the nature of claustrophobia? Do you know the expression: "doctoral exam?" Can you put yourself in the shoes of a student possessed by ambition, at the moment he stands before his judge?

In the moment of the great test, I forgot everything that I had learned, I lay in her arms shivering with fear, my frog eyes open wide, saw myself penetrated, illuminated, seen-through, scorned, humiliated, and castrated. Only once . . . in the course of the first night . . . did I pull myself together, fly into a rage, sense the desire to revenge myself, squeeze out a fearful curse, throw myself upon the countess and take her by storm for three seconds . . . or, to be more precise, for three and a half seconds.

And do you know what the countess then said to me?

"Herr Finkelstein," she said, "you are a barbarian."

"I am Jewish," I said. "Not a barbarian!"

"All the worse," said the countess.

"But our inheritance is in the Bible," I said.

"That's right," said the countess. "But did you not have contact with the ancient Greeks! And with Babylon! Did you see nothing there? And learn nothing? Nothing at all?"

It is quite clear: The countess is an anti-Semite!

Recently she has let the mask drop completely. Everyday I have to put up with sharp, scornful remarks. Only the expression "Jewish pig" hasn't been used yet, and probably she will not use it, because such and similar expressions are not part of her vocabulary. Instead the expression "Jewish pig" is served up to me in disguised form. But nevertheless quite clearly. Even the servants have noticed it. They don't even take the trouble to grin surreptitiously behind my back. They grin quit openly . . . in my presence.

Yesterday the countess said: "It is rumored that you Jews were once a proud people. A people of farmers, scribes, and soldiers. It is said that no people has fought so much for its freedom as the people of the Jews. But what's become of you?"

I said: "What do you mean?"

"What I mean is," said the countess scornfully, "history lies. Otherwise your folk could never have produced such an example as you, Herr Finkelstein. Have you ever looked in the mirror?"

What did the countess say? *Rumor* has it that no people has fought so bitterly for its freedom as the people of the Jews? What is that supposed to mean? Rumor?

History lies, she said? Did she say that? An impertinence! She wants to humiliate me.

Today, this morning—immediately after breakfast—I ordered the butler to obtain a history of the Jews for me. "I know the Bible," I said, "but that is not enough. Get me a factual Jewish history."

The butler can be relied upon. He got me a Jewish history. Namely, an outline! An outline with the most famous quotations, even excerpts from the historian Graetz. Easy and quick to read through. And besides: *The Jewish State* by Theodor Herzl, *Rome and Jerusalem* by Moses Hess, writings by Max Nordau, printed speeches by Jabotinsky, right-wing Zionist literature, and so on. I am happy with the butler's ability to track things down. I will prove to the countess that history does not lie.

A man who works as hard as I do doesn't have much spare time. Every day black market sessions and conferences. On the side, smaller jobs in the black Mercedes or on foot—even though that's really not necessary—in addition to that, at night, six to eight hours reading: Jewish history, Zionist history, and so on. In between I go to the synagogue, firstly to practice praying, and secondly because I would like to show myself in the synagogue . . . can't do any harm.

Lately . . . long discussions with the countess . . . theme: does history lie or not? I show her my books with a grin, famous names and true quotations which I have underlined with a blue pencil and of which the credibility is undoubted. It's true that the countess still makes fun of my frog eyes and my hooked nose, of my flat feet and my activities as a black market dealer, and calls me an inferior Jew, that she often rings angrily for the butler, has him bring her the newspaper album, shows me cuttings from the *Stürmer*, and says to me: "Just look at this caricature, Herr Finkelstein . . . that's how

[175]

Jews look . . . and do you or don't you look like that?" But she becomes more and more uncertain when I revoke everything she says with arguments based on quotations, documentation, and with a sure feel for the evidence.

"Look, Countess! Just look at this book! And this one! And this one!"

The countess says: "Hook nose! Itzig Finkelstein, Esquire!"

I say: "Moses!"

The countess says: "Frog eyes! Even with glasses!"

I say: "Jesus!"

The countess says: "Flat feet! Even with your fancy shoes!"

I say: "Karl Marx!"

The countess says: "A shaved head! To hide your curly hair!"

I say: "Sigmund Freud!"

The countess says: "Black marketeer!"

I say: "Einstein! You see, Countess: the basis of Western culture rests on the shoulders of Jewish heads!"

I laugh at her, tell her about Judas Maccabeus, nicknamed "The Hammer" . . . tell her about the Jewish heroes in the fortress of Masada, tell her of the Spanish Inquisition, tell her of the revolt of Bar Kokba, tell her of the exile of the Jews, tell her of the burnings at the stake, explain to her that men have died for their faith, tell her about perseverance, martyrdom, passive heroism, and say to her:

"Countess . . . two thousand years of exile for us are nothing. Nothing more than two years might be for you: because we understand how to knock off zeros . . . even if there are several zeros . . . what the Nazis could do, we also can do. Only a little differently. They knock off human zeros. We knock off the zeros of time. Nothing has changed for us. And nothing has changed for me. Here I stand, I can do no other! Who said that? Luther said it! An anti-Semite said it! But all that is shit to me. Because I, my dear Countess, say it, too. Here I stand, I can do no other! I am a Jew. And I am proud of it. And if you don't like it then you can lick my ass!"

The countess said merely: "That is something one does . . . but does not talk about. You have no finesse, my dear Herr Finkelstein!"

Every morning the butler puts the newspaper to the left of my plate. I always read the reports of mass-murder first, cut them out and keep them, underlining before I put them on file, the names of criminals already captured, and also the ones still being sought. Frequently I find the name of camp commandant Hans Mueller, and sometimes my own.

The countess scornfully watches as I go through this routine. Yesterday she said:

"Herr Finkelstein. You are a nut. And as childish as a six-year-old. You're collecting this nonsense. And underlining names! By the way: why do you underline certain names with double lines?"

I said: "Because these people are criminals from Laubwalde. Hans Mueller," I said. "And Max Schulz. Two really evil types."

"Mass-murderers," said the countess. "Just like all the rest."

"That's right," I said.

"And who is this Hans Mueller?"

"That was the camp commandant. It was in the newspapers."

"And Max Schulz?"

"A small fish," I said. "Only a small fish."

After reading about the mass-murderers I generally skim through the literary page, read the stock-exchange news, study the real estate market, read the theater and the cinema reviews, skip over articles which do not interest me, and finally read the political reports.

[177]

Of special interest to me is the unrest in Palestine. It looks serious. Every day there are headlines: "Jewish Terrorism! Revolt! Fresh English Troops Arrive in the Holy Land! Jews Demand Self-Government! Jews in the Minority! Jews Want Majority! Mass Emigration of the Jews in Spite of Blockade Continued! English Camp Attacked by Stern Group! Police Station in Tel Aviv Blown Up! Terror Organization Irgun Zvai Leumi Sinks English Ship! English Captain Kidnaped! State of Emergency! Arab Unrest!"

"What's really going on there?" asked the countess.

I say: "The Jews want their country back. Have you ever heard of Zionism?"

She has not, which is to be expected.

I explain to her: "Zionism is not a new idea. It is as old as the exile of the Jewish people."

The countess says: "And so it is not a new idea."

I say: "My people never gave up the idea of a return to the Holy Land. We have continued to nourish the thought throughout the centuries. Even in prayer—*Leschana haba ba Jerushalajim*—next year in Jerusalem!"

I say: "It is written in the books that there is not just one exile. But we are talking now of the last exile. That has lasted almost two thousand years."

I say: "You have to distinguish two phases, dear Countess, Messianic Zionism and political Zionism."

I say: "During the first phase the Jews waited patiently for the Messiah, who would take them back to the Holy Land. But the Messiah of the Jews is never in a hurry. And how long could the Jews wait? They have waited almost two thousand years. And he did not come. Do you understand that, Countess? The Jews waited like sheep, surrounded by wolves. And each sheep was afraid and was transformed. And became an ostrich. And hid its head in the sand. And did not

[178]

see the mass graves. And the gas chambers! You understand, Countess?"

"That I understand," said the countess.

I said: "Political Zionism is practical Zionism. The slogan is: Wait no longer! Hurry on ahead of the Messiah! Conquer the Holy Land on your own initiative! Through political concessions, through mass emigration . . . and when it has to be . . . through violence. And the force of arms. Do you understand that? A Jewish state! A Jewish army! A Jewish homeland for the people of the Jews! Protected by law. By our law. Jewish law. Not the law of others."

I then told the countess of Theodor Herzl, the founder of modern political Zionism with practical aims, and told her of the first pioneers from Russia, told her of the first Jewish efforts to build up the Jewish state, of new settlements, told of Trumpeldor, the one-armed folk hero, who fell at the battle of Tel Chaj, Trumpeldor, the inexhaustible warrior, Trumpeldor, the man who created the *Hechaluz* . . . the social movement of Jewish pioneers . . . told her of the first wave of immigrants and of the second and of the third, told her of other waves of immigrants, told her of our battle during the domination of the Turks . . . and later . . . told her of the battles during the time of the English mandate, told her of battles between Jews and Arabs, told her of the Haganah, the Jewish defense army, told her also of the Balfour Declaration and of the promise by England to guarantee to the Jews a permanent homeland in the Holy Land.

All that had but little interest for the countess. Nevertheless she listened to me, even from time to time felt a passing respect for me, and said:

"I really would not have thought you capable of such a thing: Conquest! Building up a country! An army! Work! I thought you were a people of cowards and merchants."

[179]

I do not know why I am trying to impress the countess. Have I got an inferiority complex? And is this complex typically Jewish? Maybe I have a castration complex.

Nevertheless I continued these discussions. I showed the countess underlined names of Jewish scholars, doctors, philosophers, artists, writers, poets, of Jewish humanists, inventors, philanthropists, politicians, revolutionaries, showed her names, underlined names, of Jewish locksmiths, cobblers, tailors, barbers . . . made it clear that we are people like anyone else, and told her:

"That is what Emile Zola tried to maintain as early as the Dreyfus case!"

Showed her that I, Itzig Finkelstein, formerly Max Schulz, knew there was no point to it all.

I cannot change the countess, I cannot change her. An anti-Semite is like a person with cancer. An evil so deep cannot be cut out.

The butler never involves himself in our discussions. When he brings the tea, or cognac, or bologna sandwiches, he pricks up his ears but his face does not change. And so he is really a true butler who acts as though he neither sees nor hears anything. A gliding Chinaman.

Today I challenged him:

"Tell me . . . what do you think of our discussions about Jewish people?"

"I was not aware, that you, Herr Finkelstein, were discussing the Jewish people with the countess. I never listen. It does not concern me."

"Now don't try to tell me that. Of course you listen."

"I do not listen, Herr Finkelstein."

"I am not asking you as a butler, but as man to man . . . one human being to another."

"In that case, Herr Finkelstein . . . I would answer as a private person, and say that you, Herr Finkelstein, have a typically Jewish inferiority complex."

"And why would you say that . . . I mean, as one man to another?"

"Because you boast, Herr Finkelstein."

"About my people?"

"Yes, about your people!"

"I don't have any alternative. Do I?"

"That's not true, Herr Finkelstein. As man to man I would say: Herr Finkelstein! A Jew who is proud of his people would not stay in Germany. He would not live here at all. And he would also not try to convince us Germans . . . if you ask me . . . with large sounding words."

"And what would a proud Jew do?"

"Emigrate, Herr Finkelstein."

"To America?"

"Not to America, Herr Finkelstein. A proud Jew would emigrate to Palestine. Get a weapon in your hand. Fight for your country. Show the world what it is to be a Jew and proud of it!"

My chauffeur is ill. His replacement, a lean, tall man with merry, small, tipsy-looking eyes, reminds me somehow of one of my five fathers, the coachman, Wilhelm Hopfenstange.

Not long ago, as we were driving downtown in the Mercedes, the chauffeur said,

"Herr Finkelstein. I have been doing a little snooping around. You are living in anti-Semitic surroundings."

"Yes, that is well known to me."

"Yesterday the cook said to the butler, 'My former boss was a Jewish university professor. Herr Hitler did him in.' And the butler said: 'Yes, that is a pity.' And the cook said: 'The

[181]

decent Jews are dead. And a man like Itzig Finkelstein is still alive.' And the butler said: 'That's life. The primitive often survive more easily.' And the cook said: 'Hitler gassed the wrong set of Jews. It would have been better if he had gassed Itzig Finkelstein and people of his type.' And the butler said: 'Yes. Or shot them. Or strung them up. Or beaten them to death.'"

Went to the synagogue today. Prayed industriously. During the intervals between prayers . . . the official prayers . . . I spoke German with my new God. I said to him: "Dear God. I do not know where you are, whether you are in heaven or simply on my tongue. But I do not care. Nevertheless I would still like to talk to you. So please listen: I, Itzig Finkelstein, have daily fights with my staff and my mistress, who actually is not my mistress but my business partner, because through her I get fantastic contacts and business deals worth millions. But that is not what I wanted to say. I just wanted to say that I have to defend myself uninterruptedly against anti-Semitic attacks. I am in despair. In my own house they want to stomp upon my human dignity. Did I become a Jew for that? I thought the Jews had won the war!"

Berlin 1947

The countess has invested my entire fortune in an unusual business. She explained it to me today over lunch: "Herr Finkelstein! It's going to be the greatest weapon-smuggling deal in history!"

I asked: "And what if something goes wrong?"

The countess: "And why should it go wrong? You see, Itzig Finkelstein, I answer a question with a question. That is your Jewish influence! It's gone that far already!"

The greatest weapon-smuggling deal in history! If that deal comes off . . . and why should it not come off? . . . then I, Itzig Finkelstein, will be able to throw up my work as a black marketeer once and for all, because I, Itzig Finkelstein, will become one of the richest men in post-war Germany; my fortune reckoned with more zeros tacked on to the end than even before.

Today I learned that a few of our best business contacts were members of the military government of the occupation forces here in Germany, in the various zones . . . some in other countries . . . especially in the capitals . . . Zürich, Madrid, London, Paris, New York, Athens, Cairo, Tel Aviv, Damascus.

"The greatest weapon-smuggling deal in history!" The countess gave a few hints of what was going on: tanks lifted from the storerooms of the conquering armies of the Second World War. Machine guns! Ammunition boxes! Bazookas! Mortars! Hand grenades! And much more besides!

I asked the countess: "I don't have vast sums of money. Who has invested besides me?"

"A few people of your sort, Herr Finkelstein."

"All Jews?"

"Jews and non-Jews," said the countess. "But all of your sort!"

Messengers! Messengers! Mail without stamps! The countess is running around excited all over the villa, forgetting to get changed, has blue shadows under her eyes. How old is she actually?

I myself, I, Itzig Finkelstein, make the following observation: my blood pressure is going up from day to day. My future hangs on a thread. Either multimillionaire or beggar!

Yesterday I moved out of the villa. That's the way it is. Precisely that way. Among other things life is often, indeed frequently, from time to time, on occasion, very ironic.

I, Itzig Finkelstein, am ruined. I have just seven black dollars in my pocket. In my trouser pocket. Because I often take off my waistcoat. Trousers are safer. Naturally you would like to know what happened? It was like this: A magnificent, unique, remarkable piece of business! The greatest weapon-smuggling deal in history! I invested my entire fortune. I left everything to my mistress, who actually was not my mistress but just my business partner. But you know how it is when one lets a Gentile do business!

It's all down the drain! And what am I, Itzig Finkelstein, going to do with seven black dollars?

Here I am squatting on my behind with not much alternative: in a small bare hotel room in the American sector of Berlin . . . gazing up at the heavens, which are black, not just because I see black before my eyes, but because in Berlin right now it is raining.

Do you believe that I, Itzig Finkelstein, can manage to begin again right from the beginning? I am almost forty!

This morning as soon as I awoke I thought of the countess. Our farewell was cool. "Herr Finkelstein! The butler will drive you to your hotel in the Mercedes!"

"Yes. Many thanks."

"Go to the Hotel Fatherland! It's shabby but it's very cheap."

"Yes. That is what I will do."

In the Hotel Fatherland there are two Jews: the Jew Max Rosenfeld! And the Jew Itzig Finkelstein!

It is said that Jews can recognize one another instinctively.

[184]

We—Max Rosenfeld and I—met for the first time in the lobby of the Hotel Fatherland, saw one another, winked at one another, walked around one another, snuffling at each other's souls, then impulsively stormed into each other's arms, shook hands, and said, *Shalom,* and asked, "What are you doing here in Berlin?" and asked, "What are you doing in the Hotel Fatherland?" and answered our questions with questions, "And what are you doing here in Berlin and what are you doing in the Hotel Fatherland?"

That was before breakfast. Later, it goes without saying that we shared the same table, had breakfast together, talked together, shared our impressions. I tried to make clear to Max Rosenfeld that we had recognized one another by our soul scent.

"Soul scent." Today I couldn't get my thoughts off this phrase. What is it precisely that we Jews give off? And when we meet one of our own kind, what is it that we snuffle around and what is it that our soul senses? What is this mysterious something? And what is it composed of? Is it our past? Our unique history? The inheritance of our fathers? Our bond with God? Our suffering for two thousand years of persecution? Our longing for Jerusalem?

On the occasion of our next evening meal together, I asked Max Rosenfeld for an answer: "We recognized each other from our soul scents, did we not? I asked the same question at breakfast."

Max Rosenfeld said: "It might be better if we leave the word 'we' out of the discussion."

"How do you mean?"

"I mean it this way: we did not recognize each other—

rather—I merely recognized you. And that meant you had no alternative but to recognize me, too."

"And how did you recognize me? By my soul scent?"

Max Rosenfeld shook his head. "Not by your soul scent, Herr Finkelstein. Just by your ugly mug!"

Max Rosenfeld said it jokingly, with a wink and a laugh, but then suddenly became serious and said: "Don't be angry with me!"

I couldn't sleep. Shortly before midnight I got up, stood in front of the wall mirror, and said to myself: "Itzig Finkelstein. There's no Jew who looks like that. It's a caricature. But everyone believes it. Even Max Rosenfeld. They've been brainwashed into believing it. What can it be?"

I lay down again. Tried to sleep. But couldn't. Stood up again. Made some diary entries. Thought: "It's already after midnight. You will have to change the date now." Thought: "To hell with the date!"

Stood in front of the mirror again. Thought in desperation: "Perhaps he recognized you by your eyes?—was looking for something in my eyes—was looking for the Jewish soul . . . but couldn't find it."

For a long time I stood like that in front of the wall mirror. And said to myself: "Your eyes, Max Schulz, have no soul. Neither Jewish nor any other. Not even German. They're just frog eyes!"

V

Once again some small-time deals on the black market. For the time being only middle-man deals. My zest for life is growing from day to day. I wonder if I will be able to get back on my feet?

Shabby Hotel Fatherland is definitely a fatherland hotel. Anyone who believes the guests of this hotel come from all kinds of countries is mistaken. Apart from us two Jews the residents here are all German.

The word naturally soon got out that Max Rosenfeld and I are Jews. Nevertheless we have not noticed any trace of anti-Semitism. On the contrary. We are respected. We seem to have a kind of favored position.

I have made the observation that everyone seems to be deferring to us. Everyone! The staff of the hotel as well as the guests. What's it all supposed to mean? People take their hats off to us, girls curtsy, even older ladies. At mealtimes we are served first. In the mornings while standing in line at the one and only gentlemen's rest room we are given preference: "Please, Herr Rosenfeld . . . Please, Herr Finkelstein . . . go ahead!"

"You see, Herr Finkelstein, for me the Hotel Fatherland is typical . . . so far as its relationship to its Jewish guests is concerned, Herr Finkelstein, it is the embodiment of a new Germany. What you see here, my dear Finkelstein, or rather my dear Herr Finkelstein—that is the spirit of the times. Nothing less than that."

I wanted to say something else, but I forgot what I wanted to say, then remembered the anti-Semitic dentists and goldsmiths of the year 1945, shortly after the capitulation, thought about it for just one quick moment, then suppressed the thought, deciding it was not important, and told him only about my experience with the countess, told him about the villa, and about my Jewish inferiority complex.

But he, Max Rosenfeld, laughed, laughed out loud. "In-

[187]

feriority complex? Herr Finkelstein! What sort of nonsense is that you're talking? What kind of Jew has an inferiority complex today? Don't you know we won the war?"

I said: "Yes. I do know that of course."

"Well then! What's that you're telling me about some countess? And a villa? You've been dreaming, I suppose!"

"Dreaming?"

"Of course! Dreaming! That sort of milieu—do you know what that is, Herr Finkelstein . . . milieu?—the kind of milieu you speak of in the villa . . . it simply doesn't exist anymore! This countess from a long time past . . . 1947 . . . a countess with a screw loose . . . new-fangled screw loose . . . and with National Socialist junk mail on her breakfast plate . . . and this butler . . . and the cheap bologna sandwiches . . ."

I said: "And what is it you find so absurd about bologna sandwiches?"

It was certainly not a dream even though I am not quite sure. What is there after all in this life that one can be sure about?

"Can't you see, Herr Finkelstein? All those Germans bowing and scraping in front of us? They feel guilty! But not one of them is in a position to bring the six million back to life. Six million murdered Jews! That's not a small matter!"

I said: "Yes. That's right."

"The Germans in the Hotel Fatherland would like to beg our forgiveness," said Max Rosenfeld, "ours, the survivors . . . but they don't know how to. And it is not easy!"

"And what do they do?"

"They take their hats off to us," said Max Rosenfeld, "or make strange sorts of bows and curtsies! But that you can see for yourself!"

[188]

I said: "And if you have to stand in line at the gentlemen's rest room . . ."

"Yes," said Max Rosenfeld, "you see . . . even there we are given priority! No creature discomforts for us! That's important. At least for the moment. Until the debt is paid off."

The new spirit is philo-Semitism. Some sort of ghost with wet eyes which one day will run dry. But when?

I do not like dreams. Dreams frighten me. Especially when I am asleep.

Last night I dreamed . . . dreamed I was in the theater. Seeing a play called *Spirit of the Times*. Saw a stage. Saw the Hotel Fatherland. Saw actors running around. Saw Max Rosenfeld. And Itzig Finkelstein. I thought: "You are in the auditorium . . . and yet there you are on the stage." I asked myself: "How can that be possible?"

VI

At last I have been able to find something out about Max Rosenfeld. He is the sole survivor of a family of six. He has the idea in his head that his wife and five children have been made into soap by the apostles of Adolf Hitler. As a barber I would have liked very much to have asked him: what sort of soap? Because everyone knows there are many different sorts. But I thought perhaps it was advisable to keep silent.

What does Max Rosenfeld look like? Max Rosenfeld looks, well, like Max Rosenfeld, that is to say just like a Jewish attorney who is no attorney because he never finished his studies . . . and so has become an accountant who takes himself for an attorney . . . who took a leading part in Zionism and came from Prague . . . about the same age as me but not quite so tall . . . in fact I would say: square build, about a head's length shorter . . . his hair already white, his face angular, wearing large, black horn-rimmed spectacles, just like mine, although mine are brown and have lenses from ordinary glass . . . his eyes, not blue as were Itzig Finkelstein's, the real one . . . but bright brown, often seeming yellow . . . like what? . . . I don't really know . . . and always able to have a different look, completely confusing everyone who looks into them.

Max Rosenfeld lives on friendship parcels sent from America. He would like to work again.

Often we discuss the future Jewish state. Max Rosenfeld is a fanatic Zionist.

"You just wait and see, Herr Finkelstein! When the time comes . . . and it will soon be there . . . we will knead an army out of the soil just like Judas Maccabeus did!"

Often we speak of the Revolt of the Maccabees and about the uprising of Bar Kokba, and each time Max Rosenfeld is very happy to see how well informed I am about Jewish history.

"Herr Finkelstein . . . you know . . . I would like to start a new life. But not here . . . over there . . . !"

"Over there . . . where . . . America?"

"No. In our own country."

"And what do you want to do there?"

"I don't know yet. Begin a new life. Start a new family."

Often Max Rosenfeld goes with me as far as the black market, even though he hates the black market. He only does it to exercise his legs . . . and have somebody to talk to.

Yesterday, too: "Herr Finkelstein: Jews like you are sitting ducks for propaganda shooters."

"How do you mean?"

"Black marketeers like you!"

"But, Herr Rosenfeld—"

"That is to say . . . you are stoking up a dying fire."

"But I ask you . . ."

"You should emigrate, Herr Finkelstein . . . go to Palestine. Take up a plow and a gun. Do some pioneer work. Help to liberate your country. Instead of lounging around here in Germany and stirring up anti-Semitism again."

Had not the butler said something very similar?

That Max Rosenfeld apologized to me later—in fact before the evening meal—was only what I had expected. Together we emptied a bottle of black wine, drank to the future Jewish state, drank to the end of the Diaspora, blessed the Nile which was swallowing the armies of the pharaoh, blessed the city of the Volga, where there was a sign, on which was written: "You armies of the new pharaoh, this road leads not to the Volga . . . but to the Nile!"

I made it clear to Max Rosenfeld that he had made a mistake.

"Now just look here, Herr Rosenfeld. Do you believe that I, Itzig Finkelstein, by working as a black marketeer, will sooner or later stir up anti-Semitism? That may well be! But believe me, Herr Rosenfeld, when it comes down to basics it doesn't matter one shit whether I, Itzig Finkelstein, am a black marketeer or wear a white collar in an office or whether I'm a farmer or a factory laborer or a tradesman or soldier. Sooner or later I, Itzig Finkelstein, will be hated! And do you know why? Because I am a Jew! *Basta!*"

Max Rosenfeld nodded his head. "But not in our country!" he said softly. "Not there."

Things are improving again. I, Itzig Finkelstein, am earning money hand over fist. True, I am not, or am no longer, looked upon as one of the "big-timers" or one of the "great big-timers," just as one of the small-timers, but not as one of the small small-timers. I live! Or rather, one lives! Or rather: one lives as one can! "Every man after his own fashion!"—as the saying goes.

To be quite honest: I don't care what the Germans think of me, the Jew Itzig Finkelstein. I am like an insect. It doesn't matter whether I buzz, whine, sting, crawl, stay in one place, or—squat. Sooner or later they will squash me to death. I am the "mote" in my brother's eye. Or the insect! Even though I am no insect! But they don't know that! Only I know that! I am a Jew!

Yesterday Max Rosenfeld and I went for a drive in the black Mercedes—I had bought myself one again: a used car, however, because I am not a big-timer or a great big-timer yet. We went for a drive in the black Mercedes into the surrounding countryside. Visited a few Jewish displaced persons camps. They are becoming emptier and emptier. The people are gradually emigrating. Many to the States, many to Canada, Australia, South Africa, but most however to the Holy Land.

Max Rosenfeld said: "The exodus of millions!"

It surely cannot be millions. Are there still as many as that alive anyway? But hundreds of thousands! That is sure! The Jews are emigrating. It has its effect on the black market, too.

The newspaper *Repentant Fatherland* is delivered every morning to the Hotel Fatherland with the unpunctuality typical of the new Germany. Today it did not come till after nine o'clock.

On the front page two pictures struck me: The picture of a blond Jewish giant; and next to it, the picture of a small, black-haired, flat-footed, bandy-legged German. Headline: Jews: A people of peasants, pioneers, and soldiers!

I say to Max Rosenfeld: "Look . . . I always knew it!"

I took the newspaper to my room with me. I read: "March of the Millions!"

An exaggeration even here. There are only a few hundred thousand left! And besides: What does the word "march" mean? Are they not using ships to get across?

I read: "Millions of survivors of the brave Jewish people in exodus to the State of Israel!"

What is that supposed to mean? The State of Israel does not exist, at least not yet. The *Repentant Fatherland* seems to be in a hurry! And then: millions of survivors? They must be crazy!

I read: "Jewish pioneers storm English blockade and break through!"

I read: "Mediterranean swarming with Jewish refugee ships: Steamers warned to watch out for traffic accidents!"

I read: "England on the watch! England refuses Jewish settlers the right to land . . . may God punish . . ."

What is that supposed to mean? May God punish whom? England?

While I am reading there is a knock at my door: Max Rosenfeld!

"Have you any matches, Herr Finkelstein?"

I give him some matches. Max Rosenfeld smokes nervously, casts his eyes over the headlines in my newspaper, and asks: "Do you know what it means . . . may God punish?"

I say: "England! It's clear enough!"

Max Rosenfeld nods his head, and says: "May God punish England! If we both keep our fingers crossed we will get the Jewish state certainly. We'll throw the English out! But not this year. Neither the Prussians nor the Jews shoot as quickly as that!"

"Next year, perhaps?"

I say: "Yes, if we both keep our fingers crossed, you, Herr Rosenfeld . . . and I, Itzig Finkelstein . . . then perhaps we will get the Jewish state next year."

At noon we listen to the news in the hotel lobby, letting every word we don't want to hear go in one ear and out the other, but pricking up our ears when we hear the word "Palestine!"

In Berlin it's raining again. Today I am staying home. The black market won't run away. During the afternoon I read the special edition of *Repentant Fatherland.* "Jewish people arming themselves for the final battle!"

So the time has come. Max Rosenfeld has packed his bags. "So you're going?"

"You can bet your life on that, Herr Finkelstein. To Palestine!"

"Then I wish you the best."

Max Rosenfeld looked at me for a long time. I almost felt that he was sorry for me. Then he said: "Come with me, Herr Finkelstein! Don't stay in Germany!"

I didn't sleep the whole night. "Come with me, Herr Finkelstein! Don't stay in Germany!"—is not Herr Rosenfeld right? Of course he is right!

I lie on my back in bed, unable to sleep. Again and again I say to myself: "Max Schulz! Max Schulz! If you stay in Germany, you will be caught sooner or later. Just think of that, Max Schulz. Just think of that. In divided Germany the victors and their new allies are combing through the country looking for old Nazis. You are not safe anywhere. Neither with the Communists nor the capitalists. You represent the uncomfortable past! Come with me, Herr Finkelstein! Don't stay in Germany!"

Max Rosenfeld is right! You should go to Palestine! No one will look for you in a lion's den!

"Herr Rosenfeld! What does it cost to go to the Holy Land?"

"Nothing, Herr Finkelstein. The fare is paid from the funds of the Jewish aid organizations. Or to put it another way: your fare, Herr Finkelstein, is paid by the Jewish people!"

I've sold the old Mercedes. My suitcase is packed already. One pigskin and another canvas, which the countess gave me as a farewell present. Canvas! An insult really!

I'm on my feet in my room and grin at myself. My gold teeth flash.

Max Rosenfeld is all excited. So you want to come with me? That is a question with the answer built in. Typically Jewish.

In a handkerchief I find three gold teeth. I had completely forgotten them. Mementos. Yes, of course. One small tooth. One middle-sized one. And one big one.

Today there was again something in the *Repentant Fatherland*. Big letter headlines: "Well-known Historians Maintain That There Is No Such Thing as Collective Guilt! Not All Germans Are Guilty!"

And more headlines: "Established Beyond Doubt That Those Against Shouted Down By Those For!"

Other headlines: "Their 'No' Was Too Soft!"

Other headlines: "Vocal Chords Regrettably Inadequate!"
And I said to myself: "So what? Men with Inadequate
Vocal Chords Are as Guilty as the Rest! Can Max Schulz
Do Anything About It? If Their 'No' Was Not To Be Heard?"
And I said to myself: "Let those against do penance for
you, Max Schulz. It can't do you any harm!"

Today I asked myself: "Who is there actually living in the
Hotel Fatherland . . . except Herr Rosenfeld . . . and except
Herr Finkelstein? Is it those who were against, doing their
penance? Or is it those who were for, doing their penance?
Or is it the people who in those days were both for and
against?"
And I said to myself: "Max Schulz! That is too complicated.
That is hair-splitting. It's too tiring. Think of the hole in
your head. It could get worse!"

"There's another lot leaving the day after tomorrow, Herr
Finkelstein. For Marseilles. We're on the list already, you
and me, Max Rosenfeld and Itzig Finkelstein. Thank God I
didn't have any trouble. As an old Zionist . . . I am well known
in the organization . . . even by the people of Bricha . . .
everyone knows Max Rosenfeld . . . and I have a good name
there, too. So what do you say? Do you have your suitcases
packed?"
"They've been packed for a long time, Herr Rosenfeld.
In any case I'm not taking too much with me. You know . . . a
Jew should travel light. That was what my father used to
say: Chaim Finkelstein, the barber."

Book Four

I

Who shot Itzig Finkelstein? The real Itzig Finkelstein? On that day . . . in Laubwalde . . . on the seventh of September, 1942?

The big question mark . . . in the dark . . . in front of my bed . . . in front of my eyes . . . not visible . . . and yet so close within my reach . . . I grabbed it already . . . with my eyes . . . the invisible . . . the fantasy . . . I have it . . . I have it there . . . could roll it up . . . but don't want to . . . could bend back the hook that makes it a question . . . could convert the sign into an exclamation . . . but I won't!

Slavitzki? What did my stepfather Slavitzki say?

"Let the rats be!" That's what he said. But I say: "Let the question be!"

Dear Itzig. You do not know who shot you. On that day in Laubwalde. You did not see him. "He" surprised you. Because "he" did not want you to see him. And because "he" was standing behind you. Two steps behind you.

He shot your father too. Chaim Finkelstein. And your mother as well. Sarah Finkelstein. "He" killed them all.

Do you know "him"? Do you know who the murderer is? Your murderer. And the murderer of your father? And the murderer of your mother? Should I let you into the secret?

I'll dangle you on a string! Open your dead eyes! And prick up your dead ears! It won't do you any good. I won't tell you the secret.

Dear Itzig. The saying goes that a man hates whatever he has to deny. I, Itzig Finkelstein, at that time still Max Schulz, have always looked like a Jew. Even though that's not really true. But people used to say so. Yes, people said: "He looks like a Jew!"

Now just think that over, Itzig. That reason alone was enough to make me hate you. To have to deny what I am not . . . if only because I was afraid I might possibly be it.

Do you understand?

Very well. You understand. So do I. Nevertheless I didn't hate you. It's strange . . . don't you think? But it's true. I, Itzig Finkelstein, at that time still Max Schulz, never hated the Jews. And why did I not hate you? I don't know. I can only say: I, Itzig Finkelstein, at that time still Max Schulz, did not hate the Jews.

Why did I kill Jews? I don't know. Because of the rods, perhaps. The yellow rod and the black rod. And other rods. Colorless rods. And there are hands, many hands, which used to swing the rods, and every blow from the rods whipped down on my behind . . . or on the behind which they called

[198]

soul . . . because that's a backside too, and sometimes it's got to bend over too!

And so. That's how it was. And I wanted my turn at swinging the rod. Or something else. More powerful. Can you understand that? You see. You understand.

And yet I could never have swung the rod or rods as powerfully and as wildly . . . if there had not been an order. An order commanding me to kill!

Do you understand me? Without an order I would never have dared to do what I did dare. I would never have had the nerve. Because I, Itzig Finkelstein, at that time still Max Schulz, was only a small fish, a nervous, timid, small fish, who could only kill because it was permitted.

We did not kill only Jews. We killed others too. There were others that we shot and hanged and gassed and beat to death . . . others . . . who were not Jews. But I was used only to kill Jews. Why? I don't know why.

It's true. I've always looked like a Jew myself . . . at least other people thought so . . . for that reason I had to be a more efficient killer than the others . . . had to show them that I was not one. I mean . . . not a Jew. Can you understand that?

How many did I murder? I don't know. I didn't count them. But believe me, Itzig. I was not an anti-Semite. I have never been one. I just went along.

Can you hear me, Itzig? And can you see me? Come! Play with me! Look for me! Where am I? Where did I hide myself?

Ha ha! You blind cow! Look for me! Come on, look for me! Where am I? In my hotel room? Wrong guess! In my bed? Yes! But not in Berlin, and not in my hotel room!

[199]

Dear Itzig. I have no room. Just a place to sleep, a bunk . . .
just like those days in Laubwalde . . . and yet not like them.
Because I, Itzig Finkelstein, in those days still Max Schulz,
am a free man.

And so! Out with it! Where am I?
I am on a ship. And the ship has swallowed me. Just for
the night. I am lying in its belly. In a big, dark room. On a
bunk. Yes. There are bunks here too.
What sort of ship? Dear Itzig? You are inquisitive. A ship,
I said. A Jewish refugee ship! So there you are. Now you know.

I, Itzig Finkelstein, or the mass-murderer Max Schulz, have
been at sea for many days. I am going to Palestine. Because
I am now you. I am Itzig Finkelstein.

Dear Itzig. Do you remember? As children . . . we often
talked about Jerusalem. . . .

Dear Itzig. This is not a letter. Or: these are not letters.
I am not even writing in my diary. I am not even writing
at all. I am just thinking. Or I think I am thinking. I am
imagining I am writing to you. To whom? To you! The dead
man!
Itzig! Come! Talk to me! Or let me talk. Listen. That's
how it is. That's how it must be and can't be otherwise.
Come with me to Jerusalem, let me take you with me.

Dear Itzig. That was not so simple as it sounds. After
we had shot you all we took down our tents and broke
camp. Order of the day: Clear out! The word was going
around: Enough's enough!

The Russians were no longer far from Laubwalde. And we didn't want them to catch us. It was a bad time. We drove with our lorries through the Polish forest, which was under snow. Toward Germany. But then the shooting began in the forest. The damned partisans. And could they shoot!

They didn't catch me. Not me. Nor Hans Mueller, the camp commandant . . . you know him, don't you? They didn't catch him either. But they got the others. Even Günther Holle. But not us. No, not us.

And what went on then? Nothing went on then! We jumped down. From where? Oh you idiot! You silly idiot . . . from the lorry! From where else? And then naturally we skipped it. Just like that.

Yes, that was how it was. And it was cold. In that damned Polish forest. And I ran. Him too . . . Hans Mueller . . . the camp commandant. We ran as though we had a fuse strung to our asses.

And it was cold. No wonder Poland was lost. There your tears freeze, and your spittle too if you open your mouth. That is Poland. And the Polish forest is there too. The Polish forest, I said . . . that damned Polish forest.

And what happened? Nothing happened. It was cold. And the heavens grinned. During the night and especially just before daylight. And I shouted at them from the top of my lungs. But they only grinned—the heavens I mean. They grinned. And didn't listen to me.

It was all over. It was all over. We had lost the war. And you had won it. The Jews. But not you. And not your father. And not your mother either. Because you are dead.

I can hardly remember what happened then. The forest path under snow at dawn. Dead comrades. Their cocks cut off. And then . . . a hut. A lonely hut. A lonely hut in the middle of the Polish forest. And a witch, Veronja.

Yes, my God. There was a hut. And in the hut lived Veronja, the witch.

She tortured me. And punished me. And scorned me. And she whipped me too. And just because I had once been a god. And I had to drink tea. And fuck her. Almost without stopping. And I yelled. And I was afraid. Because I have a weak heart. Yes, dear Itzig. It was a bad time.

Did I tell you anything about the gold teeth? No. I didn't tell you anything about them.

And so: the gold teeth. The teeth of my victims. A small fortune. In a cardboard box. Not all the gold teeth of all my victims. Because earlier we were ordered to send most of them to the Reich. Yours too. And your father's teeth. And your mother's teeth. Just one cardboard box, dear Itzig, just one. That one I took with me. And hid in the forest. And later . . . took it to the hut . . . and emptied it . . . into a sack. Not all the gold teeth from Laubwalde. Just the last few. But still. A small fortune.

Veronja I murdered. And at the other side of the forest the spring was waiting. And I, at that time still Max Schulz, walked out toward the spring. Stepped out toward home. Where to? Toward home, I said. To Germany. Of course, to Germany. Alone. All alone. But with my gold teeth. Yes, dear Itzig. Not without gold teeth.

I do not know where my mother is. And I also do not know where Slavitzki is. My mother can go to hell. So can Slavitzki.

And then I went to Warthenau. With my sack. With my gold teeth. And Warthenau was where Frau Holle lived. An old woman with a wooden leg.

And there, in the basement—there I got to know the major. He was a dead American. He was dead. And I gulped down whisky. And gobbled corned beef. And fucked a bit. But not too much.

Yes, dear Itzig. That's the story. That's it. I didn't stay long . . . in Warthenau I mean . . . with Frau Holle. I went to Berlin. With my sack. And my gold teeth.

You didn't see Germany . . . after the war! A heap of rubble. A heap of rubble! And it's your fault! Because you turned in your grave! You! The Jewish barber! And the others too! Everybody who was against us and who we did away with! And every time you turned in your grave, the houses in Germany trembled . . . walls fell . . . windowpanes cracked . . . sending broken pieces onto the street . . . just as it had been in the Night of the Broken Glass.

You did not see Berlin, dear Itzig . . . after the war . . . even though your dead eyes were everywhere . . . everywhere in Berlin. Yes, and in Warthenau too. And elsewhere . . . everywhere. . . .

What did I do with the gold teeth? I sold them, dear Itzig. As the saying goes . . . I exchanged them . . . or transformed them . . . and by the way: me too. I did a bit of a quick-change job on Max Schulz. Just like that. They're the fashion now, quick-change jobs.

It's a pity you never knew the Jewish black marketeer Itzig Finkelstein. Itzig Finkelstein in Berlin. Itzig Finkelstein . . . his black Mercedes . . . he was quite a guy, let me tell you.

Right out of the *Stürmer*. And who cut him out of that paper?
The old Nazis. Yes, the old Nazis took the *Stürmer* out of
mothballs. A picture of Itzig on the front page.

Then they cut Itzig out. And sent him to Berlin. Dumped
him right out on the black market. And later into the bed
of a blond countess.

Why did they do that? The old Nazis? I don't know.
Perhaps . . . to annoy the Zionists . . . or the proud Jews . . .
or to spread poison again. I don't know.

I lived well in Berlin. Not all the time. But most of the
time. Yes. For a time life was good to me. Really good.
And yet I was unhappy. Who? Max Schulz? No, dear Itzig.
Itzig Finkelstein was unhappy, even though Itzig Finkelstein
had won the war.

At the home of the countess Itzig Finkelstein was jeered
at. I had to defend myself because I wanted to prove to her
that I, Itzig Finkelstein, was somebody. And not just that *I*
was. But my forefathers too. I really tried very hard to prove
to the countess that I, Itzig Finkelstein, had every reason to be
proud of my ancestry. I am not very happy when people look
down upon me. I can't stand it. And so I said to her: "You
can lick my ass."

And then in the Hotel Fatherland there was no jeering.
And yet there it was still worse. They crawled at my feet
with their guilt and their complexes. Here, Herr Finkelstein.
There, Herr Finkelstein. No. That was nothing for me. So
I said to myself: "You are not Max Schulz anymore. You are
Itzig Finkelstein. He doesn't want to be an inferior being.
But not an *Übermensch* either. Itzig Finkelstein just wants
to be a human being. Nothing more. A normal human being
among normal human beings. Not a groveling black sheep.
And not a condescending black sheep.

I do not know exactly any longer when I made the decision for the first time to go to Palestine. But in any case I came to terms with this idea: I thought to myself: no one will look for you in the lion's den.

That's how it was. And yet that was not the only reason. Today I am quite clear in my mind that I, Itzig Finkelstein, would like to live among Jews, among my own kind. In my own land . . . because I, Itzig Finkelstein, no longer feel comfortable under goyim. Can you understand that?

My dear Itzig. In recent times I have occupied myself a lot with you . . . not just with the extermination . . . that's past now . . . but with your history: Jewish and Zionist history in general. Everything in summary form. And I have begun to get enthusiastic about your national cause. What am I saying? For your cause? No. For my cause, who am also one of you.

Now listen, Itzig. Prick up your ears.

Lichtenberg is a Jewish displaced persons camp in the vicinity of Berlin. It swarms with refugees. From time to time the camp empties and fills again. The Jews are well organized. Especially the Zionists. Anyone who wants to emigrate to Palestine needs only to get in touch with the Zionists. The organization takes care of everything. They bring the Jews from the eastern territories to Lichtenberg . . . and to other displaced persons camps as well . . . it just depends . . . in order to get them all together . . . you understand? . . . before the great journey begins . . . that's how we did it too . . . although our aims . . . in those days . . . and the aims of the Zionists . . . if I can put it like that . . . were of a different nature.

As a first step the Jews were collected together. And moved further on . . . across the sector and zone frontiers.

[205]

Then still further . . . across the French frontier . . . occasionally across the Spanish or the Italian or the Greek or the Yugoslav frontier . . . and then . . . down to the sea. The Mediterranean. But that is not the end of the great journey by a long way. It really only begins there. So listen:

Max Rosenfeld and I—Max Rosenfeld is a friend of mine—and so, Max Rosenfeld and I made our way with a minimum of luggage to Lichtenberg . . . but didn't let ourselves be collected in the large group . . . but instead presented ourselves to the "collectors." In Lichtenberg we received Mexican visas. Why? Was it that we wanted to go to Mexico? Nonsense! But we needed them for the transit journey to the French port. Yes. The departure was from France. It was all child's play. It didn't cost us a penny either. The organization paid everything. And so off we went to France with our Mexican visas. As far as the coast. To which point? I do not know. It was just a point. Somewhere on the coast. I was not dumb enough to ask questions. It was a secret. I, Itzig Finkelstein, was traveling illegally to Palestine . . . at the expense of the Jewish people . . . in order to annoy the English . . . to land in the dark . . . to make history . . . even though I have made history once already . . . and do you think I was dumb enough to put questions at such a moment?

So there you are! One day we got to the coast. Somewhere in France. The French were informed. They are our friends. They have short legs. And the English have long legs. They don't like the English. For that reason or because of that fact, France encourages illegal immigration into the territory of the English mandate.

Yes. And then: A ship was waiting! A Jewish refugee ship! A blockade-breaker!

There was no harbor there. Just a beach. The ship couldn't anchor. During the night we were brought to the ship in four boats, because the night is dark and because English secret agents don't see well in the dark.

The ship was really a miserable wooden box. Right away I said to Max Rosenfeld: "Herr Rosenfeld! You mean to say they want to get us to Palestine on this hulk? I guarantee you: we'll all fall off!"

But Max Rosenfeld said: "Don't be afraid, Herr Finkelstein. We'll all make history in this hunk of wood!"

So that's how it was, dear Itzig. That's how it was and no different. The Mediterranean swarmed with vessels like that. And one of them was our vessel . . . that miserable hulk *Exitus*.

Exitus? Exit? End? Death? Why choose this name? Is it supposed to be a ghost ship?

Yes, dear Itzig. It is a ghost ship. And now I know, at last, how the slogan came to being: "March of the Millions!" Because we were not millions. But the dead were making the journey with us. The six million! Millions of dead! Those clubbed to death! Those hung to death! Those shot to death! Those gassed to death! All of them are going with us! And where to, dear Itzig? What kind of a question is that? Into the historical home of the Jews! Home!

II

Formerly the *Exitus* was called *La Belle Claire*.

La Belle Claire; *Clara the River Belle*! Steamboat with pink bottom: gem of the Seine, as symbolic as the Eiffel Tower in Paris, the wonder of tourists and pride of its captain Maurice DuPont! And when was that? I don't know exactly. Around the turn of the century. At least that's what I suppose.

The organization buys whatever it can to set the millions on the march. Captain Maurice DuPont left this world long

[207]

ago, as did the steamboat *La Belle Claire*. But the organization has initiative. It brought *La Belle Claire* back from the dead, even though it was rotted, had neither flesh nor skin, and was an eyeless skeleton. Now its name is *Exitus*.

A ship from the kingdom of the dead? Yes, dear Itzig. But seaworthy.

Our captain is a Greek. His name: Teiresias Pappas. A Jewish girl I befriended here on the *Exitus*, the former ballerina Hanna Lewisohn from Berlin, explained to me what "Teiresias Pappas" means. Pappas is Pappas. She didn't know exactly. Probably a name. A Greek family name. And Teiresias? That's a name too. In this case a forename. But significant. Teiresias— so at least Hanna Lewisohn said—was the blind seer in *Antigone*, a tragedy by the Greek poet Sophocles. Do you know Sophocles? The Greek?

Teiresias Pappas is not blind. But Teiresias Pappas is a seer . . . there is no doubt about that. Because Teiresias Pappas has prophesied to us all that he, Teiresias Pappas, will bring the ghost ship *Exitus*, through the blockade in spite of the English . . . during the night. "The English will not catch us!" said Teiresias Pappas. "The *Exitus* will land! With all its dead and all its living on board! I swear it by my name Teiresias Pappas!" Yes, that is what he said.

The crew of the *Exitus* is international, my dear Itzig. Most of them are Greek and speak several languages, like Teiresias Pappas; people who have moved around all over the globe, old sailors and adventure-seekers, but we have Frenchmen here too, Norwegians, Portuguese, Spaniards, and others. When I saw the crew for the first time, I was almost afraid, because they looked like a crafty and sneaky bunch: wild, good enough for a pirate ship or for a blockade-breaker, or for that miserable hulk of a ship the *Exitus*. But our captain Teiresias Pappas holds his men in check. He has told them: "The women may not be raped! Nor the children! Looting is forbidden! And so is hitting harmless passengers! Any of you who doesn't get that into his head will be thrown overboard into the Mediterranean!"

When he talks like this Teiresias Pappas is not joking. And his appearance drives home his point: small, bandy-legged, bald, bearded, his one eye like a glowing coal. Yes, dear Itzig. He has only one eye. But he is not blind.

Who is there on the *Exitus* to protect us . . . apart from Teiresias Pappas? Dear Itzig . . . the organization . . . who else? To be precise, David Shapiro is on the *Exitus*. David Shapiro, a commander in the Haganah, the Jewish defense army in Palestine, an army illegal from the standpoint of the English but legal from ours.

Besides David Shapiro, there are others here too . . . Haganah soldiers . . . and two representatives of the Palmach . . . elite force of the Haganah in the Holy Land. And naturally also a few agents of the Mossad Aliyah Bet, which is the organization responsible for the illegal immigration of Jews to Palestine. Illegal from the perspective of the English . . . make no mistake . . . from our standpoint it's legal! And there is even a representative of Rechesch on board, responsible for the procurement of arms, a man on his way home with us after finishing a mission in Europe. So you see, Itzig . . . it's full of people who work for the organization or, shall we say, for the umbrella organization, or for the shadow government of the future Jewish state.

Are we armed? What sort of question is that? . . . dear Itzig . . . the Haganah people are armed to the teeth, as are those from the Palmach and the others too. Or do you think that Teiresias Pappas could hold his crew in check if he didn't know there were Jewish freedom fighters behind him?

There's something my mind's eye is trying to make out. It's . . . a sardine can swimming in the water. . . . The *Exitus* is a sardine can. And we are the sardines. Our dead too? They too. They're standing, lying, sitting, and squatting between us. Bodiless sardines.

There is no room here. It's almost like your barracks in Laubwalde. The *Exitus* is packed to capacity and beyond with illegal immigrants. There are sixteen hundred people on a seven hundred ton ship . . . now I know why it is that Teiresias Pappas crosses himself three times a day.

Not long ago Teiresias Pappas said: "David Shapiro, commander of the Haganah . . . if the ship is not under a spell from you Jews . . . then my name is not Teiresias Pappas! One passenger per ton of water displacement. In emergencies that is what is allowed on a small ship. A seven hundred ton ship for seven hundred passengers. But not more."

"Well, so what?" said David Shapiro.

"Logically speaking we should all go under. Sixteen hundred illegal passengers apart from the crew . . . that is a little too much."

"But we won't go under," said David Shapiro, the Haganah commander. "For one thing, because we have put the boat under a spell . . . and for another thing, because you, Teiresias Pappas, have prophesied the landing to all of us."

Yes, dear Itzig, there are too many of us. There is no joking about that. Even though the dead do not weigh anything. But we, the living . . . we weigh something! How come that we do not sink? Have the dead wings? Are they carrying the *Exitus*?

I have had good luck with my bunk. Those who don't grab a bunk have to sleep on the ground. Here, down in the hold, the air is all used up. It stinks of sweat and throw-up.

Sometimes the *Exitus* seems to be swaying like a swing, and those who are seasick throw up on the spot . . . and when they get such an attack it's not always easy to get up . . . to the fresh air . . . everywhere there are sleeping people lying on the ground . . . even in the corridors and on the steps.

I don't sleep much . . . often I start up . . . wakened up by loud screaming. What's that you say, Itzig? What is it you're asking? Why some people scream during the night . . . why they scream?—it's the survivors who do that, dear Itzig, the survivors of our concentration camps.

Yes, dear Itzig. And the babies bawl. They too.

I am always happy to see the dawn. I can hardly wait for the light of day. Always before dawn I creep out of the belly of the *Exitus,* stumble over the many bodies, and somehow grope my way up to the fresh air . . . feeling like a man suffocating to death . . . and sniff at the fresh breeze. Even during the day everything is over-full, and the people on deck make desperate efforts to walk around or else stand jammed together at the rail. But at the first light of day there is enough room on deck. Quite enough room. Even for me, the mass-murderer, Max Schulz. That's when I can exercise my legs.

As the waking God opens His eyes from sleep, throws His first sleep-heavy glance across the sea toward the boundaries of heaven at the horizon of the ocean . . . when good God coughs and night is shooed away . . . and when night says: "Gently, gently! I'm not going to be rushed! I will go but in my own good time! . . ." then, dear Itzig, that is the time that I, Max Schulz, the mass-murderer, alias Itzig Finkelstein, the Jew, take my constitutional between the quarter deck and the forecastle, moving about freely, filling my lungs deeply with salty air, breathing in the oxygen. I stand erect on the bridge, sweep out my arms, and remain there with closed eyes . . . then open them slowly . . . like good God drunk with sleep . . . see at first nothing . . . hear . . . the voice of Him who is not: "Let there be light!" . . . and the black gray ocean slowly changes color, glittering mysteriously. Then I see the first glow of day! I see how in the east heaven and earth join together . . . in a laughing blaze. We are steering in that direction. Toward the east. Toward the laughing blaze. Steering toward it with our dead! So that they will arise again!

I try to think logically. And say to myself: "You are wrong. We are taking the dead with us. That's true. But is it really only the six million? Are not all the dead with us, all those who ever died in exile, from the day of the destruction of the Second Temple, or even earlier?"

I say to myself: "Itzig Finkelstein. That may be true. But the *Exitus* is not the only refugee ship. Others have gone before it and there will be others after it. And so it is not possible that the *Exitus* has all the dead on board. If that were true the other ships or hulks would have too few."

Dear Itzig, not long ago I saw your shadow. On the rail. And the shadow of your father. And your mother's shadow.

You did not turn around. I stepped right through you. Looked at the ocean. And peered at the sun.

Your father said to your mother: "Sarah! I believe 'he' shot our son to death!"

And your mother said: "Chaim! I believe 'he' shot our son to death!"

And you said to them: "Father! Mother! I believe 'he' shot me in the back!"—and then you asked: "Who was it that shot you to death? When I was not present? Was 'he' the one? Was 'he' the one who shot you?"

Can you guess when that happened? When I stepped back in place . . . from out of your shadow . . . ?

I bumped against Max Rosenfeld. He was standing behind me . . . and said: "Herr Finkelstein!"

And I said: "Herr Rosenfeld!"

"Why so lost in thought?"

"I was thinking of my parents."

"I see . . ."

"They were shot to death in Laubwalde."

Max Rosenfeld looked right past me, staring at the sea, and at the surf caused by the *Exitus*, as though afraid to meet my eyes.

"Here . . . you see . . ." I pulled a few newspaper clippings out of my waistcoat pocket and showed them to Max Rosenfeld.

The headlines: "Mass Murder in Laubwalde! Story of Human Liquidation! Behind Barbed Wire in Poland!" . . . and so on . . . pointed to the name of Max Schulz with my finger.

"Underlined!" said Max Rosenfeld.

"I always underline him," I said.

"Why?"

"He's the one who murdered my parents."

"How do you know that? He wasn't the only SS man there, you know."

"That's right," I said. "I suppose that's right."

My collection of newspaper clippings has been going from hand to hand here on the *Exitus*. Max Schulz is unknown.

A name, just a name. Listed on the interminable roll of horror. People have long ago become blasé. Horror has been something they have known, and known for too long. Most of them read through my collection in a bored manner, but with understanding for me, because the word has already got around that I, Itzig Finkelstein, come from Wieshalle, a small town in Silesia . . . just as did Max Schulz. That I had known him surprises no one. Nor does the fact that Max Schulz— as I admit quite openly—had grown up in the same streets as I and had even served as apprentice in my father's salon, Chaim Finkelstein's . . . not in order to learn the handiwork of mass-murdering, but in order to study the honorable profession of a barber. And the people can understand why I suspect Max Schulz, more than any other of the SS in Laub-walde, even though I cannot prove it. "He must be the one who shot my parents dead! He's the one . . . and nobody else!"

People tell me: "Don't think of it anymore! Think of the future, Herr Finkelstein . . . not of the past!"

The future: that is the reason I like to stand at the rail, my eyes turned toward the Promised Land.

A ghost ship? Yes, dear Itzig. But a gay one. In spite of the shrill screams at night. Because it is not the night but the day that matters. The *Exitus* comes out of the night. But it's plowing its way toward the day. During the day people feel glad. Everyone on board seems to love the light of day. And I, the mass-murderer, am no exception. The food is bad. That's true. But as we eat we sing songs. To help it go down better. There's a lot of singing here. And dancing. Do you know the Jewish national dance, the hora? Old and young alike dance it. Even Teiresias Pappas, who after all is a Greek, dances it with us.

Yes, we dance the hora, and those who do not dance beat time with their hands.

We sing! We sing! And there are a few young boys who play the harmonica. That's something you should see! Your dead eyes would light up. Quite some fun, let me tell you.

And do the dead dance with us? Yes, dear Itzig. They dance with us. You too. And your father. And your mother too.

The weather is good. We have really been lucky. The sun seems to join in our happiness. It plays on deck with the small children and with the big children. And the sun smiles at us. It's all over, Itzig. Now we can laugh . . . even though sometimes we still might feel like crying.

And the sea? The sea seems to join in our happiness too. A storm could blow us right out of the water. But the sea is calm. Perhaps the sea senses that our ship is borne aloft by the wings of the dead? I do not know for sure, Itzig. I really do not know for sure.

The sea is calm. At the rail mothers hold out their small children—all day long—they pee in peace . . . and the sea grins up with its green eyes and says nothing, swallowing everything with tolerance, making no fuss.

Not long ago Teiresias Pappas said: "The sea is calm. The sea could swallow us all . . . all of us illegal voyagers. But the sea does not do it. Because if it did the English would be glad. And the sea knows that. The sea does not like the English because the English have been masters of the sea for too long. Yes, my friends. You just believe Teiresias Pappas!"

III

You will be amazed to learn, Itzig, if I might choose this moment to admit it to you, that I, Max Schulz, artistic hair stylist, have almost forgotten how to cut hair. After all, it's been a long time. For a long time the only practice I got was with a gun. Using it, as the saying goes, on Jewish targets . . . and had left my scissors and comb to the moths.

Shortly before leaving I bought myself a few tools: a comb, a pair of scissors, a razor blade, shaving equipment, and a few other things. You get the gist: the essentials. I told myself: "That will bring good luck!"

Do I do haircuts for the people on the *Exitus?* Of course. A man has to begin again sometimes! And here on the *Exitus* I have the ideal opportunity to get my hand in again. I am the only barber on this miserable hulk. So if you think about it I am indispensable.

It was a day to remember! The day on which I, the mass-murderer, Max Schulz, became a barber again! A man with a good solid, middle-class trade! If I had a calendar I would circle this date, with a thick, firm, unbroken ring.

Max Rosenfeld was talking on deck with the captain. He said to him: "If I were you I would have my beard trimmed sometime! People are talking and saying: 'He looks barbaric! Teiresias Pappas! Almost as bad as the crew!'"

And Teiresias Pappas said: "I'll have my beard trimmed in Haifa!"

And Max Rosenfeld said: "Why not have it done here?"

"Because I don't know of any barber here!"

"But I know one! He's a barber. And a good one at that. Itzig Finkelstein!"

That's how it started.

The captain called me to his cabin and said: "Herr Finkelstein. Could you trim my beard?"

"Yes, I can," I said. "And I can cut all that fluff off your bald head . . . and that shock of hair sprouting around your temples!"

[216]

Teiresias Pappas was enthusiastic: "But not here in the cabin. Makes too much mess. Best do it outside in the fresh air!"

We fetched a high back chair and put it in front of the guard rail . . . on the bridge . . . high atop of the flagstaff. Teiresias Pappas sat himself down on it imperiously, allowed me to wrap him in towels.

A few passengers had noticed us. Scarcely had I begun my work when they began to come to watch. More and more of them came. Soon Teiresias Pappas and I were surrounded by an excited crowd of women and children. A little later the men joined the women and children. They cracked jokes, talked among themselves about Teiresias Pappas' beard, and about his bald head, chewed at bread crusts and at their fingernails; the small children yelled and the bigger ones tried to pull Teiresias Pappas' beard, got their little fingers between the scissors, not caring two hoots about my protests or about Teiresias Pappas and his fierce, rolling eye, as he sat there wrapped up. It was quite a lot of fun, let me tell you.

Yes, that's how it began, dear Itzig. The same day the entire ship knew that Itzig Finkelstein was a barber. I began to get a lot of work. First all the fops on board the *Exitus* came asking for a genuine, fashionable haircut. And then the lines formed, family patriarchs, shy bachelors, children dragged along by their proud mothers. Now and again women came to me too. "Mr. Finkelstein. I'd like to have a man's haircut. That's the fashion these days."

Do I do shaves, too? Here on board the *Exitus*? No, Itzig. As the only barber I don't have any time for that here. Everyone can shave himself. The only thing I shave is heads. But that's something quite different. Try to understand me. The demand is too great. After all I only have one pair of hands.

I earn money too. But not much. Those with plenty pay more, the poor people pay less. I am like a doctor. If I smell the scent of money on a patient, then I start to fleece him. He helps to pay for the others. The trouble is, most of the people on the *Exitus* are poor slobs, so that I have no alternative but to serve them for nothing. It's a matter of honor. Now and again one has to do something for mankind. Is that not so?

The weather is beautiful, and working in the fresh air is a lot of fun. Here the tufts of hair do not fall on firm ground, as is the case in a proper gentlemen's hairdressing salon, but when the breeze is strong are wafted immediately into the open sea, blown by the fresh winds over the surf, spotlighted by the bright rays of the sun and followed by the happy giggling of the children, to the joy of God but to the annoyance of the hungry fish gliding along with their mouths open.

IV

Max Rosenfeld sleeps in the hold too, but on the opposite side. We sit next to each other at meals, and get together a lot on other occasions. He talks all the time I am working and when it's time for a walk saunters along with me between the main deck and the quarter deck.

Teiresias Pappas also likes talking to me: "Mr. Finkelstein. Look over there! That is the Greek coast. Out there in the sky, those are no angels, those are English airplanes, RAF . . . Royal Air Force. Yes sir, we've hoisted the Mexican flag. Did they notice the swindle? Not yet. They're only little dots, those airplanes, only little dots. But just keep watch, Mr. Finkelstein. Once we get into Palestinian waters . . . then the little dots will grow to giant birds . . . and will circle above us . . . but don't be afraid . . . don't be afraid

[218]

Mr. Finkelstein . . . Teiresias Pappas has thought out a big plan to deceive the English . . . the most magnificent illegal landing plan of all time."

And the Haganah commander, David Shapiro. He has red hair and a red mustache. Had his mustache trimmed by me. We got to talking:

"Is it true, Mr. Finkelstein, that you knew the mass-murderer Max Schulz? That's what they say here on board the *Exitus!*"

"That's true, Commander."

"What sort of fellow was he?"

I said: "A rat-catcher with bats in his belfry."

David Shapiro nodded his head, then said: "We'll get him one day. Jewish secret agents! One day! And we'll take him to Jerusalem! And hang him up on the highest tree!"

"Are there high trees there?"

"Of course there are high trees there," David Shapiro said.

Yes, that is David Shapiro. A giant of a man, with a breast like a gorilla and hands like a butcher . . . completely covered with hair, red hair, right up to the fingernails, his eyes hard as steel and blue as the sky. Runs around on deck with four revolvers, two on his left side, two on his right side . . . bouncing about shortly above the knee. Loaded . . . the terror of the crew.

Once he said to me: "Mr. Finkelstein, if ever Max Schulz fell into my hands, I'd tear him apart. I'd chop him into a thousand pieces . . . and throw him to the jackals."

I asked him: "Are there jackals over there?"

"Of course there are jackals over there," said David Shapiro.

"And what about the high trees, or the high tree, in Jerusalem? I mean the ones where Max Schulz should hang . . . I mean . . . what will happen to them if you tear him apart personally beforehand?"

"Then the hell with the high tree," said David Shapiro. That is David Shapiro. And he too took me to his heart.

My first customer every morning is Judge Wolfgang Richter. A small court judge.

Judge Wolfgang Richter is a Jew. A German Jew through and through. He looks like Churchill: massive head, bald on top, heavy smoker, cigars. He speaks only German. A German through and through whose soul-scent is very different from mine and from that of the other Jews here on board the *Exitus*. Judge Wolfgang Richter's soul smells of beer, yes, dear Itzig: beer. Of the pub, and of potato dumplings and sauerkraut.

Here on board the *Exitus* I do not give shaves. I don't have the time. I only shave heads. But shaving heads belongs really to the area of haircutting. In the case of Judge Wolfgang Richter I make an exception. I not only shave off the fluff from his bald head, I also shave off his beard stubbles. Why is it I make an exception with him? I don't know why.

He's always my first client. He is as punctual as a clock. I shave him before breakfast. At dawn I soap up the judge. As the heavens are gathering light, as the fish perform somersaults in the first light of the sun, as the mouth of dawn flashes with gold, I lather the face of the judge, not caring whether he, the judge, is napping.

Usually the judge wakes up only when I've finished putting on the lather and have begun to scratch with the razor blade. He wakes up, the judge does, blinks, looks out over the sea, which in the meantime has been bathed blood-red, and says: "Beautiful . . . what do you say, Herr Finkelstein?"

"Yes," I say then. "Your honor."

[220]

"Blood-red," says the judge, "as though the mermaids of the sea were menstruating in unison. All at once!"

"Mermaids do not menstruate," I say. "You are wrong, your honor. It's just that the sea is afraid."

"Of whom then?" the judge asks. "Of the English?"

"No," I say. "Of the sun."

"So," the judge says, "of the sun you think. And how do you then explain the red color, Herr Finkelstein?"

"It's the red of a blush," I say. "There are no such things as mermaids. Only the sea. The sea is the virgin. A chaste virgin. And is startled because the sun has surprised her as she slept."

"Are you a poet, Herr Finkelstein? An inhibited poet, perhaps?" the judge laughs. But that does not bother me. His beery soul does not understand mine. Even though his land had a Goethe and a Schiller!

One day he spoke with me about Max Schulz. "The case interests me. So you really did know him?"

"Yes. Very well as it happens."

"And he has disappeared without trace?"

"Without trace!"

"It's just not possible. There must be traces somewhere! It's just we don't have a keen enough sleuth. That's what the trouble is!"

"Does the case really interest you?"

"Yes. Very much!"

Have I introduced the rabbi to you, dear Itzig? No, not yet. He is not one of my customers. But as it happens he sleeps in the bunk above mine. And so is my sleeping neighbor!

Often before going to sleep we talk in a whisper:

"Mr. Finkelstein! Are you still awake?"

"Yes, rabbi!"

The rabbi is not really a rabbi, but just a very pious man. Imagine him to yourself: a large, rather corpulent man, draped in a long-sleeved, black robe called a "caftan" . . . bright, sharp eyes, which always have something a little sarcastic but never anything wicked in their look, a beard shot through with gray, black and gray, a pale face, framed by a hat edged with fur, which he keeps on even when the sun is shining. Does he take his hat off at night? I don't know. He sleeps above me, and in the dark I can only hear his voice. But I assume he doesn't keep his fur hat on to sleep, but wears just a round, black yarmulke.

"Rabbi! How did you survive the war in this get-up? How could anyone hide himself wearing a caftan?"

"I survived the war in the forest, Mr. Finkelstein. In the Polish forest."

"I see . . . a forest Jew?"

"Yes, a forest Jew."

"And the beard?"

"I was allowed to keep the beard."

"What sort of hiding place did you have?"

"I hid in a bunker."

The rabbi was from Kolomeija. In Galicia. Once I said to him: "My parents lived in Galicia before they came to Germany. Not far from Kolomeija."

"Where?"

I said: "In Pohodna. My parents told me a lot about Pohodna."

"I know Pohodna. Oh yes . . . the Finkelsteins from Pohodna. I knew them."

"Chaim Finkelstein and Sarah Finkelstein?"

"No. I didn't know them. They weren't there when I came to Pohodna. But Moishe Finkelstein, I knew him. And he had a brother, Chaim Finkelstein, who was supposed to have gone to Germany."

"That was my father. And so you knew my uncle Moishe Finkelstein?"

"Yes, I knew him."

"I did not know him. We never visited each other. And what happened to Moishe Finkelstein?"

"The Germans gassed him. His wife too, Rifka Finkelstein. And their twelve children. And their children's children. A large family."

I said: "Yes."

And the rabbi said: "Yes."

And I said: "Yes."

And the rabbi said: "But there's still one left . . . of the Finkelsteins . . . apart from you naturally . . . there's another . . . your cousin, Ephraim Finkelstein . . . people called him Froike. Froike Finkelstein."

"The son of Moishe Finkelstein?"

"Yes. The son of Moishe Finkelstein . . . and of Rifka Finkelstein."

"Then he must have had more than twelve children. He must have had thirteen children?"

"Yes, thirteen," the rabbi said, "thirteen."

I said: "Thirteen." And thought: "An unlucky number. Like seven!"

"And where is my cousin Froike Finkelstein now? On his way to Palestine?"

"No. He is still in Poland. In Pohodna. I met him there after the war. And talked to him."

I said: "I hope he comes to Palestine. We are the last. And I would like to get to know him."

The rabbi said: "Yes. But he is a Communist. Has a good job there."

[223]

You can imagine how deeply I heaved a sigh of relief when I learned that my cousin Froike Finkelstein is a Communist and would not be coming to Palestine. The question is merely: how long will a son of a Finkelstein remain a Communist? Will his Jewish heart not one day begin to beat like the heart of a Jew . . . to beat that way once again? And will he then not be inclined to come back? Will he not then come to us? In order to live with us in a Jewish country? —and why should I trouble my head over it now? For the time being Froike Finkelstein is a Communist, lives in Poland, and has no intention of joining me on my travels.

I often talk with the rabbi about Jewish history, and the rabbi is astounded but at the same time very happy that I am so well informed. I have admitted to him quite openly that I have forgotten how to pray properly, and have been practicing again after the war, but it still goes a little slowly, though it's not so bad anymore, that I go to the synagogue very seldom, even though I have set my mind on going there on all high holidays, and even though I don't even put on my phylacteries in the early mornings . . . my *tefillin*.

"Mr. Finkelstein," he said. "You are no typically assimilated Jew, like for instance Judge Wolfgang Richter, but half assimilated. That's what you are! A half-assimilated Jew! There's still a little tradition there. . . . Naturally: as the son of Chaim Finkelstein and nephew of Moishe Finkelstein, how could it be otherwise? A pious and very respected family . . . the Finkelsteins . . . but otherwise . . . you are no better than the others, all the other Jews who have forgotten the spirit of the Torah."

No, dear Itzig. I am not conspicuous. Most of the Jews here on board the *Exitus* are anything but pious, and think very little or nothing at all of God, many of them have declared open war on God, and their attitude toward Him, the protector who has failed, is defiant.

God is a great failure, a real letdown. What did He do when His children were toppling down into the deep mass graves? Which army did He send to their rescue? Worms! Dear Itzig, worms!—and what did God do for the others who were shot up through the chimneys? Only the clouds took pity on them, and perhaps the rain, on which they glided back down again . . . back to us on earth.

No. Most of us on board the *Exitus* do not believe in God anymore. We are going home, into the land of our forefathers, in order to have soil and earth beneath our feet, in order to found a state and an army, to prevent it all from happening again. We on board the *Exitus* don't want to be sheep anymore. Never again will we let ourselves simply be carried off to the slaughterhouse. That's what we are. We on board the *Exitus* . . . patriotic Jews, that's what we are. But not religious.

That's what I made clear to the rabbi. And that he understood. But the rabbi does not give up hope. Do you know what he said? "Herr Finkelstein," he said. "I understand your bitterness. And the bitterness of the others. One day you will find your way back to God! You and the others too!"

I can remember exactly your Bar Mitzvah, a day just as important in your family as the day of your circumcision. You went with your father to the synagogue. And when you came back you said to me: "Now I am a man. Now I am of age." And yet you were only thirteen years old. But in the faith of the Jews the day of Bar Mitzvah is the day of answering before God.

From the day of your Bar Mitzvah, you had to put on your phylacteries every morning and repeat the long morning prayer to yourself just like your father, Chaim Finkelstein, just like a man of responsibility. And in the synagogue . . . there you were called to the Torah with your full Hebrew name: Jitzchak ben Chaim! Just like a man of responsibility.

Do you know, Itzig? I asked the rabbi to loan me his phylacteries! And the black prayer book.

"What sort of black book?" the rabbi asked.

"The siddur," I said. "That's what I mean."

"And the tefillin?"

"Yes," I said. "And the tefillin . . . the phylacteries."

"Do you still know what to do, with the tefillin?" he asked. "And what the proper way of putting them on is?"

"I knew it once," I said.

The rabbi showed me how to do it . . . according to regulations . . . showed me everything I had almost forgotten, taught me and said, "That is a *mitzvah*—a good deed before God."

"Yes."

The rabbi wanted to save my soul. Lent me his phylacteries, lent me his prayer book, even though I had one myself . . . a black prayer book . . . in my suitcase . . . but I didn't want to unpack it . . . yes . . . I have a prayer book . . . but no phylacteries . . . and so I borrowed both . . . and the rabbi stood at my side and watched to see that I did it right . . . put on the phylacteries properly and according to regulations . . . even chose the right prayer . . . out of the black book . . . the long morning prayer which is mumbled to oneself slowly. At first I did it wrong . . . but then I did it right.

And do you know what happened next? Just guess, my dear Itzig!

[226]

The rabbi left me alone. Went to the toilet, left his caftan hanging on the bunk, and the fur hat too, going to the toilet only in his yarmulke, and still half undressed. I took the chance to slip quickly into the black caftan. I also put on the broad fur hat. There I stood, with my phylacteries, in the caftan and fur hat, the black book, the siddur, in my hand, murmuring my morning prayer, swaying rhythmically back and forth, just as pious Jews do.

As I was standing there, deeply buried in my prayers, I caught the attention of the children in the dormitory . . . and they surrounded me and said: "Rabbi!"

That is the rabbi. I have introduced him to you. That's him. And yet it could be me, too.

Teiresias Pappas I have introduced to you. And David Shapiro. And Max Rosenfeld. And Wolfgang Richter . . . the judge! Others I have hinted at. I will introduce others to you later. You must have patience.

V

All the children on board the *Exitus* got vitamin injections. The announcement was made in grand style by loudspeaker.

Vitamin injections, injections, final injections? Memories?

Sometimes, at our camp in Laubwalde injections were given in special cases. Phenol! Fatal!

I remember: for a time I served in the concentration-camp hospital, because one of the orderlies was ill. Easy work.

Once we killed about a hundred children. The children were brought into the examining room one by one. There was a curtain and behind it a chair. And behind the chair was the orderly Zaleski, a Pole. He held the child still, the child whose turn it was, you understand . . . and in front of the chair was yours truly, Max Schulz.

I was the one in front of the stool before the child. In front of the child whose turn it was. In my hand I held the needle with the fatal phenol. In which hand? In my left hand. I'm left-handed, you see, dear Itzig.

Suddenly with a lightning thrust I jabbed the needle into the heart of my patients, my children. They were dead on the spot. Little angels, dead.

After the ship's medical officer, Dr. Steiner, had made his announcement, I, the mass-murderer Max Schulz, went immediately to the sick bay and offered my services voluntarily.

I said: "Dr. Steiner, today the people wanting a haircut can wait. If you need help then I am at your service. I was a hospital orderly once."

Dr. Steiner was visibly happy. He didn't put any questions. Where? When? Probably he thought: with the partisans or some place like that; and asked only: "Can you give injections?"

"I can," I said.

"As it happens I don't have a single assistant, not one. That is extremely nice of you, Herr Finkelstein."

Dear Itzig. I gave the children on board the injections. As I did so I felt like a saint, a purified and transformed mass-murderer. Because not one of my children fell down dead from the chair!

Since the vitamin shots the children love me. Previously they used to call me Mr. Finkelstein. Or simply "barber." Now they just say: Chaver Itzig!

Do you know what Chaver means? It means friend! Or comrade, also! The children surround me wherever I am. I can hardly get away from their love. "Chaver Itzig! Another shot!"

It goes on for the entire day, or: "Chaver Itzig! Are you a rabbi?" Or: "Chaver Itzig! Cut my hair please!"

Five bunks, one on top of the other. The rabbi sleeps in the very top one. He is number one, if you like. But he could also be number five. I am number two or number four. That depends completely upon whether you begin counting from below or above.

Beneath me is a man. I do not know what his name is. He's just a man. And beneath the man is a woman. I do not know what her name is. Just a woman.

But just guess who sleeps in the very bottom one? Number one or number five?

In the very bottom bunk sleeps Hanna Lewisohn from Berlin, the ballerina. I mentioned her earlier. She is the one who explained to me who Teiresias was. Teiresias, the blind seer from the tragedy of *Antigone*.

Hanna Lewisohn maintains that she survived Berlin when Berlin was burned down, and that she glided out of the blazing fires dancing . . . because dancing ballerinas do not dance: they glide.

Hanna Lewisohn belongs to my female clientele. She was the first woman to have her hair cut by me: "Herr Finkelstein! A man's haircut for a ballerina!"

Now we are good friends, and already on first-name terms. She has bats in the belfry like me . . . and yet it is different. I believe she is really off her head. But we get on well together. Yes. Excellently. Sometimes it seems to me as though I were the only person to whom she could talk. You know how it is: a meeting of minds.

One night I felt sick. The *Exitus* was shaking through all its joints, had high blood pressure, its spectral eyes were rolling, it's hulk bouncing angrily against the grinning waves, its belly groaning in the night. Occasionally the *Exitus* arched itself like a wounded whale, shot out of the night waters, wanted to leap to the clouds, sank back weakly, hovered raging between the waves, turning round in a circle.

And so I clambered down from my bunk, passed the two unknowns, past the ballerina Hanna Lewisohn. Staggered over the bodies of those sleeping on the floor of the hold, trying to get up to the fresh air, but threw up while still on the steep steps. After waiting until my stomach felt settled again, and having wiped off my mouth, I staggered back, groped around in the dark for Hanna Lewisohn's bunk, and thought: this is where you have to climb up, three times one is three, and the fourth, that's yours . . . and was already on the steps . . . when two hands grabbed me!

"Is it you, Itzig?"

I said: "Yes, it's me."

"My man's haircut has slipped!"

I said: "Oh nonsense. That's not possible."

"It has," said Hanna Lewisohn. "It is possible."

She pulled me down from the ladder, grabbed hold of me, and yanked me under the cover.

In the dark I could not see her face, but I knew it well. Hanna Lewisohn's ballerina face has a childlike expression: it is the face of a six-year-old with the skin of an old woman. You should see her eyes, dear Itzig! As round as marbles, black eyes . . . eyes which can smile like lips, a delirious grin . . . yet scintillating. And her hair is black too, much too black for it not to be dyed; that was something I was able to notice right away with the practiced eye of the barber. But her hair is as soft as silk, just right for a gentleman's haircut. It suits her, back and sides tailored to the head . . . and once I said to her: "Hanna," I said. "There are only three barbers in the world who can bring off such a

first-class short back-and-sides cut for men: Chaim Finkelstein—my father—and me. And the mass-murderer Max Schulz
too."

"Him too?"

"Him too," I said.

I knew her face. And I knew the head which belonged to
her face. Yes. I knew her face. Nevertheless I fondled it with
my killer's hands, pretending that I did not know it. I fondled
her face like a blind man would fondle it. Or like a blind
mass-murderer. And Hanna Lewisohn said nothing, kept her
eyes closed, panting, panting against my hand, and against
my face, above her own, in the dark.

Her breasts smelled like corned beef, dear Itzig, like the
corned beef I had eaten at Frau Holle's . . . because here on
board the *Exitus* we eat almost only corned beef, we are
corned-beef maniacs because our provisions hoard is filled right
to the top with canned food. Chopped meat in tear sauce.
What sort of tears? The same tears, dear Itzig, from the same
well as the tear dollars of the American Jewish aid organization, which provided us with the corned beef.

Her nose is narrow and bony, but her mouth is broad.
Hanna Lewisohn lay still as I touched her face, only her breathing betraying her excitement. Suddenly she embraced me,
rolled me on my back, threw herself on top of me, slid down
my hardened member, let it disappear into her womb, sat on
top of me like a beetle, but then crept back down, suddenly
yanked up my head and pressed her lips to mine.

That was our first kiss.

Have I made you look up, dear Itzig? Do you want to know
whether she had an orgasm?

When she kissed me. Several. Then she shoved me away,
turned her back toward me and wouldn't let me touch her
anymore. She's a little bit mad. A little bit of a lot.

[231]

"And then I ran," said Hanna.

"Where to?" I asked.

"I don't know," said Hanna. "I just ran. Down a street. A dark street. Everything was dark. I ran and ran."

"Where to?" I asked.

"Into the dark," said Hanna.

"What happened then?"

"There was a house," said Hanna.

"Just one house?"

"I don't know," said Hanna. "I only saw that one house. The door was open. I ran in. Up the dark stairs. Right to the top. Until I couldn't get any further."

"Go on, Hanna," I said.

"And there at the top . . . right at the top . . . was a door, just one door. . . . I knocked."

"Did somebody open it?"

"Yes," said Hanna.

"Who?"

"A hunchback," said Hanna. "A dwarf. A man with short scraggy legs and an enormous head. And long arms . . . clutching a lamp . . . in huge hands."

"And I suppose he had fangs?"

"Yes. Long fangs!"

"A blood-sucking monster?"

"Right," Hanna shuddered. "A real bloodsucker."

"Did he bite you?"

"No," said Hanna. "He didn't bite me."

"I said to him: 'I'm Jewish. The Gestapo are after me. They'll kill me if they get me.'"

"The dwarf stared at me. He stared at me for a long time, then suddenly grabbed me, pulled me into the room and hissed: 'In here—I'll hide you!'

[232]

"A garret," said Hanna. "A bed, a table, a chair. And a long bench!"

"And a window," I said.

"Yes. And a window," said Hanna.

"And from the window you could see over Berlin, right? A rooftop view of Berlin?"

"Yes," said Hanna. "How did you know?"

"And what happened then, Hanna? Did he make a meal of you?"

"No," said Hanna. "He just strapped me down. On the long bench."

"How often, Hanna?"

"Just once," said Hanna.

"And for how long?"

"A long time," said Hanna.

"How long, Hanna? For how long were you strapped down like that?"

"For three years," said Hanna.

"Oh, sure, he took care of me. Kept me fed. Washed me. Brought me the bedpan."

"For three years?"

"For three years."

"And he never unstrapped you?"

"Never unstrapped me."

"And did he beat you?"

"No," said Hanna. "He didn't beat me."

"Rape you?"

"Not that either."

"What did he do then?"

"He didn't do anything except stare at me."

"What happened next, Hanna?"

"Then I began to dance," said Hanna.

"Even though you were strapped down?"

"Yes," said Hanna. "After all I'm a ballerina. I have to dance."

I said: "Yes, of course you have."

"And so I danced," said Hanna. "For three years I danced. You should have seen me."

"You were magnificent, I suppose?"

"Yes," said Hanna, "I was. And every day I got better. Better and better. Better than Pavlova. Better! Much better. One triumph after another. The most famous choreographers worked with me. With Hanna Lewisohn! Prima ballerina assoluta! You should have heard the cheering and clapping after every appearance. And those bright lights. . . .

"Those bright lights," said Hanna.

"Yes, Hanna."

"And the blaze," said Hanna.

"What sort of blaze, Hanna?"

"Berlin was on fire. All the houses round about us were burning. Only ours was not."

"Yes, Hanna. And you couldn't get into the cellar when the bombs came down? That's right, isn't it? Like the others did?"

"Yes," said Hanna. "That's right. And the fire . . ."

"How was that, Hanna?"

"I just danced right out of the window. Just like a butterfly . . . and fluttered down dancing into the fire."

"And burned your wings?"

"Yes," said Hanna. "I fell dead to the ground. But then one day," said Hanna, "one great day . . ."

"What about that day, Hanna?"

"One day I danced out of the ashes. That was really something to see!"

[234]

Did you hear that, Itzig? How she danced out of the ashes? She's nuts, let me tell you . . . even though I sometimes talk nonsense myself . . . in a different way. What's that you're saying Itzig? She didn't tell that story at all? This conversation between me and Hanna Lewisohn never took place? It's just something I made up?

If Itzig Finkelstein were mad . . . who would be the one to talk nonsense then? Me or you? Be careful, Itzig! Don't quarrel with me! We have to get on well with each other! The two of us! You and I!

And so: let's assume . . . that she did tell it to me. Let's assume that I understood her wrongly, which is not my fault or would not be. So let's assume:

The hump-backed dwarf is not a hump-backed dwarf. The hump-backed dwarf is some man or other, a quite ordinary normal man . . . or a woman . . . a woman, why not? Or: anyone at all . . . let's say someone who protected her until everything was over. Let's suppose the loft were an apartment, a roomy, airy apartment; even cozy. And the long bench not a long bench but a sofa . . . let's say: a plush sofa. And let us suppose: everything happened differently. Especially the strapping-down. We could well imagine in her fantasy the walls of the apartment becoming straps. And holding her captive for three years. Or the man was the straps. Or the woman. Or the hunchbacked dwarf, a dwarf and yet not a dwarf. Let us suppose: her soul wanted to fly away together with the legs of the ballerina, but could not, because that was either not advisable or dangerous.

It is possible therefore that I understood her wrongly. And she told her story intentionally, just the way she did . . . just in the way I understood it, in order to make it more vivid. Perhaps she thinks that I, a barber would otherwise not understand the truth . . . that is possible, is it not?

[235]

Every night the *Exitus* changes course. No one knows what Teiresias Pappas has in mind for us. Yesterday we were sailing toward the African coast, toward dawn we turned around and went back the way we had come. The eyes of the *Exitus* are opened wide from sheer terror. From time to time Teiresias Pappas has the miserable hulk sail around in circles as though the ship were one of my rats, chasing its own tail.

I spoke with the commander of the Haganah, David Shapiro, and asked him what was going on.

"It's an evasive maneuver," said David Shapiro. "Haven't you noticed that we change course every night? And the flag too," said David Shapiro. "Take a look next time."

That was yesterday. I wandered over to the flagstaff beneath the bridge and noticed that we were sailing under the Japanese flag.

"The day before yesterday it was the Portuguese flag. And three days ago the Swedish. And four days ago the Mexican. And five days ago the flag of the Soviet Union," said David Shapiro with a laugh, as we met again on deck. "Now what do you say to that, Mr. Finkelstein?"

"Nothing at all," I said. "What about the name *Exitus* painted on the ship?"

"That can stay for the time being," said David Shapiro. "In any case it's pretty blurred by now, and no one can read it properly."

Max Rosenfeld thinks that Teiresias Pappas is a charlatan. Or a man who likes to deceive himself. Not long ago Max Rosenfeld said:

"The most magnificent illegal landing of all time! That's what Teiresias Pappas is telling all the passengers. It's nonsense, Herr Finkelstein! If we are lucky, we'll get through the blockade without being noticed. If we're out of luck, we won't."

Sometimes Teiresias Pappas' voice booms at us in broad daylight through the loudspeaker:
"Everyone on deck go below! Only the crew allowed on deck!"

At that there always begins a race toward the steps leading down to steerage. A safety regulation. Nothing more. Necessary only when a foreign ship turns up or when there are suspicious dots in the sky. Nobody is allowed to know who we are!

And yet I, mass-murderer Max Schulz alias the Jew Itzig Finkelstein, I am convinced that the English know exactly who we are. They know that we are on the way to an illegal landing. The English are waiting patiently. As soon as we have sailed into Palestinian waters, they will overrun us with their ships and their airplanes. Then we will probably be interned on Cyprus. Or we will have to fight our way ashore.

Yesterday David Shapiro said to me: "It will be like shooting clay pigeons! We will knock off the English like sparrows. And we have Molotov cocktails too! We will fight! Like we fought in Warsaw!"

I asked him: "And will we land?"
"Of course we will land," he said.
"And then what?"
"Then the English can lick our asses!"

The closer we got to the Palestinian coast the more restless everyone became. This morning weapons were handed out: revolvers, old guns, Molotov cocktails, and a few sub-machine guns. The voice of the Haganah commander came through the loudspeaker: "Anyone who can handle weapons present himself to me."

I of course made my services immediately available. I said to David Shapiro: "How many sub-machine guns have your people got?"

"Five, Mr. Finkelstein."

"Then give me one!"

"Can you handle such a weapon, Mr. Finkelstein?"

"Of course."

"Where did you learn?"

"From the partisans."

I received my sub-machine gun. And a few Molotov cocktails. And am quite excited. A pity I am not keeping a diary right now. Otherwise I would have made the following entry:

"I, the mass-murderer Max Schulz, am from today on a Jewish freedom fighter."

I cut people's hair with the sub-machine gun hung around my neck. And I keep a few Molotov cocktails underneath the improvised barber chair. As before, women and children gabble on while I work, and now and then a few men who have nothing better to do, but nobody cracks jokes anymore. I am respected. Hanna Lewisohn has become quite wild since I became a soldier. And not only at night. During the day too. She never leaves my side and kisses me at every opportunity.

Otherwise not much happens on the *Exitus*. No one knows whether Teiresias Pappas intends to touch the Palestinian coast today or tomorrow night or whether he is intending to put off the landing still further. Perhaps tonight we will be sailing in the direction of Africa, or just sailing around in a circle, or perhaps making sneaky zigzags.

The weather holds fair. A brief rain shower would have done the *Exitus* no harm. God might have decided to give the miserable hulk a wash before its landing. No time had to be lost. And with his sun he could dry it right off. But apparently He can't do it, since it doesn't rain in this area of the ocean during the summer. It has something to do with the climate.

The weather is good and the heavens are blue. People on deck gossip with one another excitedly, and the babies peeing through the railing pee so quietly and softly without a whine or a moan as though aware of the devotional nature of the moment. For everyone here can feel it in his bones: the Promised Land is near!

Strange. Every time the rabbi looks at me, it seems to me, to Max Schulz the mass-murderer, it really seems to me as though there are doubts in his eyes, as though his eyes were not sure whether or not they really should bless me. What am I to understand by that?

I avoid his gaze. On the other hand I often get together with the judge—Judge Wolfgang Richter—and not only at dawn over his shave. He's not so easy to get rid of, and his interest in Max Schulz grows every day. He gets me to tell him all the gossip. Asks me questions. And every time assures me:

"Herr Finkelstein! The case interests me! And I can well believe that the fellow has gone underground. But he does have to be somewhere, doesn't he? Or doesn't he? And I'll bet you that I'll find out his hiding place sooner or later. Do you want to bet?"

"Very well," I said. "Let's make a bet."

"Let's bet a bottle of champagne, Herr Finkelstein!"

"Very well," I said. "A bottle of champagne!"

We made it! For God's sake, Itzig, open your dead eyes! Tonight we are going to land!

[239]

First Teiresias Pappas spoke. Quite briefly. He said only: "Tonight we land!"

Then David Shapiro spoke. David Shapiro spoke for a longer time. He said that we would land because it is our historical right: to land in our inherited homeland. "And the landing is not illegal! It is legal!" The voice in the loudspeaker seemed to be shouting at the heavens. "Who is illegal in Palestine? The English! And who was it who stayed there two thousand years as guests while we were away? All sorts of goyim! And the Arabs too! And who does the land belong to by right? To us! And who was it gave it to us? You!"

Dear Itzig. I can't remember exactly what else David Shapiro said. I can recall just one particular word: a single word. David Shapiro said: "Resurrection."

What did he mean by it? Is the resurrection really close by? And what resurrection? The resurrection of the dead? Or the resurrection of the Jewish people? And could it perhaps be so, that the dead do not really rise again? That only a people rises again? And we are the people? And with the people, its past history? And with its history . . . the dead right down to the last generation?

I do not know, dear Itzig. I only know that the people on the *Exitus* lost their heads at the word resurrection. Somebody or other shouted: "Our ship is no longer called *Exitus!* It is called *Resurrection*." And another shouted: "We will have to change the name!" And the crowd yelled: "And the flag! Down with the false flag!" And Teiresias Pappas shouted: "No! No!"

Nobody bothered anymore about the "no" from the Greek Teiresias Pappas. The evening before the landing the ship was rebaptized, the name *Exitus* scratched off. Now it is called *Resurrection!* The word streams into our eyes from all sides . . . in every language . . . the whole ship is painted with it

. . . in order that the heavens can see it too . . . perhaps, too . . . the whole world . . . and on the flagstaff, dear Itzig . . . flies now the blue-white flag bearing the Star of David.

That was our last day in exile. Or let us say: that was the last night.

Can you see me . . . Itzig Finkelstein? I am standing by the guard rail, my sub-machine gun hung around my neck.

𝔅𝔬𝔬𝔨 𝔉𝔦𝔳𝔢

I

I stood by the ship's rail, checked my weapon, hung it again around my neck, and looked out to sea. I saw the sea drinking in the sun. I saw how the last light was grabbed by the waves, sensed the silent screams of the fish, saw desperate splashes of sunlight dangled from leaping jets of foam, and thought: now our time has come! Closed my eyes, held them closed for a long time, then blinked, opened my eyes, the frog eyes—mine, not yours—and noticed that night had climbed out of the sea.

Next to me, in the dusk, stood David Shapiro. I asked: "Are we there?"

"Not yet," said David Shapiro.

I heard him coughing softly.

"At 3 A.M.," said David Shapiro. "At 3 A.M. the *Resurrection* will . . ."

"What?"

". . . reach the Palestinian coast."

"At 3 A.M.?"

"At 3 A.M."

I nodded. And looked up to heaven.

"I hope He will hide the moon when we get there," said David Shapiro. As though he were reading my thoughts.

I asked: "Who? Teiresias Pappas?"

"No," said David Shapiro. "Not him."

You can't see the ship anymore. But don't worry. The English didn't see it either.

At three o'clock in the morning Teiresias Pappas sailed our *Resurrection* across the invisible three-mile limit. We kept our weapons at the ready and trained against the foe, who was out there on the watch somewhere in the dark. Shortly before dawn the fishing boats used by the Haganah reached us. We transferred into them, like black beetles at night, clambering down the rope ladders of the *Resurrection,* bags and baggage on our backs.

We left the night behind us. As we arrived, the new day stretched its arms out to us. But very carefully. Like a man waking from sleep who does not dare to open his eyes. The beach was still dark.

The people took off their shoes and climbed out of the boats, began to cry, waded through the shallow water, waded stumbling and crying . . . waded the last few yards barefoot . . . stumbling and crying . . . had wet feet . . . and suddenly began to run. And then were standing on dry ground. There they dropped to their knees and thanked the Lord, in whom suddenly in that moment they believed again. And kissed the holy earth.

[244]

A dark beach, even though it was already daylight. All around me, men on their knees behaving as though there were nothing more important in the world to do than to kiss the sand.

You can probably imagine that I, the mass-murderer Max Schulz, felt a little confused. What should I do? Kiss the holy ground? Or not kiss it? Cry or not cry? Thank the Lord or not thank the Lord?

And so I too fell on my knees, in order not to be conspicuous, and kissed the holy earth and cried and thanked the Lord.

It is daylight. And yet the beach is dark. The sun is biding its time. The sun wishes to protect us until we are in safety.

A convoy of lorries, waiting at the side of the road. On all sides armed Haganah soldiers, young men and women in khaki uniform. Watchful shadows in the dark.

I, the mass-murderer Max Schulz, have kissed the ground. My mouth is full of sand. I raise myself, spit out the sand, notice Hanna Lewisohn standing next to me, also spitting out sand, see her suddenly turn around, throw her arms around my neck, and say: "Itzig . . . now we are home again!"

Hanna is still weeping. I weep also. Still. Hanna says: "Itzig, don't cry anymore!"

I say: "No, Hanna. We have cried enough. This is the last time."

Hanna nods her head. I can see her doing it in the dark. A shadow moving its head. A nodding shadow. Hanna says: "The Haganah have sealed off the beach."

I say: "Yes, Hanna. If the English come they'll have to fight."

And I look all around me but can see only shadows, and suppose: The shadows are khaki. With sub-machine guns. Armed Jewish soldiers.

I do not know how long all that took: the arrival, the embracing the soil, praying, the awakening, the jubilant rush across the holy beach to the street, the siege of the lorries. I know only that Hanna and I reached the convoy of lorries, that helping hands pulled us up, that Hanna stood next to me when the motor started, that suddenly dawn began to break over the landscape, that the desert revealed its contours, that the sun began to peep out from behind the dunes, and that the heavens opened.

We had lost a great deal of time. We had been waiting for this moment almost two thousand years. Now we had to move on before the English showed up.

We drove off. Only the rear guard of the Haganah stayed on the beach, to cover our retreat.

Or . . . let us say . . . to cover our advance.

II

Arab shepherds had watched our landing and naturally had alerted the English. But not until later in the afternoon. *Baruch Ha Shem*—that is to say: blessed be thy name—not until late in the afternoon, after we legal or illegal immigrants had long since vanished from sight or had found a hiding place in the sandhills of the desert. It's true that then the English snuffled around busily—and angrily too, because they had been asleep—and delivered a few blows with the withered hand of a dying empire . . . but it was too late.

You can well imagine that the press very soon got wind of the affair, and indeed the details of the ghost ship's adventurous journey became known, after a few of Teiresias Pappas' people had let out our secret over booze while on leave in Greek ports on the return journey.

The world press had shouted the news of our landing in

huge headlines. I snipped out a few of them, made a few corrections with swift strokes of the pen, and of course kept them. Do world headlines interest you?

Headlines: *Resurrection* Docked in Palestine! On 14th of June, 1947, Sixteen Hundred Illegal Immigrants Broke Through English Blockade! English Too Late! Illegal Immigrants Flee In Lorries! Wild Drive Through Desert! Units of the Jewish Underground Army Cover Their Retreat! Lorries Carrying Illegal Immigrants Disappear at Dawn! Without Trace! English Comb the Holy Land Seeking Illegal Immigrants!

Other headlines: Illegal Immigrants Get Forged Papers from Jewish Shadow Government! Forged Papers Are Legal Papers!

Headlines: Mass Imprisonment in Haifa, Tel Aviv, and Jerusalem! Mass Imprisonment in All Major Cities! Mass Imprisonments Lead to Nothing! Assumed Illegal Immigrants Not Being Hidden in Cities but in Jewish Community Settlements!

And more still! More headlines! In an interview with the expert for Palestinian affairs, Sir Edward Hunter, the writer of these lines, learned that the Jews of the Holy Land, especially those in the community settlements, are from time to time blind and deaf. Not one of them will admit to having seen or heard anything!

The Jews brought Itzig Finkelstein back into the land of his ancestors. His arrival, after an exile of two thousand years, was a historical moment. For that reason, therefore, Jewish freedom fighters kept the holy beach covered: in order to protect Itzig Finkelstein, the homecomer, in order to guarantee safe conduct in the Holy Land . . . because Itzig Finkelstein, the homecomer, was not to fall into the hands

[247]

of the English at any price, for they would have deported him . . . back into exile.

The lorries separated and went off in separate directions. The one carrying Itzig Finkelstein drove for three hours at breakneck speed through a desert of sand and stone which Itzig Finkelstein had known hitherto only from postcards.

Itzig Finkelstein had a stomach ache. He felt like throwing up. And why? Because the lorry was going over all sorts of strange bumps or because Itzig Finkelstein was being transformed anew.

Itzig Finkelstein had transformed himself too often. Out of the innocent baby which once had borne the name Max Schulz had grown a small rat-catcher, and out of the rat-catcher an educated young man, and out of the educated young man a barber. And out of the barber an SS man, and out of the SS man a mass-murderer. And out of the mass-murderer the small-time Jewish black marketeer, and now: out of the small-time Jewish black marketeer, Itzig Finkelstein, the pioneer, the homecomer, a freedom fighter.

Yes, damn it all, I felt like throwing up. I felt sick. Too many transformations . . . all the small and large Max Schulzes and Itzig Finkelsteins rumbled in my bowels, were born, were transformed, climbed ladders and fell, grew and died. The lorry raced on bumpily through the desert. I stood there jammed between other illegal immigrants, staring into the morning sun, staring at the brilliant blue sky and at the picture-book landscape. We raced through a cloud of holy dust, a long way off the main road . . . the main road which still belonged to the English. And now and then we drove past dirty Arab villages. We drove by Bedouin camps, but I scarcely noticed them, seeing them only through the film over my eyes. Subliminal pictures, formed in the dust by the new sun, all flashing past, mummied figures, tents of camel and

[248]

goat hair, mangy dogs, springing out of the "wadis"—the dried-out river beds—and snapping at us, camels, and donkeys, which scarcely lifted their heads, and herds of gray dirty sheep and strange small black goats.

We drove inland, away from the Gaza coast, taking the caravan routes into the desert, then turned around and drove northward, and finally made a broad arch and moved back in the direction of the coast.

Yes, that's how it was. At about seven o'clock in the morning we reached the first Jewish settlement: fields in the middle of the desert! Plantations! Banana and orange groves! Small bright houses with flat roofs, surrounded by trees and beds of flowers! Irrigation canals! Water hoses! Sprinklers showering their spray beneath the yellow sun! And I said to myself: "Max Schulz! A miracle! The Jews have conquered not only us, they have conquered the desert as well!"

We drove on at the same speed, driving through the transformed desert, overjoyed at the sight of the colorful fields, looking in astonishment until our eyes were popping out of our heads. Hanna Lewisohn, who was standing a little more to the front of the lorry, pushed her way through to me, lay her arm about my shoulder and said: "Itzig Finkelstein, your frog eyes are bigger and rounder now."

I tried to laugh and said: "Because the desert has been transformed!"

"Just look," said Hanna. "Jewish farm workers! There! On the field! They're waving!"

Hanna waved back. And I did the same. And the others. We all waved!

We came to a country road. Everything there were Haganah sentries, who gave us to understand through signs that the way was clear. Not a trace of English roadblocks. For a while we drove along the Tel Aviv–Haifa road. At the Haifa-Natania crossroads we took the right fork, drove through a cluster of eucalyptus trees, came to a field road, saw banana and orange groves again, drove through them, the lorry skipping from sheer pleasure, skipping first slowly, then quicker, then suddenly stopping altogether. We had arrived. In the kibbutz Pardess Gideon.

Immediately after his arrival in the kibbutz Pardess Gideon, Max Schulz received new clothes. He was given a khaki uniform, a pair of rough brown shoes, a round, small khaki hat, intended to shield his head from the hot sun—a precautionary measure against bats in the belfry—and in addition to that Max Schulz, alias Itzig Finkelstein, received fresh underwear, cigarettes, a place to sleep, and of course new papers.

No. I was not afraid. Neither of the Jews nor of the English. For the Jews I was a Jew, a homecomer. For the English I was a man with proper papers. And untouchable, a citizen of the British mandated territory of Palestine.

Name: Itzig Finkelstein. Profession: barber.

III

I've been in the kibbutz Pardess Gideon for a few days now. I have already learned a few words of Hebrew. Our greeting: *Shalom!* which means: "Peace!" And other words: *Kibbutz* . . . meaning a "community settlement" or "collective village"; the plural of that word . . . is *kibbutzim; chaver,* which means "comrade" or "friend," a word I had already learned while on board ship.

The plural of that is *Chaverim.* So make a mental note of those words: "Shalom. Kibbutz. Kibbutzim. Chaver. Chaverim." The members of a kibbutz are called kibbutznicks, and every kibbutznick is at the same time a chaver. Is that too complicated for you?

A kibbutz is a community settlement without a gentlemen's hairdressing salon. At least, that is the case in Pardess Gideon. There is not a trace of a gentlemen's hairdressing salon. Nowhere. I asked myself right away: "Where do the settlers actually have their hair cut? Where? And when? And by whom?"

I soon found that out: now and then. When it happens to become necessary! And usually . . . behind the showers . . . in fine weather . . . in the sunshine . . . and by Nathan Herzberg, the locksmith, a clever man, who can do all sorts of things . . . including haircutting.

A kibbutz is no place for a real barber!

Kibbutz Pardess Gideon: a small paradise, an oasis in the desert.

Hanna likes it here. She is happy. Hanna is working in the chicken run, and I'm working in the cow shed. We are together only in our free time. And what do we do then? All sorts of things. Mostly we go for walks. Yes. Just that.

When we go for walks, Hanna and I hold hands. Hanna would like to run off with me, but not far from here, just run around a little, but I don't let her. I hold her tight. We saunter along through the orange and banana groves, stomping through the potato fields in rough shoes. There are meadows too, real meadows. Just no gentlemen's hairdressing salon.

The houses are small. But the biggest among the small ones is the communal dining room. In Hebrew it is called: *Chadar Ochel.* That's where mass meetings take place, also social gatherings, for instance: The Oneg Schabbat, a sort of sabbath festival with songs, and folk dancing. That's something you should make a note of: Chadar Ochel, the community dining room in a community settlement or in a collective village or in a kibbutz . . . accommodating many kinds of get-togethers.

I remember exactly the bathtub in Frau Holle's cellar. She had borrowed it from Willy Holzhammer's mother, in order that I, Max Schulz, the mass-murderer, could splash around in it with nothing on. In this place there are no bathtubs for the grown-ups! Instead, there is a shower! Rather a room with a lot of showers. And hot water—not gas—hisses out of the showers . . . after you turn on the tap of course.

There is even a library here! A library with many instructive books! These Jews are strange farmers. Farmers who read books, talk about books, and have philosophical discussions. I believe that every one of them was formerly something else.

Do they earn much money here in Pardess Gideon? They don't earn anything at all. Each one does what he can and gets enough to live. That's how it is. The individual does not earn any money. Only the community. And the community builds new houses, buys new land, in order to create living space for the ones still to come.

I bet you're thinking that there's nobody stupid enough to work for nothing? Especially not the Jews? Am I sure I have not made a mistake? That they can't be Jews? But they are. They're Jews all right.

Shall I describe what it's like to live in a kibbutz? What happens on a normal working day? From the very beginning? From the first gong in Chadar Ochel? To the last? A communal meal? The working team? What the rooms are like in the small houses with flat roofs? What life in tents is like?

And why there are still tents since there are houses as well? Whether there's a space problem? Do you want to know whether the beds are large or small? Comfortable or uncomfortable? And whether we sleep here with or without pillows, on hard or soft mattresses, what the smell of the soil is like? And the sky? And the sun? Do the heavens and the sun smell? Whether they are different here? Do you want to know what distinguishes night from day here? Whether it is only light and darkness? Do you want to know whether we have screen windows? Or mosquito nets? And do you want to know how the moon looks at night seen through the window or through the slit in the tent? And what the cry of a jackal is like? Or of many jackals? And whether the desert behind the plantation whispers in the night? Or whether it is quiet? Do you want to know such things?

If I were to describe to you at length what a kibbutz is and what life in a kibbutz is like, then I would have to write volumes. But I, Itzig Finkelstein alias the mass-murderer Max Schulz, do not have time for that. For I am not writing a factual book about Palestine or about the kibbutz. Understand? That sort of thing annoys me! Go to hell! Or go and ask God. Go to His library. Ask for a factual book. Look in the catalogue. Under the letter "P" for Palestine. And under "K" for kibbutz.

I don't feel well. I would say as a trained barber who has to work in the cow shed, I feel bad.

And so: I got here on the fourteenth of June. To the kibbutz Pardess Gideon. And naturally I needed a rest. You can imagine that, I suppose? After such an exhausting journey on the ghost ship! So what! They put me into the cow shed right away!

IV

For a whole week I worked there. I was fed up to the back teeth with it. And so I said to myself: "Itzig Finkelstein alias Max Schulz. That is no place for a real barber. And besides you need a rest. Better get going on some sort of journey. It will not do you any harm. And you still have a few black market dollars."

I left the suitcases behind. For the time being. I traveled without suitcases. But with my new papers.

Nathan Herzberg, my rival, the locksmith, who from time to time played at being barber, brought me in the donkey cart to the next bus station. He is a coachman too!

"Got the travel bug, Chaver Itzig?"

"Yes, Chaver Nathan."

"That I can understand," said Chaver Nathan. "Go and take a look at your country."

"Yes."

"You haven't seen it for two thousand years."

I said: "That's true. I'm curious."

The next bus station was four miles away. We drove to it at a leisurely pace. We rode through plantations and desert. We talked.

"It's always so," said Chaver Nathan. "Newcomers work for a few days on probation. We give them clothes and new papers. And then each one goes his own way. Many prefer to live in the city, a few go to another kibbutz, some stay."

"I would very much like to stay with you, Chaver Nathan," I said. "But I am a barber. And I would prefer to be working in my own profession."

"Oh come on," said Chaver Nathan. "You can cut hair with us too. You can help me. But we don't need a full-time barber here."

"But the profession of barber is not a spare-time profession, Chaver Nathan. That's something I can't accept."

"Ah well," said Chaver Nathan, "if that's what you think, then let me tell you: work is work. If there is no hair to be cut, then there's work in the cow shed or on the field. Or in the orange grove or in the banana grove or in the kitchen or somewhere. There's always work to be done here."

That's how it was. We talked. We smoked. We sweated. The donkey stank. Two men in a bumpy donkey cart, a cart with rubber automobile tires because of the rough sand. Two men in khaki uniforms sitting on a bare seat, one of them forty years old, his name Itzig Finkelstein, the other over sixty, a man whose leathery face was forked by the weather, white hair, body like a dried-up branch.

"When I came here forty-five years ago," Nathan Herzberg said, "there was only sand and stones and mud. We took the stones away. And the sand. And dried out the marsh. That was real dirty work. And the damned mosquitoes. It was no fun."

I said: "Yes. I can well imagine."

"There were thirty men of us and nine women. That's how we began. Then more came. Today there are almost four hundred of us. It's still a small kibbutz. But anyway."

"Yes, Chaver Nathan," I said.

"The first ones came from Russia. Today there are Jews here from all countries of the earth. And there are German Jews like yourself. Are you really a German Jew, Chaver Itzig?"

"My parents came from Galicia."

"Then you're a Galician," said Nathan. "A 'Galitzianer.' That's what I thought. And do you have some money?"

"Dollars from black market deals," I said.

"Black market deals," said Chaver Nathan. "So you're one of those. You'll have to change your ways here, Chaver Itzig!"

No. I did not have difficulties. The chauffeur of the Egged Bus Company—Haifa-Tel Aviv Line—did not want to change black dollars but took me when I whispered to him that I had landed only a very short time ago. And the English? They didn't make any difficulties either. From time to time we came to roadblocks. The damned Tommies! They stop every Jewish bus. But I didn't have any difficulties. None. None at all. My papers were in order, and my clothes were inconspicuous. I was just Itzig Finkelstein, a man traveling with proper papers, a man in khaki trousers, in a khaki shirt, and a khaki hat, a man with rough shoes, a man from a kibbutz.

V

When we were marching into Russia the country seemed endless: the earth arched itself into infinity beneath the silent sky, ate the soles from our boots, and laughed at our tired feet. But here everything is narrow and limited.

I have been traveling around here for a few days, going around in circles. I was inquisitive. I believe everyone is inquisitive who comes here for the first time, especially a Jew and quite especially an old Nazi like myself. And when a man comes who is both, then two eyes are no longer enough.

My frog eyes have photographed all sorts of things, and flashed the pictures into the belfry of my head, to be registered, and retained in the memory of the mass-murderer Max Schulz or the memory of the Jew Itzig Finkelstein.

The Arab villages and cities are stiff with dirt, and the misery that I have seen has almost made me, the mass-murderer, feel pity.

I was in some nameless Arab village and there I saw a small

[256]

boy standing in the gutter. In the hot sun! With half-blind eyes streaming with pus! Grinning black flies settling on his eyes! And buzzing.

I had to blink from horror. When I looked again I saw other small boys and girls . . . and grown-ups too . . . many of them still young . . . many of them no longer young. Even the very old. Standing there where the small boy had stood. With the same eyes. And the same flies swarming about them.

And then I saw a coffeehouse. At the street side. Something stirred in my head . . . a hammer thudded at my temples: a coffeehouse! And a jabbering radio! The hot sun! And the stink! And a nameless village! And clay houses. And houses knocked out of the rock. And sand. Lots of sand. Desert sand. And dying soil. And little hungry donkeys braying. And little hungry goats bleating. And skin and bones. And sun. And sand. I felt sick in the stomach. What do you say?

I have never seen sick eyes in Jewish villages. Or grinning black flies settling on the eyes. And during the day I have never heard a jabbering radio. And not seen any men in the coffeehouse watching the flies. In the Jewish villages which I have seen . . . I, the mass-murderer Max Schulz . . . everything that feeds on matter or sucks blood . . . and buzzes . . . has been stirred up for the last lost battle, the battle against Jewry. In the Jewish villages the marsh has been raped and screams for help in the way a baby screams for help when his mother is changing his wet pants . . . the screams of the marsh have the sound of a baby's screams, for the Jews are changing its wetness. Backwardness is being raped. And the Jewish farmers are working mercilessly with their picks and shovels, ripping open the stomach of the dying earth in order to give it new life.

And in the cities . . . in the cities . . . there I saw no

beggars . . . they have fled. I assume: fled from the trade unions. Asphalt roads have covered the sandy paths and schools and hospitals and factories have made their peace with the apartment houses and with the avenues of trees and the parks so that they may together, by a strange pact, dominate the skyline of the city.

VI

There were sixteen hundred of us illegal invaders . . . on the fourteenth of June . . . early in the morning on the beach. I don't know where they are. A few came to Pardess Gideon. Me too. And Hanna.

As before Hanna is working in the chicken run. Hanna loves everything that has wings.

I went back to Pardess Gideon to fetch my suitcases. Since I did not arrive until late in the evening I had no alternative but to spend the night on the kibbutz. I slept in Hanna's tent. If truth be known I don't really like sleeping with Hanna. She is too thin. For my taste. I like fat women. As fat as my mother. You should have seen *her!* She was some woman!

It was dark in the tent. I could not see Hanna and could only feel the pressure of her lean body. We slept on a camp bed. Too narrow . . . too narrow for victim and executioner. But that . . . did not seem to disturb Hanna.

"You've seen nothing, Itzig Finkelstein. You've been traveling around for four days . . . and have seen absolutely nothing."

Hanna is laughing quietly in the dark. I can tell she only wants to provoke me. She wants to get me talking. But I don't want to.

"I saw a lot, Hanna. But I have to chew it over first."

[258]

"Did you see Jerusalem?"

"Yes."

"And the Wailing Wall?"

"Yes. That too. I even said my prayers there."

"Do you believe in God?"

"Sometimes yes, sometimes no, Hanna. Just the same as most people. I don't take Him seriously."

"Then why did you say your prayers at the Wailing Wall?"

"Tradition, Hanna."

"Tradition?"

"Yes, Hanna. Tradition."

"And what did you do there . . . at the Wailing Wall?"

"Cried, Hanna."

"Why, Itzig?"

"Tradition, Hanna. Tradition."

"Now just think, Hanna. Other Jews before me have prayed and cried there. For centuries and more.

"I remember, Hanna . . . when I was still a boy . . . I stood next to my father in the small synagogue on Schillerstrasse. He prayed. Our eyes were turned to the east. We thought of Jerusalem and of the remains of the Great Temple . . . of the Wailing Wall, which symbolizes everything for us . . . everything . . . Hanna . . . our unique past . . . freedom . . . exile . . . agony . . . semblance of death . . . and the will to be born again."

"You're a good talker, Itzig Finkelstein. Tell me more about Jerusalem."

"There are two cities there. The new and the old Jerusalem."

"How does it look?"

"I can't describe it, Hanna. The new city looks quite different from the old city. But the new city lives off the old city."

"Did you see the Church of the Holy Sepulchre?"

"Yes I saw it."

"And the Omar Mosque?"

"That too."

"And the Garden of Gethsemane?"

"Also."

"And the Via Dolorosa?"

"Yes, Hanna."

"And what did you do in Jerusalem?"

"Walked around, Hanna. Taking photographs."

"What with?"

"With my frog eyes."

Can you see us? Can you hear Hanna laughing? I light myself a cigarette. Hanna says: "Watch out. Don't set the bed on fire. And the tent with it."

I lie smoking.

"And did you see Mea Sharim . . . where the Orthodox Jews live? And is it true that the Jews who live there wear caftans and fur hats and have long beards like they used to have in the ghetto?"

"Yes, Hanna. That's true. They still live as they did in the ghetto. In Mea Sharim. And still work hard at their prayers there. It's a different world, Hanna. There it is in the middle of the world of the pioneers, standing like a monument, Hanna, to prevent us from forgetting God."

I lie still smoking. And peer upward through the slit in the tent and see a single star. It stands in the heavens above Jerusalem.

"Were you at the Dead Sea, Itzig?"

"Yes. I was there."

"And what's it like there?"

"Hot, Hanna. It's hot there."

"And what did you do there?"

"Went for a swim, Hanna. And swallowed salt water. No one can sink there. Not even a mass-murderer."

"What a lot of nonsense you talk. You're really off your rocker—and did you see the river Jordan? And the river Jarkon? And were you at the Red Sea?"

"Yes, Hanna. But leave me in peace."

"Were you in the Negev?"

"Of course I was in the Negev."

"And what does the Negev look like?"

"Like a lunar landscape, Hanna."

I didn't want to keep talking, but I went on and on. I talked of Capernaum, and about Bethlehem and Nazareth and the paths of Christ, who believed he was a God. I talked of the Jordan and of the tracks of John the Baptist. I let my thoughts spring and leap, and told of Caesaria and the Roman statues, spotted by the summer birds just as is the monument to the Führer on Adolf Hitler Square in Warthenau. I told of drained marshes, of red and black earth, of heaven and sun, yellow desert sand and rocks of white lime, of Jewish villages and of community settlements further inland, all of which are like Pardess Gideon and yet different.

Can you see Hanna? And can you see me? It is dark in the tent. Hanna has eyes like a child. Squints a little. She was strapped down once. Three years. To a bench. And one day she flew away. Suddenly could fly.

"It must be beautiful, Itzig. On top of Mount Carmel."

"Yes, Hanna. And it's woody there too. And dwarfs live in the woods. Just as in Germany. And yet the woods there are different. The dwarfs are different."

"And the bay?"

"That's further below. And if you're standing above, on the

[261]

top of the mountain . . . and look down on the bay . . . you get the desire to fly. Like butterflies."

"Like butterflies?"

"Yes, Hanna. Exactly like butterflies."

"I must try that sometime."

I nod my head and say: "Yes—Hanna. You can fly there. Fly around a bit, above the bay. The only thing you have to watch out for is the English fleet."

Hanna says: "I'm not afraid of ships."

"That's fine then, Hanna."

I creep out of the narrow bed. Hang something in the opening of the tent, because the stars are disturbing me, close my frog eyes, and feel like sleeping.

Hanna suddenly asks me: "What has impressed you most?"

"What do you mean?"

"Here in Palestine."

I say: "The young trees, Hanna. The young trees which the Jews have planted in the desert."

Hanna says: "Trees!"

I say: "Yes. The young trees. Every young tree is the soul of a dead man."

"Of a Jew? Of a Jewess? Of our dead?"

"Yes, Hanna."

"Is that really true, Itzig?"

"Yes, Hanna. That's really true."

"And how many young trees have you seen?"

"I have not counted them, Hanna. But a lot."

"Millions?"

"I really wouldn't say that, Hanna. But every day more are planted. The numbers are increasing."

"Is that the resurrection of the dead?"

"Yes. They are all coming back."

"All?"

"Yes. All who ever died in exile."

"And the others . . . who once died here?"

"They are already here. They don't need to come back."

"And will they rise again too?"

"Yes, Hanna. Slowly and gradually."

"And what about us, Itzig?"

"We have risen again already. There are two resurrections. The resurrection of the dead and the resurrection of the living dead."

"Then we are among the living dead?"

"Yes, Hanna. All Jews in exile are the living dead. They live without firm roots. It is not a proper life."

"How come, Itzig Finkelstein?"

"The living dead come here, Hanna . . . to strike roots."

"Like trees?"

"Yes, Hanna. And yet it is different."

I say: "Hanna! There is yet a third resurrection. David Shapiro hinted at it once. The resurrection of the Jewish people! That one begins where the other two resurrections . . . come together, join hands, and swirl around in a strange dance."

What have I told you? Of my last night? In Pardess Gideon? In Hanna's tent?

We talked. We made love. And then I went to sleep. I slept uneasily, had a strange dream, a dream . . . that I had transformed myself back and was Max Schulz again:

And Max Schulz, the mass-murderer, went to Jerusalem . . . to piss three times symbolically . . .

[263]

Once in the Church of the Holy Sepulchre . . .

BECAUSE HERE LAY THE BODY OF CHRIST! HERE HE ROSE AGAIN FROM THE DEAD!

And once in the Omar Mosque . . .

FOR FROM THIS ROCK OF SAKHRA MOHAMMED SOARED INTO HEAVEN! ON HIS WHITE STEED EL BURAQ!

And once in front of the Wailing Wall . . .

FOR HERE, IN THE LAST RUINS OF SOLOMON'S TEMPLE, WAS THE MOST HOLY PLACE OF THE JEWS!

At the Wailing Wall Jews stood crying, old Jews and young Jews. And I stood between them. And pissed. And not one of them saw it. Because I, Max Schulz, am a clever pisser.

But crying is catching. I found that out a long time ago. When I saw the others crying I began to cry too. And suddenly I was no longer Max Schulz, I was a Jew again. I was Itzig Finkelstein.

And Itzig Finkelstein was ashamed that he had pissed, even though he knew exactly that he had not pissed as Itzig Finkelstein . . . but as the mass-murderer Max Schulz. And Itzig Finkelstein wiped away the stains from the wall and cried bitterly.

And Itzig Finkelstein who was Itzig Finkelstein again went back into the Omar Mosque and wiped away the stains there . . . Max Schulz's stains . . . then went back to the Church of the Holy Sepulchre and did the same.

It is already late afternoon. I am sitting in the dining room. In Chadar Ochel. I am writing. Now and again I underline something. This is my last day in the kibbutz Pardess Gideon.

Today I am leaving. I have to go somewhere, don't I? Somewhere I have to strike roots! Somewhere there must be a proper barbershop where I, the mass-murderer Max Schulz, can work as a real barber!

VII

I was in Jerusalem again. But that is no city for a barber. I couldn't find work. Next I tried Petach Tiwa, Rischon Le Tion, Haifa, and finally Tel Aviv. Result: a blank.

Tel Aviv is a city for barbers. There plenty's going on. The place is teeming with barbershops and gentlemen's hairdressing salons. Yes. It's a real city. But I couldn't find work. Then there was a newspaper advertisement.

I was sitting in a café in Tel Aviv. Early in the morning. Having a good breakfast. I had changed a few black dollars, transformed them. I was just paying the bill with the right currency . . . when I saw the newspaper announcement! "Barber urgently wanted! References requested! Gentlemen's Hairdressing Salon Schmuel Schmulevitch! Beth David!"

I went there straight away. To Beth David. With both my suitcases. And my black dollars. And local pound notes and piasters. Schmuel Schmulevitch's shop was the only one in Beth David!

There are people who race off right away to satisfy their curiosity. I am different. I enjoy my curiosity. I prolong the agony intentionally, as long as possible. I said to myself: "You should really go straight away to this fellow Schmuel Schmulevitch! There's a lot of competition! And other barbers could present themselves, present themselves before you . . . and take the job away from right under your nose."

But then I said to myself: "Itzig Finkelstein. First you take a good look at the town. Because there's no point in taking a job in a town if that town is not to your liking, even if this Beth David at first sight looks like Tel Aviv, or a miniature Tel Aviv . . . but first sight is not second sight . . . it's the same as with love. You have to make doubly sure."

I, the mass-murderer Max Schulz, wandered around for two hours . . . in Beth David . . . simply wandered through the streets alone. Had a good look at the town. Listened to people talking. Asked a few questions. Walked on. Nobody seemed to think there was anything odd about me. I was not conspicuous. No one shuddered at the sight of me. No one got a shock. Not even the sun blinked.

Yes. And when I had seen enough I said to myself: "So. Now it's time to go to Schmuel Schmulevitch's. Now it's time to introduce yourself: Gentlemen's Hairdressing Salon Schmuel Schmulevitch, Avenue of the Third Temple, 33–45."

Now just think: I, Itzig Finkelstein, alias the mass-murderer Max Schulz, arrive at my destination. I stand in front of the window, feeling dumb-struck. I say to myself: "Christ, Itzig! That's real class!"

Out of sheer excitement I take off my glasses. Press my frog eyes to the window. Stare into the shop. I beg your pardon . . . into the salon. I think: Christ, Itzig! Ten barber chairs. Polished mirrors. Ten washbasins. A display counter. Shoe-shine boys, manicurists. Teams of barbers, apprentices, concealed lighting. A dream of a hairdressing salon.

VIII

Schmuel Schmulevitch was the spitting image of Chaim Finkelstein: small, one shoulder stooping . . . the left one—yes: the same shoulder . . . as though two thousand years of suffering and persecution had hung themselves from this one single shoulder, the left shoulder, the one nearest the heart, his nose dripping a little, bald-headed, large expressive eyes, wise, good-natured, well read in the Bible. Like Chaim Finkelstein.

You can well imagine what a shock I got when I saw Schmuel Schmulevitch for the first time. From sheer fright I let out a fart but Schmuel Schmulevitch pretended not to notice.

The shop . . . I beg your pardon . . . the salon . . . was full. Ten barber chairs, garrulous haircutters, apprentices pretending to be busy, shoeshine boys smirking all over their faces, elegant manicure girls with upswept hair. A bustling business, all repeated and reflected in expensive mirrors. Familiar sounds: snatches of conversation, the snip snip of scissors, scratching and scraping, whirring.

The air had a familiar smell, the smell a class shop should have. It was the kind of air that invited sniffing.

A few gentlemen were waiting patiently in comfortable leather armchairs, many with bald heads, smoking cigars, reading or leafing through illustrated magazines, others had hair, smoked cigarettes or nothing at all, a mixed clientele.

I had let out a fart but Schmuel Schmulevitch only said: "Unfortunately all the waiting chairs are full. But one will be free soon."

I stammered out: "I am not a customer . . . I've come to see about the job."

Schmuel Schmulevitch took me into the adjoining room, a narrow room, what I assumed was a dressing room, or so it looked . . . for the staff to change in or to make coffee . . . There was a clothes rack, a spirit stove, and a toilet room.

I said: "My name is Itzig Finkelstein. I read you advertisement in the paper."

"So," said Schmuel Schmulevitch. "Itzig Finkelstein?"

I nodded my head and said: "Perhaps you have heard of my father . . . Chaim Finkelstein . . . a well-known barber . . . author of the famous specialist's handbook *Haircuts Tailored to the Head?*"

"Never heard of him," said Schmulevitch. "Chaim Finkelstein? Never heard of him. But the book. Yes. Somehow the title seems familiar."

I said: "A well-known title."

And Schmuel Schmulevitch said: "That's what it's like with literature today . . . with modern literature."

And I said: "What is it like?"

And Schmuel Schmulevitch said: "It's like that. Look. People remember the titles. But not the authors. *Haircuts Tailored to the Head?* Yes, I remember. But Chaim Finkelstein. I don't remember him."

So that's what happened. We sat down on a shaky bench next to the clothesrack. I told Schmuel Schmulevitch my story, a little too quickly and a little plaintively, and showed him my Auschwitz number.

Schmulevitch listened patiently, and when I had finished just nodded his head gently, his bald head, and said: "Yes. You have gone through a lot. But I take it . . . you are still a good barber?"

"Yes. I am."

"Your father was a famous author."

"Yes. He was."

"Now I remember. A unique book. Written by a unique barber."

"Yes. That's right."

"So you had a good teacher."

"Yes. That's right."

[268]

"A few barbers have applied already . . . before you . . . but none of them was any good."

And I said: "Yes. That's life."

And Schmuel Schmulevitch said: "You see. That's how it is."

Naturally I was hired. Started work the next day. To be precise, on the fifth of July, 1947.

Allow me to introduce my new colleagues: Isu Moskowitz, Joine Schmatnick, Sigi Weinrauch, Max Weizenfeld, Lupu Gold, Michael Honig, Benjamin Jakobowitz, and Itzig Spiegel. As you see, there are nine haircutters. I am the last.

Ten barber chairs and only nine haircutters? That's right. Our boss, Schmuel Schmulevitch, works personally at the tenth barber chair.

As you can see . . . everything is well organized.

I forgot to mention the names of the two apprentices, and the names of the manicure girls, and the names of the shoe-shine boys. Forgive me. The two apprentices are Franzel and Motke; the two manicure girls are Rita and Irma, the shoe-shine boys Amos and Raphael.

Have I confused you? Is that too many names? Is your lazy mind packing up? Very well: then for the moment just remember my colleague Itzig Spiegel—blond like the real Itzig Finkelstein—but with a mustache . . . a twirly mustache, swept up boldly to two dangerous points. Eyes: not blue. Not like Itzig Finkelstein's eyes. Itzig Spiegel's eyes are green. Or: greenish gray. Voice: a little squeaky. Probably a non-smoker. Like me, Itzig is a bachelor. His parents are from Galicia. Like mine are. On the very first day he said to me:

"Mr. Finkelstein. Two Itzigs is a little too much of a good thing for one salon. From today on your name is Jizchak!"

I said to him: "It's out of the question. I'm not going to change my name."

"Very well then," he said. "Then from today on my name is Jizchak!"

I said to him: "As you like, Mr. Spiegel. It's all right with me. I just don't understand why it's not possible to have two people with the same name . . . in this salon."

"It's because of 'his' wife," he said. "She can't stand Eastern Jews. And to have two employees with a name like that . . . that wouldn't suit her I'm sure."

"Which wife are you talking about, Mr. Spiegel?"

"Schmuel Schmulevitch's wife."

"Isn't he an Eastern Jew himself?"

"Of course he is. That's just the point."

There's a real dragon for you! Schmuel Schmulevitch's wife! I completely forgot to introduce her to you. She's the boss around here. Really. Apart from Schmuel Schmulevitch. You get that all right . . . don't you? I forgot her. But she's here. Yes really. Always here. Sitting at the cash desk. And serving at the counter. She's everywhere actually, even if only with her eyes.

Mrs. Schmulevitch: the face of a mummy. I put her age at ninety. But that can't be right. I thought Veronja, the witch in the Polish forest, was a hundred and eighteen. But that wasn't right either.

No. She can't be as old as that yet. Because the eyes in her mummied face are strangely alive. Flashing little birds' eyes, which transfix haircutters, apprentices, manicure girls, shoeshine boys, and even the boss, Schmuel Schmulevitch, to their prescribed working places with hypnotic power. There's a saying here in the shop . . . I beg your pardon . . . in the salon . . . "When she looks we work" . . . full steam ahead and without wasting time. Yes, when Mrs. Schmulevitch looks over, nobody dares to pick his nose or scratch his behind or even smoke, the snipping and shaving and scraping and massaging and parting of hair are carried on at high speed, in short: *work* is the order of the day.

Not long ago Itzig Spiegel said to me:
"If you think about it, they're both very different people . . . Schmuel Schmulevitch, a man with a heart of gold . . . and his wife: a poisonous snake!"

Her hair is dyed bright blond. Usually she wears curlers, as though she wanted to show us that she, an old woman, is a long way from having given up.

She wears a silver necklace. With something hanging from it, a piece of jewelry that's hidden from sight, dangling somewhere between her two withered breasts, out of sight beneath the dress she wears . . . buttoned up to the neck.

I asked Jizchak Spiegel: "What sort of piece of jewelry is it?"

"No one has ever seen it yet," said Jizchak Spiegel. "There are just a few stories!"

"And what are the stories?"

"That it's some sort of German medal."

"Is she a German Jew?"

"Yes. She is. From Prussia."

"And Schmuel Schmulevitch?"

"A Russian."

"Oh I see!"

"Yes, you see. . . ."

"And what sort of medal is it?"

[271]

"The rumor is that it's the Iron Cross First Class. Her first husband was a Prussian officer."

"A Jew?"

"Yes. A Jew."

"A memento? The Iron Cross?"

"Yes. A memento."

A Prussian Jewess who cannot forget Prussia. That was all I needed. Especially here in the Holy Land.

Do you know what Schmuel Schmulevitch said to me not long ago?

"Mr. Finkelstein," he said. "We are comrades in sorrow. I am a Russian and you are a Galician . . . a 'Galitzianer,' if I'm not mistaken. We will have to be wary of my wife."

I said to him: "My parents are from Galicia, but I myself was born in Wieshalle, an old German town."

"That doesn't make any difference," he said. "You are a 'Galitzianer,' Mr. Finkelstein."

I asked him: "Did your wife vote in those days?"

He asked me: "Vote for whom?"

I said: "Adolf Hitler."

No. Up to now I've had no difficulties with Mrs. Schmulevitch. Sometimes she looks down her nose a bit when I talk Yiddish with the customers, but she doesn't say anything. She knows I'm good. I am a good barber. I do my job.

IX

I said to myself: "Itzig Finkelstein! You'll have to watch out! You'll have to watch out good and hard! She leaves you in peace right now. But one can never know . . . you look like a Jew. Much too much like a Jew, with a face straight out of the *Stürmer*."

In the mornings I am the first in the shop . . . I beg your pardon, in the salon . . . and in the evenings I am the last to leave . . . my industry is proverbial. I even work during lunch hour, never waste time, no picking my nose at work, no scratching my backside, and no smoking.

Yesterday Schmuel Schmulevitch gave me a key. Said to me:

"Mr. Finkelstein. My wife is impressed. Since you're always the first to come in anyway and the last to leave, from now on you can be the one to open the shop in the mornings and to close up at night."

What did I tell you!

Yesterday evening a customer came after everybody else had gone home. Even Mrs. Schmulevitch. Only Schmuel Schmulevitch and I were still in the salon. Schmuel Schmulevitch came up to me and said: "An American Jew. A tourist. And he'll have to be served. It's not possible to turn away an American Jew. After all our future state is going to need a lot of money. Don't forget that!"

"You go on home, Mr. Schmulevitch. Don't keep your wife waiting. And so far as overtime is concerned . . . don't worry . . . I've got nothing else to do anyway."

We were alone. The customer and I. We talked in Yiddish. The customer said, "I came here to write an article. About Palestine."

"Are you a journalist?"

"No. I'm president of a Jewish welfare organization. We publish a small journal. I have to write something now and then. A lead article."

"Very interesting. You're an amateur journalist?"

"I arrived yesterday. It was already dark. Couldn't see a

[273]

thing. Went first to my aunt. In Beth David. Slept there. Woke up early with lumbago. Stayed in bed all day. In the evening I got a telegram from New York. My wife in labor. Premature. Unexpected. Have to fly back today!"

"Congratulations. A son, hopefully, I suppose?"

"I hope so."

"A pity, really. You came here especially to write an article about Palestine . . . and haven't seen anything!"

"I haven't seen anything at all."

"And what will become of the article about Palestine?"

"I'll have to write it."

"Even though you didn't see anything?"

"Yes."

"And how are you going to do that?"

"I don't know."

"Perhaps I can help you."

"You?"

"Yes. Why not?"

"How can you help me?"

"I could get you some material."

"Not a bad idea."

"It's true that I've only been here for a few weeks and haven't seen much. But I've seen more than you. Because . . . you haven't seen anything at all!"

"Tell me what you have seen . . . perhaps it'll be enough for the article."

We were alone in the salon: the customer and myself. I tied the apron around him, following regulations, expertly, adjusted the barber chair with safe and sure barber hands, setting the back and with it the body at my disposition at the right slant,

[274]

rearranged the head- and footrests, showing the customer that I knew what I was doing.

First the hot compresses! That is very important! To get the beard soft! Lathering alone is not enough. I took my time.

The customer was lying there comfortably with his eyes half closed. I turned over in my mind what I could tell him. What had I seen? Yes. I would tell him that. But later. Not now. First I had to talk about history. For what is this country without its history?

First I talked about history. I began with our patriarch Abraham and his wife Sarah, explaining to my customer that we the Jews had never maintained that Sarah, our first mother, the wife of Abraham, had been made pregnant by God personally, as is maintained of Mary the mother of Jesus Christ . . . even though we would be justified in making such a claim: because this claim, which we have not made, would have been quite logical, would have seemed as it were obvious, because Sarah's pregnancy was a miracle, because Sarah was already stricken in years, that is to say very aged, an old woman, whereas Mary the mother of Jesus Christ, was still young and could have become pregnant in a quite normal way, namely: from a quite normal male member. From a member between two legs.

"You see," I said to my client. "We could easily have claimed that God in person made Sarah pregnant. Then we, the Jews, would all have been God's personal descendants!"

I grinned at my client and said: "But we do not make such a claim! It would be shameless presumption to do so!"

After the compresses I began with the shaving brush, spreading the lather briskly, and with obvious care. I spoke about the descendants of Sarah and Abraham. I spoke about Egypt, about the fat and the lean years, about slavery, spoke about

[275]

an infant floating alone on the waters, among the bulrushes, who later became leader of the people, spoke about the burning bush, spoke about the exodus from Egypt, the exodus of the children of Israel, spoke about manna and about the movement of bowels—because manna is a laxative—spoke about Mount Sinai, about Moses, who was no longer a baby floating alone in the water, but now a man with a beard, told about the Ten Commandments, spoke about forty long years, spoke about the Golden Calf, and the Promised Land.

I don't know how long I had been lathering my client but when I got to our first king, the lather had become as hard as cement: for better or worse I had to scratch it off the cheek of my client, and begin to lather it again afresh, with fresh soap and fresh foam.

I told about many kings, about the division of the Great Kingdom, about victorious and defeated enemies, about occupation and liberation, about small and large wars, spoke about the destruction of the First Temple, about the exile in Babylon, about longing and nostalgia, gave him the quotation: "If I forget thee, O Jerusalem, let my right hand forget her cunning. Let my tongue cleave to the roof of my mouth, if I remember thee not . . ." Spoke about the Talmud, and the return home, spoke about the Second Temple.

By the time I got to the Romans I again had to scratch off the lather and begin again. I got the sequence right only as I was telling about the destruction of the Second Temple. I shaved my client hastily, washed his face, using alum water and eau de cologne, gave him a face massage, dried him, puffed on some powder, dusted it off, and said:

"So! Haircut, too, sir?"

Naturally the customer wanted one. As I cut his hair I spoke about the exile, about the curse of Jesus, saying,

"Not that he meant it . . . at least not in that sense, but he

[276]

did say it: 'Daughters of Jerusalem, don't weep for me but weep for yourselves and for your children. For behold, the days are coming when they will say: Blessed are the barren and the wombs that never bore and the breasts which never gave suck.' "

I spoke about the sufferings of the Jewish people, spoke about the devil with a false cross, spoke about the shedding of blood in the name of the Lord, who knew nothing of it, spoke about the Lord who was a Lord but not the son of God, even though he believed himself to be so, or perhaps did not believe . . . for how should I, Itzig Finkelstein, know something of that nature with certainty or even try to argue the point? Spoke about the first and the last pogroms, even though I did not know whether the last would be the last . . . for how should I, Itzig Finkelstein, know such a thing with certainty or even dare to make such a claim . . . spoke of numbers . . . named the number two thousand, and said: That could be years . . . long years and short years, years of exile . . . and said: That is a number! And said: But numbers are numbers! Said: I do not like to count. I did not count the millions. Then! Said: Numbers are numbers! Said: And years are years! Said: Just years! Said: Years of agony! Said: And sometimes the dying man blinked with his eyes or twitched at the heart, sometimes arched his back: yes, and could not die. I spoke about smaller murders and larger ones, about unplanned and planned murders, spoke about black ravens, about oakwood and canvas, about locks of hair in foreheads and mustaches, about pathetic eyes, about rods in many colors, about the techniques of gassing and burning. Said: It is not easy. Said: It takes ability too. Spoke of mass graves. And they just stood there . . . and toppled back into it. Said: Just like that; yes, just like that, that's how it was.

I had cut off too much of my client's hair. But I, Itzig

Finkelstein, or the mass-murderer Max Schulz, could not make it longer anymore. What had happened had happened. The customer realized that too.

I snipped around a bit more to put his mind at ease, spoke about the uprooted fruit tree, which took roots into itself, in order that the growing fruits would not be impeded, spoke of spiritual roots, spoke of the sod, spoke of foreign soil and the soil of home, of blood and earth and the homecoming, spoke of the assemblages of Jewish people all over the world for their homeward pilgrimage, spoke of the present, spoke no longer about the past, said only:

"So! We do not want our dying to go on any longer! And if we cannot die . . . then we can just as well live!"

And the customer realized that also.

When I had finished and my client had made careful notes on everything, I desired to repeat a few things to give an expression to certain thoughts once more . . . so I, the mass-murderer Max Schulz, dictated to the American Jew Jack Pearlman—who was not as good a Jew as me because I live here and he lives over there!—dictated to him therefore the following line: said to him: "Please take down the following:

Jewish construction work in Palestine has impressed me deeply. I was impressed not only by the stinking canals, waterworks, power plants, roads, cities, schools, and hospitals . . . I was impressed above all by the fields in the desert and the young trees which the Jews have planted in the thirsty earth.

Dear Reader. The saying goes that in every tree newly planted the soul of a dead Jew lives. Of our dead. I have seen many trees. And still more are being planted. It is said that there will be millions!

Dear Reader. I ask myself: and how is it with the living

[278]

Jews? Are they in reality the living dead? The living dead of the Diaspora? Who come really alive only when they come here? Do they have to live in the Holy Land in order to rise again from the dead? And to strike roots? Like trees? Even if differently?

Dear Reader. And what should we do? We Jews in America? Should we not all arise again? That is what I ask myself. I, your president!"

I took my customer to the nearest taxi stand. Of course before doing that I put out the light in the salon . . . and locked the door. A man has to know his duty.

X

Early this morning a dead Englishman hung in front of my window.

I am a person who wakes up slowly and with difficulty. That has something to do with my blood circulation. Or with the bats in my belfry. First I yawned, half asleep, stretched myself, massaged my head on the right spot, stretched my back and my arms, then my legs, finally my flat feet, blinked first with the left eye then with the right eye, stared at the ceiling and thought: that's a hotel-room ceiling.

And then I saw the Englishman!

If you think that I jumped as though I'd been electrocuted, jumped as I did in the Polish forest on the lorry, when the shooting started, from out of the woods . . . and I jumped down from the lorry . . . and ran off . . . as though I, Max Schulz . . . had a fuse up my ass . . . then you're making a big mistake.

In certain situations I keep calm and collected. I got up in a leisurely manner, rubbed the sleep out of my eyes, padded over to the window, peeked at the Englishman a little . . .

[279]

but not too much, only a little . . . and said to myself: "Itzig Finkelstein! You had nothing to do with that!

"They can't pin this one on you. You didn't hang him. And besides, you have an alibi. No murderer would hang his victim in front of his own window! That's obvious!"

I got dressed and went out. My window opened on the back yard. Probably one reason why the Englishman had still not been found. It was still very early in the morning and in the other hotel rooms which look out on the back yard everything was quiet and sleepy. My window was on the ground floor. Very practical for the hangman. No need to climb. Who could have done it? Jewish terrorists? Of course. Who else? I had nothing to do with it.

As I was crossing the street, it occurred to me that today was Saturday. In this town on Saturday everything was closed. Our salon as well. And so today I didn't have to work. I decided to take breakfast in the Café Trumpeldor in Ben-Jehuda Street.

I sat on the sun terrace. Looking at the view. It's famous for it. For instance: the bus station! It can be seen from here, from the sun terrace of the Café Trumpeldor. It's a completely ordinary Egged Bus Station, and behind it is a street full of bungalows where new immigrants live. They're shabby bungalows built of wood with roofs of corrugated iron and dismal little slits for windows, which look with a restrained envy to the beautiful new houses of Beth David . . . the houses on the other side of the Egged Bus Station. A stroke of good luck that I don't have to live there, because I, the mass-murderer Max Schulz, still have some black dollars in my suitcase. And a steady job.

Building is going on in the southern part of the city. Beth David is expanding. One day we will overtake Tel Aviv. One day the new immigrants will leave their bungalows and move into new buildings. When will that be? One day. When the English move out. After the establishment of the Jewish state.

Today is Saturday . . . the Sabbath . . . or, as it is called in Hebrew, *Shabbat*. The building sites doze. The scaffoldings are deserted. The mood of Shabbat dominates. The shops are closed. Even the buses at the Egged Bus Station are resting.

On the Shabbat the city awakens later than usual. It is still early. The streets lie there as though lifeless, yet not quite, because the eyes of the streets are already blinking.

On the corner of Ben-Jehuda Street I notice two English tanks . . . soldiers smoking cigarettes on the turret . . . and a little later a jeep. Do they know anything? About my Englishman?

I am the first guest in the Café Trumpeldor. The waiter seems sleepy. He knows me.

"Coffee with cream, Mr. Finkelstein?"

I say: "No. Without cream."

"And orange juice? Two eggs? Toast?"

I say: "Just give me an ordinary German breakfast, not too many vitamins and proteins: coffee and rolls with butter and marmalade!"

I strain my frog eyes, peer with a froglike look into the distance: over to the palm trees and the ocean, red from the blood of my Englishman. The ocean should really be blue, and I say to myself: "Itzig Finkelstein. Englishmen are blue-blooded."

My waiter brings coffee, rolls, butter, and marmalade. As I am eating breakfast the ocean changes color. Blue tinged with red. Red merging into blue.

I say to myself: "A pity that from this sun terrace the Forest of Six Million Souls can't be seen."

My waiter has forgotten the sugar. He comes back once more, but I have finished drinking the coffee a long time ago.

"Do you think there was something going on in the night again, Mr. Finkelstein?"

"Possibly. There are tanks on Herzl Square. And I saw some early this morning in King David Street, and in Jabotinsky Street, and in the Avenue of the Third Temple, not just at the crossroads. And more than usual. There are tanks even here in Ben-Jehuda Street."

"Perhaps the terrorists have been shooting a few English-men again?"

"It's possible."

"Or stringing a few up."

"That's possible too."

"After all, the English hang Jews. Or don't they?"

"Naturally."

"Not long ago the English hung Moishe Kaplan. And Ben Gideon. And Ben Amos! And Schloime Suppengruen! Four terrorists! Four peoples' heroes!"

"That's true."

"There you are. For every Jew that is hung . . . hang an Englishman! We pay back in the same coin!"

"That's not quite right. We are killing more. We are knocking Englishmen off like rabbits. Didn't you read the news-paper yesterday? The attack on Camp Zion? One hundred and fifty-four Englishmen shot to death!"

My waiter grinned. He said. "Shot in battle. That's some-thing else again. Not many are hung. Just now and then. Only when they hang one of our people! Hanging is a punishment!"

The streets of Beth David begin to waken up. I catch sight of a few early risers. Three of the eucalyptus trees in the street become visibly brighter as the laughing sun strengthens its rays, the white houses in the center emerge from the shadow and expose their bodies to the sun. I ask my waiter for a few Palestine papers in German and Yiddish, and he goes off. I finish off the rest of my coffee.

The notorious terrorist organizations in the Holy Land are the Stern Group and Igrun Zvai Leumi. But there are many more smaller groups. In Beth David the reigning organization is the Schwartz Group—called after their leader Yankl Schwartz, nicknamed Yankele.

When my waiter comes back with the newspapers and puts the pile on my table, I ask him: "Do you believe that Yankl Schwartz is capable of hanging an Englishman in a back yard?"

My waiter says: "Impossible, Mr. Finkelstein. Yankl would never do such a thing. If he hangs somebody, he does it in the main street for sure."

"Avenue of the Third Temple?"

"Yes, and on the highest eucalyptus tree!"

"And why not in a back yard? And why on the main street of all places? And why on the highest tree?"

"So that the press gets wind of it!" said my waiter. "And so that the news gets to the general public all over the world . . . you understand, Mr. Finkelstein . . . that's what it's all about . . . so that the United Nations gets off its ass for once . . . and makes a decision!"

Do you know what that is . . . the general public around the world? That represents billions of stopped-up ears! And do you know what I said to myself? "Itzig Finkelstein. The world press will have to scream loudly! Or else the public at large won't hear a damned thing. And your waiter is right. The Englishman couldn't have been hanging in the back yard! It must have been the Avenue of the Third Temple! You must have made a mistake."

I leafed through the pile of newspapers. News releases about past mass murders are no longer important. Are on the back page. Even here . . . as elsewhere. I made the usual clippings, stuffed reports into my pocket, skimmed over the front pages with the latest reports about uprisings and terrorism in Palestine . . . then got ready to go.

I went to my boss Schmuel Schmulevitch in order to discuss the incident of the hanged Englishman.

Schmuel Schmulevitch lived in Sholom Aleichem Street. Sholom Aleichem was a famous poet, a Jew from Eastern Europe. I walked slowly. I had plenty of time. It was the Sabbath. The Englishman was on my mind. And I thought also of the stories about Sholom Aleichem, which Itzig Finkelstein had once, among other things, read to me. I stopped for a while in front of the monument on the crossroads: the monument of Tevye the milkman. I asked myself: why have the summer birds not spotted it? Then walked on.

Schmuel Schmulevitch received me in his dressing gown. His wife was still asleep. I accepted his invitation to a second breakfast, and as we partook of it I told him briefly about the Englishman and also about my conversation with the waiter in the Café Trumpeldor.

Schmuel Schmulevitch thought for a long time, then said: "The waiter is right, Mr. Finkelstein. Yankl Schwartz wouldn't hang an Englishman in a back yard."

"But I saw the Englishman, Mr. Schmulevitch. I even poked him a little."

"Then there's only one possible explanation, Mr. Finkelstein."

"And what would that be?"

"Were there any hooks, large or small, by your window?"

"Yes, Mr. Schmulevitch. I hung my washing up not long ago and had two pretty solid hooks fitted."

"Is your window the only one in the back yard that has hooks?"

"I suppose so, Mr. Schmulevitch."

Schmuel Schmulevitch offered me another roll, as well as butter and marmalade, poured me some coffee, watched me devour the roll, and the butter and marmalade, and how I drank up the coffee.

"German breakfast?"

"Yes. It was my wife who introduced it."

Schmuel Schmulevitch offered me a cigarette, but I declined. "I don't smoke on the Sabbath, Mr. Schmulevitch."

"Oh? I didn't know you were pious, Mr. Finkelstein."

"I am not pious, Mr. Schmulevitch."

"Then why don't you smoke on the Sabbath?"

"Out of tradition, Mr. Schmulevitch."

"Then I suppose you don't drive on the Sabbath either."

"Generally not, Mr. Schmulevitch. Only when I have to. In an emergency. I don't have to smoke. It's a matter of discipline and nothing more."

Schmuel Schmulevitch nodded his head. I could see he wanted to light a cigarette . . . but he suppressed his wish. . . . I suppose out of piety. He didn't want to hurt me.

"I presume you come from a pious home, Mr. Finkelstein."

"Yes. My parents were pious people."

"Mine too," said Schmuel Schmulevitch. "But their piety didn't help them any."

I asked: "Auschwitz?"

"No. They were too old for Auschwitz. They lost their lives as early as nineteen hundred and three. In Russia. The po-

[285]

groms. But to get back to your Englishman, Mr. Finkelstein. This is how I imagine it:

"Yankl Schwartz captured the Englishman shortly before daylight—I mean, he and his men. They then carried him off to the Avenue of the Third Temple in order to string him up there according to plan . . . as your waiter said quite rightly: from the highest tree. But that didn't work. You understand, Mr. Finkelstein . . . with the English patrols on the street."

"Yes, I can imagine it."

"He and his men ran right into an English patrol. At the last moment they saved themselves by getting into a yard, into the nearest available back yard."

"My back yard?"

"Right. The back yard of the Hotel Beth David. They decided to wait there, until the air was clear. Then they saw your window. Saw the two hooks. And strung the Englishman up there for the time being."

"Very logical, Mr. Schmulevitch."

"They let him hang there for a while. Let us say for a half an hour. Temporarily, let us say. And then, you, Mr. Finkelstein, happened to wake up. You saw the Englishman, shambled over to the window, and gave the Englishman a little shove. Yes. That's how it went. And you had no means of knowing the Englishman was only there temporarily, you couldn't know that."

"No. I couldn't know that."

"Meanwhile he's now in the Avenue of the Third Temple. Been there a long time already."

"I don't get it."

"But it's quite simple," said Schmuel Schmulevitch. "Let's begin at the beginning again. Yankl Schwartz and his men strung up the man temporarily in the back yard. Then . . . when the coast was clear . . . they unhooked him . . . dragged

[286]

him over to the Avenue of the Third Temple, and hung him
up again."

"From the highest tree?"

"From the highest tree."

"Because of the world press? In order that the incident
would not go unnoticed?"

"Right."

"So he is no longer hanging in front of my window?"

"You can bet on that. He's been gone a long time."

"So I don't need to worry my head about it?"

"No you don't, Mr. Finkelstein."

After breakfast Schmuel Schmulevitch and I went to my
back yard to investigate. The Englishman was gone. Later we
went to the Avenue of the Third Temple. Found a jam of
people there. We couldn't see much. The street was crowded
with sensation-seekers, jeeps, police, and military personnel. I
asked a woman at the street side. And the woman said:

"An Englishman was strung up over there. They've taken
him down already. An Englishman with a sign on his breast."

I asked: "What was on the sign?"

And the woman said: "Schloime Suppengruen is avenged!"

XI

What does a bachelor over forty do? A man who on Saturdays
doesn't smoke, doesn't ride on trains, and doesn't drive a car?
—except when there is no alternative—who has not been here
for very long, has no girl friends—what does such a man do
on his day off?

He could go to the soccer game: Maccabee Tel Aviv versus
Hakoa Beth David at the Max Nordau Stadium behind Herzl
Park. He could go swimming, watch fat and lean thighs,

maybe touch one if he's in luck while he's in the water, surreptitiously as it were, he could gaze at the sun. He could go for a walk, for instance; to the Forest of Six Million Souls . . . one mile from here . . . but that is a forest without shadows because the newly planted trees are still low . . . they still have to grow . . . grow a lot . . . he could go back to the Café Trumpeldor, talk to the waiter, drink coffee, gorge himself on whipped cream.

On the way to the Café Trumpeldor I began thinking of Hanna Lewisohn. Began suddenly to get stabbing pains in my stomach. I couldn't get rid of the idea: "Something has happened to Hanna!"

I turned around and went in the direction of the Egged Bus Station.

I felt hot. My khaki trousers and white shirt were sticking to my body. My pointed beard was wet, my spectacles steamed up, my frog eyes strained and red, I had red rashes under my armpits and down my thighs, could feel but not see the inflamed spots. They itched.

I, Itzig Finkelstein, walked in the direction of Egged Bus Station. I said to myself: "Itzig Finkelstein! It's true that you don't go for rides on the Sabbath . . . but this is an emergency. Something has happened to Hanna!"

Then it occurred to me that the buses were not running today . . . because we, here in Beth David, have made a pact with the good Lord: no bus is going to drive and desecrate the holy Shabbat! Only private cars and taxis, because that is a private matter!

I turned around again, and went in the direction of the taxi stand. Next to Herzl Park.

On the day of the soccer game it's not easy to find a taxi. You have to be lucky. I found a taxi. Got in. And said: Kibbutz Pardess Gideon, on the Haifa–Tel Aviv road. And fast.

What did I tell you! Something has happened to Hanna!

I arrived at the kibbutz Pardess Gideon and received the following information: "Gone mad!"

I said: "She was always mad!"

"But never like that!"

"How do you mean?"

"Cracked! All of a sudden she began screaming. Day and night."

"And where is she now?"

"Was taken away. Guggenstein Clinic. In Tel Aviv."

I went there, of course, straight away. But I was not allowed in. One of the orderlies was friendly enough, gave me the information:

"You can't see her."

"My name is Itzig Finkelstein. She knows me!"

"You can't see her, Mr. Finkelstein. She's in a strait jacket!"

"A strait jacket?"

And the attendant said: "A strait jacket."

After that we had a cozy little conversation.

I said: "During the war Hanna was strapped to a bench for three years."

And the attendant said: "That's something she just imagined. She was just kept in hiding. Like many others."

"She was strapped down for three years. And now she is in a Jewish country . . . and is being strapped down again."

"There's nothing I can do, Mr. Finkelstein. You see, she wanted to fly away!"

"Fly to where?"

And the attendant said: "From the roof top of the Guggenstein Clinic to the carob tree in front of the gates."

I asked: "Like a small bird?"

And the attendant said: "Yes. Just like a small bird."

My taxi was waiting in front of the Guggenstein Clinic. I said to the taxi driver: "Drive me to the nearest brothel!"

"Was it as bad as all that?" asked my taxi driver.

I nodded and said: "Yes. It was bad."

We crawled our way through the Tel Aviv traffic, jerking forward with screaming brakes through clouds of dust and sunlight, lining up behind small private cars and unconcerned pedestrians who preferred to take their strolls in the middle of the road. The city was sweltering beneath the Sabbath sun, the houses lining the streets reflected the sunlight and the trees at the edge of the road seemed to perspire. We drove through King George Street, penetrated through to Mugrabi Square, reaching a little later Dizengoff Street, with its coffeehouses and cute little poodles.

I couldn't get the picture out of my mind. Hanna in a strait jacket. Tried to think of Hanna's lean thighs . . . felt sick.

"Find me one with a fat ass!" I said to my taxi driver. "That's the sort I want to fuck today!"

"Then we are going in the wrong direction," my taxi chauffeur said. "The Hotel Queen of Sheba has only slender girls."

"Slender ones?"

My taxi driver nodded his head. "Yes, slender ones. Yes indeed. I wanted to recommend Zippora for you. I've had her myself once. When she moves . . . her bones rattle."

I said: "That's not for me. Don't you know another brothel where there are girls with some meat on them?"

"Not in Tel Aviv," said my taxi driver. "Maybe in Jaffa."

We drove to Jaffa. Hotel Abdulla!

"You'll like Fatty Fatma," said my taxi driver. "I've had her too, once or twice."

[290]

"Fat ass?"

"And how!" said my taxi driver. "Round as a full moon. And gentle brown. Two warts for good measure, one on the left side and one on the right. She's really got something on. And she's got long, fat, sweaty breasts. You can fuck her between her breasts, if that's the sort of thing you like!"

On Saturdays Tel Aviv smells of sunlight, flowers and trees, dust, villas, and bright houses, of good and bad perfume, or fresh-scrubbed poodles, of coffee, of whipped cream, of pastries known the world over, of salt water, of fruit juice, of the sweat of waiters, of powdered feet, powdered armpits, powdered thighs and powdered private parts, of capitalism and socialism, of Mediterranean and salt-sea air. And of course of shaving lotion. Of ladies' and gentlemen's shoes and of lots more. In short: it smells like Beth David. Even though Beth David is smaller.

In Jaffa the smells are different. Here the fresh sea air mixes with the stink of garbage. Here it smells of sick cats, dogs in rut, decayed houses, of fried fish and mutton, of Turkish coffee and arrack, of pepper, nuts, halva, sweaty feet, syphilis, flies, dirty underwear, little kids, water closets, and many other things.

By the time we got to the Hotel Abdulla I was feeling sick. I did not get out of the car right away. My frog eyes took in a narrow alley with high, patched-up houses decrepit with age, round arched gateways, an old fountain in the middle of the alley . . . even here a swirl of people: children in rags, women all muffled up, some uncovered, men in light and dark garments. Arabs. In front of the Hotel Abdulla—on the pavement—some men sat in a half circle smoking water pipes and drinking Turkish coffee out of small, round cups. A few of them had "keffiyehs" on their heads, others were wearing embroidered, colorful caps. They glared at our taxi. I lit a cigarette and leaned out of the window. Observed that it was the same sun as over Tel Aviv. Only the sun's brush used different colors here.

My taxi driver said with a cough: "Yesterday two Jews were murdered in Jaffa. Did you read about it in the paper?"

"Yes," I said.

"Have you a revolver in your pocket?"

"No."

The taxi driver grinned: "Then I would not advise you to go into the Hotel Abdulla alone."

"So you think something could happen to me! Something bad!"

"A knife in the back," the taxi driver said. "Or your throat slit! It's hard to say beforehand. One or the other."

My taxi driver asked for a cigarette. I gave him one.

"But nothing happened to you . . . when you were with Fatty Fatma?"

"But that's a long time ago. In those days the political situation was different."

I had been looking forward to Fatty Fatma, had already allowed my thoughts to dwell on her giant behind and her sweaty breasts . . . and my own sword, my normal cock, roused and stiff and trembling . . . had already been saying to me:

"Itzig Finkelstein! You haven't had a woman for a long time! And today is the Sabbath. And on the Sabbath no Jew should drive a car! But you only drive when it's absolutely necessary. And this detour to Jaffa was necessary. Because fucking is an urgent matter!"

But then I said to myself: "Itzig Finkelstein! Better alive on top of spindly Zippora in the Jewish brothel in Tel Aviv

. . . than with a knife in my back or my throat slit straddling Fatty Fatma in the Arab brothel in Jaffa!"

So I said to my taxi driver: "Back to Tel Aviv!"

We drove back to Tel Aviv. Stopped in front of the Hotel Queen of Sheba. I climbed out, went inside, gave the ladies the once-over, spindly Zippora included, found them all too thin, turned around and went back to my taxi. I said to my taxi driver: "I can't make up my mind. Back to Jaffa."

I talked to give myself courage. Said to myself: "Itzig Finkelstein! Everything is very exaggerated! They're definitely not going to stick a knife in your back! Not to speak of slitting your throat!" But as soon as we arrived in Jaffa and stopped in front of the Hotel Abdulla, my heart sank back into my shoes.

We drove another few times back and forth between Hotel Abdulla and the Hotel Queen of Sheba, without my making up my mind. I felt like that famous donkey who because he couldn't make up his mind starved to death between two haystacks . . . though this is not a good comparison, because I, Max Schulz, am no donkey, and a backside is not just hay. And I didn't starve to death, because I, Max Schulz, found a way out in the end. A mass-murderer is self-reliant.

XII

Have bought myself a textbook of the Hebrew language. Am making good progress. And I'm learning English too, a language with some relationship to German.

I've been playing exciting games. Last week I counted trees. Counted all the trees in the Avenue of the Third Temple, and those in Jabotinsky Street, Sholom Aleichem Street, Ruppin Street, Anski Street, Peretz Street. And I wanted to count the trees in King David Street too as well as those in the street next to it and those in Herzl Park and the palm trees on the beach. I even considered going into the Forest of Six Million Souls. But I didn't.

It's a dangerous game. I do not like counting. You know that. I didn't like counting then either. Asked myself: "Why do you count when you don't like counting?"

Said to myself: "You'll get the shakes!"

Said to myself: "If there's such a thing as a last judgment . . . and if everyone there can choose his own punishment . . . then you will say to God: I don't mind what punishment you give me . . . only don't make me count trees. It gives me the shakes!"

Please don't think that I, the mass-murderer Max Schulz alias Itzig Finkelstein . . . failed to take account of practical considerations . . . I mean to say: during my walks. Not long ago I was wondering where I should open my future barbershop or gentlemen's hairdressing salon. You understand what I mean! I don't want to be an employee forever! I want to make myself independent someday!

I have looked over all the streets in Beth David for a suitable spot. The shop has to be on a corner, since the "Man of the World," my father's salon, was also on a corner—on just the right corner!

I said to myself: "Itzig Finkelstein! First get to know the country and its people better. Learn the language. Snoop around a little. Keep your eyes and ears open. Weigh the pros and cons. Carefully. And read the papers. Hold off a little. The English will withdraw soon. And then there'll be war here. And if you have to go to war . . . it won't be good for a new business."

In the gentlemen's hairdressing salon of Schmuel Schmulevitch everything is as it was. A gold mine. It's enough to make a man's eyes pop out. Mrs. Schmulevitch, from Prussia, is as always annoying the personnel, feared by us all, including Schmuel Schmulevitch.

Schmuel Schmulevitch is as popular as ever. Doesn't have a lot to boast about. He is basically a man to be pitied. Does she whip him at night? I don't know. Naturally we are loyal to him.

Everything as before, I said. Nothing has changed. The two manicure girls are arrogant, the barbers garrulous, the shoeshine boys have smirks on their faces the whole day, the two apprentices are clumsy and lazy.

Not a soul suspects me. When I speak Yiddish, I am a Galician, a "Galitzianer," though one whose Yiddish is not good, since I have never lived in Galicia. It's understandable. I'm not a proper Galician. Just called a Galician, a "Galitzianer" as a joke. When I speak German I am a German Jew. And when I use words from the vocabulary of the Black Corps then I am a concentration-camp victim. I picked up a bit of the lingo. Basta! And why not? How could I help it. I wasn't there of my own free will!

In the gentlemen's hairdressing salon of Schmuel Schmulevitch everything is as it was. Even the political discussions. My latest regular customer, Daniel Rosenberg, who owns a textile factory—and who is rumored to be the future mayor—asks me the same question every morning: "Mr. Finkelstein! What is your opinion of the political situation?"

My answer is always the same: "And what do you think of it, Mr. Mayor?"

To that he usually says: "I am not mayor yet."

My answer then, of course, is: "But you soon will be, Mr. Mayor. I'd like to take a bet on it!"

The political situation is serious. I would even go so far as to say: very serious!

Terrorism has increased. Recently two English ships were sunk by Jewish terrorists. And an English general murdered. Nine tanks blown up with Molotov cocktails. A goods train held up, an English arms depot.

Last night the houses in Beth David shook. There was a powerful blast. I fell out of bed. Went down to the street. Couldn't see much. Saw some flames. The sky was red.

I learned what was happening only this morning. Yankl Schwartz and his men.

Shock Troop Batallion A . . . attack on Beth David Prison. Blasted the building. All terrorists formerly imprisoned by the English liberated. During the mission a number of ordinary criminals escaped. Could not be avoided.

Shock Troop Batallion B . . . street cleaning. English tanks at street corners destroyed. English street patrols shot up. Slogan . . . this is a Jewish city!

Shock Troop Batallion C . . . attack on the police station at the corner of Sholom Aleichem Street and Pinsker Street. Twenty-five dead.

A state of emergency has been declared in Beth David.

But that's nothing. New English troops are landing every day. It makes me laugh! England is bankrupt! Guerrilla warfare of this kind is much too expensive! They can't afford to stay here. The English will withdraw. And soon! And what will happen then. There will be a no-man's land right in the middle of Palestine. And two groups of the population at each other's throats: Jews and Arabs. War. There'll be war here soon!

Yes, damn it all. The political situation is serious. Of course we have to reckon with the Arabs. They're sharpening their knives and loading their guns already. Right now they are only practicing. Nothing more.

Have you read it in the paper? There it is, black on white: "Jews slaughtered in Jaffa!" Lucky I didn't go to Fatty Fatma!

Yes, it's in the papers. Headlines: "Jewish Bus Fired upon by Arab Snipers on Mountain Road to Jerusalem! Synagogue Burned Down! Arab Attack on the Kibbutz Quar Joseph Ben Nathan!" The pigs have set fire to our fields! Burned banana plantations. That was yesterday. And last week? Then we had the affair with the three Jewish villages. Did you read it? They just pushed their way in . . . into our villages . . . armed Arab men, carried off two women, burned houses down, looted. . . .

Have no fear. Once the English are gone we can take a reckoning. They're going to get a knocking. And I, Itzig Finkelstein alias the mass-murderer Max Schulz or vice versa, do not intend just to play the spectator. I'm going to join in the game. You can rely on that!

Three days of this state of emergency! Now it's over! It looks like the English want to negotiate with Yankl Schwartz. I can't really tell.

Fresh English troops have moved into Beth David.

Do I know where he is? Yankl Schwartz? No idea. Not even Schmuel Schmulevitch knows. And he is a famous barber!

No one knows where Yankl Schwartz is hiding! Nor what he looks like. I imagine him to be a giant. A Jewish giant! Perhaps he looks like the Biblical Samson.

XIII

Among my colleagues are two German Jews, Sigi Weinrauch and Max Weizenfeld. Personally I, the mass-murderer Max Schulz, consider Max Weizenfeld to be a good Jew. Whether he is pious I don't know. But a Zionist . . . that he certainly is. I would say: an idealist! An active member of the Haganah. He was a kibbutznick too and planted the first trees in the Negev.

But the other one . . . Sigi Weinrauch, he's an enemy of the people. Cracks jokes about Zionism—we used to call that sort of thing "corruption of the truth"—insults our leaders—we used to call that sort of thing "Führer defamation,"—and is always talking about the lost cause—what we used to call "dissemination of enemy propaganda and defeatism"—but the worst thing of all is that Sigi Weinrauch loves Germany!

Can you understand that? A Jew who loves Germany! In spite of the six million souls! He is no better than my boss's wife . . . the one with the Iron Cross . . . Mrs. Schmulevitch . . . Iron Cross hidden between aging breasts.

The two of them are in cahoots. That's obvious. They talk openly about the beautiful Rhine and the Moselle, about beer and sauerbraten, bread dumplings and white sausages. Those two don't like it here.

Not long ago I said to Sigi Weinrauch: "If you don't like it here, Mr. Weinrauch . . . why don't you go back to Germany?"

He said: "I'm waiting for Germany to recover."

And Mrs. Schmulevitch put her snout in also. And said: "I, too, await Germany's recovery."

And my boss, Schmuel Schmulevitch, said: "You're not really thinking of going back!"

And Mrs. Schmulevitch said: "Of course I want to go back!"

"Without me! And what about the salon?"

"The hairdressing salon . . . we'll sell it!"

As for Sigi Weinrauch, he just grinned, said nothing, just grinned. That made me real mad!

That's the sort of thing I can't understand! Practically no idealism. I gave it to both of them right down the line. Forgot completely that I had to be discreet because of my job! But Mrs. Schmulevitch didn't say a word. Just laughed scornfully.

We quarrel all day. I, the mass-murderer Max Schulz, take the attitude that our homeland is Palestine, while the two German Jews, Sigi Weinrauch and Mrs. Schmulevitch, maintain that their homeland is Germany.

A barber should entertain his customers. I talk the whole day about history, our history, Jewish history. I repeat what I, mass-murderer Max Schulz, taught his customer the American Jew about our history, talk loudly and clearly, so that everyone in the gentlemen's hairdressing salon . . . can understand . . . including Mrs. Schmulevitch and Sigi Weinrauch.

I've made myself the following schedule: on Sundays—because Sunday is a working day here—I talk about the exile of the children of Israel from Egypt. On Mondays, about the conquest of the land of Canaan. On Tuesdays: about the division of the kingdom. On Wednesdays: about the revolt of the Maccabees. On Thursdays: about the heroes of the fortress of Massada. And on Fridays: about the revolt of Bar Kokba.

This week I changed my program . . . in order to make Sigi Weinrauch and Mrs. Schmulevitch still more angry. I'm not afraid of Mrs. Schmulevitch anymore, because . . . it's a matter of honor!

On Sunday I spoke about the exile of the Jews, kept it brief.

On Monday I spoke about the turning point, a man writing a book, inspired by the Dreyfus case . . . a man called Theodor Herzl, the book: *The Jewish State!* An idea is born . . . or not born . . . merely transformed, given life . . . Ahasver leaps into the young fountain . . . a flame is sparked . . . the revolution begins.

Tuesday I spoke about the first Jewish settlements in Palestine, mentioned the First World War and the heroic deeds of the brand-new Zion mule-corps and the Jewish legion, which fought side by side with the English against the Turks, in the end forcing the Turks to flee. Talked about the Balfour Declaration and England's promise of a Jewish homeland in Palestine.

On Wednesday I spoke about mass murder, and said: "Ahasver's children!" And asked: "Why did they not come earlier? What were they waiting for?" Yes. That's how it was. On Thursday I spoke about the present. And today . . . on the last day of the week . . . I spoke about the future.

XIV

The entire morning I kept quiet. Gathering strength. Leaving the talking to my colleagues. For they are a lot of gabblers.

By afternoon my colleagues had talked themselves into exhaustion. That was what I had been waiting for.

Then I spoke in detail about the exodus of the English, while I cut several hair-stylings, all quite beautiful. Later I shaved several clients while speaking about the foundation of the Jewish state and wars with the Arabs—wars which lay before us. Shaved well and cleanly, didn't cut anybody, didn't leave any stubble, did a good job.

The more I talked the more excited I became. Little hammers knocked in the corner of my head, where my bats in the belfry were. Veils of mist wafted before my frog eyes. I cut still another short back and sides, but with my next customer I started to make mistakes, the words now coming thick and wild. I had visions, spoke of millions of small children, spoke of atom bombs, spoke of expansion, spoke of the tiny land of China, spoke of domination of the world! Felt my backside starting to itch, my member stiffening, took off my glasses, looked in the mirror, saw two giant frog eyes, saw a curl of hair flop over my forehead, and the mustache, talked louder and louder, intoxicated by my own voice . . . which . . . sounded so very much like . . . or exactly like . . . the voice on the Mount of Olives behind the altar.

My speech over, everything in the gentlemen's hairdressing salon was shaking, that is to say everything not screwed or nailed down. The shining mirrors bathed the room with reflected light. I did not know whether the customers, the staff, and Schmuel Schmulevitch and his wife had really understood the last part of my powerful speech, but was sure the tone of my voice had not failed to exercise its hypnotic effect. Because when I stopped talking, for seconds it went completely quiet in the salon, as quiet as on the day on the Mount of Olives after that mighty oration. But all at once the customers sprang up from their chairs, not bothering anymore about scissors and combs, shaving machines and razor blades, brushes and soap, and screaming like madmen: "Amen! Amen! Amen!" And the staff were screaming too! "Amen!" And so were Schmuel Schmulevitch and his wife.

[301]

I really don't care one shit whether you believe me or not. Take or leave it. I intend to tell everything. Nothing less.

That sort of thing gets around. After all, we are . . . the gentlemen's hairdressing salon of Schmuel Schmulevitch . . . the only barbershop in Beth David. Everyone comes here! Here every class of society is represented, in short: the people!

Since my speech the people have been here in long lines. Men who before had their hair cut only once a month now come very often. Many get two shaves a day or come in under some kind of pretense, for heat treatments or massages, for trims or dandruff shampoos, or manicures! Business is booming. Mrs. Schmulevitch appreciates it. She has no intention of firing me.

Not long ago Schmuel Schmulevitch said to me: "Mr. Finkelstein . . . have you noticed anything?"

I asked: "Noticed anything?"

"Yankl Schwartz's people! Terrorists!"

"What about them?"

"They're lurking about here . . . about my gentlemen's hairdressing salon. Looking through the window. Peeking at Itzig Finkelstein."

"Wonderful, Mr. Schmulevitch!"

Schmuel Schmulevitch looked at me earnestly. Very earnestly. And said: "I had a feeling in my stomach they were Yankl Schwartz's men. What's more, I believe Yankl Schwartz himself was here not long ago to take a look at you."

"Do you really believe that? . . . would you recognize Yankl Schwartz? Tell the truth! Do you really know who he is?"

"No, Mr. Finkelstein. But I can't get the feeling out of my bones: Yankl Schwartz was here in the shop. . . . I mean to say in the gentlemen's hairdressing salon."

One evening . . . on the way home from the Café Trumpeldor . . . two men blocked my way.

[302]

The street lighting here is bad, even though it's a modern town. My glasses were a little steamed up. I could hardly tell what was happening. I started to notice khaki uniforms, sun-burned faces, sleepy houses, from the windows of which fell dim light . . . saw lanterns in front of the entrance to Herzl Park, asked myself: what made you come this way? . . . saw an English tank going off in the opposite direction . . . then I, the mass-murderer Max Schulz, was dragged unceremoniously off the pavement and shoved into a taxi . . . into the front seat . . . the man sitting behind me grabbed hold of me, put a blindfold around my eyes, and stuffed a handkerchief into my mouth. The end, I thought. Now they've got you!

During the drive I began to think more clearly: who could it be? Agents of the Jewish Secret Service in Palestine? Or Yankl Schwartz's men? What was it they wanted? What did they want from me? Did they know something? Or did they know nothing?

The taxi drove slowly. Probably in order not to draw anyone's attention to it. And why had they put me on the front seat? It's different in films. In films the victim of the kid-naping is always put in the back seat . . . jammed in between his captors! What the devil had they in mind? Did they want to shoot me in the back? Just as "he" had shot Itzig Finkel-stein in the back?

I sat there stiffly. Stayed calm. But kept on the watch. And said to myself: So. Now we have driven around Herzl Park. They can't deceive me. And now . . . we're heading south! Building sites! So! Here it's bumpy. Not real pavement any-more. The building site. Is that where the headquarters is?

They pushed me out of the taxi. The ground was uneven. The night smelled of moonlight, cement, mortar, wood scaf-folding, road metal, sand, unborn children. Somewhere there were steps. They took me to them. . . . Then down the steps. Here it smelled like a cellar.

They took off the blindfold and pulled the handkerchief out of my mouth . . . right out of my mouth. I could talk again. And see again. But I said nothing. Just looked around me: a cellar, as I had supposed. Even here bad lighting. But different. A long rope. No. Not for stringing somebody up. Just a long piece of rope hung from the low ceiling of the cellar, with a few flashlights attached to it. Bright light. Yes. But not electric. It was the building site, as I had supposed.

My frog eyes . . . took in a broad-topped writing desk. And the man . . . behind the desk. Others in front of the desk. Sitting there in a semi-circle like the Arabs in Jaffa before the brothel of Fatty Fatma. But they were not Arabs . . . many of them were wearing khaki. Many not. Two had bald heads. But not the others. One was wearing a hat. Saw a woman too, in a light calico dress. Necklace around her neck. But no Iron Cross. Saw the Star of David.

Somebody shoved a chair under my ass.

The headquarters of Yankl Schwartz! Yankl Schwartz does not look like Max Schulz, the mass-murderer, had imagined him to look. Yankl Schwartz had an oversized head, horn-rimmed glasses, left eye short-sighted and dark—his ghetto eye, his right eye visionary and bright—the eye of freedom . . . one eye looking one way . . . and the other another . . . past and future behind the same spectacles . . . and where is the present?

I cannot describe his body, because I only saw his head and his eyes . . . as for his feet they were hidden beneath the desk. And I didn't want to bend down. Because bending down can be hazardous.

He was sitting behind the desk. The man behind the desk was him: Yankl Schwartz!

His voice was somewhat hoarse. I guess the past still stuck in his throat like a lump which he had to spit out.

He said to me: "Mr. Finkelstein. Not long ago you proclaimed the conquest of the world by Jewry!"

I said: "Proclaimed as a prophecy!"

Yankl Schwartz smiled. He looked straight into my frog eyes. With the one eye of the past and the other eye of the future. His looks struck me like blows, even though it was one single look.

Yankl Schwartz said: "That's not what we're after, Mr. Finkelstein."

I asked: "What do you mean?"

"To conquer the world," said Yankl Schwartz.

"Then what do you want, Mr. Schwartz?"

"To give the English a knock on the head!"

"And what else?"

"To establish the Jewish state!"

"Where, Mr. Schwartz?"

"Here, Mr. Finkelstein. Within the framework of our historical frontiers."

"And what next, Mr. Schwartz?"

"Nothing next, Mr. Finkelstein. After that we want to live here in peace."

"And what about the gate, Mr. Schwartz?"

"It will stay open," said Mr. Schwartz.

"To the millions?"

"To all . . . who want to come," said Mr. Schwartz.

Yankl Schwartz polished his spectacles, taking them off for a few seconds, then putting them back again.

I asked: "And the Arabs?"

"I don't know what's going to happen to them," he said, still smiling, although his voice seemed slightly strained. "We painted the benches in Herzl Park bluish-white," said Yankl Schwartz. "And we put a sign up in Arabic, saying: 'Be seated on the benches of the Jews!' When the time is ripe, all the benches within the lines of our historical frontiers will be painted bluish-white. And we will set up the same signs everywhere. That is a very opulent offer, Mr. Finkelstein!"

"Yes it is," I said. "That's true. But supposing they don't want to sit? What do we do then?"

"I don't know that yet," said Yankl Schwartz.

"It's a problem?"

"Yes," said Yankl Schwartz. "It's a big problem."

I said: "So that's how it is."

And Yankl Schwartz said: "Yes. That's how it is."

Suddenly I noticed my apprentice Motke among those sitting in a semi-circle. I hadn't noticed him before. So! Him too! A terrorist!

"Your sermons about Jewish history are amateurish," said Yankl Schwartz. "But you preach with enthusiasm, Mr. Finkelstein! That has impressed me!"

I saw Motke grinning. He winked at me. An impertinence! An apprentice!

"You were in a concentration camp, Mr. Finkelstein?"

"Yes."

"In southern Russia too?"

"Yes. That was earlier."

"We know that already! In your barbershop—that is to say Mr. Schmulevitch's hairdressing salon—you've remarked on it already. On your exploits in southern Russia. In conversation. And put on all sorts of airs. Am I not right?"

"Possibly. I can't remember everything I say when I'm working. You know how it is. One talks and talks."

"So it's correct? You were there? In southern Russia?"

"Yes. I was there."

"And what did you do there? Really do?"

"I used my gun to shoot with!"

"So it is true!"

"Of course. I got some shooting practice."

Yankl Schwartz nodded his head. "That's what Motke told us. So it's right."

"Yes. It's true."

"How many people did you shoot, Mr. Finkelstein?"

"I don't know. I didn't count them."

"And what sort of guns did you have, Mr. Finkelstein? Russian-made guns?"

"No. German-made guns!"

"Good," said Yankl Schwartz. "That's excellent."

Cold sweat was breaking out of my forehead. As you can imagine. But I reflected. I could still think.

It was obvious that Yankl Schwartz thought me to be a former partisan who had fought with weapons stolen from the Germans . . . on the right side . . . not on the wrong side.

"Are you still a good shot, Chaver Itzig?"

Do you notice it? The change in tone? The change in manner of address? Chaver Itzig?

I said: "Yes I am, Chaver Yankl."

"Good," said Chaver Yankl. "That's good."

XV

I could easily tell more about what went on in the cellar, but I prefer to make only a short note.

After the conversation with Yankl Schwartz coffee was

served. We had a nice friendly chat. The mass-murderer Max Schulz shook many hands, was introduced to everybody except to Motke, because he knew him. Hard liquor was served after the coffee. Then meat from the spit. Then coffee again. Everyone puffed away merrily. There are no non-smokers there. Or vegetarians. They are all normal. Or so it seems to me. Or that's the impression I had.

Did I become a member? Would you like to know? Member of the notorious terrorist group of Yankl Schwartz?

It is not for me to decide. Yankl Schwartz decides who becomes a member. He's the one who makes the final decision. No one else.

Naturally, I, Itzig Finkelstein alias the mass-murderer Max Schulz, am a member.

During the next weeks I heard nothing from Yankl Schwartz. Not until my wedding night!

What's that I said? My wedding night. But I'm getting ahead of myself. I don't want to do that. So let me tell the story chronologically:

This is what happened:
At the end of August the two manicurists Rita and Irma were fired without notice. Reason: arrogance.

Mrs. Schmulevitch said: "That's something I can allow myself. Arrogance! Because I'm at the cash desk. But when a gentleman entrusts his hand and especially his fingernails to a woman . . . parts of him which as everyone knows give away what a man does or doesn't do . . . then he is sensitive."

Yes. That's how it happened. Then one day there was a big blow-up . . . and one thing led to another . . . as the saying goes.

[308]

As a boy I once went to the circus. And there I saw the fattest woman in the world. Her name was Johanna. I fell head over heels in love with her. But that's a long time ago.

The new manicurist is called Miriam or Myra. And she is even fatter than my own mother. And fatter than Johanna, the fattest woman in the world. And if I am not mistaken, fatter than Fatma in the brothel Abdulla, even though I have not seen Fatma.

For a few days we were without a manicurist. And Mrs. Schmulevitch was nervous. Schmuel Schmulevitch too. They began to quarrel. And Mr. Schmulevitch said:

"There isn't one in Beth David!"

And Mrs. Schmulevitch said: "There isn't one here!"

"Then I'll call up the Histadrut in Tel Aviv."

"The Histadrut? What's that?"

"It's high time you learned Hebrew. That's our union!"

"I don't want anything to do with the union."

"Then we'll have to try the Mankelevitch Agency!"

"Still less with that. They're the ones who sent Rita and Irma."

That's it in a nutshell. The two could not agree. This time Mrs. Schmulevitch was also against advertising in the newspaper. There remained just one alternative: Myra!

My boss Schmuel Schmulevitch thought about it for a while, then said: "All right then. We'll take Myra!"

Myra? A niece of Schmuel Schmulevitch's from the kibbutz Degania. Not far from here.

The same evening, after the great decision to take Myra had been made . . . I, the mass-murderer Max Schulz, was invited to dinner at Schmuel Schmulevitch's house.

[309]

We were having a nice, pleasant talk:

"She was in the salon before," said Schmuel Schmulevitch, "in the spring . . . and worked well. But then she left. Went to the kibbutz."

"Why, Mr. Schmulevitch?"

"Because there's plenty to eat there."

"Does she eat so much?"

"Yes," said Schmuel Schmulevitch. "She eats a lot."

On that evening at Schmuel Schmulevitch's I learned a lot about Myra. Even if not everything:

Myra comes from a small town in the Ukraine called Wapnjarka-Podolsk. In 1941, along with all the other Jews in the town, she was shot to death in the cemetery. Which cemetery? The Jewish cemetery!

No, she isn't dead!

"She is alive and kicking," said Schmuel Schmulevitch, "even if mute. From the shock."

And so: mute.

Miriam or Myra managed to crawl out of the mass grave. Note: I assume because the SS were bad shots.

Continuation of the report:

Myra did not crawl out alone. There was another woman. An old woman.

And the old woman, who is now in Palestine and knows Schmuel Schmulevitch, told him the following:

We didn't want to stay anywhere near the cemetery. And so we went away. Anywhere. On foot. And Myra was mute and couldn't speak. But she was a good walker. Better than me. Because I was an old woman. And Myra was young.

One day we were captured. Somewhere or other. And were deported. Somewhere or other. To a concentration camp. And there we stayed. We were not shot. And not gassed. But the only thing was there was nothing to eat there. Or almost nothing.

And when we came out again in 1945, Myra was as thin as a skeleton: a stew of ribs with eyes . . . eyes which sometimes moved.

And then Myra began to eat. To eat from morning to night: even dreamed of food in her sleep! A mute eating machine.

I asked Schmuel Schmulevitch: "And how are you going to tempt such a 'freak' back from a kibbutz . . . to your hairdressing salon?"

Schmuel Schmulevitch said to me: "With a promise, Mr. Finkelstein. I'll say to her: 'Myra, my child. Naturally you can live with us again. We will be good to you. And so far as my wife's cuisine is concerned: from now on we'll have a cake every day, as much cake as you can eat!' "

When Myra came to work for the first time . . . a little late . . . I got such a shock I let my razor drop to the ground. I had never seen anything like it! Schmuel Schmulevitch was right: an eating machine. Gigantic. Mute. A mouth condemned to silence. A fat backside that has had its revenge on the years of hunger.

Myra gave us all her hand. Twenty-eight perhaps, I thought to myself. Or thirty. No more. A pretty face with dimples. But the eyes . . . like a fish, I thought. A dead fish with moving eyes.

I gave not another thought to Yankl Schwartz. I could only think of Myra. During the day in the shop . . . I beg your pardon, I meant to say in the gentlemen's hairdressing salon . . . I obviously found it difficult to concentrate. I mean on my important and responsible work. At noon I

[311]

got my meal down somehow, hardly knowing what I was eating. And of course it was the same at breakfast. And in the evening. For I eat three times a day.

The meals were not appetizing anymore. I had no nose for them. They had no smell.

At night I lay awake thinking of Myra, tossing and turning in the lonely bed . . . because suddenly it was lonely there.

Since Myra came into my life . . . with all her fat and all her mute screaming . . . I masturbate day and night. I can hardly stay on my feet. During the day I do it in the rest room of the gentlemen's hairdressing salon of Schmuel Schmulevitch, at night I do it in my lonely bed.

You see, for me Myra embodies something. I think I know what it is and yet can't be sure. Whenever I think of her the urge to destroy wells up within me, I feel an overwhelming desire to smash the world around me, to swallow it piece by piece, till it runs along my blood, swells my veins, I lose good semen, once I have lost the semen I want to spit it all out again, stick everything together again, stroke it, pat it . . . but not let go, as though I had to hold on in order to take new mouthfuls.

You see, I have become a different person . . . and yet . . . when I think of Myra . . . then I want to go through everything . . . somehow . . . again . . . the past . . . only differently, you understand . . . go through it all with Myra . . . no other way! . . . experience myself as I was and am no longer or perhaps still am even if different. You understand that? And the present too I would like to go through with her. And all our tomorrows!

Do you know what love is? I do not know exactly. But I believe the feeling that I, the mass-murderer Max Schulz, have for Myra . . . must, I think, be it . . . what I mean is . . . love!

Was I there? In Wapnjarka-Podolsk? At that place . . .
where all the Jews were shot . . . except for two . . . an old
woman and a young woman . . . even though they were
among those shot . . . but not hit for keeps?

I don't know. I saw a lot of forests and a lot of cemeteries in Poland and in the Ukraine. And certainly we were
in the area too. I mean . . . Myra's area. But I really made
a note only of the names of big cities. Wapnjarka-Podolsk
was an unimportant place . . . a paltry hole. I don't know
anymore. Perhaps I was there. Perhaps not. We never stayed
long in one place. For a few hours or a day . . . in small
and unimportant cities . . . we did our job . . . fulfilled
our duty, didn't stay long and went on.

XVI

Yesterday I had a date with Myra. We went to the Café
Trumpeldor! The waiter stared at us with open mouth and
bulging eyes.

For myself, mass-murderer Max Schulz, I ordered one piece
of cake, and for Myra I ordered ten pieces . . . five apple
pies, three pieces of chocolate cake, a piece of raisin cake,
and a cream puff.

Since Myra could not speak I had no alternative but to
carry both ends of the conversation.

What did we do next? Do you want to know? We went
to the movies. To see a film with Ingrid Bergman.

The seats were too narrow for Myra. But the owner of
the place, Mr. Mandelstamm, was kind enough to bring
one of the broad leather armchairs from the lobby, which
he set up next to the emergency exit. We held hands. I
didn't dare do more. This is Beth David! Not Wapnjarka-
Podolsk.

Myra is a good worker but not a quick one. Because she keeps stuffing herself as she works. Without stopping. And it takes time to stuff yourself!

The white apron Myra wears for work has large pockets. And they are full to bursting with all kinds of tasty morsels: figs, dates, nuts, raisins, hard bread crusts, and dumplings made from artificial flour and sawdust . . . a store of delicacies rousing Myra's appetite constantly.

The customers know Myra and bring her sweets and chocolate, as well as old bread, leftovers, scraps usually saved for their pets, because they know she likes such stuff. They were in the concentration camp too . . . many of them at least.

Are all concentration camp escapees so eager to stuff themselves? No, not all. Only a few. Most of them have gotten over their hunger. Gotten their revenge in a different way. Somehow.

As far as the staff is concerned, we have great sympathy for Myra and always leave something for her to eat from our early morning coffee breaks. All sorts of other things too . . . apple cores, cake crumbs, the pits from plums or peaches when there's still something left on them: we just put them down somewhere, carelessly—so it seems—usually in some corner, because Myra gets real pleasure out of these things only when they aren't offered openly, and are difficult to find. When they have to be hunted out, as it were.

Today I once more stood for a long time in front of the mirror, looking at my gold teeth. What would my mother say if she knew that I intended to marry Myra? She would certainly say: "Anton, come here! Max wants to get married! At forty. What do you say to that?"

And Slavitzki would certainly say: "At forty not every ass looks alike. That's when a man gets choosy."

My mother would say: "That's right, Anton."

And Slavitzki would say: "It has to be a good ass."

And my mother would say: "A Jewish ass! And moreover, fatter than mine! That's what appeals to my Max!"

The die is cast. I have proposed marriage to Myra. She just nodded her head.

My future wife: Miriam Schmulevitch! Daughter of Joseph Schmulevitch . . . shot to death on the ninth of July, 1941. At the cemetery in Wapnjarka-Podolsk.

XVII

I have no family over here. But Myra does. Schmuel Schmulevitch and his wife. Of course. But others too. Not her father. He was shot to death like I told you! And not her mother either. Nor her five brothers. Nor her six sisters. They were all shot to death. And so were her aunts and uncles and cousins, male and female cousins, from Wapnjarka-Podolsk. They were all shot to death by us. But the family Schmulevitch is large.

Myra has still more family. Apart from Schmuel Schmulevitch and his wife. Other aunts and uncles, other cousins, male and female. And where do they live? In Mea Sharim. The Orthodox Jewish quarter in Jerusalem. They are pious Jews.

I have no family over here. That's true. But Myra has family. And soon her family will be my family. We have invited them all. To the wedding. All of them.

Myra and I were married on the third of September, 1947, in Beth David, under Jewish law, by the rabbi Nachum

Nussbaum. My father Chaim Finkelstein was married in the same kind of ceremony. My mother, too, Sarah Finkelstein. Under the *baldachin!*

Rabbi Nachum Nussbaum had scarcely begun with the ceremony when my new relatives began to sob. And when I spoke the decisive words just as my father Chaim Finkelstein had one day spoken them to my mother Sarah Finkelstein, the sobbing from my relatives became still stronger. I said: "Behold! thou art betrothed to me with this ring, in accordance with the law of Moses and Israel!"

After Rabbi Nussbaum had read aloud the marriage contract and had sung the Seven Blessings, we took sips of the ceremonial glass of wine just as my father had done, Chaim Finkelstein, and just as my mother Sarah Finkelstein had done. Then I took the wineglass and threw it to the ground, breaking it into a thousand pieces, for that was the custom, and my father Chaim Finkelstein had done the same.

When we came out from underneath the *baldachin,* a newly joined married couple, my new relatives congratulated us as did a number of customers from the gentlemen's hairdressing salon of Schmuel Schmulevitch whom I had invited, and the staff added their good wishes too. They shook us by the hand and shouted: *"Mazel tov!"*

Shouted: *"Soll sein mit Masel!"*

The reception was held—out of consideration for my pious relatives—in a strictly kosher hotel: the Hotel Cohen round the corner from the Café Trumpeldor. We had rented the banquet hall for the evening.

Just imagine: long tables covered with white cloths. A festival banquet: gefilte fish, noodle soup, boiled beef with potato pudding and sweet carrots—my mother Sarah Finkelstein called them *tzimmes*—and dessert, stewed apple with raisins, nut strudel, apple strudel, cherry strudel, dates, figs, and of course coffee and tea.

Look at it in your mind's eye: a mixed bunch of guests. We, the emancipated Jews, sitting on the left, the pious ones from Mea Sharim on the right.

Imagine it: A band like in those old days, not like ours in Wieshalle, but like the one in Wapnjarka-Podolsk, playing Yiddish songs. And playing gypsy music.

And just imagine: the band playing for dancing. The pious Jews from Mea Sharim, in long black caftans, caps and fur hats, dancing among themselves, forming circles, snapping fingers, beards twitching—the *Mitzvah Taenzel.*

The pious Jews drag me, the mass-murderer Max Schulz, down from his seat—a friendly gesture—and invite me to dance with them.

We are all a little groggy from drink. The pious Jews laugh, snap their fingers, swish with their beards, and dance around merrily in circles. Sweeping me with them. I dance with them. Feel groggy. Everything looks different. Myself included: I see myself with the sack of gold on my back. See myself dancing. See my victims. They're joining in the dance.

A dance of death. And we, the living, are in the middle. And the music is playing for us.

No! No dead corpses are going to make me weak. If the dead want to dance with me I have nothing against it.

I stagger back to my seat, plunk down in my chair, hold my head in my hands. One of my relatives gives a loud laugh. I can't stand it. A laugh like that. What is there to laugh about!

I hear voices: "He danced well! That's how a bridegroom should dance! But he's drunk!"

Damn it all. I'm not drunk!

Was I there? Or was I not there? In Wapnjarka-Podolsk? And what happened to the press? My name is not mentioned anymore? Nowhere. But I keep on with my collecting: reports about the mass murder. See other names. Never mine. Isn't it important anymore?

No. I'm not drunk. Not really drunk. But why not? Why should I not be?

I emptied a few bottles of wine . . . good wine . . . sweetened. Sank under the table. Wanted to sleep off my thick head.

Myra then took me home.

Schmuel Schmulevitch advised us to live for the time being in my hotel room, until the new apartment houses in the south of the city were ready and we, Myra and I, took his advice to heart. My room has space enough. Only the bed! Too narrow! Much too narrow!

When Myra and I arrived home after the festivities there was a happy surprise awaiting us: a new bed! Delivered secretly during the afternoon. A present from Schmuel Schmulevitch and his wife. A gigantic bed. You've never seen anything like it. There was a card on it: "For Itzig and Myra, with sincere good wishes, Mr. and Mrs. Schmuel Schmulevitch."

Naturally you will want to know whether Myra was a virgin and if so, whether I, the mass-murderer Max Schulz, penetrated this important secret during the wedding night?

I tried to find out. I tried seven times. But seven is an evil number.

I said to myself: "Itzig Finkelstein! You're drunk. And

[318]

your snake is asleep! In a firm deep sleep! He's not stirring!
Not even the fattest woman in the world can rouse him
now!"

I fell asleep. At two o'clock in the morning there was
a knock on the door. First, very soft. Then, a little louder.
Angry, I took a look. Who could it be?
It was the terrorists!

XVIII

I said to Yankl Schwartz's men: "It would have to be tonight,
my wedding night."
They said: "Get dressed, Itzig Finkelstein. Tonight is the
night!"
I said to them: "You know what? I've been thinking about
it. I don't want to have anything to do with it anymore. I've
done enough shooting. It's all over for me!"
And do you know what they said to me: "Get on with
it! Get dressed. Don't start making a fuss now!"
"And suppose I don't want to?"
"An order is an order!"
And I said to them: "That's what they used to say too!"

The terrorists are fighters, genuine freedom fighters. In those
days . . . all you did was murder the defenseless! The innocent! And women and children and old men!

I got dressed. Kissed my wife good-by: Said to her: "Myra!
The fatherland calls!"
Then cleared out.

We left the town by roundabout ways. Behind the building
sites, in the south of the town, the desert began. The night

was damp and hot and quiet. In the Forest of Six Million Souls the jackals howled.

I marched as the last in the line of men and women. Noticed my apprentice Motke. He slowed up his pace, waited for me and suddenly began to jog along beside me.

I said to him: "Now, Chaver Motke. I've really got myself into something this time!"

"Chaver Itzig. You were always such a good talker!"

"Yes, Chaver Motke. That's true."

We passed through a dried-out river bed. A pale moon hung over the landscape. Strange animals lurked among the white lime rocks, we shooed them away, they slithered across our path and vanished. We stumbled over skeletons—of beasts or men . . . difficult to say which in the darkness . . . croaking birds beat their wings against the walls of the ravine.

I said to Motke: "Not one of us is carrying a gun!"

"We get the guns later," said Motke.

"Where?"

"In the Wadi El Bakar," said Motke. "Yankl Schwartz is waiting there for us with the rest of his men. It's a river valley further to the south."

Motke laughed softly. "And we're going to get English uniforms too, to make us look like Englishmen."

"Like Englishmen?"

"Like Englishmen, so that we can get right up to the barracks."

"Which barracks?"

"The English barracks," said Motke. "The Empire Barracks near Tulkarem."

"And how do we get there?"

"In lorries."

"And what do we want with the Empire Barracks?"

"Steal weapons—a few lorries full, hopefully. We're going to need them."

"For the War of Our Future?"

"Right," said Motke.

My apprentice stumbled, and I grabbed hold of him. "Keep your eyes open, lad!"

"Yes, Chaver Itzig."

"When is the attack, Motke?"

"Not till dawn."

"Why not in the dark?"

"I don't know, Chaver Itzig. But I think it's because we're going to drive right up to the barracks in English uniforms just as if we were a normal convoy."

A short while later, as we were marching through the Forest of Six Million Souls, I broke out in a cold sweat.

In the Forest of Six Million Souls, I could hear the ancient trees praying . . . even though no ancient trees are there. I could see them and I could hear them. I could see their foliaged eyes uplifted toward heaven and I could hear the words: *"Shema Yisrael, Adonai Elohenu, Adonai Echath!* Hear Oh Israel: the Lord our God, the Lord is One!"

No reptilian creatures anymore, as there had been in the dried-out river valley, but I saw giant black birds, much more gigantic than those in the valley. Birds circling above the treetops, necks cocked and beaks wide open as though panting for air: up there above the trees they circled and croaked their song toward the yellow moon.

The ancient trees in the Forest of Six Million Souls blessed their brothers, stretched higher than the other trees, spreading wide their gnarled branches. I saw how younger male trees pressed female trees to their barked chests, how female trees acquiesced and stroked the males . . . with one hand only . . . while the other leafy hand patted gently the crowned saplings which sprouted below them, boughed faces hidden beneath the flowered aprons of their mothers.

And I saw all that as we were marching and I caught too the stench hanging stale upon the forest. A strange smell that made my stomach retch and my throat grow acid. I'm not sure what it was, but I think it was the smell of gas and gun powder and wet prayer books, but also the smell of fear, of fear strangled at prayer, the smell of a fear different from the other fear we all have known . . . and it was the smell too of our dear beloved God. Just a little. Just a teeny bit the smell of our dear beloved God.

I said to my apprentice Motke: "Chaver Motke, I don't like the smell around here."

"It smells of young trees, Chaver Itzig."

"Didn't you see the old trees?"

"No, Chaver Itzig. We only planted the forest two years ago."

"And did you see the Six Million?"

"Not them either," said Motke. "We haven't planted as many as that yet. This is only the beginning."

And Motke said: "The beginning, Chaver Itzig."

Yankl Schwartz attacked the Empire Barracks with two hundred people. We fought with the rising sun at our backs, mowing down the English with our sub-machine guns as they were blinded by the sun and before they had had a proper chance to come to their senses and ask the important question: "What's up?"

I fought in Shock Troop Unit C. Our unit arrived a little later, after Shock Troop Unit A and Shock Troop Unit B were already in the interior of the camp and the barrack yards and had cut a path through the barbed wire, blown up the broad entrance gate with holy hand grenades and holy dynamite, and blown the three watchtowers out of the holy earth.

Our losses were negligible. Our booty was large: ten lorries full of ammunition and weapons for the War of Our Future.

XIX

After his first mission the mass-murderer Max Schulz took part in six further missions: blew up a bridge, derailed a train, robbed a bank, attacked two military camps and an English tank and lorry convoy on the Tel Aviv–Jerusalem road.

Rumors about me are going the rounds. No one knows anything for sure. Especially in the gentlemen's hairdressing salon of Schmuel Schmulevitch!

It's not just that I'm "sick" so often . . . but the negligence of my apprentice Motke. He opened his trap not long ago, Motke. He himself is not suspected. But: Itzig Finkelstein is!

In the gentlemen's hairdressing salon of Schmuel Schmulevitch it is known that Finkelstein is a terrorist . . . even though they cannot tell for sure.

Mrs. Schmulevitch is scared of me. She has taken off the necklace with the Iron Cross and put on an extra-large Star of David. And that she doesn't hide between her aging breasts. She wears it openly and obviously. Not long ago she said: "Mr. Finkelstein! Every night I pray for the final victory!"

The old witch—she just wants to impress me. I said to her: "Those were the words the Führer used, Mrs. Schmulevitch!"

Immediately she corrected herself and said: "I pray for

the freedom of the Jewish people! And for the resurrection!"

On the street no one fails to greet me. Even my waiter in the Café Trumpeldor has behaved toward me lately with an exaggerated attention which is almost embarrassing. Keeps my papers off to one side and cuts out the reports about mass-murderers for me, in order that—in his own words— "Mr. Finkelstein can drink his coffee in peace, coffee with cream!"

I have noticed: when the waiter serves me coffee, his hands tremble.

No. Here we have no traitors. The English don't know anything yet.

Time goes by quickly. That's true. It's already the middle of October. I'd already been on six missions. Then I was on my seventh. And seven is an evil number.

During the seventh attack . . . the attack on the English tank and lorry convoy on the Tel Aviv–Jerusalem road, our men were chopped up. Yankl Schwartz was killed.

After that the Schwartz group disintegrated. A few people went over to the terrorist group of Irgun Zvai Leumi, others to the Stern Group, but most of them, among them myself, joined the Haganah, the Jewish underground army.

I said to myself: "Max Schulz! Back in 1933 you made a wrong choice! And lost! No man can afford to be a two-time loser! Or to choose wrongly twice! You will continue to fight for the Jewish state. With body and soul. And if there's no such thing as soul then just with your body! Max Schulz! These Jews can reckon with you!"

The decisive battle of the future still lay before us. But military maneuvers continued. The Haganah trains every week, sometimes in one place, sometimes another, mostly in the Judaic mountains.

On the average my new comrades in the Haganah are younger than me. But here every man is needed. And I'm a good shot. Very good. A talent such as mine cannot be turned away.

XX

Itzig Finkelstein broke both his legs on the first of November, 1947, during a maneuver.

The Haganah people took Itzig Finkelstein into the Hadassah Hospital at Beth David.

Further: he stayed there until the twenty-seventh of November.

On the twenty-seventh of November, Myra took him home.

On the twenty-ninth of November, his room door was open. His neighbor's room door also, his neighbor who had a radio, which Itzig Finkelstein did not have.

On the twenty-ninth of November Itzig Finkelstein's neighbor had turned his radio up very loud. Because of that, Itzig Finkelstein learned of the United Nations decision . . . even before his fat wife Myra brought him the happy news . . . because she happened not to be there, that is to say, not at home.

On the twenty-ninth of November, 1947, Itzig Finkelstein heard . . . from his bed . . . through the open doors . . . his own door and his neighbor's door . . . that "the plan to divide Palestine has been passed by the Plenary Session of the United Nations with a vote of thirty-three against thirteen with ten abstentions!"

Further: that meant the English would withdraw!

Further: that meant . . . two independent states in Palestine. An Arab state! And a Jewish state!

At last! A Jewish state! Even if only a small one, chopped

and abbreviated and not so long and broad as Itzig Finkelstein and Yankl Schwartz had hoped, namely following the demarcation lines of the historical frontiers . . . but nevertheless: a small state! Better a small state than none at all! After all wouldn't it be possible to make it bigger?

As soon as Itzig Finkelstein understood or grasped the full implications of what he had just heard on the radio, he leaped out of bed, jumping for joy. But he was jumping the gun! Because for the time being the state existed only in the filing cabinets of the United Nations.

Further: Itzig Finkelstein broke one of his legs again. Because the fractures had not yet healed properly.

I was taken back to the Hadassah Hospital. Stayed there until January 1948.

On the twenty-second of January, 1948, my fat wife Myra took me home. I had to stay in bed until the fourteenth of May. I had to wait till the fourteenth of May before I could jump for joy again. I jumped out of bed with a single bound.

On the fourteenth of May, 1948, or, to be more precise, on the fifth of Iyar, 5708, by the Jewish calendar, the last English troops withdrew . . . and the Jewish state was officially proclaimed: the state of Israel!

When I leaped out of bed with a single bound early in the morning all this was quite settled. But I knew: today is the great day! The sun had already risen and no one could take this day away from us! This time I was not jumping the gun!

Schmuel Schmulevitch had closed the gentlemen's hairdressing salon . . . at three o'clock in the afternoon already in order to go home in time to hear the radio. Myra and I collected him at the shop since we were invited to dinner.

My legs were still fairly weak . . . as was our young state
. . . but I didn't show it . . . we sauntered at a leisurely pace
along the Avenue of the Third Temple. The crowd on the
street was excited, but had not yet begun to celebrate, waiting
for the great "historical proclamation" which the loudspeakers
were about to give.

"Today is Sabbath eve," said Schmuel Schmulevitch, as we
turned into Jabotinsky Street. "On the Sabbath we always have
gefilte fish and noodle soup and boiled beef, sweet carrots and
stewed apples and nut strudel and apple strudel," Schmulevitch
said. "I've insisted on that."

Myra nodded. And I said on her behalf: "Yes. Myra likes to
eat that."

"Me too," said Schmuel Schmulevitch. "But not my wife."

"So . . ." I said.

"Today she didn't want to," said Schmuel Schmulevitch.
"She didn't want to cook what I like. She's made sauerbraten
and potato dumplings instead. I couldn't help it."

"It's really not suitable," I said. "Today of all days when
the Jewish state has just been proclaimed."

"It's because we had a quarrel yesterday," said Schmuel
Schmulevitch. "It's my wife's way of getting her little own
back."

"Making sauerbraten and potato dumplings?"

"Yes," said Schmuel Schmulevitch.

I asked: "Will we be eating them this evening? After lighting the Sabbath candles?"

"No," said Schmuel Schmulevitch. "Because my wife missed
her lunch today. So we'll be having dinner earlier tonight."

"Before lighting the Sabbath candles."

"This afternoon," said Schmuel Schmulevitch.

I really felt sorry for Schmuel Schmulevitch. Lucky that I,
mass-murderer Max Schulz, am not married to such a woman.

[327]

Mrs. Schmulevitch obviously had put herself to some trouble: the sauerbraten was first class, just as were the dumplings. We dug into them with a healthy appetite, even though it was not yet evening.

As soon as the voice on the radio began to read the first words of the Declaration of Independence, Myra raised her massive head uneasily. I could see a thick German potato dumpling sticking in her mouth. She could neither swallow it nor spit it out.

We all looked at Myra. The radio droned on. The whole world was listening along with us. It was a great historical moment.

Suddenly I leaned over, pulled the German potato dumpling out of Myra's mouth . . . and put it back onto her plate. Myra looked at me with her strange staring eyes.

The voice on the radio carried on undisturbed. Suddenly Myra began to cry. I had never seen Myra cry before. We others sat there as though transfixed, as though nailed to our seats. And Myra wept. And the voice on the radio spoke to us, telling us that now everything was past. The Eternal Jew had laid down his pilgrim staff. At long last The Eternal Jew could take a rest. And Myra wept. I saw: the numbness in her eyes become liquid, melted, flow down from her eyes, flow out from the mirror glass of her soul, over cheeks and chin, dropping onto the mashed-up potato dumpling . . . now lying on her plate.

At first Myra wept without a sound. But Myra wanted to weep loudly. Her mouth was gaping open. But no sound came from this mouth. The thought ran through my mind: what a lot of potato dumplings must be in there! And she wants to spit them out!

I thought: the invisible potato dumplings. Those are the

[328]

right potato dumplings. And while I stared at Myra, I kept hoping that she would spit them out!

Myra was trembling throughout her whole body. Her fat face was shining with sweat. I wanted to bend over and embrace Myra, but Schmuel Schmulevitch held me back.

The voice on the radio was talking to Myra. And Myra was weeping. Weeping with open mouth. And spitting out her potato dumplings. And the voice on the radio was talking. And carrying on undisturbed by Myra.

Suddenly a convulsive thrill shot through us all . . . for Myra had uttered a scream . . . and then . . . all at once . . . Myra . . . the mute . . . began to speak!

XXI

During the first night of our independence, I had not slept. Myra my wife was to blame, because she talked incessantly, as though trying to make up for lost time. I lay there awake, holding open my tired frog eyes and watching Myra's potato dumplings come spilling out into the night.

As morning dawned I received my call-up orders.

War! All over the streets loudspeakers babbled: five Arab armies on the march across our new frontiers!

Do you remember my prediction, that one day the major war of our future would begin?

The minor war with the Arabs had begun a long time ago. I had missed it because of my broken legs. But that war was not too important for me. It was merely a kind of civil war, between Jews who were for and Arabs who were against the plans to divide Palestine, a war which had taken place under the very eyes of the angry English during the last months of the

[329]

mandate. The large Arab armies, assembled beyond the frontiers of the mandate, had not involved themselves directly, and could not, as long as the English were still here. But the large Arab armies merely kept themselves at the ready to march in one day . . . on the key day! . . . to destroy our new state, and throw the Jews into the ocean . . . including me, the barber Itzig Finkelstein.

The large, official war of our future, on which I had counted and for which I had waited, was a war for our future, and it was logical for it to begin in the dawn of the new future.

The large Arab armies were all over us with their heavy tanks, and their airplanes flew quicker than the "Hamsin" . . . the mischievous desert wind, which even the ancient prophets had feared.

I said to myself: Itzig Finkelstein! The Jews should cross themselves!

During the first weeks of war our convoys of tanks consisted for the most part of old buses, disguised a little of course . . . protected by steel plates and provided with dangerous spy holes and hastily mounted machine guns; and we had in addition, lorries, private cars, taxis, all similarly protected, and of course at the head of our tank convoy the maneuverable milk and honey carts of the firm Nudelman and Co. Milk and honey had been the things to entice us here formerly, and when symbols are driven to the front, then it is a time of bitter earnest.

During the first weeks of the war we were no better off for airplanes. The Haganah had bought them up somewhere, I do believe out of the moth-eaten airplane collections of anti-Semitic antique dealers, who were hoping that we would break our necks. Sure they could fly, but no higher than the clouds above Beth David during the rainy season . . . and no quicker. We had bombs too: wooden boxes filled with dynamite. They were heavier than air, and fell, following the law of gravity, always downward, exactly what we wanted.

And we had big guns, too. Even a few new models, but most of them were ancient and called up memories inside me, memories of history books which I had read as a child: the battle of Waterloo! Napoleon's famous cannons!

Yes, that's how it was. Exactly so and not otherwise.

Naturally we had revolvers and rifles, and other weapons, even bazookas and mortars, sub-machine guns and light and heavy machine guns. But it was not enough. That was the truth of it: we didn't have enough!

Where there was no bazooka, there was the heroic spirit of the Maccabees! Our boys leaped onto the enemy tanks with hand grenades and Molotov cocktails. Units of the Haganah with no real mortars attacked the foe with the "Davidka," that is to say the "Little David," a homemade Haganah mortar loaded with dynamite, which made one hell of a bang— and—so the saying went—made the walls of the Omar Mosque shake, and not only the walls, also the shrine inside, the Sakhra Stone, as well as the strands of beard from the prophets which were kept there.

We were fighting a foe far superior to us in arms and equipment. But we held our position. We fourght boldly. Because we knew what we were fighting for!

Then ships reached our harbor. More weapons were delivered. Were distributed hastily. The first Jewish tank units of any size—this time real ones—rolled to the front. New guns appeared in our units. New mortars and other kinds of weapons. And high up in the sky appeared new airplanes —airplanes displaying the Star of David, flying higher than the clouds and quicker, even quicker than the "Hamsin."

Naturally you will want to know whether I, Itzig Finkelstein alias the mass-murderer Max Schulz—a man with a weak heart —was at all fit for war service?

I have been keeping something quiet. I had a medical examination some time ago . . . by the Haganah doctors. They laughed at me . . . the doctors, I mean, when I told them of my heart troubles in the past. They just said: "It's all in the mind! You're fit as an ox! Itzig Finkelstein!"— naturally I tried to explain my case, and not because I wanted to get out of anything . . . on the contrary . . . I wanted to fight . . . merely in order to establish clear relationships with them, the Haganah doctors, and make them understand that I, Itzig Finkelstein, a man with heart trouble, was ready at all times in spite of my illness, to go to war. I told them: "In the past . . . gentlemen . . . because of my heart . . . I was transferred . . . to the back lines . . . the Hinterland I mean . . . as far back as possible . . . namely . . . by order of the medic in our unit."

They just looked blankly. Not understanding what I was trying to say, not knowing what kind of Hinterland nor what doctor and what unit I was talking about. Merely said: "The doctor in your unit just wanted to do you a favor, Itzig Finkelstein. And so he wrote you down as sick." I said: "And what about my dizzy spells? And my anemia? I had all those then!"

"That was for other reasons."

"And the heart attack in Veronja's hut?"

"That was no heart attack," said the Haganah doctors, even though they had no idea what I was talking about.

"Could that have had something to do with my bats in the belfry?"

They laughed and said: "It's possible."

In the first weeks of our great war for the future, I, Itzig Finkelstein, alias the mass-murderer Max Schulz, fought in the "Jerusalem Corridor." The city of Jerusalem was under siege. We had to break a corridor through the enemy surrounding lines in order to be able to establish a lifeline into the city. Then after I had fulfilled my mission, was transferred to the Egyptian front, conquered one village after the other, one city after the other, and finally on a beautifully clear and sunny autumn day, marched into Beersheba.

During the first month of the rainy season we had driven the Egyptians out of the Negev, and stood before the Sinai Peninsula with our victorious troops. But we were not permitted to go further, had received strict orders to stay put, even though our boys would very much have liked to go on to Cairo or even further.

During the summer of 1948, our army had been transformed. Out of the Haganah, basically a bunch of civilians thrown together for fighting purposes, had in the meantime developed the fully equipped, fully uniformed Israeli Army, the *Zahal*. I myself, Itzig Finkelstein alias the mass-murderer Max Schulz, was a newly promoted sergeant and damned proud of my rank.

That's how it was. But you know how it is: the better things are going, the more demanding one becomes. It was the same with our army. The officers began to cast a critical eye . . . upon my feet. There was something they didn't like although I was after all a sergeant and a real one.

Toward the end of December 1948, I was demoted to

[333]

behind-the-lines supply duties because of my flat feet. There was nothing to be done.

Then came the incident:
I received orders to bring fresh provisions to the front line. There was not much of it left. Of the front, I mean. It had been shot and maimed. Hung there like a motionless curtain, light at day, dark at night, between our victorious troops and the defeated Egyptian Army.

I left with my men to get the provisions. I sat in my jeep, next to the driver, sub-machine gun across my knee, ammunition belt fastened, hand grenades on my left hip, watching through the mirror the lorries in my charge coming up behind me . . . and my boys. My driver drove at a comfortable speed, supposedly into the Hinterland . . . but started off in the wrong direction.

It was my fault, I had lost my compass. That was the truth.

We drove straight ahead, kept going straight ahead, and by the time our convoy finally stopped . . . we were hard by the Suez Canal.

I said to my driver: "Now, Yankl (his name was Yankl too), are you under the impression that this is the river Jordan?"

And Yankl, my driver, said: "No, Itzig (he called me simply Itzig), I am not."

"So what do you think it is, Yankl?"

"The Suez Canal!"

I left my jeep, took my shoes off, washed my flat feet in the Suez Canal, then went back and climbed into my jeep.

I sat in my jeep, thinking. We hadn't met any Egyptian troops anywhere. There was no opposition. I was in a position to order my men to cross the Suez Canal and march on in the direction of Cairo.

But what would happen then? I began to think of the political consequences. For the moment Egypt was still in the English sphere of influence. The Sinai Peninsula too. A Jewish invasion into these territories would force England to intervene. Could we—a small, new-born land—afford a war with England?

I spoke with my driver about my misgivings. He said: "In the event of English intervention, I could telegraph my uncle in America. And he would demand an audience in the White House."

"You mean to get the Americans involved on our side?"

"Right."

"The Americans won't do that. Not against England."

"I suppose you're right there," said Yankl.

"You have an uncle in France as well, don't you, Yankl?"

"Yes—but I don't think that the French will go to war."

"Now listen, Yankl. In the event of English intervention our defense minister would have no alternative but to ask for Russian troops. And you know what that means?"

Yankl nodded his head. "A Third World War!"

Irresponsibility! No more of that for me, mass-murderer Max Schulz. Now I was Itzig Finkelstein! And so I gave my men the order for a "tactical return," not to be confused with a "strategic retreat."

Once more we got back to our own lines. We were arrested. Reason: "Advance against Orders!" We all were court-martialed. But acquitted. Reason: a mistake!

The press reported the incident with headlines. With of course, diplomatic embellishment. The text ran: "Chief-of-staff brings back the barber sergeant Itzig Finkelstein personally."

That was to make a good impression abroad. I read several different newspapers, and came across headlines like the following: "Itzig Finkelstein, the Wolf-eyed Warrior!"

Or: "A Jewish Hero!" Or: "Judas Maccabeus Has Risen Again!"

Or: "Ghetto Jew a Thing of the Past!"

Shortly after that incident, I, Itzig Finkelstein, was demobilized. When I got back to Beth David the whole town was in an uproar about the victory. Everywhere there were blue and white flags. In the windows, on top of roofs, balconies. The flags waved merrily in the wind, stretching upward toward the sun, as it gazed out tired and exhausted from behind the clouds. Because the rainy season was upon us. Big heavy clouds hung over the city.

That was just the beginning. Much more lay before us.

When I got home I was astounded. Myra had lost weight. We kissed long and passionately!

Myra asked: "What about the war?"

"We won!"

"Did the Arabs sign?"

"They will sign."

"A peace treaty."

"No."

"What then?"

"An armistice agreement."

"And what about the peace?"

"That's something we'll have to hope for, Myra."

XXII

Schmuel Schmulevitch has died. A heart attack!

I went to his funeral and even bought myself a black top hat, though that's not the custom here.

For a few weeks I rested. Not until the beginning of March, a few days after the signing of the armistice agreement between us and the Arabs did I, Itzig Finkelstein, go back to work at the gentlemen's hairdressing salon of Schmuel Schmulevitch. That was still its name.

I was astounded at how much everything in the salon changed with Schmuel Schmulevitch's passing. There were huge numbers hung on the barbershop chairs. Number one, number two, number three, number four, and so on. There were extra chairs with extra numbers in the dressing room, and two barber chairs without numbers were placed each in one corner near the wide show window.

I asked my colleague Jizchak Spiegel: "What is all this supposed to mean?"

"We're just following a new order of Mrs. Schmulevitch's, Mr. Finkelstein."

"A new regulation?"

"Yes, Mr. Finkelstein. Take a look: barber chair number one, the one by the window, the best barber chair in the salon, right by the window, you understand . . . that one . . . is reserved for German Jews!"

"Oh I see! And what about barber chair number two?"

"That's for Jews who come from other West European countries."

"And number three?"

"For elite Eastern European Jews."

"And who are they supposed to be, Mr. Spiegel?"

"The Russians and the Lithuanians."

"And barber chair number four?"

"For Jews from the rest of the Eastern European countries. Except Rumania."

"And where do Rumanian Jews sit?"

"On the last chair reserved for Jews from Eastern Europe. On chair number five."

I looked at Jizchak Spiegel horrified. Thought of the house door number—33/45! Thought: "Aha! So that's how it is!"

Jizchak Spiegel explained to me next that barber chair number six was reserved for the elite of oriental Jews: namely the Yemenites, after which came the others: on the last chair reserved for oriental Jews sat the Moroccans.

Jizchak Spiegel shrugged his shoulders apologetically, then explained the rest of the sequence which went right into the dressing room.

Then I asked: "And what about the two chairs without numbers near the window?"

"One is reserved for the 'sabras,'" said Jizchak Spiegel. "Those are the Jews born in this country, Mr. Finkelstein. We can't classify them."

"And what about the other one, Mr. Spiegel?"

"That one is for non-Jews. For new citizens of the state who are not Jews. For foreigners too. We let them sit by the window as a gesture of courtesy."

I said to myself: "Itzig Finkelstein! Not everything here is in order. But why should everything be in order? Things don't go quickly. We need time. And patience. Yes, patience above all. Ahasver has swallowed too much dust. After all he was on the road for two thousand years!

[338]

"Just bide your time. Have patience! We can bring about miracles. We have got the state. We can also get the model state!

"Think of the birds circling above the young new trees. Don't they have to bide their time? Until the trees have grown? Don't they have to wait for leaves to come? And the fruit?

"We are only at the beginning!"

Book Six

1950: Moved to a new address. The apartment of Mr. Daniel Rosenberg, the future mayor of Beth David. Because he had a large apartment, but was having financial problems.

1951: Moved to yet another address! Our new house! In the new, completed southern part of the city of Beth David. A one-family house with a huge sun terrace. Made the down payment . . . with black dollars. A very pretty house it was. All new furnishings, not too expensive, but tasteful.

1952: Inherited some money. From Myra's uncle in Mea Sharim. Uncle Abraham Rabinsky, a brother of her mother, who had emigrated in time. Died in 1952 after a short illness.

1953: Bought the gentlemen's hairdressing salon of Schmuel Schmulevitch from the widow of Schmuel Schmulevitch!

No. She did not move to Germany. She was an old, tired woman. Moved to her pious relatives in Mea Sharim.

I, Itzig Finkelstein alias the mass-murderer Max Schulz, became in 1953 the proprietor of what he had always dreamed. Of course I gave to the shop—I beg your pardon I meant to say the gentlemen's hairdressing salon—another name. I called it: "Man of the World," proprietor Itzig Finkelstein.

Does it lie on a corner? Of course! It's situated on a corner. And on the right corner too!

1954: Redid the furnishing of the salon. Comfortable leather armchairs for customers awaiting their turn. Cocktail tables. Ashtray stands. Newspaper and magazine tables. Walls decorated with pictures.

Because of the competition! You understand! We were no longer the one and only gentlemen's hairdressing salon. Beth David had undergone massive expansion since the great victory. There were new houses, new barbershops, new hairdressing salons.

The competition! Don't make me laugh! Who is there who can compete with Itzig Finkelstein? Respected! An idealist! An orator! A terrorist! A member of the Haganah! A man who fought at the front! A man who washed his feet in the Suez Canal? In the sign of the Star of David! A hero of the people! And apart from all that: a good barber, a first class barber, and a true artist.

The numbers! On the barbershop chairs! Gone! It wasn't me who took them down, even though I, Itzig Finkelstein, was against the numbers. My employees took them down! Now what do you say to that?

Confidentially, that sort of thing couldn't last! The people are against numbered barbershop chairs! There are a few barbershops and hairdressing salons which still have them but they are becoming fewer and fewer. Disappearing one by one.

We don't have a model state yet. But we are working at it. And we are making progress. We are on the way to it.

After the great victory of 1948–49, after we had opened the gates of the Holy Land to all Jews, a flood of new immigrants began pouring in . . . the first million . . . the beginning of the many millions we had counted on, and which we had waited for, and which we prayed would one day come.

There were many idealists among the newcomers, people in the mold of Trumpeldor, the one-armed hero of Tel Chai. But there were others too. There were people who could not adjust. People who had neither the will nor the energy. These people wanted to leave again: to go back to Europe or even to America.

I am the sort of person who flies into a rage when a Jew tells me that he doesn't like it here. I can, however, understand a lot of these people: the concentration-camp survivors. Many, like Myra, were able to recover, but many could not. We had driven them into the ground, finished them off. Deadened their souls. What can you expect from such people? Can you expect them to be enthusiastic about anything? What nonsense!

Many of these dead souls came to my hairdressing salon. I took them under my wing, spoke with them about history, about our mission, about the great work of construction which lay ahead for the Jewish people. I told them: "Here we need every hand, every arm and every head. Those who go back to Europe are traitors! And whoever goes to his aunts and uncles in America is just as bad!"

I failed to convince these people. But I did hypnotize them. These people did not leave. They stayed and helped us build.

Yes. That's how it was. And one day . . . one day future mayor Daniel Rosenberg said to me: "Mr. Finkelstein! Everything gets talked about! Including good deeds! You have done a good job!"

And then said: "And when I'm drinking coffee with the Minister of Culture next time . . . I will not forget your name."

There was a certain newspaper announcement, which for me was the most important event of the year 1954.

It goes without saying that a posh hairdressing salon subscribes to foreign newspapers. And what is it that I discovered one day? An announcement! A certain announcement in the Munich *Observer:*

GENTLEMEN'S HAIRDRESSING SALON OF ANTON SLAVITZKI
HUBERT ROSNERSTRASSE 20
NEAR STACHUS
MUNICH.

Now what do you say to that. So he was in Munich! My mother too, surely!

Did I write to them? Or make any other kinds of attempt to come into contact with them? No, I'm not that dumb! Both of them are surely under observation by the police. They're just waiting for me, the mass-murderer Max Schulz, to run into such a trap one day.

II

After the great victory in 1948–49, the victory of the stronger will, our tiny land began to develop at a hectic pace. At last the desert was freed from the lordship of the goyim. Once again it demanded our attention, not waiting any longer it began to roll angrily its gritty sand eyes, bare its crunchy teeth, and whip out its hot wind; in short: it was jealous of the narrow band of land made arable.

[344]

That was the situation. You have to understand it. There's no joking with the desert. That was something our government realized. Ambitious plans were made, a new extensive construction program, intended to overshadow all that the old pioneers had done for us before the foundation of the state. The government had new streets built which were better than the new streets of the old pioneers, and new villages and new towns better than the new villages and new towns the old pioneers had built. New names began to appear as dots on the map, and our new Chalutzim had their hands full to do better than the old pioneers had done. The desert screamed for all sorts of things, but mainly for more trees, partly because, I assume—or so the rumor goes—trees attract rain.

That's how it was. The desert screamed. And our new Chalutzim heard the scream.

I saw it all, kept my frog eyes open. I saw how here everything changed, flourished and grew, was happy about the new cities and villages, about new meadows and fields . . . most of all about the specially planted trees.

No. I have stopped counting the trees. I have not tried it ever again. It's hopeless. There are far too many now. And who wants to go nuts trying to keep count? Not me, that's for sure!

1955! An important event: foundation of a local society for the prevention of cruelty to animals—SPCA! President: Itzig Finkelstein.

To this humane concern I, Itzig Finkelstein alias the mass-murderer Max Schulz, have applied all my energies during the year 1955. And my essay—an attack on modern chicken farms—appeared in the largest daily newspapers of Beth David, under the headline: "We Demand Freedom of Movement for Chickens!"

That's how it was. In 1956 not much happened. Apart from a short war which only lasted a few days. I missed it, unfortunately—had the flu—and when I got out of bed again, the war was over.

Make a note of its name: the Sinai Campaign.

III

In 1957 I put up a giant sign in the window of the hairdressing salon "Man of the World." On the sign were the words: "Itzig Finkelstein, inventor of the newly discovered hair-growing lotion *Samson* V-2." In order to promote the old alongside the new, I put a second sign next to it, a smaller one of course, not so striking, about a well-known but useless recipe for night cream. On it was written: "Itzig Finkelstein's Night Cream for Men, from a tried and true formulation:

200	grams of beeswax
300	grams of spermaceti
500	grams lanolin
500	grams olive oil
10	grams borax
10	grams attar of roses

During the next two years the mass-murderer Max Schulz planted a small flower plot, and in the little earthen patch behind his idyllic, small, one-family house a vegetable garden of tomatoes, onions, radishes, and parsley. Besides that Max Schulz had acquired a rabbit hutch and a chicken run. I must add at this point, however, that the doors of the chicken run and the doors of the rabbit hutch were always open and are still open, leaving the little animals free to choose between staying in the hutch and wandering about to their heart's content.

Otherwise nothing important has been happening, I mean, during the two years that followed. Not until 1960 . . . when I had trouble . . . in the matter of war reparations.

One of my customers, attorney Dr. Franz Bauer, a German Jew, started talking about it one day while getting a haircut. He said: "Mr. Finkelstein! Are you aware that the new West German government, which is going through an economic miracle, is paying Jews reparations?"

I said: "Of course I know."

Dr. Bauer then said: "The Germans are shelling out for bone dust, heart soap, concentration camps staggers, diarrhea, fear of death, and so on . . . also property losses, career damage, damage to your health, imprisonment compensations, and so on. So you, Mr. Finkelstein, as a former Auschwitz prisoner, could surely get quite a lot! If you like I can take over your case."

I got hot and cold shivers down my spine. The last thing I wanted was investigations. I didn't want to fill out forms, give data, produce papers, look for witnesses, apply for documents. That was precisely what I didn't want.

"Dr. Bauer, as a prideful Jew I cannot accept such money. How can you calculate the cost of fear of death in your very marrow in terms of money? I don't want to talk about it. Not even about loss of property or damage to my career. This money stinks of ground bones! Let my parents rest in peace!"

I had raised my voice on purpose. And as so very often . . . the affair was soon being talked about.

The very next day one of my customers approached me.

"Mr. Finkelstein. As president of the Association for the Prevention of Cruelty to Animals in Beth David, would you be willing to be president of an association for the refusal of reparations also?"

It seemed a good idea. I said: "Noblesse oblige!"

And the customer said: "Very well, Mr. Finkelstein. Noblesse oblige!"

On the third of February, 1960, I, Itzig Finkelstein or the mass-murderer Max Schulz, founded the "Association for the Refusal of Reparations."

Since our membership was unfortunately very limited, I placed an advertisement in our local daily newspaper once a week. And in order to make the club more attractive, especially for young ladies, I invented the "anti-reparations haircut for ladies."

The idea did not fail to have its effect. Young ladies—including of course some of the older generation—joined our movement, teeming into my salon, in order to have the anti-reparations haircut for women executed by the president of the Association for the Refusal of Reparations in person. A brilliant piece of business!

My attorney Franz Bauer crossed over unfortunately to the competition, after however first writing me a letter. He wrote: "Mr. Finkelstein! You refused these monies! And now have the impertinence to make capital out of the indignation of your association members!"

One observation: I have shaved off my beard! And thrown away my glasses! Under the pretext that I don't need them anymore: my eyes have improved. I have let my hair grow again! It is ice-gray, even though I am only fifty-three years old. But that's how it is. I can't change anything. And I've gotten fat. And have a double chin. Who could possibly recognize me now?

In 1961 my cousin from Poland came over, Ephraim or Froike Finkelstein, a former Communist, now a Zionist, the one surviving son of Moishe Finkelstein, the brother of my father, Chaim Finkelstein. My cousin's wife and his ten children had been put to death in the gas chambers. But my cousin had married again and now had another wife and another ten children.

You can imagine how glad Myra and I were. The same month yet another cousin came over, from America. He was here by chance as a tourist and had seen my announcement in the newspaper, just as had Froike my other cousin, who had read the advertisement even though he was not a tourist.

Of course we had a big celebration. As you can well imagine. A family party just like in Pohodna.

My cousin Froike said: "I saw a picture of you once. As a small boy. At that time you were blond and had blue eyes."

And I said: "Oh, come on, dear Froike! The years don't pass without leaving their traces! The nose changes when you give it a bash—and I got a few bashes in the concentration camps—and hair turns gray with time even if it was once blond . . . when a man has seen what I have seen, dear Froike, blue eyes easily become fish eyes."

Then jokingly I added: "Or frog eyes."

That seemed reasonable to my cousin.

IV

If only we had peace here. Yes, if only we had peace. But we don't!

I don't think I ever told you about the Arab refugees . . . about the crowds of them who fled . . . during the great first decisive battle.

We did not drive them out. On the contrary. We had

painted our benches bluish-white. We wanted them to sit down next to us. But most of them did not want to.

Many of them stayed. Many fled. Why did they flee? I do not know. Perhaps because they were afraid of people like Yankl Schwartz, even though Yankl Schwartz was not opposed to the sign . . . you know the one I mean . . . the sign in Arabic which invited them to sit down next to us: on the bluish-white benches!

But now they cannot come back. We do not want them anymore. That you must understand. It's a question of the bluish-white benches.

You see they want to come back in order to paint our bluish-white benches in their own colors. We know that. And they know it too. And that is what cannot be. Reflect a moment: we are a small people. And we have wandered for a long time. And the bluish-white benches have to stay put somewhere! And somewhere they must stay for good! Because there must be a place where we ourselves decide whether or not we have the right to sit down . . . can you understand that?

And I never told you anything about the disturbances on the frontiers! Or the Arab terrorists who cross our borders at night. Or about the mines. Or about being shot in the back. It is not quiet here. Yet it is beautiful. I have seen this land grow. And I love this land. And I love the bluish-white benches.

In the spring of 1967 the smell of war was already present. It was still not quite round the corner, but there was something in the air. I could tell.

The great Arab states are up to something. The small ones too. They are lining up behind the refugee barracks. They want our country. They are using the refugee bungalows as a pretext. That's what. And behind the refugee barracks, and

[350]

behind the large and small Arab states . . . stands the Soviet Union. Waiting to swallow us all. It doesn't look good. Not good at all.

Yet I had other worries. Quite suddenly my wife Myra became pregnant. What do you say to that? After so many years! After a childless marriage!

We went to the doctor. He asked me: "How old is your wife?"

I said: "Fifty. Or forty-eight! I don't know exactly!"

And Myra said: "Forty-five."

And I said to the doctor: "Oh hell. Why do you ask a woman how old she is? What does it matter? She's pregnant. *Basta!*"

For Myra and me there could be no doubt: it could only be a son! And we decided between us to call our son Judas, after Judas Maccabeus, the great Jewish freedom fighter. Myra then said: "Or Jehuda! It sounds better!"

So I said: "All right then. Jehuda!"

Smirkingly I told Myra of the announcement in 1907, when I, Itzig Finkelstein, first saw the light of the world, told her about that unique birth announcement which my father, Chaim Finkelstein, had put into the *Jewish Spectator* in my honor and said to Myra: "We must do the same thing! In honor of our son Judas or Jehuda! Let's draft it now!"

"Is it not a little premature, Itzig?"

"No. Important things have to be prepared for!"

I got right down to work, full of anticipation, feeling already what it was like to be a father, and drafted the birth announcement, similar to the one of 1907, or at least sounding like it:

"I, Itzig Finkelstein, barber, owner of the well-established gentlemen's hairdressing salon 'Man of the World,' former member of the Schwartz terrorist group, Haganah soldier,

sergeant in the Israeli Army, veteran of the year 1948, first
Jewish soldier to reach the Suez Canal at the head of his
men, on the thirtieth of December, 1948, president of the
Association for the Prevention of Cruelty to Animals in Beth
David, president of the local Society for the Refusal of
Reparations, inventor of the famous hair-growing tonic *Samson*
V-2, have the honor to announce the birth of my son and
heir Judas or Jehuda Finkelstein."

I then drafted the answer of the citizens of Beth David,
which I would hand over in good time to the mayor, Daniel
Rosenberg—for in the meantime he has become mayor.

"We, the citizens of Beth David, are happy to congratulate
barber Itzig Finkelstein, former member of the Schwartz
terrorist group, Haganah soldier, sergeant in the Israeli
Army, veteran of the year 1948, first Jewish soldier to reach
the Suez Canal at the head of his men, on the thirtieth
of December, 1948, president of the Association for the
Prevention of Cruelty to Animals in Beth David, president
of the local Society for the Refusal of Reparations, inventor
of the famous hair-growing tonic *Samson* V-2, on the birth
of his son and heir Judas or Jehuda Finkelstein."

V

And then came the war. A war that was over just as fast as the
one in 1956. Before you could say hey-lads-hey it was a thing
of the past.

Naturally I wanted to go to the front. I said to myself:
"Itzig Finkelstein. Your wife is pregnant. She is going to present you with a son. And he should be proud of you. Because
this time . . . Itzig Finkelstein . . . it's an important war. You
must join in. It is the third battle of decision. And all good
things come in threes. And there is much more at stake. The
bluish-white benches are at stake. And the old historic fron-

tiers are at stake, a long way from our present boundaries. And Jerusalem is at stake. The old city is at stake. Because the Wailing Wall is in the old city—the remains of Solomon's Temple, the most holy shrine of Jewry!"

And then I said to myself: "Itzig Finkelstein! One day your son should be able to say: 'My father, Itzig Finkelstein, was the first Jewish soldier to reach the Wailing Wall.'"

But they didn't want me. Too old, they said. I then went and rescued my old uniform from the moths in the cupboard and rummaged out my old marching orders, from the General. Then I fetched my sub-machine gun from its hiding place in the cellar, and ammunition. And my steel helmet. And hand grenades. And food from the kitchen. And out of the garage the old shot-up jeep as well.

Myra was in Tel Aviv with my cousin Froike Finkelstein. Visiting. Myra knew nothing. Did not know that I, Itzig Finkelstein, intended to do my bit in the war.

I had my jeep hastily repaired and next day left: in full battle dress and with the General's marching orders in my pocket, after having changed the date on them.

I left for Jerusalem very early in the morning. My head held high. Above, squadrons of airplanes flew. New jets bearing the Star of David. They eclipsed the sun, blacked out the sky. Here below the streets were blocked by our tank convoys. But I got through!

As I was driving through the Forest of Six Million Souls, I had a flat tire.

I said to myself: "Didn't you just have the jeep repaired?

"By the time you've had it towed away and put right, the war will be over.

"And the Wailing Wall recovered!

[353]

"This damned forest! And these damned trees! It's their fault!

"Six million souls!

"And who will reconquer the Wailing Wall?

"A Jew! . . . no other may reconquer it.

"Are you not a Jew?

"I am one . . . but not from the perspective of these trees . . . of these six million souls!

"Because only they know the truth!

"You cannot fool them. Even though you are circumcised. They know exactly who you are.

"Yes, damn it all. They know that my circumcision is worth nothing! They know that circumcision is a bond with the Lord, the unique and eternal God, and God has never made a bond with you, Max Schulz.

"Then God knows the truth too?

"I shit on God!

"And who are you? If you are no Jew, not a real Jew?"

And I heard the answer of the trees.

"You are the last. The last in rank. Among the circumcised. And among the uncircumcised."

I asked the trees: "And why am I the last?"

The trees said to me: "The last of the last!"

I asked the trees: "And why? Is it because I have shot people to death differently or hung them differently or beat them to death differently . . . than the last of the last?"

The trees said to me: "Because you do not acknowledge your guilt! Because you deny it! And hide yourself! Among your victims, of all places . . . the surviving and dead victims!"

I bet you would like to know whether Myra had a son? Yes. It was a son. He had neither arms nor legs. He had

[354]

neither body nor face. He had only eyes. Gigantic frog eyes. And they fixed themselves upon me once, then closed forever.

VI

The ghost ship! The *Exitus!* The *Resurrection!* Do you remember? A phantom, that ghost ship. Like life. Does it or does it not exist? Did it or did it not happen? Was it all a dream?

I never visited Hanna Lewisohn again, and as for Teiresias Pappas—occasionally I read something in the newspaper about him, and I never saw Max Rosenfeld again, nor any of the others . . . except for one!

Yes. One of the passengers on the *Exitus* or the *Resurrection* showed up later . . . once again . . . after the third war of decision . . . in December . . . December 1967.

Do you remember Judge Wolfgang Richter? The small-time county court judge from Germany, a Jew without soul-scent, smelling a little of beer, the pub, potato dumplings, and saurkraut. He had taken an interest in me then. And in the case of Max Schulz!

What did he look like? Can you really not remember anymore? The one who looked like Churchill. And he smoked cigars too!

One day without warning he turned up in my salon.

Judge Wolfgang Richter is an old, tired man. Eighty at least. Or more! Lives not far from us. Lives on a pension and reparations money. Moved to Beth David because Beth David looks like Tel Aviv but is smaller and is not so damp and not so noisy. Of course he discovered my barbershop . . . you can't miss it . . . saw my name too . . . above the door

. . . and on the signs in the window, and thought: or probably thought—Itzig Finkelstein! Judge Wolfgang Richter. An old, tired man. And lonely. Very lonely.

Myra often invites him to dinner: she feels sorry for him. That's how it is. Confirmed bachelors are in general not popular, but when they are as old as Judge Wolfgang Richter, as old and as tired and lonely, then people feel sorry for them.

Once—during the evening meal—Myra said to him: "Have you seen Itzig's collection?"

And Judge Wolfgang Richter said: "No. But it interests me."

"Itzig is a collector," said Myra. "He bought himself a filing cabinet and has folders in all possible colors. He has a stamp collection. And a butterfly collection. And other collections. All possible kinds of collections."

I said jokingly: "I collect letters too. But I don't show them. Too personal."

"I'm not interested in letters," said the judge.

"The important ones are in code," I said. "No one can read them anyway."

"I'm not interested in letters," said the judge.

Myra laughed. And said: "Sometimes Itzig gets fanciful."

After the meal we moved back into the living room, since we don't have a smoking room. Judge Wolfgang Richter smoked a cigar and I smoked my usual Camels.

"Now I remember," said the judge. "You were already a collector on the ship. Unless I'm mistaken what you were collecting then was reports about mass murders?"

"Right," I said. "I still collect them."

"You told me in those days . . . about a certain Max Schulz?"

I nodded my head. And said: "That's right. A mass-murderer whom I knew personally."

[356]

"Was he ever caught?"

"He was never caught."

We smoked, and drank cognac. Myra was in the kitchen and didn't disturb us.

"In 1945," I said slowly, "I found an article and cut it out. There were all sorts of things in it about Max Schulz!"

"What was in it?" asked the judge.

"All sorts of things," I said. "All sorts of things. But you know that already! I used to carry the article in my pocket . . . on the ship . . . in 1947 . . . I showed you the article. You read it."

"Possibly," said the judge. "But after all that's more than twenty years ago. I can't remember what was in it."

The cognac was good. French cognac. Judge Wolfgang Richter was astounded to be able to drink such good cognac at a barber's.

I told him everything that was in the article: about the first murders in Poland, then the mass shootings in southern Russia, about Max Schulz's supposed heart attack, his transfer into the Hinterland . . . back to Poland . . . into the Hinterland, even though in those days even southern Russia was Hinterland, and told him about Laubwalde, the concentration camp without gas chambers . . . and the mass shootings there, which were so very similar to those in southern Russia and yet a little different. Told him of documents which have been found . . . about Laubwalde, told him what was written in the article, told him about the first troops of the Red Army . . . and about the flight of the SS through the Polish forest. And about the partisans. And about the last ambush. And about how the SS had been wiped out. Except for two who escaped: Hans Mueller and Max Schulz. I told him everything that had been in the article.

I said: "The names of the two hunted criminals used to

appear from time to time . . . in the papers . . . then suddenly they disappeared."

The judge smoked and drank his cognac. "Hans Mueller doesn't interest me. Only Max Schulz interests me!"

"Me too. Only Max Schulz!"

Myra came out of the kitchen and sat down with us, but saw that we didn't want to be disturbed and went away again.

"You were very interested in the case on the ship," I said. "In the case of Max Schulz. Can you really not remember anymore? You promised me to clear up the case one day!"

"I can't remember," said the judge. "It's too long ago."

"Oh come now. It's definitely true. We even made a bet. A bottle of champagne."

"I can't remember," said the judge. "It's too long ago."

The old man was not lying. It was too long ago. He could only remember the name. The name Max Schulz . . . and also the fact that I was a collector, a collector of reports about the mass murder. Nothing else. I had refreshed his memory.

The conversation began to be great fun. I held off awhile before telling my secret, and for the time being told him only about the childhood of Max Schulz, and how this childhood had seemed through the eyes of his playmate Itzig Finkelstein. After I had told him everything about the childhood of Max Schulz, I said:

"Dear Judge. Many years ago I told you that Max Schulz shot my parents to death. At least, I hinted at it. On the ship. In a conversation. Do you remember?"

"No," said the judge.

"They were in Laubwalde too."

"So . . ." said the judge. "And you are still convinced it was Max Schulz who shot your parents to death?"

"Still," said I. "Just as before!"

[358]

"But you can't know for sure," said the judge. "You were not there!"

I said: "But I assume so."

"Max Schulz was not the only SS man in Laubwalde!"

"That's true," I said. "And yet I assume so."

And then I told him my secret.

"Look here," I said to the judge. "I imagine the following scene:

"A truckload of Jews arrives in Laubwalde. The Jews are driven out of the wagons with whips and barking dogs. My parents are among the Jews. And among the SS men is Max Schulz. My parents see Max Schulz! And Max Schulz sees my parents!

"My parents know what they are in for. They didn't know it before. Or at least nor for sure. But now . . . behind the barbed wire . . . now their eyes are opened. They see the dogs. And the SS. And the long, open graves. And those who have already been shot lying in the graves. They catch the smell. They know everything.

"My father is the first one to discover Max Schulz. Sees him standing over there . . . between other SS soldiers. Runs up to him. Goes on his knees in front of him. Begs. No. Not for his own life. Begs for the life of my mother.

"My mother sees my father. And sees Max Schulz. And runs over. To the two men. And drops to her knees. Begs. No. Not for her own life. Merely for the life of my father.

"My father weeps. Calls out: 'Max Schulz! You were my apprentice. We were good to you.'

"And my mother calls out: 'What have we done to you?'

"The SS officers laugh. They watch Max Schulz. Max Schulz can smell the question: Did you know these Jews? Were they your friends?

"Max Schulz wants to clear himself. He cannot deny that he has known the Jews, because they knew his name. But they were not his friends. He could never admit that. They were just Jews. Nothing more. Of no importance to him.

"Max Schulz points his guns at the heads of the two kneeling Jews.

"Max Schulz shoots them."

"It's possible, I suppose," said the judge. "Your version almost convinced me."

For a while we were silent. I offered the judge a couple of Myra's homemade flat cakes. But he declined.

"He would have shot Itzig Finkelstein too," I said to the judge.

"Perhaps," said the judge. "But Max Schulz couldn't do that, since Itzig Finkelstein was not there. After all you're here."

I said: "Yes I am. But it could have been done."

The judge smiled. I said: "Just imagine . . . if Itzig Finkelstein . . . had arrived in Laubwalde in another cartload."

"Would the same thing have happened to him then?"

I shook my head, saying, "No. It would be wrong to think that. Itzig Finkelstein would never have gone on his knees."

"So it wouldn't have happened."

I said: "Not like that!"

The judge asked: "How then?"

"Approximately as follows," I said. "You see, it is well known that Laubwalde was no work camp but a death camp. But, after all, workers were needed even in a death camp! For digging graves, burning corpses, cleaning the latrines in the barracks and all sorts of other jobs. You see my point. And they needed people in the camp kitchen too!

[360]

"Max Schulz sees Itzig Finkelstein. Picks him out all of a sudden among the newly arrived prisoners. Max Schulz draws the attention of his seniors to Itzig Finkelstein, saying to them: He looks strong! He can still work! And one of his superior officers says: 'Yes. Bring that one out of the group!'

"Itzig Finkelstein is put to work in the camp kitchen. Max Schulz visits him often. After all they were friends once.

"The other SS soldiers notice. One day one of his comrades says: 'Watch out, Max. Don't talk so much with the Jew. Jew fraternizers are sent to the front!'

"Max Schulz wants to clear himself. He has to do something!

"Max Schulz shoots Itzig Finkelstein to death! But not from the front, from behind!"

"And why from behind, Herr Finkelstein?"

I said: "Because he was afraid to look him in his eyes!"

The judge thought I was a garrulous old fool. We kept on talking for a while. Then the judge nodded off. Later Myra came into the living room, woke him up, and said:

"Judge Richter. It's after ten o'clock. We're just ordinary middle-class folk. We go to bed early. And my husband has to go to the hairdressing salon very early tomorrow."

I accompanied the judge part of the way, purely out of courtesy. As we said good-by, the judge asked:

"Did we really bet a bottle of champagne, on the ship . . . more than twenty years ago?"

"Yes. If you cleared up the case of Max Schulz."

"Strange that I had forgotten that. I am getting old."

"That's how life is."

"And does the bet still stand?"

I said: "Of course."

[361]

VII

The judge had not come around for a long time; then one day he came into my hairdressing salon triumphantly and said: "Herr Finkelstein! I've come to claim my bottle of champagne. I've solved the problem!"

I asked: "What problem?"

"The whereabouts of Max Schulz. And why the press has kept quiet all these years!"

I was shaving Mayor Daniel Rosenberg, and had to take care, could not let my hands tremble, but I did tremble, nicking him neatly underneath the chin—good that it was not his jugular vein . . . dropped the blade to the ground, picked it up again, apologized, and said: "Something is wrong with my blood circulation."

It was quite simple.

Judge Wolfgang Richter is a man who easily gets bored, who is retired, doesn't have a decent job, lives on a pension and reparations money, in short: a man who has time, enough time to write boring letters . . . letters to the proper authorities: to the authorities responsible for hunting down mass-murderers on the loose!

Did Judge Wolfgang Richter achieve anything? Of course he achieved something.

He cleared up the case!

The result of Judge Richter's inquiries:

Max Schulz is dead! His body was found on the second of June, 1947, by the Poles! Judge Wolfgang Richter even succeeded in drumming up a newspaper article dated June 10, 1947, in which there was a short factual report about the death of Max Schulz in a small German provincial newspaper: the Warthenau *Advertiser*. Apparently the only newspaper which considered my death important, or important enough to report.

I have read the article. I, Max Schulz, froze to death during the winter of 1945 in the Polish forest. My body was found by Polish farmers close to a section of the woods where an ambush by partisans on a lorry convoy carrying retreating SS soldiers had taken place, a few miles from Laubwalde, a former concentration camp. The Polish peasants who found me cut off my head. And my member. Then took my boots away. And took my money and papers and other things I had on me, burning everything they didn't need, but leaving my uniform!

Monstrous, isn't it? The peasants didn't even report the incident. Not until June 1947, when some lumberjacks found my corpse, which had already decomposed. And had no head. And no penis. And no boots. And no papers. But was in uniform!

You can take my word for it. I am not being hunted anywhere. Not by any authorities in the whole wide world.

The world has forgotten me. And who am I? Max Schulz, a sergeant! I was a sergeant in the Israeli Army. And was a sergeant in the SS. The two things are not the same. But I am a sergeant. And a sergeant is not important! A small fish is not important either. And I was after all only a small fish among many other small fishes. There were thousands like me, small-time mass-murderers, who later went underground somewhere. Naturally there were large, very large fishes as well among the mass-murderers, whose names had made headlines in the important papers, or were still making them.

The world has forgotten me. And Judge Wolfgang Richter had informed himself well. With good old German stubbornness. Just one paper had carried a report of my death. No others. It wasn't important enough. That is sad.

I said to the judge: "A pity that I overlooked the article in the Warthenau *Advertiser*."

And the judge said: "Dated the tenth of June, 1947. We were on the high seas then, and there were no newspapers with the latest news!"

I said to the judge: "How can the authorities tell that the corpse really was that of Max Schulz?"

"Because everything was gone over carefully. Time of death, place, uniform, and so on. As a former judge I could tell you a lot about such things, but after all it's more than twenty years ago. It's not important anymore. Forget it."

"But in those days there were other SS units in the Polish forest," I went on stubbornly. "Marching through the Polish forest on the retreat toward Germany. Surely it could have been another SS man?"

"But it was Max Schulz," said the judge.

"It could also have been Hans Mueller," I said. "The camp commandant, who managed to get away along with Max Schulz on that day. Yes. Why could it not have been Hans Mueller? He was there too."

"I don't know that," said the judge. "But put your trust in a former judge: the authorities have proof that the dead man was Max Schulz and not Hans Mueller. You have to trust the judgment of the authorities!"

I said: "It was not Max Schulz!"

And the judge said: "But it's been established! Do you want to be cleverer than the authorities?"

VIII

My trial took place in March 1968. On a Thursday!

We—that is to say Myra and myself—often have visitors. Mostly neighbors. I could describe them, and I would do it. But I find them boring . . . and I, Itzig Finkelstein, have at the moment no patience to describe boring people. The only ones among our frequent visitors who are not boring are Jizchak Spiegel the barber, with whom I share professional interests, and Daniel Rosenberg the mayor, who is an important man . . . but I don't need to describe them, since you know them already.

On Sundays the Ruckensteins, who have a grocery store, come over, and on Mondays the Blumenthals come . . . ladies' underwear. Moishe Lewi, the motor mechanic, comes on Tuesdays—he's the one who mended my old jeep—on Wednesdays, Jizchak Spiegel and his wife and on Fridays Daniel Rosenberg, the mayor, who comes with his whole family.

Yes, you're right. I left out Saturday and Thursday—purposely. On Saturdays or on the Sabbath or on the Shabbat Myra and I have developed the custom of going on an excursion. And on Thursdays Myra, my wife, has her coffee circle. That begins in the afternoon and goes on until ten o'clock at night.

I, Itzig Finkelstein alias the mass-murderer Max Schulz, am excluded from that. The coffee circle is only for ladies!

Some thin, some fat, some pretty, some not pretty, some still young, some no longer young . . . Myra's friends.

On Thursdays, I play cards: gin rummy with Wolfgang Richter, the judge. Since men are not welcome in my apartment on Thursdays . . . because of the coffee circle . . . we play in the gentlemen's hairdressing salon "Man of the World."

This is how it happened:
We were playing cards. We stopped at about nine-fifty P.M., because I go to bed at ten o'clock . . . and so we stopped playing, put the cards back into their packs, laid them on the newspaper and magazine table, and were just about to leave, when the judge made a remark which made me, the middle class barber who goes to bed early rather than late, forget the time. The judge said:
"They buried him cockless and headless! He didn't deserve any better!"
I asked: "Who?"
And the judge said: "Max Schulz!"
I don't know why the judge started off that way. It was obvious that the judge had no desire to go home yet, into his lonely room, his lonely bed, had no desire to gaze at four bare walls and a bare ceiling, wanted to talk a bit, knew very well that I . . . Itzig Finkelstein . . . would forget the time, would forget that it was almost ten o'clock, that I was a simple homely type, and that my wife was waiting at home . . . he knew I would stay and talk with him . . . if he began to talk about that subject . . . began to talk about Max Schulz . . . he knew that . . . he knew that this subject was my weak spot . . . and he took advantage of it
The judge began to make jokes about the death of Max Schulz, especially about the cutting off of his head and the cutting off of his penis, squinting at me through amused eyes, provoking me, causing me finally to make an ill-considered observation. I said:
"He is not dead. He is alive! He is as alive and kicking as a Sabbath carp that hasn't been caught."

[366]

"And how come you can know that so exactly?"
In a rage, I blurted out: "I just know it!"

"I can understand you, Herr Finkelstein! You are hunting him. Hunting him in your mind. You are not satisfied that he, Max Schulz, died without a trial. I can understand why you, Herr Finkelstein, want him to be alive, to be caught, condemned, and executed. You busy your mind with him. I can understand that. For after all you believe that he was the one who killed your parents. And you believe that he would have killed you too, if you, Herr Finkelstein, had been there, in that concentration camp . . . in Laubwalde. But he is dead! Dead as a stone! He froze to death in the Polish forest. And he has been found. Without a head! And without private parts!"

Sometimes lack of an imagination amuses me, if it's found in a woman like Frau Holle. But to be quite honest I would have expected more from a man like Wolfgang Richter. I was annoyed! I said:

"For you things are simple. You want to spare yourself the trouble of thinking. That's typical for a small-time county court judge. Max Schulz froze to death. Case closed. But let me tell you, Judge, things are much more complicated than that, much more complicated than you imagine complicated things to be!"

We had sat ourselves down again around the card table.

I said: "In the Polish forest it is cold. During the winter I mean. And it was winter then. It was cold then. So cold the spit froze in a man's mouth. And the tears on your lashes. The lashes too. Yes. Where was Max Schulz supposed to be going? The forest was swarming with partisans. And the Red Army had already arrived. The evening before. They had occupied the forest as day was dawning. So where was Max

Schulz supposed to be going? To the local peasants perhaps? They would have eaten him alive in their huts!"

I took a deep breath and went on: "It's true Max Schulz should have died in the woods. Because the Polish forest is a Polish forest. A man like that doesn't come out of it alive. Not under those circumstances, or at that time of year. Because it can be assumed that he had no food with him . . . or had had no time to take food with him . . . because he jumped down from the lorry . . . like Hans Mueller . . . that's well known . . . or it was well known . . . jumped down and ran! Without food! And without a place to go! In that devilish Polish cold! Frozen to death! Starved to death! Done with! Case closed! But things are not so simple, your honor!"

I gave a jeering laugh and continued:

"Max Schulz ran into the forest, looked around for a trench, some abandoned bunker, by chance found one, and as it were fell over himself getting in. And there it was warm. Or rather: not warm, but not so cold as outside or above ground. You follow? And then . . . next morning . . . Max Schulz crawled out of the bunker . . . wandered around in the forest for a while . . . stumbled over the dead . . . his own comrades . . . but didn't stay long . . . where the dead were I mean . . . but kept on going and wandering around . . . and looked for and found a warm farmer's hut!"

The judge laughed: "You have quite an imagination, Herr Finkelstein! That I can truly say! And what was in the hut? A Polish peasant I presume? And he beat him to death? Right?"

I said: "Wrong. There was no peasant living in the hut. Just an old woman. She saw Max Schulz. And thought he was a god. But one who had lost his power. And she kept him in her hut in order to give beatings to the powerless god. And to rape him! And put him to shame!"

"You're out of your mind, Herr Finkelstein. You're going too far. That sort of thing is pure fantasy."

[368]

I went on cautiously: "I am giving loose rein to my imagination, only to demonstrate to you that there are possibilities or were possibilities . . . for Max Schulz I mean . . . possibilities!"

"To survive?"

"Yes. Your honor!"

I told the judge my story. Told him about the winter. And about the spring. And how I wandered through the Polish forest . . . with the gold teeth in the sack on my back . . . walked . . . in the direction of Germany. Told him about my circumcision. Told him about Max Schulz, who changed his name. Told him about his new name. Told him about Itzig Finkelstein. Told him about the countess. And about the Hotel Fatherland. And about the *Exitus*. And about the *Resurrection*. Told him everything. And when I came to the end, I said: "Your honor, I am Max Schulz!"

The telephone rang.

Of course I have a telephone. Two in fact. One at home. And one in the shop . . . I beg your pardon, I meant to say the gentlemen's hairdressing salon! I'm not badly off, thank God!

At the first ring, the judge stood up, picked up the phone shouted, "Oh, it's you, Mrs. Finkelstein! Yes. We're still here. Your husband has gone mad!" Then went on a little more calmly. "No. You don't need to come over. Better not. I'll look after him."

IX

I said: "Just imagine I am really Max Schulz! And imagine . . . this hairdressing salon is a courtroom! And just imagine . . . I am the accused. Just imagine: You are my judge!"

I am convinced that the judge did indeed think I was mad

. . . and went along with the game merely in order not to provoke me any further . . . it could of course also be that he was enjoying the game, because I, Itzig Finkelstein alias the mass-murderer Max Schulz, had placed him for the last time in the judge's chair, him, an old man living in retirement: but above all, I, Max Schulz, offered him, the former small-time county court judge, a major trial—a murder trial!

The judge asked me: "Where is the jury: And where is the clerk of the court? And where are the witnesses? And where are the attorneys? And where is your laywer? And where is the court doctor? And the police? And the public? And the reporters? And all the others?"

I said: "We don't need them!"

"Why not, Herr Finkelstein?"

I said: "Herr Schulz. Please call me Herr Schulz!"

"Why not then, Herr Schulz?"

For a while I kept my eyes on the judge. Saw a few tiny hairs in his nose and his ears, and thought: "Sometime I must cut those off." Then thought: "Why not now?" And so I pulled him, the judge, down from his seat, eased him onto the first barbershop chair, near the window, took a pair of scissors, cut the hairs out of his nose and ears, sat myself down next to him in the second barbershop chair, and said: "So you see? The accused is not standing before the judge! He's sitting next to him! They are sitting next to each other: judge and accused!"

"And what is that supposed to mean, Herr Schulz?"

"An unusual judicial procedure. We are going to renounce the usual procedures, and get on without an attorney, a defense, and all the other appurtenances. We are working together as partners!"

"As partners?"

"Yes, indeed, your honor. Let me assure you that I, Max Schulz, have the same aim as you!"

"And what would that be?"

"To work out a punishment for me that would satisfy my victims."

Did I tell you already about my new icebox? In the dressing room. Yes. I have a new icebox there.

I brought out a bottle of wine. White wine. Chilled. Refreshing. Then took two wineglasses. Went back into the salon. Poured out some wine. Had a drink with the judge. Said:

"Let's go through with it in a quite unconventional way. In order to emphasize our partnership. Just straight through."

"Unconventionally?"

"Yes. We can even call each other by our first names. I'm Max. You're Wolfgang. Understood?"

The judge drank his wine and lit himself a cigar . . . invited me to sit down, and said:

"So, Max, sit down next to me!" And said: "I've never been through a trial like that before!"

A hairdressing salon! Two men! In a gentlemen's hairdressing salon!

See it before you: a long wall mirror. Four eyes. The eyes of the judge. And the eyes of the accused.

"Guilty!"

"I went along with what was done! Just went along with it! Others went along with it. It was legal in those days!"

"Guilty!"

"And besides I have bats in the belfry, Wolfgang. Don't forget that. I've always had them."

"Guilty!"

"Yes indeed. Guilty! It's a matter of opinion. But if you like, Wolfgang, I'll go along with it. And so: I am guilty!"

"In this case . . . my sentence is: death by hanging!"

"How many times, Wolfgang?"

"Six million times!"

"But we don't know whether it was six million, Wolfgang. It could have been a little more, or a little fewer. Besides I didn't kill them all. I mean: not all six million. I was just involved."

"How many did you kill with your own hands, Max?"

"I don't know exactly. I didn't count them."

"Approximately, Max."

"Approximately ten thousand. But it could have been a few more. Or a few less. But to give you a round figure, ten thousand!"

"Let's agree on that, Max!"

"Fine, Wolfgang."

"And so: ten thousand it is!"

"Yes, Wolfgang!"

"Then my sentence is: death by hanging ten thousand times!"

"Now listen, Wolfgang. You can't really want to hang me ten thousand times?"

"Oh yes I can, Max!"

"But that's not possible, Wolfgang! I only have one neck!"

"That's true, Max. What are we going to do?"

"I don't know, Wolfgang."

"Then we'll just hang you up once!"

"But that's not possible either, Wolfgang."

"And why should that not be possible, Max?"

"Because we started out with a certain premise, Wolfgang."

"What was that, Max?"

"To find a solution that would satisfy my victims."

"So what, Max?"

"They would not be satisfied with that punishment."

"What do you mean, Max?"

"My death will be just one death. One death for ten thousand deaths. That would be unjust."

"That's a problem, Max."

"Yes, Wolfgang. That's a problem!"

"Let's assume, Wolfgang, let's assume that I had ten thousand necks. And that you could string me up ten thousand times. Do you think that my victims would be satisfied?"

"I don't know, Max. I'll have to think about it."

"I'm sure they wouldn't, Wolfgang. My victims would not be satisfied with it."

"Why not, Max?"

"What would they get out of it, Wolfgang? They're dead."

"Yes, Max."

"It's true that they're growing again as trees, Wolfgang. But it's not the same."

"What do you mean, Max?"

"I mean . . . it's a different sort of life. Not the same. Not the one that I, Max Schulz . . . snuffed out."

"I don't understand that, Max."

"Just reflect a little, Wolfgang. What I snuffed out I cannot give back. Not even if I wanted to. I cannot. Do you understand that. I cannot. It is not within my power."

"Yes, Max, and so what?"

"Wolfgang! Why can't you understand? That's what they want, my victims. My dead. They want their lives back. They don't want to hang me up or to beat me to death. Or shoot me. Not even ten thousand times. All they want is to have their lives back. Nothing more. And that I can't give, Wolfgang. That is something Max Schulz can never give them back. I cannot even strike out the fear of death that they had. It's not possible, Wolfgang. There is no punishment that could reconcile my victims."

Our voices became more quiet. Only the echo of our words bounced around the room, banging in desperation against the shining mirror, and hitting our eyes, our eyes in the mirror as they sought what they could not find.

The judge was helpless. I offered him more wine but he declined. For a long time we were silent. Then the judge said: "The best thing to do is adjourn the trial."

I said: "Adjourning it is of no use. There is no solution. Not even at the next trial."

Once more we began to play cards. Neither of us wanted to go home.

The judge was thinking. Trying to find a solution. His mind was not on the cards. Not as usual. We only played two hands. Then the judge nodded off.

Try to see us in your mind's eye. Two helpless men. Who have played a game. Who are tired. Especially the judge. He has dropped off. And now is waking again. He looks at me. And says:

"Max Schulz. There is no solution. It's a dirty game."

I say: "A sentence must be pronounced."

And the judge says: "I am tired. I cannot think of one now. And it's a dirty game. And I am an old man."

I asked: "Shall I pronounce sentence?"

The judge nods his head, saying: "I'm tired. What is the sentence?"

I say: "Acquitted!"

And the tired old man nods his head. And says: "Acquitted!"

X

Every day the judge comes in for a shave: face and head. He grins when he comes into the salon. Every morning his greeting is:

"Shalom, Herr Schulz. How are you, Herr Schulz? Why do you call your famous hair-growing lotion *Samson V-2*? What does Samson's hair have to do with the German rockets? And what do you think, Herr Schulz? Should I try it? At my age? What do I need hairs for anyway? An old man? Who should I be trying to please? What do you think, Herr Schulz?"

The customers in the hairdressing salon "Man of the World" know the game we play and either crack jokes or express sympathy for me. Mayor Daniel Rosenberg has recommended his own doctor to me. He said:

"It's true he's not a psychiatrist but just a general practitioner. But he's a man with great compassion. You should put yourself in his hands."

Not even my wife takes me seriously. I've been on strike for several weeks. When visitors come I isolate myself in the den. My study. I want to have peace and quiet.

Nowadays I often go into the Forest of Six Million Souls! I talk to the trees, tell them stories, tell them of the salt of the earth, that is not salt but merely dust . . . the dust of beings that have been, of God's creatures. I tell of the dust that wanders. I tell of the wandering dust.

"And one day the dust arrived. And was transformed."

I tell them of growing and becoming. And how men and plants strike roots. And why.

I was sitting in the shadow of the trees and let myself get provoked. The trees said to me:

"One day you will die. You are no longer young, Max Schulz!"

I said: "I never said I was. Although these days a man is not old at sixty-one. People live longer these days."

And the trees said: "That's true."

And I said: "That's true."

"But one day you will die."

"Of course. Everyone has to come to terms with that thought sometime."

I played a guessing game with the trees. I said to them: "Now come on, start trying. Start rummaging around in your leafy brains! How am I going to die? Let's see if you can guess: the cause of my death!"

"We don't care two hoots!"

"All the same. Just guess. It's all a game."

"You'll get caught and hanged," said the trees.

I laughed: "That's not likely. Most of the mass-murderers are free. Many of them are abroad. But most of them back in the old homeland. Don't you read the newspapers? The mass-murderers are doing well! They're barbers. Or something else. A lot of them have their own businesses. Many own factories. Are industrialists. Many are in politics again, even in the government, are high up and command respect. And have families."

I grinned and said: "Verily I say unto you, that is the whole truth. They are living in freedom and laughing at God and the world. Yes. And at the word 'justice.'"

I said to the trees: "For instance I could die on some Sabbath eve. Because my wife makes good fish. Fish just like her mother made in Wapnjarka-Podolsk. So I could, for instance, choke on a fish bone. And suffocate? That would be more probable! Or I could get something else stuck in my throat—a large bone? That would be more probable too! I could slip and fall down. On the street. That would be more probable, too. I could die of an illness. That would be probable. Or of old age. That would be possible. But it would probably be heart trouble . . . a heart attack. It could happen at night. In my sleep. And I wouldn't even notice it.

"And of course it could happen during the evening. In my apartment. Namely at five minutes to ten. Just before going to sleep. That's when I sometimes make love to my wife. At five to ten. Always on the dot. Just before going to sleep. That's how we arrange it. Now and then. Not too often. And it could happen that my heart will give up. It's possible after all!"

For a long time still I spoke to the trees, making suggestions, wanting them to guess at my cause of death. The trees could not decide on anything.

XI

Yesterday after lunch I lay on the sofa in the living room, trying to have my usual afternoon nap, but could not get to sleep, so just lay there with half-closed eyes.

It was oppressively hot. "Hansim" weather. East winds. Comes out of the Arabian desert, to torture people and animals and plants. That's what it is. The Arabs don't dare to send their airplanes. They do dare to send us their wind.

I lay on the sofa, got into breathing difficulties and began to feel worse. My wife was pottering around in the laundry room. Steam filtered through the half-opened door to the living room, floated along the wall, wound around my sofa and finally completely enveloped me.

I had a waking dream, believing I was really at death's door.

[377]

My wife's excited voice at the telephone: "Doctor. It's happened! My husband! A heart attack! After lunch. What? A heart transplant? You have three Arabs in storage? Two tourists? An Englishman? And a German? Five hearts are available? Just a moment. I'll have to ask my husband. Excuse me. Yes. He can still manage a whisper."

"Can't be done, Doctor. I've asked my husband. He doesn't want an Arab heart. And not an English one either. And especially not a German heart. My husband wants a Jewish heart!

"What do you say? You don't have one in store? No Jewish hearts? Not even one?

"Excuse me? Tomorrow perhaps? Or the day after? There's always something happening? In occupied territories? A mine? A bomb? Shot in the back? Or maybe someone will die in bed? That too? So we just wait?

"Excuse me? A stroke of luck? Someone's just died? Not quite dead? Just dying. Wants to donate his heart?

"Excuse me? What do you say? A rabbi? A rabbi's heart? Whether my husband agrees?"

I'm on a stretcher. Being carried away. I lose consciousness. Then I come to again.

Where am I? Probably in the Hadassah Hospital. In a ward for serious cases. I can't even think. Only fog. Nothing but fog. But I hear voices. Some voices:

"He was unconscious for a long time. He doesn't even know that he's had his operation. Doesn't know anything at all."

"Is that right? He has a rabbi's heart now?"

"That's right!"

"Who was it?"

"I don't know. A rabbi."

"Will he live?"

"I don't think so. Something didn't quite work out."

"So he's . . . dying again?"

"Yes."

Voices, voices, voices: "Yes. Yes. Yes."

"Yes."

"Yes. Yes. Yes."

What's all that, damn it? I don't hear voices anymore. And I don't see anything. It's dark. And quiet.

No. I don't feel anything. And yet I can see. I can imagine things:

I can see my thoughts slipping out of the belfry, freeing themselves to worm around my eyes, to burst forth from the frog eyes, begin to hover, hover about in the room, on the ceiling, stare at me, whisper something to me.

Judge Wolfgang Richter says: "Max! You are lying at death's door!"

And my thoughts, squatting on the ceiling, after having long escaped from the slimy mass, the gray pulp behind the frog eyes . . . say: "Yes. I know, Wolfgang."

"I could not condemn you here, Max. Not here on earth. But I have thought of something."

"And what have you thought of, Wolfgang?"

"Something quite original!"

"And what's that?"

"I hand you over to another judgment!"

"That's nothing original."

"I give you over to God, Max."

"Perhaps He does not exist."

"I knew it."

"What . . . did you know?"

"That you would be afraid, Max."

"How do you know that, Wolfgang?"

"I can see the sweat breaking out on your forehead. And your open mouth."

"That can't be, Wolfgang. How can my body sweat . . . from fear . . . when my fear is squatting on the ceiling?"

"That's all in your mind, Max."

"Yes. I'm afraid."

"Yes."

"How do I look, Wolfgang?"

"So-so, Max. A pity that you can't see yourself anymore. Your frog eyes are wide open. Your mouth too."

"Is that really so?"

"Yes. That's so. At the very end. A man like you dies . . . with 'their' fear."

"Whose fear?"

"With the fear your victims felt before they died."

"Is that supposed to be the just punishment?"

"No."

And suddenly I can see again. I see white curtains. And I see the open window. And I can see the wind too. I can see it!

And to me it seems as though the wind were coming from the Forest of the Six Million Souls. The wind! And the wind seizes the white curtains at my window. Shakes them.

And gradually they become darker. The curtains on the window. Become darker and darker, come off the hooks, become wings, black wings, begin to flutter, let themselves be carried by the wind, by the wind that came from the forest, the Forest of Six Million Souls. And the wings seize me, hook themselves firmly onto my outstretched arms, and the wind rises, carries my wings, me with them. Somewhere. There!

And there was a courtroom. There a trial took place. The trial of Max Schulz!

I stand before my judge. I stand before "Him," the One and Only and Eternal.

And the One and Only asks: "Are you the mass-murderer Max Schulz?"

And I say: "Yes. I am the mass-murderer Max Schulz."

"Are you circumcised?"

"No. I am not circumcised. My foreskin grew again. On the way here."

"Have you the heart of a rabbi?"

"No. It fell out. On the way here it dropped out. On the way here. I have my own heart back again."

"Where is your false Auschwitz number?"

"It has vanished."

"And the SS tattoo?"

"It is back again. Where the scar was."

"Are you really the mass-murderer Max Schulz?"

"Yes. I am really the mass-murderer Max Schulz."

And the One and Only asks: "Guilty?"

And I say: "I went along with it. I just went along with it! And others went along too. It was legal in those days."

"Is that your only excuse?"

"That is my only excuse."

"What about the bats you have in your belfry?"

"No bats in the belfry."

"Guilty?"

"Yes. Guilty!"

"Do you expect a just sentence?"

"Yes. A just sentence. I, Max Schulz, expect justice from a just authority."

And the One and Only spake out with mighty voice: "Then I condemn you!"

But I say: "Just a moment. First I have to ask you something!"

And the One and Only says: "Ask away! But quickly!"

"Where were you? In those days?"

"What do you mean . . . in those days?"

"In those days, during the executions?"

"What do you mean?"

"The execution of the defenseless."

"When?"

"When it happened."

I ask: "Were you asleep?"

And the One and Only says: "I never sleep!"

"Where were you?"

"When?"

"When it happened!"

"When it happened?"

"If you were not asleep . . . where were you?"

"Here!"

I ask: "Here?"

And the One and Only says: "Here."

"And what did you do if you were not sleeping?"
"When it happened?"
"Yes. When it happened!"
And the One and Only says: "I watched!"
"You watched? Only watched?"
"Yes. I just watched!"

"Then your guilt is greater than mine!" I say. "If that is true . . . then you cannot be my judge!"

"It's true," says the One and Only. "I cannot be your judge!"
"That's true!"
And the One and Only says: "That's true."
And I ask: "What do we do next?"
"What do we do next?"
"That is a problem!"
And the One and Only says: "Yes. That is a problem!"

And the One and Only climbed down from his seat of judgment and placed Himself next to me at my side. And so we both wait! For a just sentence! But who is there who can pronounce it?

M9